CAPTIVE ICE

by
Karin Richardson

A Deer Creek Mystery

CAPTIVE ICE is also available as a Kindle edition
from Amazon.com

10 9 8 7 6 5 4 3 2 1

ISBN 978-1-57550-080-5

Printed in the United States of America
Cover Art by Johanna M. Bolton

CAPTIVE ICE is a work of fiction. All the characters
and events portrayed in this book are fictional, and
any resemblance to real people and incidents is
purely coincidental.

Dead before Christmas!!!

"Unless you give me what I want, you will be dead before Christmas," the voice on the phone snarled. And he meant it too. Someone had already tried to kill Ruth Ann's cousin, and now a dangerous operative has kidnapped Ruth Ann!

And of course, it was Blue Ice that the man on the phone wanted! But there is help as always from friends, including one very sprightly old ghost who appears to Ruth Ann in her dreams.

CAPTIVE ICE brings back the delightful cast of characters, residents of Deer Creek, a peaceful ... well, a relatively peaceful little town in the Rocky Mountains of Colorado. Add members of Ruth Ann's family from Sweden and you have an intriguing cast for this new mystery! CAPTIVE ICE also introduces yet another villain, a dangerous adversary who collects precious gems and will stop at *nothing* to add Blue Ice to his collection!

Here's what readers have to say about Richardson's mysteries:

☆ ☆ ☆ ☆ ☆
Jaw Dropping – kept me on the edge of my seat! (TT)

This book was so suspenseful from start to finish. The voice of the characters was so strong I felt like I was right there with them all searching for the necklace! Awesome, quick read!

☆ ☆ ☆ ☆ ☆
I loved this book. Every time I thought I had it figured out there was another twist and turn. A great read and now I anxiously wait for the next one!

☆ ☆ ☆ ☆ ☆
Love the dialogue between characters. East to pick up if set it down. Keeps you guessing.

☆ ☆ ☆ ☆ ☆
A charming mystery!!

☆ ☆ ☆ ☆ ☆
A great read. Perfect for a book club. Looking forward to the next one in the series!

☆ ☆ ☆ ☆ ☆
What a great, fresh, new read by an up and coming author!

☆ ☆ ☆ ☆ ☆
Great read!! Love Ruth Ann! Can't wait for the next book!

Captive Ice and all the books in the Deer Creek Series will and always will be dedicated to my grandmother, Ruth Ann.

There's barely a day that goes by that I don't remember the kindness and unbelievable strength she displayed during happy, sad, and trying times. I only wish I could be as good of a person as she was. She's dearly missed but I feel she's happily watching from the one place she couldn't wait to get to at almost 94, Heaven!

Chapter 1

Christmas was looming. I was in a hospital in Stockholm staring into the comatose faces of both Prunella and Alex. Axel sat next to me, silent. I longed to be back in Deer Creek, enjoying my home, my family, my friends and my antique shop. I longed to put the drama I'd lived for the last three months behind me. I almost wished I had never inherited, much less seen, that priceless aquamarine, Blue Ice. That necklace has been more pain then pleasure. So many have tried to steal it. Too many have been murdered, kidnapped, cursed or injured. I'm one of the fortunate ones; I've only been kidnapped.

A wave of self-pity came over me, but then I realized that my dear Prunella and Alex would be strangers without Blue Ice. My life would have never been blessed with Axel, Inga, Sherman, Cassandra, Isabella, Meme and Carlos. I was slowly understanding my role in the mystery of Blue Ice. The gem would always be a part of me, for better or worse.

I remember the exact moment when Prunella's eyes opened and she saw me sitting by her side with Axel. I was deep in thought, barely aware of her. Axel was sitting next to me in a chair reading business e-mails on his laptop. He glanced up and jumped when he noticed her piercing blue eyes staring at the two of us. Without speaking, he grabbed my arm and gave it a rough tug.

1

"Hey," I snapped. "That hurt!"

"Ruth Ann," he said slowly. "Look, look at Prunella!"

I turned away from glaring at Axel. "It can't be!" I said ever so slowly and quietly. "Is she awake?"

"I don't know, Ruth Ann," he replied. "Look at her eyes, they aren't moving. They're just staring at us, blankly."

"I'm going to get the nurse," I said, hopping out of my chair. "They need to know she's opened her eyes."

I ran out of the private hospital room and grabbed the nearest nurse in the stark white hallway. "Please, help me!" I said, out of breath. "I think my cousin just woke up!"

The nurse didn't understand me at first because I spoke English, and she only Swedish. When I pointed to Prunella's room, she nodded and hurried to the nurse's station and picked up a telephone. She spoke rapidly and then rushed past me into Prunella's room. I followed her, and when I stepped inside the room, I paused at the door watching the nurse hover over Prunella. She asked Axel to step back, and when he spotted me in the doorway, he walked to meet me.

"She asked me to give her some space while she checks her vitals."

"She doesn't speak English, so you'll have to translate for me." I added, "I like the nurses on duty that speak both languages, but this one doesn't."

"It's okay, Ruth Ann," Axel said, taking hold of my hand and squeezing it. "I'm here for you, and I'll let you know everything she says."

"Do you think this is just something involuntary? Or do you think she might actually be waking up?" I asked him, scared I was getting my hopes up for nothing.

"I really don't know, Ruth Ann," he answered, worried. "We've been sitting here day after day waiting for something

2

to happen."

I looked at him oddly and asked, "What do you mean by *something*?"

"I don't mean anything by it, Ruth Ann," he snapped, irritated. "I didn't mean I wished her dead, if that's what you're thinking! I just wanted some sign from her."

I wasn't going to take his remarks personally given the situation. "I'm sorry if that's what you thought, Axel. I just meant ... I really don't know what I meant. I'm tired, confused, and just want to go home. It's time for her to wake up so we can get her back to Deer Creek."

"It's okay, Ruth Ann. I feel the same way. I want to get back to Colorado, too. I don't mean to snap at you. Let's just wait to see what's going on."

We stood off to the side of the door and watched as a doctor entered, and between the nurse and the doctor we felt something serious was happening. It took quite a long time before the doctor asked us to step into the hall.

"What is it?" I asked, impatiently. "Is my cousin alright?"

Axel added, "Is my wife awake?"

In English, the doctor answered, coolly, "We're not sure yet. She's showing slight signs of brain activity which makes me more hopeful than I've been lately."

"What's that supposed to mean?" I bellowed. "Are you telling us that you thought Prunella was never going to wake up?"

The doctor held his hand up and said, "Ms. Conroy, I'm going to be upfront with you. The longer she's in a coma, the less likely she is to wake up. It's been quite a while, and I was starting to have my doubts. However, with her current brain activity, and opening her eyes, I am hopeful she'll wake up

3

very soon."

"I'm sure glad you're telling us the real truth after she's shown signs of brain activity!" I exclaimed, agitated with the man.

"I need you both to go back in and keep talking to her. Be loud and ask her lots and lots of questions. Hopefully, there will be a topic that'll snap her out of her semi-unconscious state." He added, "Can you both do that for me?"

"Yes!" I cried. "I know exactly the topic we can use to snap her right out of it!"

"Whoa," Axel answered, shaking his head after reading my mind. "I don't know if what you're thinking of using to wake her is smart. It's a very stressful topic, don't you think?"

"Yeah, but it'll get her heart pumping and she might sit right up and start yelling at us for putting her in such a dangerous spot."

The doctor watched our exchange with confusion. "I don't know if I really want to know what you're referring to, but, I will add, I don't want anything too stressful thrown at her right away. Maybe, there's something positive or news that is good and exciting you could talk to her about?"

Axel and I looked at each other and I shrugged my shoulders. "Wow, now that you mention it, I can't think of anything exciting that happened lately that's positive. Can you, Axel?"

"I, I don't know," he replied, baffled. "We've had so much heartache and trouble lately, I can't think of anything."

"Well," the doctor said, sternly. "You better come up with something or else it could put her into a deeper coma." With that statement, he turned and went to another room.

"Hey," I said, angrily. "What does he mean by that? Why didn't he explain himself?"

"It's kind of an obvious statement, don't you think?"

Axel asked, rhetorically.

I thought about it for a nanosecond and realized we needed to think of something happy to talk to Prunella about, and that topic wasn't Blue Ice.

Chapter 2

Axel and I sat by Prunella's side. We didn't say a word, watching her blue eyes stare into space. "One of us has to say something!" I spat out.

"Ruth Ann," Axel said, whispering in my ear. "I seriously can't think of anything positive to get her attention."

I turned my head away from Prunella and moved my chair a little closer to Axel. "I know. With her losing the baby, and Sherman's death, what are we to talk about?"

A little too loud, Axel said, "Well, not that bloody Blue Ice necklace!"

Suddenly, out of nowhere, Prunella started wailing, her arms in the air, shaking her head back and forth violently.

"Stop her, Axel!" I shouted.

Axel hopped out of his chair and grabbed Prunella's arms so she wouldn't hit herself. As he laid across the upper half of her body, he bellowed, "Go get the doctor!

I ran out of her room as fast as possible. Thankfully, the doctor was still at the nurse's station sitting behind the desk typing into the computer. I rushed over, hollering at him to get back to Prunella's room. Something horrible was happening. He responded immediately and followed me back into her room.

"What happened?" he asked, in English.

"We were just sitting talking to each other when she started moving violently. Her arms were thrashing back and forth and her head was whipping from one side to the other." I took a breath and added, "Please, help her!"

The doctor loosened Axel's hold on Prunella just as the nurse rushed in the room holding a needle. "Put it in her thigh," the doctor ordered. "I need it in her bloodstream stat!"

"What, what are you putting in her?" I begged, terrified at what was happening.

"It's just a sedative, Ms. Conroy."

Axel and I stood back a few feet to let the doctor and nurse do their jobs. Within a couple minutes, Prunella calmed and her arms fell limply to her side. Her head was to one side, and the nurse gently put it back into a comfortable position.

"Okay, she's still now," the doctor said, standing and moving toward Axel and me. "Please, come with me into the hall, *again*."

Axel and I marched behind the doctor into the hall. I felt better the last time we met in the hall. I really thought she was waking, but now, I wasn't feeling very confident. Axel looked worried, and I didn't blame him. What if her body was shutting down? I didn't know how to move forward if something horrible happened to her.

The doctor said, "Your wife, and cousin, was sedated to keep her safe. I really didn't want to do that since she was just starting to show signs of activity. This may put her back into a deep coma."

"Are you saying my wife may never wake up after this episode?"

"No, but it wasn't what we wanted to happen." The doctor paused, and looked at the two of us and asked, "Did either of you say anything that could possibly upset her or threaten her?"

"Us?" I asked, resentfully. "We were just whispering."

Axel looked at me and said, "It's my fault. I said something I shouldn't have too loudly."

"What?" the doctor asked.

"I brought up the reason she ended up in this hospital."

"Axel, I doubt what you said could've caused that reaction."

"Would one of you tell me what you're talking about?" the doctor demanded.

"Let me," I said to Axel. He nodded, and I explained as briefly as I could about the necklace and it's cursed past.

The doctor's eyes opened wide, and out of nowhere, he started laughing. I was so surprised at his response, I snapped, "I'm not telling you a story. It's all true!"

"No, way," he said, snickering. He looked from Axel to me, and back to Axel. He saw the irate looks in our expressions and changed his demeanor. "If what you're telling me is true, then no wonder this woman ended up in the hospital!"

"She ended up in the hospital because she was cursed by a person who desperately wanted our necklace!" I exclaimed. "Prunella and the necklace have both been ridden of their respective curses, but Prunella collapsed and ended up here. Nobody you've met had anything to do with what happened to her. We love her and have been by her side ever since it happened."

"And is that why the young man ended up here, too?" the doctor asked, referring to Alex.

"Yes, but his injuries were physical," I answered. "He was an innocent person who got mixed up in this whole affair."

8

Axel added, "But, Alex is in grave condition, correct?"

"Yes. I'm recommending he be transferred to a private clinic dedicated to coma patients."

"We were told," Axel said, sadly. "I heard they want to transfer him in the next day or two."

"Yes," the doctor replied, dispassionately. "I'm just a consulting physician for him, but I do agree with the transfer."

"I'm sick about it," I said, upset. "I need to go and check on him."

"Soon, Ruth Ann," Axel said. "You've been by Prunella's side, and Alex's side for a long time. I think the specialized clinic will give him the attention he needs right now." Before I could respond the wrong way, accusing him of giving up on Alex, he said, "I'm not saying it's hopeless, Ruth Ann."

"Many patients wake up after being in comas, right doctor?"

"Well, there are some, but many, I'm afraid, do not."

Axel's face turned beat red, and I had to admit, so did mine. I thought Axel was going to lunge at the poor doctor, but I grabbed his arm and held him back. I quickly tried to calm myself down and think rationally. "Are you saying Alex will be in a coma for the rest of his life?"

"No, I'm not. I'm just saying that he could. I have to be completely forthright with you both. I'm not trying to deflate any of your hopes for Alex to make a full recovery at some point."

"*At some point?*" I asked.

"It depends on how long he stays in a coma, Ms. Conroy. If he comes out of it soon, he'll make a quicker recovery. The longer he stays comatose, the more time he'll need to relearn basic tasks such as speaking, walking, eating on his own, taking a shower and going to the bathroom."

"Doctor, will you answer one more question?" The doctor nodded. "Are you telling us all of this because you think Prunella could be in the same predicament as Alex?"

Axel glared at me and snapped, "Of course he doesn't mean that, Ruth Ann. He's only talking about Alex."

"Well," the doctor began. "If your wife falls back into a coma, then those conditions would apply to her too."

Axel was about to protest vehemently, but instead, he turned and walked down the hall into the stairwell. I was about to go after him when I changed my mind. He needed time alone, and I wasn't going to chase after him. He needed to cool off before going back inside Prunella's room. I did, too, but I also wanted to get back in and grab her hand and beg her to wake up! What a huge mess this was, and I had to think of some way out of it!

Chapter 3

The doctor left me standing alone in the hall just outside of Prunella's room. He had another emergency down the hall. Room 402's patient was having trouble breathing. He excused himself and sprinted down the long hallway. I stood debating whether to go after Alex or go inside and force my cousin to wake up! The latter won out. I stood a little straighter, forced myself to have a better attitude, and marched inside Prunella's room.

I watched as she lay peacefully in bed. She was sleeping soundly due to the sedative, but I hoped and prayed that was the only reason she was so still. I must've sat next to her for over an hour when I felt a funny sensation in my front pants pocket. "My cellphone," I said to myself. I reached into my pocket and looked at the display. "Inga!" I answered. "I'm so glad to hear your voice. How are things going back home?"

"Not so good, Ruth Ann," she replied in a weak voice so unlike her. Inga, Axel's longtime housekeeper, was a large, middle-aged woman about my age, who was as sturdy and strong mentally as she was physically.

"What's wrong now?" I asked, worried. "Are Isabella and Carlos alright? And what's going on with Cassandra? I hope John isn't giving her a hard time!"

"Well, it's not John who's harassing Cassandra, it's that

detective, Judy."

"She's a pain in the ..."

I thought about Deer Creek's Chief of Police and my boyfriend, John, for the first time in weeks. Well, he *was* my boyfriend. He's strong, handsome, and very stubborn. He and I have dated for years, but just within the last year or so we became exclusive. Even though I lost my husband over twenty years ago, I'm not ready to marry again. I've tried his every nerve. John has saved from my reckless behavior handling crimes against my family and the necklace more times than I can list, but each time he grows angrier and angrier with me. However, when I've been even slightly injured, he's right at my side, being more attentive and sweet than I can tell. We've hit a rough patch the last month or two. It wasn't his fault, though. I've been so busy trying to save my family and stop the nonsense with the constantly cursed necklace, that I have to admit I've neglected him. I haven't told him yet, but now there's more to this than I thought. And that 'more' is actually a 'who,' Axel Eklund. Axel is a rich and powerful shipping mogul in Stockholm whose family fought and struggled for decades to acquire Blue Ice. We met when my cousin Prunella, who feared Axel would steal Blue Ice from her, sent it to me in Colorado for safekeeping. I didn't even know I had a cousin in Sweden until that fateful package arrived. Driven to obtain Blue Ice at any cost, Axel purchased a massive mountainside estate in Deer Creek, sent his henchmen to steal it, and kidnapped me to Sweden. Despite his crazed lust for the gem, I knew Axel was no killer. Eventually, he saw the light and reformed. The Swedish courts exonerated him, he moved to Deer Creek, reconciled with Prunella and proved to me that he was truly an honorable man.

Axel and I are closer in age than he and Prunella. He's in

his sixties, and I am, well, very close to that decade. Prunella, on the other hand, is in her mid-thirties like my daughters. I know what everyone's thinking, but I'm not having an affair with Axel. Yes, we've grown close, very close, but nothing inappropriate has ever happened. Axel has given me every indication that he would like to pursue more with me, but I've put my foot down! We've had countless heart to heart talks while waiting for Prunella to wake up from her coma, and even though he's married to her, he thinks it might have been be a huge mistake. He married Prunella after losing his first wife, who was horrible I might add, and jumped into Prunella's arms without enough time to really get to know her. I truly believe he loves her, but maybe not the kind of love that a husband and wife share. That's why I'm so confused.

"Ruth Ann!" a voice called out from inside the hospital room, startling me.

"Axel," I said, holding the phone away from my ear. "It's Inga, and she just started telling me Judy's harassing poor Cassandra."

"Well, she did commit a lot of crimes, Ruth Ann," he replied, shocking me.

"So, did you!" I snapped.

"Exactly," he said. "That's why I know it's not going to be easy for Cassandra. She needs a good lawyer and I'm not sure that'll happen in Deer Creek."

"Then get a good lawyer for her!" I demanded.

"Hello? Hello?" a voice cried from my cell phone.

"Oops. Sorry, Inga. I didn't mean to ignore you. I was just filling in Axel on Cassandra. What is Judy doing to her?"

"She's making her life difficult while she's out on bail. She tells her to enjoy what time she has because she'll be locked up for life soon enough. She's being a big bully."

"What if I make a call to John and tell him what she's doing? He'll get Judy off her back. We just have to patiently wait for the trial where all of us will be witnesses for her. They'll let her off her crimes after what she's done to make amends."

"I don't know, Ruth Ann," Axel said. "I got lucky, and it'll take a miracle to get Cassandra off. She held onto serious revenge against our families."

"But, she didn't kill anyone or kidnap anyone. That was Svenson. He's a horrible man and a terrible lawyer!" Suddenly, a thought popped in my head. "Hey, why can't we get Prunella's lawyer, Michael Svenson's cousin, Steven to come and help Cassandra?"

"Great idea, Ruth Ann," Inga shouted from the phone. "I'm sure Mr. Eklund could make that happen, right?"

Axel looked uncomfortable, but said, "I guess I could call him. I'm terrified of that name, though. Anything associated with the name Svenson scares me."

"But, Steven's a good guy. He'll do anything to help Prunella," I reminded said.

"True," he admitted. "I'll make the call."

"Thanks!" I said, and then returned my attention to Inga.

"Anything else going on back home? How are my daughters Lynne and Nancy? I hate that I've been away so long."

"They're fine, Ruth Ann," Inga told me. "I went to Lynne's new store at the resort. Her famous balls are selling like hotcakes! Or should I say hot balls!" We both enjoyed a rare laugh, and I loved thinking about Lynne's bakery. "Carlos and Isabella are pitching in here big time. It's not the same without Sherman, but Isabella's cleaning and Carlos is managing the household. I really have become dependent on them and hope they don't plan on going back to Jamaica."

"They won't, Inga. Carlos can't really go back to his family and Isabella doesn't have any other family except for Cassandra."

"I forget that they are half-sisters," Inga said.

"I think they'll be very close some day. They both have to heal from their past, but in time, they will."

"How's Ms. Prunella?" Inga asked, hesitantly. I knew she was dying to ask, but fearful of my answer. It's always been the same. No change.

"Well," I said, trying to figure out how to tell her what happened today. "There have been some changes."

"WHAT?" she screamed through the phone. "She's not worse, is she?"

"No, no, Inga. She opened her eyes."

"Ms. Prunella's awake, finally!" she hollered, so happy. I wasn't going to tell her the whole truth but gave her something happy to cling to for a change.

"She's not awake, Inga. She opened her eyes and then she had a bit of a tantrum. We're not sure why, but the doctor had to sedate her. He's still hoping once the sedative wears off that she'll open her eyes and wake up."

"Oh, well, it's not great news, but at least there were some changes. Maybe that fit will snap her out of her coma."

"We hope so, but until then, no changes."

"Stop saying that, Ruth Ann," Inga snapped. "I'm beginning to hate those two words!"

"Sorry."

"My next dreaded question ... how's Alex?"

"Unfortunately, he hasn't woken up. He's being transferred to a specialty clinic nearby for coma patients. Axel has promised me he would get the best of care, and we can pray that someday he'll snap out of his coma."

"Oh, that's not good news at all, Ruth Ann," she said, quietly. "I feel so bad for the young lad. He's got his whole life in front of him, and now this."

Alex recently entered our lives as a young, newly graduated college man. Like all my new family, he came in search of Blue Ice. He had promised his mother on her deathbed that he would claim the gem for himself. That didn't happen. Alex didn't have it in him to be violent or threatening, and sadly he was beaten and rendered comatose in our Jamaican adventure to break a curse on Blue Ice. As I was realizing, Blue Ice was part of his destiny too.

"Time will tell, Inga. Anything else going on at home? Have you heard anything about my store? I feel so bad putting Meme in charge for so long."

"Oh," Inga exclaimed, cheering up. "I forgot to tell you that Carlos is over at your store every day! He loves running it with Meme. He even lets Meme go home and take care of her little son. I think your sales are skyrocketing since he started working there. It's fantastic! He's very happy there, and people love buying stuff from him."

I wasn't sure if I was happy or not. On the plus, my sales were soaring. On the downside, he was more successful than I was. I shook my head to rid my mind of negative thoughts.

"That's great," I answered, truthfully. "Please tell him to keep up the good work and if he needs anything from me to call."

"I sure will, Ruth Ann."

Carlos was very special to me. He's gone through a lot in his life, but he's a strong, brave man who will find a new path. Again, because of Blue Ice, I met him, Isabella, Cassandra and Martika in Jamaica. Isabella and Cassandra's sister, Martika, another victim under the gem's curse, forced Carlos to marry her. He feared that his wealthy and very rigid parents would disown him if they found out about his homosexuality, and so, allowed Martika to blackmail him to keep his secret. Martika was a nasty, vicious woman whose only goal was getting her hands on Blue Ice. She tried everything to get my necklace, but in the end, she was killed during her struggle.

"Well, I'm going to get back to Prunella. I'll keep you posted on any changes, okay?"

"Sounds good. Tell Prunella that I need her here, and she needs to wake up immediately!"

"I will. Thanks, Inga." I ended the call and put my cell phone back in my pocket. Axel wasn't in the room anymore so I stood and went into the hall. I spotted him down the hall in the waiting area on his phone. I bet he was calling Steven Svenson about representing Cassandra.

I didn't go straight back inside Prunella's room but went toward the elevator and pushed the button. I was tired and hungry, so I decided to go get something sweet to eat in the cafeteria. Unlike most, this hospital had the most delectable foods and treats. I've been eating better than I have since Inga was cooking three meals for me. This morning, I had ginger pancakes with lots of maple syrup and a scoop of whipped cream. I ate the entire pile and could've eaten a couple more right about now. It was after lunchtime, and I figured I was due to eat. Maybe I should get a couple sandwiches and grab a couple pieces of cake for Axel and me.

The elevator door opened to the first floor, and I followed the signs to the cafeteria even though I had walked this path countless times lately. It was fairly empty except for a few tables filled with doctors and nurses devouring food quickly so they could get back to their jobs. I walked into the line designated for sandwiches, burgers, and other hot foods. I was thankful they understood English and ordered two turkey and swiss sandwiches on marble rye, my ultimate favorite combination. I grabbed a couple bags of potato chips and water bottles, and then I headed for the baked goods area. I spotted different puddings and jellos ... no thank you. I wasn't in the mood for jiggly desserts. I never have been, actually. I slowly walked through the line and saw heaven. A freshly baked chocolate cake with chocolate filling and devil's food icing! I know it sounds like a lot of chocolate, but times were rough, and I wanted it.

I grabbed a large hunk of the cake for me, and a slice of apple pie for Axel. He loved the apple pie here because it had a crumbly topping that was a mixture of butter, cinnamon, sugar, and a little flour. I didn't grab a bowl of vanilla ice cream this time because I wasn't sure how fast he would eat it once I brought it back to Prunella's room.

I walked to the cashier, whom I recognized, and whipped out my credit card.

"Ms. Conroy," Elsie, the older woman called out. "Ah, I see you found the chocolate cake! My recommendation to try this new bakery worked out. You're going to be the first person to try this cake."

"I will?" I asked, surprised.

"Yes, and will you do me a huge favor?" she asked, sweetly.

"Of course, just tell me," I replied.

"After you've eaten it, will you please let me know, totally honestly, if you like it?"

"Well, why don't I just give it a try right now and I can tell you immediately," I said, happy to oblige.

"Really?" she asked, amazed. "I figured you'd want to eat your sandwich first."

I laughed, and said, "Dessert is good any time during, after or before a meal!" I grabbed a plastic fork from the container near the register and took a big bite that included the icing, cake, and the filling. I slowly let the piece slide off the fork into my mouth. "This is unbelievable!"

Elsie looked worried, "Unbelievably good or unbelievably bad?"

I didn't want her to hang on too long, so I answered, "It is unbelievably fantastic! My daughter's a baker, and she would rate this one five stars!"

"Oh, that's fantastic!" Elsie said, smiling broadly.

Out of curiosity, I asked, "Why do you care so much? Is it because you recommended this bakery?"

"Kind of," she said. "It's also my granddaughter's bakery."

"Ah, now I understand," I said. "Well, you have my full support if you need a reference."

"Thank you, Ms. Conroy."

"Please call me Ruth Ann," I said, for the hundredth time.

"Yes, Ruth Ann."

"I'll see you soon, Elsie," I waved and headed toward the elevator back to Prunella's bedside.

Chapter 4

I stepped out of the elevator and walked toward Prunella's room with my tray. I stuck my head inside her room but didn't see Axel. I looked down the hall where I had seen him last, and at first, didn't see him, but then I looked at a group of chairs near a television and there he was, sitting alone. I walked to him, thinking it might be nice to eat in the waiting area for a change.

"Axel," I said, startling him. "I brought lunch."

"Oh, yeah, we did miss lunch, didn't we?" he said, appearing a little out of sorts.

"Are you hungry?"

"I guess so. We had a large breakfast, but I can eat again." He looked at me oddly and said, "After all those pancakes you ate, I'm surprised you're even hungry."

Offended, I said, "It's been over six hours since we've eaten. I can't help it if I'm hungry again."

"Sorry, Ruth Ann," he said, perking up. "I didn't mean anything by it. I just lost track of time."

"Do you think I should be watching my weight?" I asked, suddenly self-conscious about my intake of food.

"Absolutely not!" he replied, quickly. "I forget, you can really eat. You must have a fast metabolism."

"I don't sit still a lot," I answered. "I get antsy."

"Yes, you do, Ruth Ann," he said with his handsomest smile.

I felt a surge of warmth run through my body. He was an extremely handsome older man. He was distinguished, intelligent, and in excellent shape for being about ten years older than me. His thick gray hair was neatly cut and he always wore fashionable clothes. Today he was wearing a pair of gray wool pants and a light gray cashmere cardigan with a plaid buttoned shirt underneath. He smelled wonderful, too. I'm not sure what cologne he was wearing, but it had an earthy tone that was quite pleasing. I smiled at the thought that I was falling for the man who had kidnapped me just 3 months ago.

I snapped out of my momentarily dream-like state and noticed Axel stood and was trying to take the tray from me. "Ruth Ann," he kept calling my name. "Let go of the tray so I can set it down for us."

"Oh, sorry, I was just thinking about something else."

"Anything interesting?" he asked.

"No, just wondering if I'll ever get home and get back to Inga's cooking."

"Soon. I really feel it'll be soon," he said, waiting for me to sit down on the couch so we could eat.

We sat in silence and devoured our sandwiches. Before we started dessert, Axel said, "I've grown to love this turkey and swiss sandwich!"

"Thanks," I said, swallowing my last bite. Before picking up my fork to eat my chocolate cake, I said, "Hey, I forgot. When I left to go to get food, I noticed you were in here on the phone. Did you get ahold of Steven Svenson?"

"I didn't call him, Ruth Ann."

"Oh, then who were you on the phone with?" I asked, realizing that was rude of me. "I'm sorry. If it's private, you don't have to answer that."

"No, no, it's not that. I was speaking with one of my business lawyers to ask them for a referral for a criminal lawyer."

"So, you really don't want to use Steven, do you?"

"No."

"I get it. There's too many bad memories associated with him. Prunella used him when she was trapped in your attic pretending to be dying. He was helping her, and you think he might not be willing to work with *you*, right?"

"Yes," he answered. "I'd like a clean start, and my team of lawyers at my company can help me."

"Did you get any names?" I asked, curiously.

"Yes."

"But, are they here in Sweden?" I questioned him. "Cassandra's being tried in Colorado."

"I know. Don't worry, Ruth Ann. I've got a great lawyer I can use who is practicing in the states."

"Oh, that's good, then."

"So," he said, eyeing his apple pie. "Can we eat our desserts now? We should get back inside Prunella's room soon."

"Yes!" I exclaimed, picking my fork up and taking a large, scrumptious bite of my cake.

"You look like you're eating gold," he said, snickering.

I explained about the cake and Elsie down in the cafeteria. "I love helping young bakers."

"Like your daughter, Lynne," Axel said, kindly.

"Exactly." I felt a deep sensation of sadness overwhelm me. I set my plate down after taking just one bite of the delicious cake. My stomach did a little flop, and I realized just how much I missed my daughters, and well, everyone.

"It's okay, Ruth Ann," Axel said, reaching out and putting his hand on my thigh. "I can see how homesick you are.

I've got an idea."

"Oh, no," I said, before he could continue. "You're not going to get rid of me that easily."

"I can handle it here by myself, Ruth Ann," he said, releasing his hand from my leg. "You should go home and be with your family. It's almost the holidays, and I'm sure you're dying to get back to your store."

"You're right about it all, Axel, but, I'm not leaving. It's more important that I stay here with Prunella ... and you."

"Me?" he asked, innocently. "I'm alright sitting here alone."

"I think you need me for support as much as Prunella does. Unless I'm speaking out of turn?"

"No, no, Ruth Ann. I love spending time with you. You keep me on my toes all the time!"

"Well, then it's settled. I'm not leaving until Prunella's discharged from this hospital and on a plane back to Deer Creek."

"Then why don't you finish your cake?" he asked.

I eyed the piece sitting on the coffee table littered with old magazines I can't even read since they're in another language. My stomach was back to normal, and I was ready to indulge. "Sounds like a good plan to me!" I reached down and devoured every last bite of my cake.

Once we were through, Axel stood and reached his hand for me to grab. "Ready?"

"Yep," I replied, taking a hold of his soft, but firm hands. "Maybe the sedative is wearing off and she'll have her eyes open."

"I sure hope so. I'm very curious to see if Prunella's actually starting to wake up." He stopped before entering her room and turned to me. "You know, once she wakes up, things will be different with us."

"What do you mean?"

"You and I have spent a lot of time together. Talking, eating, walking, waiting, and getting to know each other much better than before."

"What are you implying, Axel?" I asked, suddenly shaking a little.

"Ruth Ann, you know that we've grown close, and well, I've developed ... " I held my hand up and told him not to say what I thought he was about to say.

"We can't deny our feelings or the truth, Ruth Ann."

"Yes, I can!" I said and stormed inside Prunella's room. What I found in there stopped me dead in my tracks.

Chapter 5

I let out a little yell, and Axel came flying in the room. "Ruth Ann," he cried, out of breath. "What's the matter?"

I didn't have to answer. He stood frozen, like me, staring in the direction of Prunella's bed. "What are you doing?" I demanded, walking toward the stranger who was holding a pillow over Prunella's head.

"Axel didn't wait for the stranger's answer but attacked at full-force. I didn't know whether to help Axel or get help. I couldn't tell if the person was a man or a woman because they were dressed from head to toe in black. The head was covered with a black hood, and even the hands had black leather gloves on them. I watched as Axel lunged at the person, who I'm presuming was a man, and threw him away from his wife and onto the floor. He didn't take long to recover. He quickly stood and without looking at Axel, ran past me, shoving me against the wall by the door, and disappeared.

"Go after him!" Axel shouted, while checking on Prunella to see if she was still breathing.

I flew into the hall and looked both directions. He was gone as fast as he came. I ran to the nurse's desk and asked the one and only nurse sitting staring into a computer screen. "Did you see that man?"

"What man?" the nurse asked, casually looking up from

her computer.

"The man all dressed in black, who ran out of my cousin's room after trying to kill her!"

The nurse popped up so fast, she knocked her chair to the ground. She ignored me and rushed into Prunella's room. I followed as quickly as I could and watched as she asked Axel to step aside so she could check Prunella. I saw her take her phone out and page the doctor. She turned to Axel and me and bellowed, "Please leave until we can assess if any damage has been done."

"I'm not leaving!" Axel snapped. "Look what happened when we stepped out of the room for just a few minutes."

"Don't argue with me, Mr. Eklund. If you want me to help your wife, I suggest you leave until the doctor comes and talks to you." She turned her attention back to Prunella, obviously not accepting any more protests from us. As we were about to step into the hall, the nurse called out, "Who did this? Do you know the man who assaulted your wife?"

"No," I answered for the both of us. I turned to Axel to make sure he didn't know, and when he shook his head I felt a sense of relief that it wasn't someone he actually did know.

"We need to contact the police," the nurse said. "Either we will do it after we make sure she's stable or you may make the call now."

We stood outside Prunella's door as the doctor walked past us and into her room. I looked at Axel as he stared inside the room until I broke his attention away. "Axel, we need to contact the police."

"No."

I was stunned. "Why not?"

"Let's wait and see what the doctor says, and then we can talk."

Well, that was weird. Why wouldn't Axel want to contact the police and go after the person responsible for trying to kill his wife? I desperately wanted to grill him, but it wasn't the time.

We waited about ten minutes, when the doctor marched out of the room shaking his head. "Let's go to the waiting room and talk."

Uh-oh, that didn't sound positive. Axel and I followed the young, tall doctor into the empty waiting room. Axel and I sat on the same couch where we had eaten our sandwiches, and the doctor sat on a chair next to us. "So, your wife's alive. I want to reassure you that, first. The strangest thing has happened though."

"What?" I demanded, terrified.

He held his hand up and said, "No, no, you're reading me wrong. She woke up!"

"Are you kidding?" I asked, stunned.

"Hold on, let me finish, please," the doctor began. frustrated. "I checked all her vitals and everything is fine. You saved her in the nick of time. If whoever it was continued suffocating her for even a minute longer, she might not have survived."

"Wow," I mumbled, horrified at the thought and thankful we went back into her room when we did.

"Yes, yes, be grateful, not revengeful," the doctor suggested, looking directly at Axel.

Axel stood up, and hovered over the young man and exclaimed, "Someone just tried to kill my wife! You're telling me not to seek revenge, aren't you?"

"Mr. Eklund, if you go after this person you could be killed. Or worse, your wife or Ms. Conroy."

Axel plopped down on the couch. "I'm sorry, doctor. I'm

at my wits end lately. So much has happened this year. I'm exhausted and my patience has been worn to the bone." He looked at the doctor and held out his hand. "Will you forgive me?"

"Of course, sir," he replied, taking his hand and shaking it firmly. "You're under enormous stress, and it's only natural for patient's families to lash out once in a while. But, just don't do it again. I'm on your side, remember?"

"Yes, I promise. Thank you, doctor."

"So, can we get back to one very important point you just told us?"

"Yes, Prunella is awake, sort of."

"Here we go again," I murmured. "What do you mean by that?"

"The jolt to her system when that man was trying to suffocate her allowed her to react, and her reaction was to open her eyes and move her body."

"Is she alert enough to know where she is?" Axel asked, concerned.

"I don't think so. Her eyes are open and her arms, legs, and head are moving around. I think it's urgent you both go in and talk, talk, talk to her! Get her to wake up even further. You have the power to do it."

"What are we waiting for?" I bellowed, standing up, ready to go.

"Hold on one second, Ms. Conroy," the doctor said, standing up himself. "Please, please don't bring up any dangerous topics, if you know what I mean."

"I promise. It'll be happy, motivating, and hopeful words we speak to her."

"That's what I want to hear," he said, walking with us to Prunella's room. "I'm going to go in for a while and see if she has any reactions while you're talking to her."

"I'd feel more comfortable if you were there, too, doctor," I said.

"I'm ready," Axel said, taking a deep breath and heading inside Prunella's hospital room.

We entered side by side, after the doctor. He walked confidently to her bed and took a little light and shined it in her eyes. For the first time in weeks, Prunella's head jerked from the bright light. "She's awake," I whispered to Axel. "She just reacted to the flashlight."

"I saw that, too, Ruth Ann," Axel said, quietly. "I'm actually nervous."

"So am I," I admitted. "It's been such a battle, and now she's coming back to us."

"I actually am beginning to believe you this time, Ruth Ann," he said, after doubting Prunella would ever wake up.

The doctor turned toward us and said, "Don't be afraid to come closer. Prunella's definitely improving. Come and talk to her, but remember," he warned, "Happy, happy, happy."

At all cost, I wasn't going to mention anything remotely controversial. Like our Blue Ice necklace. That was the last thing I planned on bringing up. However, I was still racking my brain trying to think of what I could talk about. What is something positive I could tell Prunella that would get her attention? I didn't have to think too long when Axel took the lead. He walked over to Prunella, sat down on one of the two chairs permanently placed next to her bedside and said in a loud, almost too cheerful, voice. "Prunella, can you hear me? It's Axel, your husband."

The doctor patted Axel's back and suggested, "A little more natural, and maybe not so loud. There's nothing wrong with her hearing."

"Sorry, I'm a little nervous."

"Just be yourself and talk to her like you would on a normal day."

"Normal!" I laughed. "There's nothing normal about us."

"I'll say," a weak voice called out from the bed.

"Prunella!" I hollered, rushing to her side. "Did you just say that?"

Chapter 6

The three of us stood stunned. She had just spoken, and even joked with me. Once the doctor did a quick exam with us in the room this time, he smiled and said, "Keep talking. She's clearly waking up."

I took her delicate, frail hand and gave it a hearty squeeze. "It's so good to see those beautiful blue eyes of yours."

Prunella blinked several times and tried to smile. She was able to give a slight grin, and said, "Where am I?"

The doctor answered for us. "You're in the hospital, Prunella. Do you know where?"

She squeezed her eyes shut, straining to remember, and even though I was momentarily worried they wouldn't open again, they did. "I'm in Sweden, right?"

"Very good," the doctor said. "Do you know what time of year it is?"

Her face tensed, and she clearly seemed flustered. The doctor didn't want to push her so he quickly said, "Don't strain, Prunella. I think we'll leave the questions alone for now until you're less groggy."

"No, no," she begged. "I'm not tired! I want to know what's going on. Why am I in the hospital, and how long have I been here?" She tried to sit up, but the doctor gently pushed

31

her back down so her head could rest on the pillow. "Please, I need some answers, and, what's wrong with me?"

Axel stood and went up to the head of her bed and leaned over. "All your questions will be answered, Prunella. Let the doctor make sure you can handle everything first." He was so sweet and gentle with her that Prunella nodded and agreed to rest a little while longer.

The doctor asked if he could take her to run a few tests, but Prunella insisted she was fine. "It's necessary for the doctor to make sure everything is running properly, Prunella," I said. "You'll be right back, and then we can talk."

Prunella agreed, and once the nurse and doctor wheeled her out of the room, we sat in our chairs, silent, not knowing what to say.

Finally, after several minutes, I couldn't take it any longer. "What are we going to tell her, Axel?" I said, frustrated. "We can't exactly say she was cursed and tried to kill all of us!"

"No, we can never speak of that."

"But, too many people know," I said, terrified. "Can she be arrested for what she's done?"

"Absolutely not. She was under the influence of drugs and an odd Jamaican curse. Nobody would hold her accountable for anything during that time."

"I hope so. Look at Cassandra. Judy's giving her a real hard time back home. They're aren't giving her a break at all."

"I know, I'm working on that. But," he started to say, "Look at me! I committed quite a few horrible crimes, and I'm a free man. It'll be alright, just give it time."

"What do we tell her in the meantime?" I asked.

"I'm trying to think about that now, while she's away getting those tests."

We went back into silent mode, both of us racking our brains trying to figure out how to explain, not only how she ended up in the hospital, but how she ended up in Sweden!

Prunella was gone for about an hour. Once she was settled back in her room, she was able to sit up and communicate much more clearly than before. The doctor warned us not to discuss any stressful topics until she'd had more time to recover. Axel and I came up with a plan, actually a huge lie, to tell her until she was strong enough to hear the truth. We knew we could not speak of her beloved Uncle Sherman, and how he died. I really don't know the truth myself actually, but one thing was certain, Prunella would blame herself for his death.

"So," Prunella said in a strong voice. "Are one of you going to start explaining?" Her eyes bore deep into ours as she finished asking.

"Um," was all I could muster.

"Come on!" she demanded. "I know something really bad must've happened."

"I have an idea," Axel said. "Why don't you tell us the last thing *you* remember?"

That was good, Axel, I thought to myself. We watched as she searched her sleepy brain to recall her last memories. "What is wrong with me? I can't remember anything at the moment."

"Don't force it," I said. "It'll all come back to you in time."

"But you can tell me. That'll speed things up."

"No, Prunella," I answered. "That could make you worse. The doctor wants you to take it easy and filling you with too much information could set you back."

"Set me back where?" she demanded. "Back into unconsciousness?"

33

"Yes, Prunella," I replied. "We don't want you to slip back into a coma. It's bad enough Alex is still in one." OH, NO! I screamed inside my head. I can't believe I just said that.

Axel's head turned and stared at me in shock. "Ruth Ann!" he said, through gritted teeth. "Why did you say that?"

"I, I didn't mean that," I said, trying to dig myself out of this hole. "I meant, you were unconscious for a while, and look, now you're sitting up talking to us. All is good."

"Ruth Ann!" Prunella snapped. "Don't you do that to me! You can't say that I was in a coma and take it back! And then.you said Alex is in one, too!"

"Yes, well, I didn't mean to tell you that, yet," I said, bumbling. "It's too much too soon."

"Look at me!" she ordered. "I'm very conscious and getting angry. If you don't spill it now, then I'm going to get even angrier!"

"You need to fill her in on Alex, Ruth Ann," Axel said, quietly. "But carefully."

Prunella's glare was menacing. She was peeved and wanted answers. I wanted to run and come back later when she was stronger, but I was caught, and had to get myself out of this without too much damage. "Well, you were in a coma, but now you're not. You've woken and look healthy and clearly able to communicate."

"Was I shot?" she asked.

"No, no, you weren't shot," I replied. "You just kind of, well, you kind of fell." That's it! She fell. I didn't add that she was cursed and acted like a crazy woman.

Prunella's eyebrows raised, skeptically. "*I fell*?"

"Yes, Prunella, you fell and hit your head," Axel answered for me. He knew I was having difficulty pulling off this lie, so he took over. "It's a long story, but you've heard enough for now."

"No, I have not!" she barked. "How did I fall, and why am I in Sweden?"

"I had to come here on business, and you and Ruth Ann came with me."

"Then how did Alex end up in a coma? And where is he right now?"

"He's here, too," Axel said.

"I thought you said it was you, Ruth Ann and me in Sweden?" she asked, quickly.

"He came with me for business, Prunella," Axel said.

"Oh, yes, he does work for you now, doesn't he?"

"Yes, he does," I said, hoping he would be able to work for Axel again someday.

"Okay, so the four of us came here, and you and Alex worked while Ruth Ann and I did what?"

My, she's an inquisitive little thing, I thought. "Yes. We were at Axel's office when you had your accident."

"Accident?" she inquired, curiously. "I had an accident?"

"Yes," I said, suddenly coming up with a plan. "You were up in Axel's office with us, and you fell. You hit your head and here you are."

"What about Alex? Did he fall and hit his head, too?" she asked, doubtful.

"No," Axel interrupted. "It's completely different than your situation. Alex ingested something he shouldn't have, and he had a bad reaction."

"He did?" she asked, looking like she was starting to believe us. "What?"

"They're looking into that now," Axel answered. Good one! Let's try not to make the lies bigger than they need to right now. Deflection was good, very good.

"So, he's in really bad shape?" she asked, worried.

"Yes, Prunella. I don't want to upset you, but he's not waking up, and they're planning on moving him to a special clinic," I said.

"For coma patients, right?" she asked.

"Yes," Axel answered. "But, I plan on giving him the best treatment out there.

"That's good, Axel," she said. "You do have a kind heart."

"I try, Prunella. I really do," he said, looking like he regretted lying to his wife.

The doctor popped in to check on us. "I think Prunella needs to have some quiet time. Maybe you two can go get some rest and come back later."

"No!" she cried, popping her head off the pillow. "I've been asleep for too long, and I want to stay awake. I'm scared if I fall asleep I won't wake up!"

"Of course, you will," I assured her. "You're getting better now, and will continue to get stronger, but we need to listen to the doctor. Axel and I will only be gone a short time. I could use a shower!"

"Okay, I guess," she said, resting her head back on her pillow. "But, don't be gone long."

"We won't," Axel said, leaning over and kissing his wife on the cheek. "You do what the doctor orders, got it?" he said, smiling.

"I will," she said. "I want to get out of here as soon as possible."

"That'll happen soon," the doctor said.

We walked out with the doctor, leaving a nurse inside to check on Prunella. I had a horrible thought, what if that man came back and tried to kill her?

Chapter 7

"You need to contact the police," the doctor reminded us. "Or I can do it for you."

"No, please, don't," Axel asked. "I'll take care of it. In fact, I'll make a quick call and have her room guarded. Then this won't happen again."

"But, Axel," I pleaded. "There's someone out there who tried to kill Prunella. Why can't we let the police help find that mad man?"

The doctor also waited for Axel's response. I realized, by the desperate look in Axel's eyes, that he wished I had kept my mouth shut. "I agree with Ms. Conroy," he said, firmly.

"I will handle protecting my wife, doctor," he said. "Can I speak with you in private for a moment?" he asked the doctor.

"Hey!" I bellowed.

Before I could protest louder, he pulled me aside and said, "Please just let me speak with you after the doctor. I haven't told you everything. Just let it go for a few minutes."

I wasn't happy, in fact, I was quite irritated. I nodded but didn't say a word since my words wouldn't be too kind. I pulled back a few steps and let Axel and the doctor talk privately. I watched as the doctor nodded several times, and then walked away. Axel quickly walked back to me and said,

"Let's go."

"But, you haven't told me anything!"

"In the car, Ruth Ann," he said, taking hold of my arm and leading me down the hall toward the elevator. "We can speak freely there."

"Fine," I snapped.

We went down to the first floor, past the front desk, coffee and gift shops, and out to the parking garage. Axel left his car here without a driver so we could come and go as we pleased. He led the way to his luxury black sedan and opened the door for me. I reached around the back seat and grabbed a long, fur coat that I had borrowed from Axel's estate and put it on. It was December, and quite chilly.

We sped through town toward his estate. I was waiting for him to begin explaining, but he was focused on the icy roads. "What time is it?" I asked, looking at his dashboard to see the hazy blue light flashing 8:00 p.m. "I don't even know what day it is."

"It's just over a week until Christmas Day, Ruth Ann," he replied. "We got a Christmas miracle, didn't we?"

I looked at him oddly, wondering what and why he was postponing telling me whatever it was he promised. Finally, I couldn't take it any longer. "Axel! Aren't you going to fill me in on this preposterous idea of not contacting the local police? Your wife was nearly killed in the hospital today!"

"I'm brutally aware of that, Ruth Ann," he said not looking at me, but gazing straight ahead. "I planned on starting this conversation while I was driving, but as you can see, the roads are very icy."

He wasn't wrong. The road had an obvious sheen and pellets of ice were hitting our windshield at an alarmingly fast rate. "I can wait until we get home."

He briefly turned toward me and smiled. "You just called my estate here in Sweden, home, Ruth Ann."

I fumbled for words, because I surprised myself, too. "I meant *your* home, Axel."

"No, you didn't, Ruth Ann. Just admit that the house that once held you captive, is now a place you can call home. I'll take that and be happy."

"I guess I do think of it as my extended home."

"I'll take it!"

We drove the rest of the time in silence. My mood felt lighter since Prunella was finally awake. However, the thought of someone trying to kill her brought a rush of anxiety. Just as we made it home, Axel received a call through his car. He looked at the number, turned his car off, and let the call transfer back to his cell phone. That wasn't very nice, I thought. Obviously, he didn't want me to hear his conversation.

I did hear the beginning of the call as we walked up the heated steps to his estate. He pushed a couple numbers in the keypad and the front door unlocked. He let me go in, and just as I was about to listen some more, he quickly retreated into his library and told me he would meet me in the kitchen.

I wasn't thrilled, but what was I going to do? I walked past the impressive staircase in the middle of the foyer and headed down a hallway to the left. I passed the formal living room, the long and narrow dining room, and pushed through a door that opened into the expansive kitchen. I expected to see Inga working hard over the stove or washing dishes at the sink, but she wasn't here. She was back in my hometown waiting for our return. It was a lonely estate here in Stockholm, and a sudden urge to get out of here overwhelmed me.

Finally, after what seemed like an hour, Axel marched

into the kitchen. I had prepared a plate of sandwiches and had tea whistling in the teapot. Axel rushed over, turned off the knob and took hold of the teapot. "I'll pour," he said, grabbing a potholder.

"The mugs are on the island, ready to go," I said. I had already put two teabags of my favorite decaf tea in the mugs.

I watched him pour the steaming hot water. His hands were shaking, and I noticed his face was tense and he looked tired and stressed. His once firm, handsome face, was now pale and dark circles had formed under his eyes.

"What's wrong?" I quickly asked him. "You look terrible!"

"Gee, thanks, Ruth Ann," he replied, setting the teapot back on the stove. "I look that bad, huh?"

"Well, for you, yes. You look totally wiped out and stressed."

"I am."

"What happened with that phone call, Axel? You need to be upfront with me."

"I know," he admitted, yawning. "Can we sit and drink our tea while I fill you in?"

"No more distractions, promise?" I asked.

"Yes, I promise."

We took the plate of sandwiches and our tea and sat at the large wooden kitchen table. Usually, Axel would eat in the dining room and be served by Inga, but well, nobody was here except the two of us. I actually wondered how the place was getting cleaned while we were here because it was immaculate. I've done what little dishes we've used while stopping by to change our clothes and take a short nap, but he must've hired an agency to come in and do the other household duties.

"Spill it, please," I said, sipping my tea and eating a peanut butter and jelly sandwich.

"Okay, here goes. Don't get mad, and please, Ruth Ann, wait until I'm done to either yell at me or ask questions." He looked at me pathetically and added, "Please?"

"Fine, but it doesn't sound good."

"No, it's not good news." He took a swig of tea and a bite of his sandwich and began to describe a nasty mess of a situation.

"Here goes. More has been happening since Prunella and Alex were admitted to the hospital. Once we convinced Inga, Carlos, Isabella, and Cassandra to leave Jamaica with John and Judy, I started receiving threatening calls."

"Threatening?" I bellowed, but slapped my hand over my mouth and whispered, "Sorry."

"The calls came in as 'no caller id', so at first I didn't answer. As you know, we've been kind of preoccupied at the hospital, so I didn't check my voicemail for a long time." I was about to ask how long, but I refrained. "I'll answer your thoughts, Ruth Ann. Until about five days ago, I didn't realize how serious these threats were. The first of several messages was to call an unrecognizable number back or else I'd be sorry. I ignored them, of course, but then they became more viscous, stating if I didn't contact this person they would make sure I'd regret it."

"Oh, no!" I blurted out, without thinking.

"I was stupid and still didn't call back. I was thinking it was a prank of some sort. Somebody who got a hold of my private number. I didn't think they would carry out their threats."

"To kill Prunella, right?" I asked, ignoring his request to hold off my questions.

"Yes. Let me continue, there's a lot more." I nodded and he continued. "About five days ago, when I noticed how many calls were made, I couldn't take it any longer. When we were home showering and taking a rest one night, I called the number." He looked at me with my eyes wide open, dying to ask questions, but I still didn't. "A man answered the phone. A low, gargled voice spoke to me, obviously trying to disguise whoever he was."

"That means we would know who he is!" I cried.

"My thoughts, at first, but then I realized it could've been someone we *might* run into instead of someone we know." Good point, I thought without saying it out loud. "Maybe we would've run into the man at the hospital for instance." He paused, took a large bite and chewed it quickly. "So, when I asked what he wanted and why was he threatening me, he told me to shut my mouth and listen. He told me not to question him or contact any police. That's why I was so adamant about not contacting the police."

"Here we go again," I mumbled, quietly.

"I just don't know, Ruth Ann. At that point, I didn't think he was any danger to us or Prunella, but now ... "

"He is."

"Yes, I believe we need to take him very seriously now."

"Please, go on and tell me what he wanted."

"He told me that if I don't comply with his demands, he will first kill Prunella, and then ..." he stopped, swallowed hard, and said, "you, Ruth Ann. He said if I don't do as he asks both of you will be dead by Christmas."

"Me?" I cried, loudly. "What do I have to do with any of this?" And then it hit me like a ton of bricks ... Blue Ice.

"I can tell by the look in your eyes you've caught on."

"The necklace, right?"

"Yep, once again, someone is after that bloody necklace!"

"This is getting really old, Axel. Why don't we sell it or give it away so they deal with it?"

"You know that can't happen, Ruth Ann. Remember, Meme, on her deathbed in Jamaica told you it's a part of us, and we'll never be rid of it or its powers."

"You're right and after everything we've been through, we can't dismiss his threats." I said.

"I agree. I didn't take him seriously until that hooded man was hovering over Prunella trying to suffocate her!"

Now that I was allowed to ask questions, I wasn't going to hold back. "Is that who called you when we pulled into your estate?"

"Yes."

"Please tell me exactly what he said to you five days ago."

"He told me that I'd never met him before and that anyone who does business with him never ignores his calls. He did catch me off my usual game, because if I weren't dealing with Prunella and all the troubles we've had lately, I would've eaten this guy alive. I've had years of experience dealing with men like this."

"You have?" I asked, dumbfounded. "I knew you ran a shipping business, but you've had to deal with criminals like this before?"

Axel laughed, and said, "Of course, I have. Many men are ruthless when it comes to their business or their pride. This guy's pride was bruised because I ignored him. However, I think he has more power than I thought, and now I'm definitely taking him seriously."

"What did he say, *exactly*?" I asked, trying to get him to

be more specific.

"He went on and on about his power and how everyone who deals with him fears him until I cut him off. I didn't have the time or the need to sit and listen to this bully brag. Well, he didn't take it kindly, and threatened to ruin me and my family. He said if I didn't hand over the gem, he would make our family pay, and he added, that we will regret the day we try to betray him."

"This is ridiculous," I said. "It sounds like a gangster movie."

"I know, right?" he said, smiling, but quickly halting. "He isn't kidding. I've done a little research since I learned his name. I don't think we're dealing with sane people, Ruth Ann."

"What's his name and is he here, in Stockholm?"

"His name is Manual Marquez."

"*Manual Marquez*?" I questioned, baffled. "That doesn't sound very Swedish."

"Nope. That's because he's not Swedish, Ruth Ann, he runs his business down south, way south."

"Like South America?" I asked, trying to figure it out myself.

"There, and Mexico, and ..." he hesitated, and added, "Jamaica."

"NO WAY!"

Chapter 8

"Did you say Jamaica?" I asked, hoping I misunderstood him.

"Yes, Ruth Ann. This guy is really dangerous, and he deals mostly in drugs, illegal drugs."

"Then why does he want our necklace?" I bellowed.

"The gem, actually. He could care less about the rest of it. He dabbles in stolen gems, high-priced gems, Ruth Ann."

"How do you know all of this?" I asked, curiously.

"I did a little research and talked to a few business associates of mine from the past."

"You mean you know people who conducted business with this man?" I asked, stunned.

"Well, yes, but not for drugs or stolen gems. They've used him to get money for their businesses. This guy has more money than you or I could even imagine."

I was dumbfounded, wondering why and how this man would want to deal with little old me. Well, actually, he contacted Axel. "How on earth did he find out about our necklace?"

"The gem," he reminded me, again. "Our past escapades here and in Colorado made news, remember? He must've heard about your rare, priceless blue aquamarine and realized he had to have it."

"So, you're saying this extremely rich and powerful man

put on a black hoodie, black pants, and black gloves, and snuck his way into Prunella's hospital room and tried to kill her?"

"I highly doubt that Manual Marquez did the dirty work, Ruth Ann. He probably used one of his lackeys."

"That makes more sense, I guess," I said, and then blurted, "Hey, if this guy is so dangerous, why not let the police get involved. I bet they've tried to get him in the past for his crimes."

Axel laughed heartily, nearly choking on a bite of his sandwich. Once he recovered, he took a sip of his cooled tea and said, "Men like that don't get caught. They let other people do their dirty work, and if they get caught, they don't rat on the big guy or else they'll be killed."

I stood and walked to the stove and grabbed the teapot. I was trying to let Axel's information sink in as I refilled our cups. "I'm so confused," I mumbled. "I just don't get this. Why does this keep happening to us?"

"I know, Ruth Ann. It's hard for me to believe my own words right now. I took it as a joke in the beginning until this guy started sounded downright angry in his voicemails. Once I heard his name, I knew I had to take it seriously and figure out a way out of this mess."

"So, five days ago you learned about this man and you waited until now to tell me?" I asked, quite annoyed.

"Yes."

"Why? I didn't deserve that, Axel. We could've prevented that attack on Prunella today."

"I realize that, Ruth Ann," he admitted. "I feel sick over it."

"Now what do we do? Have you figured out how we're going to deal with this man?"

"I called in a few favors and hired a guard for Prunella's hospital room. I couldn't tell the doctor what was going on because he would either force the issue and contact the police or kick Prunella out of the hospital."

"He couldn't do that!" I spat, panicking. "The doctor wouldn't throw a coma patient out onto the streets!"

"I'm not so sure about that. He couldn't risk the hospital and the other patients, could he?"

"No, but I really think that would never happen." I took a sip of my hot tea, and asked, "Now what?"

"This is all so new. I'm trying to figure out how to handle it myself. I think we need to get out of Sweden sooner than later."

"But, we can't leave Prunella or Alex behind," I bellowed.

"Alex will be in a safe and secure facility while he's still in his coma. I doubt Marquez will go after him in his condition. Now Prunella, she's awake and very susceptible to harm."

"Why did we leave the hospital?" I asked, terrified.

"She's under close watch, Ruth Ann. I've been receiving constant updates via text from the guard. There's been no one lurking around the corridors or trying to see Prunella. I've already asked that no visitors be allowed except you and me."

"That's good, so far, but it won't last. This man sounds ruthless, and he's not going to let a little guard standing at her door stop him." I hesitated and said, "It makes no sense. It's not like Prunella has Blue Ice with her."

"No, but with Marquez' contacts, I'm sure he knows what happened to her recently, and being kidnapped by a lunatic drug lord will definitely put her over the edge." He stood and started pacing around the table. "I need to stop him!"

"But, how?" I asked, getting dizzy watching Axel go around and around the table. Finally, I snapped, "Will you stop, please!"

"Sorry," he replied, landing on a stool at the island. "I'm so anxious and that's not usually how I act."

"No, you're the coolest, calmest man I know, Axel."

"Not anymore. This mess is taking a huge toll on my nerves."

"I hear you," I agreed.

We remained in the kitchen for quite a while. I couldn't think of any solutions and couldn't imagine outsmarting a drug lord. Out of curiosity, I asked Axel, "Have you done any business with a man like this before?"

"A drug lord or an illegal gem thief?" he asked, glaring at me. "You think I'd do that?"

"No, I just wondered if you ever needed money like the other men you know. I wasn't implying you have, Axel. I was just curious."

"Oh, well, no. I've had investors, but they haven't been of the illegal sort. I know you're thinking about my shady past and how I didn't handle things ethically, but I would never stoop so low and deal with a man of Marquez' stature. He scares even me."

"That doesn't reassure me, Axel. If you're afraid of him, then I think we're in over our heads and need to bring in some help."

"Like who?" he asked, getting up and placing his mug and plate in the sink. I watched and a silly thought entered my head. Who did he think was going to clean his dishes? Inga was thousands of miles away, and I wasn't his hired help. I quickly dismissed this inane thought and tried to think of anyone who could help us. "I know!" I hollered loudly, startling

Axel off his stool.

"Don't do that!" he barked, sitting back down. "My heart's not young anymore, it can't take a jolt like that."

"Sorry, but it just hit me. Why can't we make a phone call to John?"

"John?" cried Axel, laughing. "You think John can handle this man?"

"Well, it's a thought," I said, offended at his reaction.

"John's a small-town cop, Ruth Ann. This is a world-class criminal who kills more people in a day then John's dealt with in his entire career!"

"Don't exaggerate, Axel," I said.

"I'm not."

"At least I had an idea. What about you?" I asked.

"I'm thinking. I keep coming back to one thought ... get Prunella out of Sweden."

"Why? I thought this guy can reach us anywhere."

"He can, but we can protect her more easily back in Deer Creek. It's a small town, and any strangers hanging around will be immediately noticed."

"That's not exactly true, Axel," I said. "It's high season in Deer Creek."

"*High season*?" he questioned.

"Yes, for the resort. Our town's main income is tourism.

"So, what you're saying is that if there are a lot of visitors hanging around town Marquez' men won't be noticed?"

"Maybe," I answered, truthfully. "Most tourists are local to the area. They aren't from a foreign country, so possibly anyone Manual Marquez sends there would be spotted."

"That's hopeful," he replied. "But, we can't depend on it."

"I like the idea of going home, though. We have Inga,

Carlos, Cassandra and Isabella waiting for us. They'll be a lot of help watching and caring for Prunella."

"I agree," he said. "Let's get some sleep and then get back to the hospital. I want to have a talk with the doctor."

"I don't know how I'm going to get any rest with this new information. I would feel better just napping in her room."

"She's safe for now, Ruth Ann," he responded. "There's one more thing I need to mention."

I was just about to drag myself to my room on the second floor. "Now what?" I asked exhausted, mentally and physically.

"There's another reason why I want to get back to Deer Creek."

"What?" I asked, not sure to what he was referring.

"I think we're both so tired we're not thinking clearly. The necklace is in Deer Creek, inside my safe in the library."

I panicked. "We need to warn the others back home right away!"

"I already thought of that, Ruth Ann. I hired a couple guards today to monitor the estate."

"But, won't Inga and the others be suspicious of why they're being guarded?"

"I plan on calling Carlos before I lie down. He's the calmest one there, I think."

"Who knows," I said. "What will you tell him?"

"Not much. Just that I've hired a security firm to monitor my estate and business. Hopefully, he won't ask too many questions."

"Good luck with that," I said, knowing his explanation wouldn't get by Inga. She was suspicious of everything. I'm not so sure about Carlos. Maybe he'd just take Axel's word for it and pass it on.

"Let's get a little sleep, Ruth Ann," Axel said, standing and holding his hand out for me. I took it, even though I was capable of walking on my own. But, as Axel said, we were exhausted and not thinking clearly. Thank heaven I was sane enough to head straight past his room and to my own.

Chapter 9

I took a long hot shower and threw on some comfy pajamas. I decided to lay out fresh clothes in case I had to dress in a hurry. The minute I lay my head on my soft, plush, silky pillow I was out. Sheer exhaustion won out over my anxieties. I woke up to a loud knock on my door. It took me a minute to recognize the sound, but then I sat upright immediately. I figured it was Axel since there was no one else here except the new guards he had hired to roam the property.

"Come on in, Axel," I called out. "I'm not up yet, but it's okay to come in."

Axel opened the door and stepped inside my bedroom. "You had me worried, Ruth Ann," he said with a worried expression. "I've been up for hours."

"Hours?" I questioned him. "What time is it?"

"It's ten in the morning."

I threw off the down comforter and stood too quickly. I lost my balance and swayed momentarily, scaring Axel. "Are you alright?" he asked, rushing to my side and grabbing my arm just as I sat down on the edge of the bed.

"I got up too quickly but I'm fine now," I said, reassuring him.

He put a hand to his heart and said, "I can't take anymore."

"I hear you, Axel. I'm at my wits end, too. However, I am perfectly fine, and intend on staying that way."

I told him to go into the kitchen and get a pot of water going in the tea kettle, and I'd be down in ten minutes. He nodded and headed out, leaving me to hurry and get ready. I was thankful that last night I washed my hair and laid out my clothes. As I slipped on a pair of soft, stretchy blue jeans, I realized I forgot to ask Axel if the hospital had contacted him during the night.

Once dressed, I grabbed my purse and headed down into the kitchen. I pushed open the door and found Axel in front of the refrigerator staring at the contents inside. "What are you looking for?" I asked him.

"Something to eat."

"I'm fine with cereal and orange juice. Aren't you okay with that, too?"

"I guess so. I miss Inga's cooking, but don't ever tell her."

I laughed and walked over to help. I grabbed a couple bowls from a cupboard and went inside the large walk-in pantry to grab some cereal. I felt rejuvenated after all the sleep I had and was hungry and ready to get back to the hospital. "I want to have those sugar-coated flakes, but I think I'm going to grab some bran. What would you like?"

"Whatever you get me," he replied, solemnly.

I eyed him suspiciously and noticed he didn't look as refreshed as I was. His eyes still had black circles under them, and he was still staring blankly inside the refrigerator. "Are you alright?" I asked him. "You are kind of spacing out there."

He closed the door after grabbing the orange juice and milk. "I'm just indecisive this morning, that's all."

"You didn't get a lot of sleep, did you?" I asked him,

curiously.

"I got enough," he replied, setting the liquids on the island.

"Did you spend a lot of time on the phone? I know you were going to call Carlos. How did that go?"

"He was fine."

"Can you try and be more specific, please?" I asked, trying to shake him out of his funk.

"Sorry, he accepted my reason for having extra guards roaming the grounds without too many questions. However, Inga and Cassandra didn't let it go. Carlos was in the room with them. He put me on speakerphone even though I asked him not do that."

"That must've been frustrating, Axel," I said, grinning internally. I could just imagine the interrogation Inga gave him. "Go on."

"At first, Inga only wanted answers about Prunella's condition. But, when she heard me mention guards, she went ballistic."

"I can envision her now," I said, smiling.

"You think it's funny now, Ruth Ann," he said, not smiling. "But, I'm the one who had to answer all their questions."

"So, do they know the truth?" I asked, wondering just how much he divulged.

"No."

"Come on, Axel!" I stammered. "Stop with the vague answers."

"I'm just a little tired, forgive me." He took a spoonful of cereal and continued, "I only told them that since we were just out of danger with Svenson and the twins, I felt uncomfortable leaving them unguarded back in Deer Creek. I didn't tell them anything about Manual Marquez. I didn't feel it was best until we were there in person. Are you upset I didn't tell them, Ruth Ann?"

"No, I guess I understand why you left the part about a drug lord demanding we hand over Blue Ice!"

"Exactly," he said, digging into his cereal with more gusto.

"I forgot to ask you if you heard from your guards or anyone at the hospital? Is Prunella okay?"

"She's awake, but still groggy. Her memory hasn't returned, and I think it's a good thing for now."

"For now, yes, but the doctor does think she'll eventually regain her memories, right? I thought that's what he told us."

"Yes, he did, but he couldn't tell us when or where we'll be when it happens," Axel said.

"She's going to have a horrible breakdown when she finds out about Sherman, and her hand in his death."

"It wasn't her fault," he said, looking disappointed with my comment.

"I didn't mean it accusingly, Axel," I said. "I just know she's going to blame herself, and you know it, too. I'm worried about that, and also when she finds out she was cursed and all the horrible things she said and did to us."

"It's going to kill her," he said, concerned. "We'll have to be there to support her and get her the counseling she'll definitely need."

"We can arrange anything that's necessary, Axel," I said. "I'm a huge proponent of therapy. It got me through one of the toughest times in my life."

"When your husband was killed in the plane crash, right?" he asked, curiously.

"Yes, I didn't know how I was going to go on with my life. If it weren't for Nancy and Lynne, I don't know what and where I'd be right now."

"They're wonderful young women. You should be extremely proud of yourself for raising such lovely women."

"Thank you, Axel. I am proud of them. They've been there for me, and I hope they'll say that I've been there for them. I just wish ..." I stopped and shut my mouth.

"I know what you were about to say. You wish your daughters would settle down and get married. You want grandchildren, don't you?"

"I never thought about grandchildren! I guess I am old enough for those, but you're right about wishing my girls would meet the right men and settle down."

"They're fiercely independent, Ruth Ann." He smiled, and added, "Kind of like you!"

"Me?" I questioned him, stunned. "You think *I'm* independent?"

"Of course, you are," he answered. "You are one of the most independent woman I know."

I was so shocked by his observation that I became speechless. That's a rare occurrence, so even I enjoyed the moment of silence. However, it didn't take long to get back to business. "Ruth Ann, are you almost ready to head back to the hospital? I'm feeling anxious and want to get back. We've been gone over twelve hours. That's the longest we've been gone since Prunella was admitted."

"We had good news yesterday and thought we could take a breath but now we have to worry about Manual Marquez. My emotional state is more up and down than a yo-yo!"

"Mine, too."

"I'm ready. Let me rinse these dishes and put them into the dishwasher. Hey," I said, turning toward him while I was rinsing dishes. "Who put food in the pantry and refrigerator?

Also, I think my bathroom was cleaner than I left it."

"I hired a service to come in and clean and stock necessary items for us. They come here while we're at the hospital." He quickly realized a huge problem with what he just told me. "I need to stop it immediately!"

"Why?" I asked, confused. I kind of liked having those things taken care of for me.

"With Marquez threatening us, I don't want anyone entering this house except for my hired guards."

"You're right! They could poison our food or hide out inside waiting for us to come home."

"Exactly." He told me to meet him in the foyer so he could make a quick call to the agency to cancel the temporary housekeeper. He rushed out of the kitchen, and my guess, into his library. It didn't take me long to get the dishes in the dishwasher.

I was the first one to arrive in the foyer. I glanced at the closed library doors. I put my ear against the door. I'm against violating a person's privacy, but sometimes it was, well, necessary. Unfortunately, I couldn't hear a word. I accepted defeat and went to the front door. It was a bright, sunny late morning, and when I looked out the sidelight, I spotted a light coating of snow. "Great," I said out loud. "So, now there's snow on top of the ice."

"Yes, that sounds logical," a male voice called out.

"Axel!" I bellowed. "Don't sneak up on me. You startled me."

"Sorry. You were looking out the window so peacefully that I didn't want to disturb you."

"Are you through with your call?" I asked, changing the topic.

"Yes, we're all set. Nobody will be allowed in here except my guards when they do their indoor rotation."

"That's a good idea."

Axel grabbed my elbow and led me down the front steps and to his car. The guards had cleared and salted a path for us so it wasn't too bad. I sat in the front seat and noticed how warm it was inside the car. "I can start it from my phone, remember?" he told me.

"I'll have to have that installed in my truck back in Deer Creek," I said, making a mental note.

"I'll remind you."

We drove about twenty minutes and parked inside the hospital garage. It was a heated garage, and I was thankful for that. I was wearing the borrowed fur again, but there was clearly a chill in the air. Was it the weather or something else I was feeling?

Chapter 10

When Axel and I stepped off the hospital elevator, we knew something had gone terribly wrong. Axel took off running toward Prunella's room, and I grabbed this first hospital employee I could find.

"What happened?" I snapped at the young nurse's aide.

The girl had to be in her early twenties and froze. "I, I don't know, ma'am. I just got to this floor. All I'm doing is passing out trays for the patient's lunches."

"I'm so sorry. I didn't mean to scare you," I said, releasing my grip. "I just saw the police and I got worried for my cousin who's a patient up here."

"That's okay," she replied, walking away and heading to a large cart filled with trays. She picked one up and hurried into a room. She couldn't get away from me fast enough.

I rushed to Prunella's room and found Axel inside with the doctor, a nurse, and two policemen. "What happened?" I asked, out of breath.

They turned and saw me in the doorway, and the look of disgust on the doctor's and nurse's faces scared me. Obviously, something had happened or there wouldn't be two policemen standing over her bed.

"Come over here, Ruth Ann," Axel said, waving his arm

in the air. "I don't want the whole floor to hear this."

I hurried over, passing the nurse, and stood by Axel. He was closest to Prunella's side and blocking my view of her. As soon as I got close, I noticed she was sitting and awake. Phew, I was worried she had either been harmed or slipped back into a coma.

"Prunella!" I cried. "You're alright."

"Yes, Ruth Ann, I'm OK, now."

"What does that mean?" I asked, anxiously. Before anyone answered, I noticed there wasn't any guard around. "Hey, where's the guard? I never saw him out in the hall or in here."

Axel responded, "He was attacked, Ruth Ann."

"Attacked?" I bellowed. "Who attacked him?"

Axel stared at me uncomfortably, and then it hit me. A hired thug of Manual Marquez must've taken out the guard. "Is the guard okay?"

"I'm afraid not," the policeman said. "He was murdered, and that's why we're here. We need to find out why this lady needed a guard."

I stayed silent. It wasn't my place to say a word. I waited for Axel to clear it up and figure out what we needed to do next. I was so relieved that Prunella was okay, I felt insensitive toward the poor, dead guard.

"I told the police that I hired a guard because of what we just went through with Svenson and the twins. I know Svenson is tucked away in jail, but he's escaped before, and I didn't want to take any chances."

"And," I added, unwisely. "The twins are dead."

The policeman in charge turned toward me and gave me a quizzical look. "And what do *you* know about it?"

I turned on the most innocent look I could muster. "Me? I know nothing about why anyone would attack my cousin, officer. I'm offended you would think I had anything to do with it."

"We never said you had anything to do with it, ma'am." I got the feeling the officer didn't believe me.

"Axel, we need to protect Prunella. How are we going to keep her safe? There have been two attacks in two days."

The lead officer whipped his back to me and spat out, "Did you say this woman has been attacked *two times*?"

Axel decided it was best to shut me down. "I'm sorry, officer. Ruth Ann only meant that Prunella was attacked today, and when she first came to the hospital in her coma."

The officer eyed me suspiciously, "Is that what you meant, Ms. Conroy?"

I hated to lie, and especially to a police officer, but I didn't have a choice. "Yes, I'm sorry, I've been sitting in this hospital room for so long, time has escaped me."

I was relieved when the officer wrote me off as a spacey female and turned his attention back to Prunella. He started questioning her rapidly, when the doctor cut him off and demanded he let her rest. "She needs to stay calm. You can come back tomorrow."

The officer slapped his notebook shut and stormed out of the room with the other office trailing. The doctor, knowing Prunella had been attacked yesterday, turned to Axel and barked, "Why did you lie to that officer?"

"I didn't have a choice," Axel replied.

"Why is that?" the doctor asked. "I could've blown your lie apart by telling them what really happened yesterday. I gave you the benefit of the doubt after you hired a guard to watch over your wife. However, your guard proved to be of no use." The doctor stood tall, arms crossed over his chest, waiting for an answer.

Axel was about to comply, when I cut in. "Can someone tell me what happened today? Before we argue about who's lying and why, I need to know what happened to that guard and who got inside the room."

"I'm in this room, too, Ruth Ann," Prunella snapped. "Stop treating me like a child. I'm awake and capable of answering questions."

"You're in a delicate state, Prunella," the doctor said, smiling gently. "Let me describe what I saw before the guard was killed."

"Thank you, doctor," I said waiting.

"I started my rounds early this morning around nine. Everything was quiet on the floor for a couple hours until suddenly a nurse came running into the room of a patient I was examining. She told me that a man wearing a black hoodie just came off the elevator." He raised his hand to ward off our questions. "Before you ask, I warned the floor staff to be on the lookout for a man in a black hoodie and pants."

"And black gloves," I mumbled.

He scowled at me and replied, "Yes, and black gloves." I mouthed that I was sorry, and he continued. "I immediately left the patient in the care of the nurse and headed into the hall to see if he was still lurking around. That's when I noticed the guard wasn't standing outside Prunella's room. I rushed in and found the guard and the man in the black hoodie fighting on the floor. My main concern was for my Prunella, so I yelled to the nurse to call the police immediately, and then I rushed to Prunella's side avoiding the men on the floor."

"You stepped over those men?" I couldn't help but ask.

"I completely avoided them. They didn't even notice that I came inside the room."

"Really?" Axel asked, surprised.

"Yes. I checked on Prunella, who was sedated and sleeping, and was relieved to find her alive."

Prunella's eyes flew wide open. "You thought they *killed me*?" she asked, terrified.

"Of course, I did," the doctor exclaimed. "They tried just yesterday to suffocate you!"

"Go on, please," Axel said, eagerly trying to understand what happened during the fight.

"Once I knew Prunella was safe, I turned my attention to the two men beating each other up on the floor. I have to give it to the guard, the poor guy. He fought till the bitter end."

"That's horrible!" Prunella cried.

"I don't want you getting upset, Prunella. Would you like another sedative?" he asked her.

"No!" she replied, frustrated. "I don't want any more drugs. I want my head clear, and I want to remember what's happened to me!"

"In time, Prunella," the doctor said, gently. "You've had a traumatic experience and your brain needs time to heal. It will happen, so please be patient ... and calm."

"Doctor," Axel said, irritated with the disruptions. "Please tell me, what you did next?"

"I told Prunella to stay still and not say a word. I picked up the nearest item I could reach and threw it at them, hoping they would disengage and take it out of the hospital." He stopped and pointed to the bed tray on the floor. "I threw a full tray of food at them. It startled the wrong man, I'm afraid. It gave the hooded man enough time to grab the guard's neck and ... well, kill him instantly."

"He broke his neck?" I questioned, sickened by the description.

"Yes. At least it was quick and he didn't suffer long," the

doctor added. "I'm not saying I'm happy he died, but if he was in pain, it was only for a second."

I didn't have any further questions, except one. "What happened to the hooded man?" I asked.

"He stood up, looked at Prunella and me, and ran out of the room."

"Did you see his face or anything that could identify him?" Axel asked, curiously.

The doctor's expression took on a look of terror. "Yes. His hood accidentally slipped off his head for a second, and I saw his eyes, and face."

"Can you describe him?" I asked. "And did you already tell the police all of this?"

"No. I don't know why I didn't tell them about seeing his face, but I wanted to speak with you first."

"Thank you, doctor," Axel said. "Please, describe his face."

"He had long dark hair pulled up in a high bun. It was very greasy, and his eyes were black, jet black. I felt like his eyes were empty, and it made me cold, very cold. He looked young and very strong."

"Anything else? Like his ethnic background?" Axel inquired.

"He looked of the Spanish or Mexican descent."

That convinced me that he was one of Manual Marquez' men. I knew it, and this man just murdered an innocent guard.

The doctor looked intently at Axel and asked, "What do we do now?"

"*We* do not do anything. I will handle this by myself," Axel replied.

"That's not a good enough answer for me," the doctor said, fiercely. "If you don't give me the answer I need then I plan on telling the police I remember seeing his face."

Astonished, I said, "But, you told them you didn't see his face. Don't you think they'll question you?

"I could easily say I was distraught at first, and now I'm recalling everything."

"Doctor," Axel began. "I'm not saying nothing is going to be done. I'm in the process of figuring out who is doing this to Prunella and my family. If the police get involved, I'm afraid it'll make matters worse."

"Please tell me you're close to finding whoever committed these horrendous crimes?" he asked, pleadingly.

"Yes, I am." Axel looked at me, and asked the doctor to give us some time alone with Prunella. He nodded, but made it clear we needed to get answers immediately or he would contact the police and make a statement.

Axel waited until the doctor left the room. He walked over and closed the door. "Okay, we're alone," Prunella said. "Why did you need to speak with Ruth Ann and me alone?"

"I think we need to make some changes with your stay at this hospital," he said, matter of factly. "It's not safe, and I don't want to risk another guard's life."

"I don't blame you, Axel, but how can we watch over Prunella if a licensed, professional guard can't?" I asked.

"We'll have our guards, Ruth Ann, but I want to get Prunella out of this environment. It's too easy a target. Anyone could dress up as a doctor or nurse or even a volunteer. I want to move her, and immediately."

"But," I said, anxiously, "She's not ready to leave the hospital. She just woke up from a long coma!"

"I'm fine, Ruth Ann!" she belted. "I think I could leave here."

"But, you don't have your memory back," I said, terrified

of the time when she did remember.

"The doctor told Prunella he didn't know when, and *if*, memory of the events leading to her coma would return, Ruth Ann," Axel said.

"What do you mean by *if*?" Prunella angrily asked her husband. "The doctor said when not if!"

"Yes, yes, you're correct, Prunella," Axel agreed, even though he and I knew it might not be true. The doctor told us in confidence that some people don't ever remember tragic moments.

"I don't care," I bellowed. "I think it's too soon to move Prunella." I added, "And where do you presume to move her?"

"I'm working that out right now, Ruth Ann," he replied. "In fact, I need to step out for a moment and make a call."

"Where, and who are you talking to?" I asked, confused and frustrated. "Why not make the call in here? Prunella and I want to hear your plans, too."

"Yeah!" Prunella declared, strongly. "I am the patient, you know."

"I'm brutally aware of that, Prunella," Axel said. "The truth is, I don't get very good cell service in here." He added, "And, it is against the rules to have cell phones on in here."

"It is?" I asked, surprised. "We just talked to Inga in here yesterday."

Axel looked guilty. He scrambled, and said, "It was just for a second, and this might take a while. Please, just let me go for a few minutes and hopefully I'll have more details when I return."

"Am I safe in here without you and a guard?" Prunella asked, worried

"I'm just going to be in the hall, and I doubt that lunatic will come back this fast."

"I'm here, too!" I exclaimed. "I know I can't fight a killer, but I can sure scream loud enough to get help in here immediately."

"There," Axel said, walking to the door and opening it up. "I'll leave it open, and I swear I'll be able to see your door the entire time."

Prunella and I nodded, and he took off into the hall. I walked closer to her bed and plopped down in a chair, exhausted, even though it was only early afternoon. Prunella watched me intently, and finally said, "You look exhausted Ruth Ann."

"I am. It's been a really long year so far!" I declared.

Prunella looked disheartened. "I'm sorry that I've caused you such heartache and aggravation. I wish we could turn the clock back and do it all over again. I would never put you in such danger!"

"I wouldn't change anything, well, there are *things* I would change, but hear me loud and clear ... I never have regretted meeting you or anyone else close to us. It's a privilege to have you in my family, and I can't tell you enough that I don't want anything bad to happen to you. I'd give my own life to protect you!"

"Ruth Ann," she said, tears streaming down her rosy cheeks. "I feel the same about you. If I could only remember the last few weeks. Are Inga or Sherman here?" she hesitated and asked. "How are they?"

Uh-oh, I thought to myself. How was I going to handle this? I couldn't tell her poor Sherman had been killed, yet alone possibly by her own two hands. Quickly, I replied, "I just spoke with Inga yesterday. She's back in Deer Creek, with the others, waiting for us to go back home."

"That's so nice, Ruth Ann," she said, smiling. "Tell me,

what's going on back home?" She smiled so innocently, I couldn't help but wish that what happened when she was cursed was a just nightmare and not real.

"Inga's being Inga, fighting with everyone to keep control. Isabella and Carlos are adjusting to the cold weather and helping Cassandra acclimate too."

Prunella looked at me quizzically. "Everything you just said to me sounds like words I don't understand. Outside of Inga, I have no idea who you are talking about!"

"Really?" I asked, completely stunned. I had an idea. I decided to ask Prunella what her last memory was. She strained to think of it, but finally, she told me.

"We were back in Deer Creek and we were eating Thanksgiving dinner."

"Are you sure that's your last memory?" I asked, praying she recalled a little more than that.

"Yep. That's the last thing I remember. That's why I'm so frustrated. Nobody will tell me how and why we ended up in Stockholm! I know you've said for business, but why can't I remember that?"

"It takes time, Prunella," I answered. "Don't force it. You need to keep gaining your strength, and I bet when you're a little stronger, your memories will come flooding back."

"I hope so."

"Let's sit and wait for Axel," I said, wondering what he was up to now. If I felt Prunella was safe in her room, I would be listening in on his call right this very moment. Instead, Prunella was bombing me with questions I wasn't comfortable answering.

"So, tell me about these others, Ruth Ann? You mentioned Isabella. I know I know her, but from where? I'm trying to remember our holiday dinner in detail. I do recall people besides your daughters, Inga, Axel, and oh!" she cried out loudly. "How's Sherman? I miss him so. I can't believe he's not here by my side. He's so loyal to me, especially now that we know he's my great uncle."

"Remember, we just came here for a short business trip."

"I know, but once I was seriously injured, I just thought he'd make the trip, and Inga, too!"

"Sherman was pretty old, Prunella," I said, not realizing the blunder I made.

Thankfully, Prunella didn't catch it, or I didn't believe she did. "He's still vibrant for his age, Ruth Ann. He's old, but very stubborn, and nosy."

"Yes," I said, carefully not putting him in the past tense. "He is a handful, isn't he?"

"But, he loves me so. He moved with Inga from Sweden to Deer Creek to be by my side. I guess I'm just a little surprised they aren't here."

"They didn't have a choice, Prunella."

"You mentioned Isabella and, who else?" she asked, confused.

"Carlos and Cassandra."

"Who are they, again? I should know this, right?" she asked.

"Yes. You will. Give it more time, Prunella."

"Please, Ruth Ann. You're not telling me anything! I need to know more, and I'm asking you, no, I'm demanding you tell me!"

I decided to start slowly. "Do you remember coming down to Jamaica to help me find John?"

She looked at me blankly. "I did?"

"Yes, but if you don't remember going to Jamaica, then you won't remember meeting Carlos and Isabella."

"What about the other woman?"

"Cassandra," I answered. "You'll definitely not remember her, either."

Before she could protest any further, Axel and the doctor marched inside the room. I was relieved, and terrified at the same time. Relieved, that I didn't have to answer any more of Prunella's questions, but terrified about what we would soon learn.

Chapter 11

"You're crazy!" I hollered at Axel. "We can't fly Prunella home in her condition!"

Prunella looked positively radiant. "That's terrific news! I want to go home, Ruth Ann. Please don't fight Axel."

"But, you just woke up from a coma!" I objected vehemently. "Doctor, are you telling me you're okay with this?"

"Well, normally I would not advise moving a patient in her fragile condition. However, these aren't normal conditions."

"But, what about her health coming first?" I demanded.

"I've agreed to hire a nurse to fly with us, Ruth Ann. We'll be taking my private plane, and I believe for Prunella's safety, and our own, that we need to get away from here."

"They could follow us," I quickly responded.

"Maybe, maybe not," Axel answered. "I feel, and so does the doctor, that going back to Deer Creek will help Prunella heal both physically and mentally.

"Hey," she cried out. "What do you mean by *mentally*? I'm not crazy, you know."

"Your memories, Prunella," the doctor answered, finally participating in the conversation. "I agree with Axel."

Now he's Axel? Before, he was Mr. Eklund. Obviously, they'd become quite friendly with each other.

"Prunella," Axel started. "Are you comfortable going back home? Do you feel you're strong enough?"

She sat bolt upright and said, "Yes! I want to go home. I want to see Inga and Sherman, and your daughters, and these new people you told me about."

Axel turned toward me, and I could see the anger in his eyes. "Excuse me?"

I quickly doused the fire. "I asked Prunella what her last memory was, and she told me it was Thanksgiving dinner. I mentioned Inga, Carlos, Isabella, and Cassandra, but she didn't remember anyone but Inga."

Prunella speedily interrupted, "And Sherman! Don't forget about him!"

The blood drained from Axel's face. I didn't want him to think I said anything about Sherman's death. "Yes, she asked how they *all* were doing back in Deer Creek, and she was surprised Inga and Sherman weren't by her side right now."

"And you said ..." Axel asked, confused.

"I told her we were only supposed to be here a short time, and they stayed back home in Deer Creek."

"I thought once they heard about me being in a coma, they would've rushed to Sweden to be with me," she said, hurt.

"We told them not to," Axel said, finally catching on. "They needed to hold down the fort back home."

"Oh," she said, still appearing offended. "Oh, we forgot about Alex! We can't leave without him, too."

"He has to stay behind, Prunella," the doctor answered for us. "He's actually being transferred in the next hour or so. So, if you want to see him, it's time."

"I want to see him, too," Prunella requested. "I know all of you will tell me no, but I'm not asking, I'm telling you."

"That's fine," the doctor said. "I'll have a nurse put you into a wheelchair, and then we'll see how strong you are. If you do well, then I'll feel better releasing you to fly across the ocean to the states."

"Good. Let's do this," she said, adjusting her personal nightgown. "Um, do I have a robe somewhere?"

I marched to the small closet, opened it and reached in. I pulled down a beautiful silk robe I brought from Axel's estate. "Here," I said, bringing it to her.

She smiled, and said, "I remember this robe! It's so cheery, and bright with the flowers."

"I'm glad to see you know that robe," the doctor said, smiling. "I feel confident your memories will come back soon."

I knew the doctor was happy, but Axel and I weren't. The last thing we wanted was for Prunella to remember all the horrible things she did. We watched Prunella happily slip on her robe, proud she felt a connection with it.

"I'm ready, let's go see Alex and try to wake that man up!"

The three of us didn't have the heart to tell her it wasn't going to happen and might never happen. Instead, we put on fake smiles, and watched as Prunella swung her legs around to the side of the bed and, with help, stand. The nurse and doctor let her do most of the work, and then she sat in the wheelchair. We were impressed with the strength Prunella showed. She just might be strong enough to fly home!

Every day since Prunella and Alex were admitted to the hospital, I have visited Alex, too. I didn't spend as much time with him, but I was told he was in a deep coma, and Prunella needed more of my attention. I felt horribly guilty that I didn't give more time to Alex. He needed me, and I felt I let him down. It wasn't that I didn't visit him, but I had a difficult time watching him lie there so lifelessly. It terrified me, and I couldn't face it. Watching Prunella was bad enough, but she seemed more alert somehow. Alex, he just looked as if he had already left this cruel world for a better place. I had a hard time watching him slip away.

Axel and the doctor assured me that he would get the best care at the clinic, but I worried he might never wake up. I put on my best smile and took over from the nurse and wheeled Prunella in Alex's room.

Her face turned pale, and she started to weep. "Maybe this isn't a good idea," I said, stopping.

"NO!" She cried. "I want to go by his side. We need to speak with him and let him hear our voices."

The doctor nodded, and I wheeled her to his bedside. "Talk to him, Prunella," the doctor said. "He knows your voice. He may not wake up, but many experts say he can hear you talking."

Prunella grabbed his still hand. "Alex," she said so kindly. "It's me, Prunella. Ruth Ann and Axel are here, too. We need you to wake up! Please, Alex, we want to go home, and you need to come with us." She waited for him to respond, but when he didn't, she said, "Please Alex, show me a sign. Squeeze my hand or wiggle your fingers."

We stood frozen, watching Alex and Prunella's exchange. "Don't get your hopes too high, Prunella," the doctor said. "Alex hasn't shown any reaction to anyone."

Suddenly, out of nowhere, we all spotted movement. "Look!" Prunella cried, loudly. "He just tried to move his fingers!"

"I saw that," I said, amazed. "Did you, Axel, doctor?"

"Yes, I saw that, too," Axel said.

"I can't believe it," the doctor mumbled. "He moved."

Prunella looked at the doctor and asked, "That's the first sign from him since he arrived here?"

"Yes."

"How long has it been, doctor?" she asked, smartly. We hadn't told her how long she had been here.

The doctor caught on to her motive immediately. He responded, "A very long time, Prunella."

"How long?" she repeated, becoming agitated.

"Calm yourself down, Prunella. Or I'll have to insist you return to your room to rest," the doctor said, firmly.

She stopped her inquisition and turned her attention back to Alex. "Please, Alex, wake up."

I noticed the doctor slipped out of the room and returned with a nurse. "Can you please give us a few minutes alone with the patient?"

"But, we just got here!" Prunella stated.

"You can wait in the hall, and when we're done, I'll let you back in."

He didn't wait for us to respond, but had the nurse wheel Prunella into the hall, and we followed. "What could he do to Alex that we couldn't watch?"

"I guess an examination to see why he moved his fingers," Axel answered.

We waited for what seemed like hours, but it was actually only about fifteen minutes. The nurse came out first, and when Prunella asked if we could go in, she said a flat out, "No."

"Well, she was rude," Prunella said, irritated.

We didn't have to wait long when the doctor stuck his head out the door and held a finger up. "Just give me a second more."

The nurse returned without glancing our way. She obviously didn't want us to ask again if we could go inside.

"What's taking so long?" I asked, getting quite frustrated myself.

"Maybe it's good news," Prunella said, excitedly. "He might've woken up like I did!"

"Sorry, Prunella," a voice said from the doorway. "Alex hasn't come out of his coma yet. However, he has more brain activity. I think Prunella talking to him was exactly what he needed. I think spending more time with him is a good thing."

"But, I thought he was being transferred to the clinic," I reminded them.

"Oh, that's right," the doctor said. "The transport is probably almost here."

"But, that's not fair!" Prunella cried. "If he's trying to wake, and he's shipped off somewhere else, he'll never hear our voices. I think he should come home with us."

"He's much too fragile for the flight, Prunella," the doctor said. "I don't know if he would survive."

"He's still that bad?" I asked, sadly.

"He's in serious condition. His body hasn't recovered yet."

"I'm confused. I thought he was just sick?" Prunella questioned him.

The doctor looked uncertain, but he quickly regained his thoughts and said, "He was, is, Prunella. I'm just saying that since he's been in his coma for so long, his organs are having a difficult time. He needs to be monitored and stay put until he's stronger." He added, "I feel confident after seeing more brain activity that it will happen. I'm sorry that he has to be moved too, but we don't have a choice. Plus, you're going to be flying back to Colorado very soon."

"So, we have your approval?" Axel asked.

"Yes. The more I think about it, and the more I've seen Prunella talk and move, I'm sure she'll be better off back home."

"I'm happy, yet sad," Prunella replied. "I really don't like leaving Alex here without any of us."

"He'll be home soon," I said, trying to reassure her. I didn't like any of it either, but for her safety we needed to leave right away.

The doctor let us go back in and wait for the transport team to take Alex to the clinic. It wasn't a long wait. Prunella spent every second talking and pleading with him to open his eyes or give a sign, but nothing happened. Once she caught sight of the team waiting to place Alex on their gurney, she finally asked us to wheel her away from the bed. She was crying heavily, and I felt horrible for her, and Alex, but I knew it was the only choice we had.

We watched as they lifted the young man off his hospital bed onto the gurney. He seemed so frail, it broke my heart. I watched as his eyes never flickered or opened, making Prunella start to cry again. She kept talking to him until they disappeared into the elevator.

"That was horrible," she said. "I can't believe we're just going to leave him alone!"

"What other option do we have, Prunella?" Axel asked her.

"There has to be something we can do, Axel! We can't abandon him!!"

I saw the look of despair in Axel's eyes, and quickly grabbed hold of the wheelchair and whisked her down the hall. "Hey, where are you taking me?" she asked me, wiping the last of her tears away.

"Just a little stroll down the hall before I take you back to your room."

Axel caught up with us and reminded me quietly that Prunella wasn't safe out in the open. "I forgot," I said, mad with myself for putting her in more danger. "Let's go back to her room and ask the doctor when we can leave."

"I was just on the phone trying to arrange for my plane so we can get out of this country right away. They have to make their flight plan, and get it okayed. It shouldn't take long. My pilot said he'd call me back right away."

The nurse followed us into her room and let Prunella get herself up and out of the wheelchair without assistance. She was stronger than I thought and I knew she was determined to prove herself. My guilty feelings for wanting to go home so badly suddenly overcame me. I grabbed Axel's arm while the nurse was situating Prunella in her bed and told him I, too, felt horrible about abandoning Alex.

"He's already on his way to the clinic so we can't stop him now, but maybe I can call over there later and discuss his condition. The doctors there may have a different opinion and let us take him home with us."

"How? He's not even awake!" I stammered. "No doctor in their right mind would let us move him."

"Then why are you asking me?" he asked, exasperated.

"Let me vent, Axel," I said. "I know what's right, but it doesn't make it any easier for me.

"What are you two whispering about?" Prunella called out. "You're not changing your minds about taking me home, are you?"

"No way!" I replied, loudly. "We're just waiting for the okay from Axel's pilot, and then we'll be on our way."

The doctor popped in just as I said this. "I won't release

Prunella unless the nurse is here to accompany her on the ride to the airport."

"When will she be here?" Axel asked, anxiously. "We really need to get out of here for Prunella's safety."

"We are expecting *him* any moment."

"*Him*?" Axel questioned, skeptically. "I don't know this nurse's background and if *he* can be trusted."

"He's on our list for hire. We regularly hire out nursing staff to assist with patients when we send them home."

"Can I have his credentials at least?" Axel asked.

"Of course. I recommended him myself since he will be going such a long way, and he jumped on the chance to go to the United States."

"Why?" Axel asked, suspiciously.

The doctor glared at Axel and replied, "Because he has no family left, and he's been alone most of his life. He's British, and said he only knew of an older brother, but they were separated years ago."

"Axel," I interrupted. "I'm sure this nurse is more than qualified or the doctor wouldn't have recommended him."

"I know, but do you blame me? We've had a bit of a difficult time lately, don't you think?"

"Yes, but this is different," I replied.

"How?" he asked, getting on my nerves quickly.

"The doctor knows this man, and he has worked with this hospital. Do you think some unknown criminal would have planned on working at this hospital, knowing we'd be here someday so he could swoop in and go after us? Sounds pretty ridiculous even to me!"

I could see the wheels spinning in his head. "I guess so. I'm just paranoid."

Just then, the doctor burst my bubble. "Well, Ruth Ann.

I really don't know this particular nurse that well. He has worked in this hospital as a sub, but only in the last few weeks."

"Aha!" Axel bellowed. "I told you something wasn't right."

"No, Axel," I said. "That doesn't mean anything is wrong. I think you need to take a step back and breathe. It'll be alright," I said, smiling. I turned to the doctor and asked, "Can we meet him first? I mean, if we talk with him, and he passes Axel's interrogation, then maybe Axel will approve."

"Great idea," Axel said, waiting for the doctor to answer.

"Sure. I'll bring him in here the minute he arrives," he said, and then turned to leave.

Prunella was lying on her bed sleeping. The emotional stress of watching poor Alex being taken away exhausted her. Axel had a flash of terror in his eyes, but relaxed when I told him she was just taking a nap.

It was another long day. We sat and waited in Prunella's room for a long time, when the doctor peeked his head inside. "We have a slight delay."

"What?" I asked, worried. "Is the nurse not coming?"

"Not tonight. He said he was waiting for his passport to arrive from England via express mail. It was supposed to be here today, but there was a delay and it's coming tomorrow."

"But, he could've come here to meet us," I said, feeling a little twinge of my own anxiety creep in. "We haven't approved of him yet."

"Exactly," Axel agreed. "Why not come here first?"

"I, I guess he didn't feel it was necessary," the doctor answered unsure. "It's okay. It's too late to discharge Prunella tonight anyway. Maybe you and Ruth Ann should go back to your estate and get some sleep. You can come here first thing in the morning."

"Are you insane?" Axel hollered. "My wife isn't safe here. How could I leave her here alone?"

"I'm sorry, I misspoke. Maybe one of you can spend the night with her. I can have the nurse set up a cot."

"I'll stay," I said, quickly. "Axel probably needs to get some work done, and I don't have a lot to pack."

"Ruth Ann, you're not safe either. We need to stick together."

"But, you must have plans to make so we can leave!" I took a deep breath and added, "It's only a little more than a week to Christmas and I want to get home."

"We'll be fine, Ruth Ann," he responded.

The doctor decided to intervene. "Look, if you would like to leave Ruth Ann here, I will personally make sure they are both safe. I'm on duty all night, and I can make sure if I'm not in this area, hospital security will be. We'll make it impossible for anyone to take a step on this floor without passing through us."

"Well," Axel said, thinking about it. "I guess I can leave for a couple hours and pack up. I'll make all the arrangements and be back soon."

"Get some sleep, Axel," I added. "I'll camp out here, next to Prunella." I looked over at the peaceful Prunella snoozing away. "She's wiped out and will probably sleep all night anyway."

"I did give her a slight sedative so she could rest peacefully," the doctor mentioned. "Go, really, they'll be safe."

"Okay," Axel said, grabbing his overcoat from the tiny closet in Prunella's room. "I'm going to be checking in constantly, so answer your phone, Ruth Ann."

"But, I'd like to get a little sleep, too," I said, complaining. "You text me when you get home, and I promise to reply.

Then, I'll text you repeatedly when I'm awake."

"If you don't answer, I'll bug the staff here," he said, authoritatively. "You can pack when I come back to relieve you. We should be able to leave tomorrow mid-morning, if that's alright with you, doctor?"

"Yes. I think it's best. I'll promise her safety tonight, but I can't do it for an extended length of time."

"Fine," he replied. "I'll be back soon."

Axel finally left, and I waited for the nurse to roll in a cot. They were so cooperative and kind, bringing sheets, a blanket, and a pillow. On top of the cot were two trays of food. I wasn't sure what I was going to be eating when I noticed a note on top of one of the trays.

Elsie, the cashier in the cafeteria, wrote me a sweet note telling me she made a fresh apple pie, and threw in a small container of vanilla ice cream to put on top. I smiled as I lifted the cover on the plate and found a hot dog with mustard and pickles, waffle fries, and a huge piece of apple pie. I know it wasn't the healthiest of dinners, but I needed comfort food, and Elsie nailed it!

Now, Prunella's dinner wasn't as good as mine, so I decided I should eat it before she stirred. Her red, jiggly jello, soft green beans, and unknown mushy pile of meat didn't look too appetizing, but she was just beginning to eat solid food again.

I jumped on top of the cot and dug into my hot dog. Elsie made it just the way I liked, with lots of yellow, tangy mustard, and two long dill pickle spears. I took a big bite of the plump hot dog and the juices dribbled down my chin. I grabbed the napkin and dabbed my chin, anxious to eat some more.

It didn't take long for me to finish. I was starving, and a

little nervous with everything going on. I wondered if I would be able to use a staff bathroom to clean up a little when my cell phone rang. "Axel, you made it home fast."

"Yep. I'm not going to waste any time. All okay there?"

"All good," I answered. "I just ate some food, and Elsie even gave me a special piece of apple pie. It was warm, and not too gooey. I'm just glad the rest of the pie isn't anywhere near me or I'd eat another slice."

Axel laughed, feeling relieved that nothing bad had happened since he left. "That's good, Ruth Ann. I'm in my library getting our plans confirmed. I'll pack a bag and head back to the hospital."

"Get some sleep first, Axel," I said. "I really believe we'll be okay tonight."

"I'm not comfortable leaving you and Prunella there without me. I'd be less anxious just being with you."

"Do what you need to, Axel," I replied, wondering why the last part was only about me.

We ended our call, and I decided I was going to lie down and close my eyes for a few minutes. Prunella hadn't woken to eat her tray, so I moved the table away from her and put the lid back on. She had an IV going so I felt she was being sufficiently nourished. I hopped on the cot, pulled up the thin hospital blanket, propped up two pillows and laid my head down and closed my eyes. That's all I remembered until I was wrestled awake by Axel.

"Wake up!" Axel cried, worried. "Ruth Ann, are you okay?"

I felt a mild irritation building inside me. I didn't want to wake just yet, but I knew I had to. I opened my eyes to find Axel hovering over me. "I'm up, Axel. Why'd you wake me?"

"Because it's morning!" he replied, nervously. "Prunella's papers are almost complete, and then it's time to go. Well, actually, we're still waiting for that nurse to show up!"

"I forgot about him," I said, sitting and rubbing my eyes. "I can't believe I slept so long. What time is it?"

"It's seven in the morning. I got here around three in the morning and didn't have to heart to wake you."

"What have you been doing since you got here?" I asked, curiously.

"Watching you two sleep, and doing a little work on my computer," he replied. "I figured we can stop by the house on our way to the airport. It shouldn't take you too long to pack, right?"

"Nope," I answered. "I didn't pack much when we came here."

"Prunella will be in my limo and I'll keep her warm and safe while you run in and shower and pack for the two of you if that's okay?"

"No problem," I said. "But, why can't Prunella come inside the house while I'm getting ready?"

The doctor stuck his head inside the room and answered my question. "Because I don't want her in and out of different places. I'll only okay her to go to the airport and get on the airplane. Once she's landed back in your hometown, she can only go to your home and from there I'll give the nurse the instructions." He quickly added, "Oh, he's on his way. I believe you'll be happy with him. He's very knowledgeable not only in physically taking care of patients, but also psychologically, too."

"What's that supposed to mean?" Prunella chimed in, waking up. "Are you telling me I need mental therapy?"

The doctor hurried to her side and answered, "No, no,

Prunella. You just woke from a coma and your memories are a bit jumbled. Nigel will be able to help you slowly confront your recollections."

"Nigel?" I inquired. "Is that the nurse's name?"

"Yes. I don't really know him personally, but he comes highly recommended."

"What's his last name?" Axel asked, curiously. I knew he wanted to run a check on him before he let Nigel treat his wife.

"Emory," the doctor answered. "His name is Nigel Emory."

Immediately, Axel pulled out his cell phone from his sports jacket pocket and started typing away. "He's doing a check on him," I pointed out to the doctor.

I turned my attention to Prunella, eyeing the uneaten tray of oatmeal and toast next to her. "So, how are you this morning? You slept really well last night. I don't think you ate anything for dinner and looks like for breakfast, either."

"I don't want oatmeal," she complained. "I could use some fruit, maybe."

The doctor said, "Not yet. That's harder to digest. I want you to get used to boring, plain stuff first."

"Just eat the oatmeal, Prunella," I suggested. "If you hold it down, then you can eat what you want."

"Exactly," the doctor said, walking toward the door. "I'm going to see if Nigel has arrived."

Prunella skeptically picked up her spoon and dug into the bowl of lukewarm oatmeal. She lifted it to her mouth and took a smidgen of a bite. "It's disgusting, Ruth Ann."

"I know, but just do it so you can eat better things."

She eyed me, irritated. "What did you get?" she asked, gazing to another tray near my cot.

"I don't know. I haven't looked yet." I didn't want to peek just in case Elsie snuck in another one of her treats.

"Just lift the lid and tell me what *you* got!" she demanded.

I walked to the tray and lifted the lid. I was embarrassed to find a large cinnamon roll staring up at me, all gooey and smelling wonderful. Another note was attached, telling me it was a special recipe. Just for me. "Well?" Prunella inquired. "Do you have oatmeal, too?"

"Um, no."

"What do you have?" she asked, moving her head around trying to see the tray.

"It's a cinnamon roll, Prunella. I'm so sorry. I met a friend down in the cafeteria and she keeps making me special things. I won't eat it."

"Yes, you will," Prunella snapped. "I'll just eat my disgusting oatmeal and watch you stuff delicious bites of the roll in your mouth."

I was becoming a little irritated with her at the moment and decided to step into the hall. Axel followed me out. "Don't let her get to you, Ruth Ann. She's been through a lot, and I would be nasty too."

"I feel horrible for her!" I cried. "I really would throw it out, but it won't matter. Even if I stuffed a bowl of that oatmeal down my throat, she would still be annoyed with me."

"Give her time, Ruth Ann," he said, gently. "I'm pretty sure I'll be next. I'll do something to tick her off, and then the heat will be off of you."

"Who knows," I mumbled. "I think it's best to get her out of here immediately." I was about to take a walk to the bathroom down the hall when I spotted the doctor near Prunella's room. "Look, Axel. I think Mr. Emory has arrived."

Axel turned and watched intently as the doctor spoke with a strange, older man. I say strange because he wasn't dressed in scrubs or a nurse's jacket and pants. He was decked out in a formal suit, vest, and bow tie. He was older, maybe around Axel's age. It was hard to tell because an English driving cap covered most of his face.

"Let's go meet him," I said to Axel.

"In a minute, Ruth Ann. My search hasn't shown anything for a Nigel Emory."

"You mean the name doesn't exist?" I inquired.

"Well, it was a quick search, but yes, it came up empty."

"I guess we could ask him about his past, and if you feel unsure about anything, just ask him."

"And you think he would tell me the truth?"

"Why not?" I asked him. "He doesn't know us, so why lie?"

"I can't help being paranoid after everything we've been through."

He had a point, but I didn't think this dapper older gentleman could hurt us in any way.

Chapter 12

Axel and I walked to the nurse's station right outside of Prunella's room. The doctor was quietly speaking with Mr. Emory. We approached and startled the two of them.

"I'm sorry," I said, quickly. "We didn't mean to interrupt, but we figured it was about Prunella."

The Englishman retorted, "Excuse me. You did just interrupt our conversation and it's not polite. If you and your friend will step back a little, the doctor and I can finish our conversation about a very sick patient."

Axel looked like he wanted to punch the man. He was rude and had no idea that the patient he was referring to was Axel's wife and my cousin, and that we had every right to kick him to the curb.

The doctor saw Axel's face redden and quickly averted a verbal showdown. "Mr. Emory, I would like to introduce you to the patient's husband ... and her cousin."

Nigel Emory turned slowly toward Axel and me. I pulled Axel a few feet back so he wouldn't tackle the old guy to the floor. "I'm very sorry, sir," he said, directing all his attention to Axel and ignoring me completely. "I thought you were trying to get the doctor's attention, but I misspoke."

"Yes, you did, Mr. Emory," I said, wondering if he'd look at me, but he kept his eyes solely on Axel.

Axel calmed down a bit and said confidently, "You do realize, Nigel, that it is *our* choice to employ you. My wife will be in your hands, and if you don't have a compatible meeting with us and her, you will not be hired."

Nigel Emory straightened up and reached his shaky hands to adjust his already perfect bow tie. "I do understand that, sir. I assure you that my education and experience will impress you enough to let me take care of your wife."

"We'll see about that," Axel answered, walking away into Prunella's room. I was about to follow when I thought I'd add my two cents.

"Sir, may I call you Nigel or would you prefer Mr. Emory?" I inquired, assuredly.

"Nigel, is fine with me, ma'am."

"Ruth Ann," I said, not liking being called, "ma'am".

"Yes, Ruth Ann. I am sorry about my rude behavior before. I will assure you that I will take my position very seriously if you and Mr. Eklund hire my services."

"Well, that's good to hear. Why don't we all go in and meet Prunella."

The doctor nodded, and gently nudged Nigel in the right direction. "Prunella's in a delicate condition still, Mr. Emory. I don't want any stress or arguing in there with Mr. Eklund. He's in protection mode with his wife."

Nigel stopped in the doorway to Prunella's room and turned back to the doctor. I was one step ahead, but I wanted to hear what Nigel was about to say to the doctor. I pretended not to be listening, but I could hear every word Nigel said.

"Excuse me, doctor. What do you mean Mr. Eklund is in protection mode? Is there some reason I should worry for my safety?"

"No, no, Mr. Emory," the doctor replied, caught off

guard. "He's just being a typical protective husband." I watched as the doctor blatantly lied to Nigel. Why did he do that? Did he think he would refuse to come with us to Deer Creek if he knew we were being targeted by a drug lord from South America?

Nigel didn't respond but turned his attention back to the patient lying in the hospital bed. Prunella was sitting up alert and smiling. Axel was by her side, making her laugh. I had a momentary twinge of jealousy for some unknown reason, but I shook it off, smiled, and walked toward them. "What's so funny?" I asked, curious.

Prunella answered, "Oh, nothing. I guess you had to be here when Axel made the joke."

"Oh," I said, not knowing what else to add.

Axel quickly caught on to the awkward moment and said, "Prunella, we have someone to introduce you to."

"Ah," she said, waving Nigel closer. "This must be my nurse."

"Nurse?" Nigel asked, confused.

The doctor immediately said, "I'm sorry, Mr. Emory. You are her official caretaker and I referred to you as a nurse."

"I'm not a nurse," he stammered. "I have an extensive medical background. I am actually a nurse practitioner by trade. I can prescribe medications and treat a patient just like a doctor."

"Oh, I'm sorry, Mr. Emory," the doctor said. "I wasn't filled in on your background. That's even better!"

Prunella watched the exchange between the doctor and Nigel with deep curiosity. Nigel decided it necessary to explain his ridiculously boring medical background to us. After about fifteen minutes, Axel put his hand up. "I get it, Nigel. It seems you're more than qualified to care for Prunella."

"Yes, it surely does." I said. It seemed that Nigel needed a lot of attention, and I was wondering if Axel thought the same.

Prunella wasn't getting as irritated with Nigel as Axel and I plainly were. She was smiling and trying and win the old guy over. Kind of like Sherman. She had Sherman wrapped around her pinky. That old butler would've done anything for her. I just hoped that she didn't remember what happened to him. In fact, I shuddered when I realized we would soon have to tell her that Sherman was no longer alive.

"Mr. Emory," Prunella began. "You sound like you've had a wonderful past helping people. I'm sure glad that my life will be in your perfectly capable hands."

Nigel stood taller than his five foot seven or so frame allowed and said, "Why thank you, Ms. Prunella. I feel comfortable saying that you and I will get along smartly!"

"Prunella," she replied to him. "Please call me Prunella, not Ms. Prunella."

"Oh, I guess, that's fine," he said, stumbling through his words. "May I ask when we will be jet setting to America?"

Axel didn't want Prunella to answer him in case he wasn't going to be traveling with us. "We're planning on this afternoon, Nigel. If you and I could have a discussion in the waiting room?" Axel nudged him toward the door with a nod, and Prunella complained.

"Hey, why do you have to leave my room?"

Axel coughed a little and said, "We just need to hammer out the details. Nothing sinister going on."

I waited to see if I was going to be invited, but Axel didn't say a word to me. I took it upon myself to follow anyway. I told Prunella to rest for a few minutes because it was going to be a *very* long day.

Chapter 13

"You don't need to be here, Ruth Ann," Axel said before Nigel caught up with us. "I have a few more questions for Mr. Emory, and then I'll make the final decision."

"I should be here, Axel. I want to hear what he has to say, too. I could tell he was irritating you back there."

"Fine," he conceded. "But, let me do most of the talking. Please."

I nodded just as Nigel entered the small sitting area. I walked to a small grouping of upholstered chairs scattered around a large round coffee table. I plopped down and waited for Axel and Nigel to join me. Axel walked over to the coffee machine and grabbed two coffees and a steaming cup of decaffeinated tea for me. I hurried over to him and took my tea so he didn't spill the full load.

Axel handed a cup to Nigel, who was seated in one of the chairs directly across from me. Axel was about to sit between us. "Thank you, Mr. Eklund," he said, grabbing the hot cup of coffee. "I appreciate that you knew to put cream in it."

"Yes, and a sugar packet, if that was okay?" Axel asked.

"Yes, yes, we English do like our sugar in our coffee," he replied, taking a sip.

I could smell the rich aroma of the coffee. I wish hot tea had a better aroma. Many people get turned off by the smell, even though it doesn't taste anything like it smells. My mind wandered a moment, and then I realized Axel and Nigel were staring at me. I had my paper cup up to my nose, breathing in the steam when I noticed the two of them. "What?" I asked. "I was enjoying the steam."

Axel laughed softly, and then turned his attention back to Nigel. "So, Nigel, you clearly stated your medical background, but I would like to hear about your personal life."

Nigel's bushy, gray eyebrows raised extraordinarily high. "And, why would you need to know about my personal life, Mr. Eklund?"

Axel could see he hit a nerve. Mr. Emory obviously was offended by Axel's question. "Because, Nigel, you will be caring for my wife, and Ruth Ann's close cousin. We need to make sure she'll be in stable, caring, hands."

"I am over qualified for this position, sir," he said, snidely. "My personal life is just that, personal."

Axel stood and said, "Well then, I guess we're through here."

"What?" I exclaimed.

"Ruth Ann," Axel said, turning to me and away from Nigel. "If Mr. Emory, excuse me, Nigel, doesn't want to discuss his life, then I will not need his services. I'll tell the doctor he didn't work out for us."

A disgruntled Nigel quickly retorted, "Fine. I will tell you anything you would like to know."

Axel smiled and slowly sat back down. He crossed his legs and grabbed his paper cup with such elegance that I thought we were sitting in a luxury hotel's lobby. "Go on, please."

"How far back do you want to know?" Nigel asked, feeling duped into spilling more than he expected.

"Well, you're about my age, so how about starting with your family. Do you have any siblings? Children? Grandchildren?" Axel inquired.

"No, I have no family that I am aware of."

"None?" I asked, not able to help myself. "You don't have any relatives whatsoever?"

"No, well, I had a brother years ago, but we lost touch. Our parents were killed when we were teens, and we were separated. We were sent to foster homes until we were of age to take care of ourselves."

"You never looked for him?" I asked, perplexed.

"We were taken to separate homes, and after a couple years, I went to school and started my adult life."

"Did you ever marry?" Axel probed.

"No."

"So, you have no wife, no parents, no other siblings than a brother you were separated from years ago?" Axel questioned, inquisitively.

"That is correct, sir."

"What have you done with your life outside of your work?" Axel inquired.

"I have an extraordinary chess talent and I enjoy long walks. I also love to cook and I've taken several culinary courses. Outside of that, I've always taken care of other people's families."

"Sounds like a full life," I said, hoping not to sound sarcastic. I didn't know why Axel would have a problem with this man. He sounded totally boring and unadventurous.

Axel told Nigel he was going to make a few calls, and then he would be back to let him know if he would be joining us on our trip to Deer Creek. He stood and headed down the hall. I was left alone with this man who looked at me like I was a child.

"So, Nigel, are you interested in coming to America?"

"Not really. I'm perfectly content staying on this side of the ocean."

"Then, why do you want this job?" I asked, baffled. He didn't look like someone who needed the money. He was dressed in expensive clothing; his manners were so proper.

"Because the agency that works with this hospital referred me to your cousin. As you can see, I'm getting up there in age, and jobs don't come my way as easily as they do to the young recruits."

"Why don't you retire?" I asked, feeling as if I pushed the boundaries too far.

"Because I want to work. I don't want to sit in my flat feeling sorry for myself. I still have lots to offer!"

"I'm sure you do," I said cheerfully, hoping I hadn't insulted him. "Oh, here comes Axel." I was happy to end our awkward conversation and see what Axel had to say.

"It looks like you check out, Nigel. If Ruth Ann agrees, then you're hired to accompany us, and take care of my wife until she's strong enough to get cleared by the doctor."

"Sounds like we have a deal. My agent takes care of the money end, so, I will accept your offer."

"Ruth Ann?" Axel inquired, looking at me for my approval.

"Yes, I think Nigel will do just fine." I truly believed that Prunella would be fully recovered quite soon and that poor Nigel might be making this trip and turning around to go right home.

"Okay, that settles it," Axel said, reaching his hand out for Nigel to shake. "I'm going to fill the doctor in and see how fast Prunella can be discharged. How long do you need to get ready?" Axel asked Nigel.

"I'm packed and ready to go," he replied, securely.

"But, how did you know you we'd hire you and when we planned on leaving?" I asked him, suddenly feeling apprehension building inside me.

Nigel looked uncomfortable. Axel and I eyed each other suspiciously and waited for his response. "The hospital told me the details of your case and that you wanted to take your ailing wife to a small town in Colorado to recover. They asked if I had any reason why I couldn't do the job and I said, 'of course not'. The doctor was the one who told me that you wanted to leave right away."

"But, you just met the doctor a little while ago. We saw you two speaking, remember?" I asked.

"Yes, I do. I packed after I agreed to take the position. All I have to do is run to my rental and grab my bags. It won't take me long."

Smooth, I thought to myself. He had an answer for everything, but, how much of it was the truth? I wondered if Axel and I were making a mistake hiring this man. What could he possibly do to us? He wasn't young or in shape for that matter. He had a thick, round middle and short, stout legs. I didn't feel the slightest threat from him. However, I was starting to wonder if there was more to this man than I originally thought. Maybe he was running from the law or an unhappy client.

For some odd reason, Axel ignored Nigel's remarks. He suggested we tell Prunella the good news.

"That's great, Axel," Prunella exclaimed, thrilled that Nigel had accepted the position. "Can we go now?" she asked, eagerly.

"I just finished the paperwork," the doctor stated, walking into her room. "You can get dressed, and by the time they finished packing, I'll be ready to discharge you, under strict conditions of course."

"Conditions?" Prunella asked, raising an eyebrow.

The doctor looked oddly at Prunella. "Well, of course there are conditions, Prunella. You just woke from a coma. Your body needs time to heal and get stronger."

"Just tell me the conditions, doctor," Prunella asked, slightly annoyed.

"First, you'll be taken from your bed in a wheelchair all the way to the plane. There will be no walking until you've landed in Deer Creek and had a few therapy sessions with Mr. Emory."

"I can't walk at all?" she asked, stunned. "But, I feel fine and want to get up and move."

"No." He waited for more complaints, but she pursed her lips and crossed her arms like a little child who was told she couldn't stay up late!

"Also, you'll be on a strict diet until we know your stomach can handle solids. I'll attach a list of acceptable foods." He held up his hand to stop her from arguing, again. "It's only for a couple more days. Once you've properly digested these foods you can go back to foods you like to eat."

"Great, because I want cheeseburgers, pizza, pasta, a great big piece of chocolate cake ..." I watched her lick her lips and dream of those foods that I knew she would normally never eat. Prunella was a picky eater, and barely ate enough to keep her alive! I wasn't about to call her out but let her continue. "Mac and Cheese, ice cream, and ... oh, some of Lynne's famous balls!"

"Excuse me?" the doctor and Nigel said at once. "Balls?"

I quickly intervened. "Not what you're thinking! They're small truffles shaped into perfectly round balls and covered in a rich dark chocolate, milk chocolate or white chocolate. She has a bakery and a small shop in our town's ski resort."

"Oh, good for her!" the doctor said, smiling. "Sounds pretty yummy. Maybe you could send me a box of her best-selling items. I'd love to try them. I sure do have a sweet tooth!"

"You do?" I asked, surprised. "I thought most doctors ate healthy foods and stayed away from sugar."

"Well, yes, but sometimes chocolate heals wounds." The doctor let out a boisterous laugh, and said he'd return in a few minutes with her discharge papers.

Nigel remained quiet until after the doctor left. "So, I'm going to run to my apartment and pick up my luggage. Where can I meet you? At the airport?"

"No, no, you come back here for Prunella," Axel said, surprised he would even suggest not caring for Prunella from the start. "She needs you by her side the entire time."

Nigel shrugged his shoulders and said he'd be back within the hour. He called out a formal goodbye and marched out of Prunella's hospital room. "Well, he's an interesting per-son," Prunella said, trying to swing her legs to the side of her bed to get up.

"Hey, where do you think you're going?" I demanded.

"I'm going to grab my clothes and go into the bathroom to clean up and change."

"The doctor just told you not to walk," Axel said, exas-perated. "Can't you let us pack your items, and bring your clothes to you?"

Prunella snapped, snidely, "I don't think he meant in here. I'm in a hospital surrounded by people who will come to my aid if I can't make it the five feet to the bathroom!"

"Easy, Prunella," I said, trying to divert an unnecessary

argument. "Why don't I help you, and Axel can wait outside in the hall. I'm sure he has phone calls to make to his pilot?"

Axel got the clue and agreed. He made me promise to stand by her side if she insisted on standing. Of course, I agreed. The minute he stepped outside her room, she asked me to close her door. I quickly complied and returned to the side of her bed. "Why'd you rush?" she asked me.

"Because I know you well enough. You were about to get up by yourself without my help."

"I really am fine, Ruth Ann. I need to try and stand. I can't stand being cooped up in this bed a minute longer!"

I felt badly for her, but still insisted I give her a hand. She nodded and swung her legs all the way over the edge of the bed and nudged her body so her feet were touching the ground. "I'm glad you have their slipper socks on," I said. "The floor could be dirty, and who knows what germs are on them."

Prunella let out a howl. "Are you serious? We're in a hospital, Ruth Ann. I'm sure you could eat meat off that floor."

"Oh, yeah, you're right, sorry. Old habits," I said, reaching out to grab her elbow as she slowly put weight on her feet and pushed off the bed. "Easy, now, Prunella."

"I'm good, this feels great!" she said, excited to get out of bed.

I helped her stand. She didn't resist, which made me feel better. "Okay, let me try to stand on my own, Ruth Ann," she proposed. I nodded, pulled my hand off her elbow and stepped a foot or two back. "If you need help, just tell me," I said, watching her closely.

"Just give me a moment to get my bearings," she said, wobbling a little. "Don't tell Axel, but I am a little weak."

"Of course, you are!" I pronounced.

I waited and watched as Prunella swayed, until she lifted one of her feet a few inches off the ground and tried to take a step. Just as her one foot left the ground, she lost her balance and tumbled to the ground so fast I didn't have time to react. Unfortunately, Axel wandered in just as she hit the ground.

He rushed to her aide, and nearly pushed me over. "Prunella! Are you alright?" He turned his head around to face me and asked me, "Ruth Ann, I thought you were helping her? How did she end up on the floor?"

"I was watching her, Axel!" I said, angrily. "I only stepped two feet away when she tried to take her first step."

"Axel," Prunella intervened. "Ruth Ann didn't do anything wrong. I asked her to give me a little breathing space and when I lifted my foot off the ground I fell. I'm fine, by the way, just a bruised ego."

"Phew," I mumbled. "I'm so sorry I didn't grab you in time."

"If you did, you'd probably be on the ground next to me!" Prunella laughed. "Actually, you almost were. Axel nearly knocked you to the ground."

"She's right, Ruth Ann," he said. "I'm sorry, I lost my head for a moment. I didn't mean to plow right into you."

"It's alright," I said, thankful to Prunella for coming to my defense.

To add to the drama, the doctor walked in to see Prunella on the floor, Axel by her side, and me sitting on the edge of her bed. "What happened in here?"

"Nothing, doctor," Axel said, taking hold of Prunella's underarms and lifting her to a standing position. "Prunella took a little tumble while trying to walk."

The doctor's enraged expression was justified. He was

normally a calm, rational man, but not at this moment. "I thought I told you all that Prunella wasn't allowed to walk until *after* physical therapy sessions with Mr. Emory." He forcefully crossed his arms and added, "Did you not understand my explicit instructions or do we need to keep Prunella here, in Stockholm, under a doctor's care?"

"No, no," Prunella pleaded. It was time for her to put on that sweet charm. "I promise to listen from now on. I truly thought I was able to walk like I remember. I know now that I need more time. Please don't make me stay here. I'll be a good patient from this moment on!" She smiled broadly, displaying her perfectly white, straight teeth and rosy cheeks.

The doctor caved, and replied, "Okay, I'll let it slide this time. But, if I find out any of you let Prunella do more than she's ready for, I'll either keep her here or put her into another hospital, even in Deer Creek, Colorado!"

"We understand, doctor," Axel said, getting Prunella to sit on the side of her bed, safely.

"I'll help Prunella to the bathroom, and I won't leave her side. Is that acceptable?" I asked.

"Actually, *I* will get her to the bathroom, and then you can take over inside there," Axel insisted.

Prunella allowed me to help her change, wash up, and fix her hair. I was thankful that this hospital had kept her clean, and even washed and dried her hair while she was in bed. It didn't take long, when I called for Axel to help us back to her bed.

"You look great!" Axel and the doctor said after seeing Prunella cleaned and dressed.

"Thanks, I don't feel like I do," she said, primping a loose strand of hair from her pony tail. "I need a good long soak in my tub."

"That may have to wait until you're back in Deer Creek," I said.

"I know, but that'll give me something to look forward to on the long plane ride back home."

"Everything's ready to go," the doctor said, handing Axel a pile of papers. "All your instructions for your wife are in this packet. Please don't skip any of them. She needs time and care, and then she'll be back to her old self."

"Old?" Prunella stammered.

"Not old, as in old, Prunella," I said, smirking. "He meant how you used to be."

"Yes, of course that's what I meant."

"Oh, sorry."

"All we need now is Nigel to come back," Axel said, looking a bit agitated that his new hire hadn't come back yet.

"I'm here, I'm here," a voice called out from the doorway. "Looks like we're ready to go."

"I'll go get the wheelchair," the doctor said after getting the necessary papers signed.

"Finally," Prunella said. "Time to go home!"

Chapter 14

We wanted to get far away from the hospital as soon as we could. I was anxious to get home and see my daughters, Lynne and Nancy, and Inga, Carlos, Isabella and Cassandra. I also felt I needed to make an appearance at my antique store, Ruth Ann's, even though Inga had assured me that Carlos and my assistant, Meme were doing very well.

During the ride, Nigel badgered us with questions about Deer Creek. I finally tuned him out after the first fifty questions. The man was really getting on my nerves, and I strongly felt I was missing something about him.

"We're here," the limousine driver called to us. The driver pulled inside the private hangar and drove us right up to the plane. Axel's pilot was waiting for us, and even opened the back door once the limousine stopped. "Welcome, sir," the tall, middle-aged man said.

"Stephen," Axel replied, smiling as he stepped out of the limousine. "Are we ready to go once we're aboard?"

"Yes, sir, Mr. Eklund."

Nigel slid out of the side seat and with the help of the driver, grabbed the portable wheelchair and opened it for Prunella. "Hey," she bellowed. "You can't wheel me up those stairs!" She pointed to the steep set of stairs that led to the cabin of the plane.

Nigel nervously said, "I can't carry her!"

Axel glared at the man and barked, "I wasn't asking you! Stephen and I will carry her in the wheelchair."

Stephen said, "Of course I will, sir. Unless you'd rather I just pick Mrs. Eklund up and someone else carries the wheelchair. That might be easier than manipulating the narrow set of stairs."

"Perfect," Axel responded. "I'll carry the wheelchair. Let's get on board so we can get home."

I watched as Stephen easily swept Prunella up the stairs. Nigel followed, and then Axel waited for me. "Go ahead, Ruth Ann. Are you alright?"

"Yes, I was just watching. I can't believe we're finally going home."

"Yes, we are."

We got ourselves situated in our seats on his luxurious plane and waited for the massive hangar door to open. Axel had one attendant on the plane who came around asking if we'd like anything to drink. The young man looked like he was in his twenties, tall, handsome, and very slim. He wore a navy long sleeve shirt, and tightly fitted navy pants. He had a yellow bow tie on, looking ever so the Swede. I asked for a cup of hot tea, and he suggested I wait until we were at a safe level before handling a hot beverage. I settled for a warm chocolate chip cookie, and a small container of chocolate milk. Axel smiled as I took a sip through the tiny plastic straw, enjoying every ounce. "Happy?" he inquired.

"Oh, yes," I answered, content. I devoured the cookie and milk and waited for the plane to take off. I leaned back in my seat and closed my eyes. I must've dozed off, because when I opened them, we were high in the sky. "Wow, how long have I been asleep?"

"A couple of hours," Axel replied.

"I seem to do that a lot, don't I?"

"Well, yes, but you've been through a lot, and you're exhausted."

"I guess so," I said. I asked what time we would be landing. "We took off around six in the evening and it'll be about a twelve-hour flight, however, the time difference will have us in Grand Junction around ten in the evening," Axel answered, confusing me. He noticed my dazed expression and quickly added, "It's a twelve-hour flight, but Stockholm is eight hours ahead of Colorado time."

"Oh, that's good. We'll get back just in time to go to bed!" I said, thinking that's not so bad.

The next couple hours went smoothly. Prunella was sleeping most of the time, Axel was on his laptop plugging away at work, and Nigel was snoring away at the back of the small, but comfortable plane. I wanted to contact my daughters and tell them I'd see them in the morning, but I had no service, and I didn't want to ask for help. I chose to pull out my electronic reading device and open a book I was currently reading. I hadn't had a lot of time in the past, but the last couple weeks I'd spent a lot of time sitting in a hospital room, alone, with Prunella deep in her coma. I had started a wonderful mystery series by an author in Chicago who specialized in woman's mysteries. She had a flare for keeping one's interest in the mystery all the way to the end. Plus, I chose it because it was one of those books you could set down and pick up anytime without having to go back to remind yourself what was going on. Those are my kind of books. Carefree, adventurous, a little romance and mystery!

Axel had the cabin lights dimmed for those who were sleeping. I was wide awake since I had napped for a couple hours. I looked around for the attendant to see if there was anything to eat when a loud scream came from the cockpit. I unsnapped my seatbelt and started to head toward the scream. "No, Ruth Ann," Axel ordered gently, but forcefully pushing me back into my seat. "Let me. I can't imagine what's wrong. The plane is riding smoothly."

"Please hurry," I begged. "That scream didn't sound good, and it was a man's scream. It scared me!"

Axel passed Prunella who was still asleep. I looked around to the back and noticed Nigel was still out, too. How did they not hear that scream? I couldn't just sit here waiting, so I walked to Prunella, who was sleeping on a long sofa close to the cockpit door.

I waited a couple minutes and didn't hear a sound. Figuring it was safe, I walked toward the closed cockpit door. Before I could reach for the handle, the door flew open and what stood before me rendered me speechless.

Chapter 15

"Ruth Ann, go back to your seat," Axel said, barely able to get the words out. "Please," he muttered quietly.

"What the ..." I said, then was forced backward until I reached Prunella's couch.

"Don't say a word or he'll die right in front of you!" a male voice ordered.

I wanted to move, but I was frozen sitting at the end of the couch where Prunella lay asleep. The stranger shoved the gun he had sticking in Axel's ribs up to his head. "Is this what you want to see?" he barked. "Get back to your seat, NOW!" he screamed, finally stirring Prunella.

I stood, rushed to my seat and sat down hard. It was only a few seats from where I was, but I was out of breath. Prunella was still asleep, unless she was faking. I noticed Nigel had woken, and his eyes were opened wide, staring at the man holding a gun to Axel's head.

"What is this?" I requested, feeling my heart beating so hard I thought it was going to burst out of my shirt.

Axel shook his head, obviously urging me to stay silent. The strange man, dressed in black from head to toe, shoved Axel down near me and tossed him into the seat across the narrow aisle. "Don't say a word," he whispered, trying not to upset the stranger.

When I got my wits about me, I realized it had to be the same man that tried to kill Prunella back in the hospital. But, how did he get onto Axel's plane? Someone must've told him our plans, and he hid away on the plane until we came aboard. But, who?

I had so many questions but didn't dare ask. Axel watched me intently, hoping I would behave. I can be a bit rambunctious, but with a gun pointed in our direction, I was smart enough to keep quiet. We waited to see what the man was going to do or say next. It didn't take long.

"Hey," Axel hollered, as the stranger walked to Prunella and bent over her.

He whipped his head around and gave Axel the nastiest stare I've ever seen. "Shut up!" he barked.

It was my turn to keep Axel in line. I whispered to him to not irritate this man. Finally, after he inspected Prunella for what seemed like an hour, he straightened up and walked to the seat right in front of me.

He stood in the aisle and glared from Axel to me, and back to Axel. "So, finally I've got you."

I was about to ask what he meant, when Axel subtly shook his head my direction. The stranger laughed wickedly and said, "It might be best to keep your mouth shut, Ms. Conroy."

How did he know my name? "I know what you're thinking. You want to know how I knew who you were? Well, I'm not allowed to say too much, but I will tell you both a few things."

He looked back at Nigel and snickered. "That weak, old man back there led me right to you. He sang like a canary when I threatened his poor little life."

"He, he made me!" Nigel bawled from the back. "He was

going to kill me!"

"Shut up, Nigel!" the man hollered. The three of us watched poor Nigel sweating in his seat. He looked pathetic and weak minded, not what I expected after initially meeting him.

"Now, you probably want to know why I'm chasing you." He looked at me first, but I refused to respond. He turned to Axel, who was glaring daggers at the man. "Well, if you don't want any answers, then I'll retire to the front of the plane to monitor the pilot."

He started to walk toward the front of the plane when I yelled, "What do you mean *monitor the pilot*?" Suddenly, I felt a panic attack forming inside me. Where was he taking us?

"Ah, finally, Ms. Conroy can't take it any longer. She figured out that we're not going home to your precious little town so you can see your daughters and friends."

"What do you know about my family?" I screamed. "You better not have threatened them!"

"Ruth Ann!" Axel snapped through gritted teeth.

"You'd better listen to your cousin's husband or is he *more* than that to you?" he said, snidely, implying Axel and I had a much closer relationship than we did.

It was Axel's turn to blow. He flew out of his seat and rushed at the young stranger. Unfortunately, it didn't bode well for Axel. The stranger was tall, athletically built, and much younger. Axel was thrown to the floor with one swat. "Don't ever try that again!" the man hollered, angry. "Get back to your seat, and if you want me to restrain you in there, I will."

Axel slowly got to his feet and sat down. I noticed he was bleeding a bit from his mouth, but I think his ego was bruised more than his body. He didn't want to admit that his age was the factor, and I felt horrible for him.

"Now, let me tell you a few important things before we get to our destination." He ordered Nigel to sit behind me in an empty seat, and Nigel did exactly as he was told after he saw what happened to Axel.

"Good. We're all snuggled close together," he said, mockingly. "First, let me state one thing very clearly. I haven't threatened or contacted any of your family, Ms. Conroy." I felt a little bit of relief with his statement, if he was telling me the truth.

"Second, we definitely are not going back to Deer Creek." He held his gloved hand in the air to stop me from asking where we were going. "My boss has given me strict instructions not to tell you the specific location. But, I can tell you we're not headed to a cold, mountainous region, but to a warm, tropical, blissful place. Well, blissful for me, I should add."

"Mexico? South America?" I couldn't help but ask.

"Nope. You're not getting that information out of me just yet. When we land, I'll fill you in."

"Then what did you want to tell us that's so important?" Axel asked, irritated with the man. "All you've told us is that nobody in Deer Creek was contacted, and that we're going South."

"You are correct, Mr. Eklund," he answered, sarcastically. "I do have more to discuss."

"Stop teasing us!" I bellowed, exasperated. "Just tell us what's going on."

He ignored my frustration and went at his own, slow, teasing pace. "I have plenty of time to divulge information. Right now, I need to give your sleepy wife another dose of her sedative."

Axel made his second attempt at taking the man down, and once again failed. This time, the man pulled a long cord out of his hoodie pocket and wrapped Axel's wrists behind his seat. I wasn't surprised that Axel didn't fight because he still looked dazed from the blow the man gave him.

"If you do that again, you won't be so lucky!" he snapped, walking away toward Prunella.

I was terrified that whatever drug he was giving Prunella would put her back in her coma. I couldn't help but tell the man, but he didn't care. "She'll be fine."

I watched as the man disappeared into the cockpit. After the door closed behind him, I stood and tried to help untie Axel's wrists. "I can't do it without a knife," I said, struggling with the thick cord wrapped around his wrists.

"I think we're beat on this, Ruth Ann. Just sit down and wait for the jerk to tell us more."

"You're not giving up, are you?" I asked, surprised he was being so calm.

"What do you propose we do? He's holding all the cards right now. I'm not giving up, just seeing what happens next. We need to find out what's really going on and where we're going. I think we're heading to either Mexico or South America. I know one thing for sure, we'll be meeting Manual Marquez eventually."

"So, now we're fighting off a drug lord?"

"Appears so."

"Why don't we just hand the necklace over and get on with our lives?" I asked, aggravated.

"It'll come back to haunt us, Ruth Ann," he said. "Meme and Isabella even told us that the gem will always be a part of us."

"I don't believe that!" I barked. "We need to come up with a plan, and quick."

"How can we plan for something we don't know?" he asked, making sense. If all they wanted was our Blue Ice, then I say good riddance to it. I'd lived most of my life without it anyway.

Chapter 16

The time passed slowly. The strange man stayed in the cockpit for quite a long time. I stood up and went to check on Prunella. She was peacefully sleeping, and I thought about shaking to wake her, but didn't want to scare her. I opened a few compartments throughout the cabin, looking for a possible weapon, but all I came up with were blankets, snack size foods, slippers, and those eye covers for blocking out the light so you could sleep.

"What are you doing, Ruth Ann?" Axel whispered. "You need to come back and sit down.

"I can't just sit and wait, Axel," I said, irritated. "What's Nigel doing behind you?" I noticed Nigel changed seats and was behind Axel.

"AHA!" the old man bellowed too loudly. "I did it!"

"Did what?" I asked as I rushed to the middle of the plane where Axel and Nigel were.

"I freed Mr. Eklund," he exclaimed, proudly.

"You did?" I asked, stunned.

Axel wriggled his wrists and I watched the ropes fall to the floor. "He did!"

Unfortunately, at that exact moment Nigel freed Axel, the cockpit door opened and our stranger returned. "Did you really think I wasn't surveilling you back here? I've been watching your every move from up front. You do realize there's a camera up there?"

"I forgot," Axel mumbled.

"Yes, your advanced age must be causing your brain to malfunction," he chortled. "I'm only going to spare you this time because you didn't know Nigel was doing it." He looked at Nigel, hovering behind Axel terrified. "Now, for you, Nigel, what should I do with you?"

"Please, don't hurt me! I'm not strong, and I can't fight back."

"No, you can't," he said, laughing boisterously. "Just go back to your seat at the back of the plane. If you stay a good boy, I'll spare you, for now."

"For now?" Nigel asked, meekly. "Are you planning on getting rid of me?"

"I don't know yet. You've been helpful to us, so who knows. Maybe your pathetic life will be spared."

I was sick and tired of his teasing and mocking us. I couldn't take it any longer and decided to get to the point. "Are you going to tell us more? You said you had more to reveal."

"I guess I could say a little more." He walked toward Prunella and checked on her. He leaned over closely and appeared satisfied. "She's resting nicely, don't you think?"

"Yes, I know you drugged her. You must be able to get drugs pretty easily since your boss is a known drug lord!" I said, misguidedly. I really thought I messed up, but he ignored my comment and went on without hesitation.

"I've been instructed to tell you that my boss," he said, as he eyed me suspiciously after processing my sarcastic comment. "My boss, runs a successful jewelry business, and he would like to obtain a specific piece I believe you have in possession."

"Are you serious?" I stammered. "Your boss wants our necklace because he runs an *illegal jewelry* business along with *illegal drugs*."

Axel nearly passed out as he watched me blurt those stupid words. I knew I pushed it this time because the man's face turned beet red. Before he could retaliate, I quickly added, "I realize what I said was wrong, but do you blame me? You hijacked our plane, drugged my cousin, and are threatening our lives. All for a bloody necklace!"

He calmed down and I was fairly relieved. He slowly walked toward my seat and leaned very close to my face. His warm, stank breath made my stomach turn, but I didn't react. I wanted to push him out of my personal space, but obviously, that would be a bad decision. So, I waited until he was ready to give it to me.

"You've got quite a smart mouth, don't you, *Ruth Ann*?" I noticed he wasn't calling me Ms. Conroy any longer.

"Can I ask you a question?" I asked, trying not to breathe too deeply. He nodded, slowly. "What's your name? I'd like to call you by your name since we're in such close proximity."

He backed off a little, not much, but enough that I didn't want to throw up any more. "Please," I swiftly added, hoping that would help.

"Viktor."

"Thank you, Viktor," I said, smiling. Axel watched me, confused at what I was trying to accomplish. "Now, please fill us in."

I truly believed I confused the big oaf. He obliged and said, "My boss only deals in private transactions with the most affluent customers. He's not running an illegal drug or gem business, Ruth Ann. He's honored back in our home town, and people do anything he asks."

"Because they are afraid of him, Viktor," I said, sincerely. "Do you work for him because you're afraid of him and what he might do to you or your family?"

"I'm not afraid of anyone!" he bellowed, snapping right back into his bad mood. "Even you!"

I laughed and said, "Like anyone could be afraid of me."

"I've heard *all* about you, Ruth Ann, and the tricks you've played on people to get them on your side. Like those twins who were killed back at Eklund's shipping business."

"You know about them?" Axel inquired, stunned.

"I know everything you've been up to lately. I do my job to the best of my ability. That's what my boss demands from me."

"Commendable," Axel said, about to clap his hands, but he chose not to.

"Enough of this nonsense. I need to check on your pilot to make sure he isn't trying any funny stuff."

"Hey, wait, Viktor," I said. "Please, tell us more before you go."

"I'll tell you only this. You and Mr. Eklund need to figure out the best way for us to get your precious necklace before we land." He turned to leave but stopped and added, "Oh, and we'll be landing in about two hours."

"What?" I exclaimed. "That's impossible."

"I really don't care," he said, and disappeared into the cockpit.

"Axel, what are we going to do?"

"I need some time to think, Ruth Ann. Can you just leave me alone for a few minutes?" He saw the hurt in my eyes and quickly amended his last comment. "I'm sorry. I really didn't mean to snap at you. I'm so upset I can't think straight. We're in big trouble, Ruth Ann."

I decided to let his unkind comments go. "I know, Axel. However, we can't let them know where the necklace is, can we?"

"No way!"

"Then what can we possibly do? Viktor's boss is expecting us to hand it over when we meet him."

"Wherever that is," Axel said. "We don't have a clue where we're going, and if you think about it, why would we have the necklace on us anyway?"

"I agree, but these people don't care," I answered. "I think we need to reach out to Inga or Carlos back home."

"How?" he asked, baffled. "We have no means of communication."

A low clearing of the throat sounded from the back of the plane. Axel and I turned to see Nigel sitting in the very last seat smiling up at us. "What?" Axel demanded. "Why are you smiling?"

Nigel reached down and pulled out his cell phone. "It's no good up here, Nigel," I said, wondering where he was going with this.

"No, but the minute we touch ground we can," he replied, waving the cell phone in the air. "One of us should be able to get service and make that call of yours to your hometown."

"He's right!" I screeched, too loudly.

The cockpit door flew open and Viktor ran out. "What are you three up to?"

I realized that blasted camera in the cockpit might've just caught Nigel with his phone in the air.

"Nothing," Axel answered, hoping Viktor missed looking in the camera.

"Then why did Ruth Ann scream?" he asked, skeptically.

I tried to think fast. "I, I pinched myself with the seatbelt. I wasn't wearing it, and I felt some bumps in the air so I put it on."

He didn't know how to respond. Did he believe me or think I was up to something?

I must've lucked out. "Oh, well, don't do that again," he stated, and marched back inside the cockpit.

"Ruth Ann, you can't do that," Axel said, crossly. "That could've cost us our only chance at letting someone know what's happening to us."

"Plus," Nigel added. "Once we land, we'll know where we actually are."

"Good point, Nigel," Axel said. "Let's take some time and think of what we're going to say, and how we can keep everyone back home safe from these criminals."

We sat in silence for quite a while when I heard a groan coming from the front of the cabin. It had to be Prunella. I unbelted my seatbelt and hurried to the front. Axel was free, but he chose to let me go so we wouldn't alert Viktor.

"Prunella," I called out. She was moving her head back and forth, obviously in distress. I wasn't sure if she was in pain or having a nightmare. "Prunella!"

Finally, she opened her eyes in horror. She sat up and without speaking looked around to see where she was. "We're still in the air?" she asked, oblivious to what has occurred. "When will we be landing in Colorado?"

I looked desperately back at Axel wondering what I should tell her. He waved me back, but I couldn't leave her. I decided to go rogue. "Prunella," I began. "We're still flying, but you've been asleep most of the time. Are you still tired? I'm sure you're exhausted after everything that's happened to you."

"No," she said, stretching her arms in the air. "I feel pretty good."

"Are you hungry?" I asked, even though I didn't know what to give her. "Nigel," I called out. "Can you come up here, please?"

"Hey, why isn't Axel getting out of his seat?" Prunella asked, turning her head to see him waving at her and trying to smile.

"He, he ..." I stopped, literally not able to find the next words. My mind went blank. Thankfully, the next think I knew Axel was sitting at her side.

"My foot was asleep, Prunella," he said, quickly. "If I stood up, I think I would've fallen."

Prunella laughed, and then asked for something to drink. "I'm so thirsty," she said.

"Nigel, can you bring Prunella some juice from the refrigerator behind you?" Axel asked.

He hopped out of his seat and brought Prunella a small glass filled with orange juice. "Thanks," she said, eyeing us oddly. She took a sip as we stared at her. "What's going on with you three?" she demanded, noticing our odd behavior.

"Nothing," I replied, quickly. "Just happy you're feeling better."

"Oh," she said, skeptically. "Something's up, what is it?"

That's when the cockpit door flew open and a man she'd never seen before (outside of trying to suffocate her) stood before us. "What are you doing out of your seats?" he asked, mainly directing his attention to Axel.

"Prunella needed me," he replied, matter of factly.

"But, I told you not to move after Nigel untied you."

Prunella's eyes widened and she realized things weren't

going as planned. "Who are you and why did you restrain my husband?"

Viktor reached into his hoodie pocket and pulled out a syringe. "It's time for another injection," he said, walking closer to Prunella.

"Wait, what?" she screamed, terrified. "Axel, what's he doing to me?"

"Enough!" Axel yelled, pushing the big brute away. "She doesn't need to sleep anymore. She just got out of a coma you monster!"

Viktor's glare forced me to take a step back. "Axel, please don't make matters worse."

"Worse?" Prunella asked, confused. "Why does this man want to give me drugs?"

Viktor got to her before we could. "You're a hostage on your husband's plane, along with those three," he said, pointing to Nigel, Axel, and me.

"Hostage?"

"We aren't flying to your boring little town, but to Santa Marta where you'll meet my boss. He needs to have words with your group."

Prunella was rendered speechless, but Axel and I just found out our destination!

"Santa Marta?" Axel questioned him. "What large city is that near?" he asked, smartly, trying to pinpoint where we were going so we could tell our family and the authorities.

"Bogota, in Columbia," he answered, ignorantly. "But, pretty far from there. It's a small town in a clearing in the jungle."

Prunella got her voice back, and it wasn't pretty. "How dare you take us hostage! You brute, let us go and maybe, just maybe, we'll let the police go easy on you." She added, angrily, "Who's your boss? Why does he want us?"

It suddenly dawned on her what the motive could be. "No way," she said, slowly. "Don't tell me it's because of Blue Ice?"

Axel and I ignored Viktor for a moment to ask Prunella if she remembered what Blue Ice was, and if her memory was coming back. "No, I'm still quite foggy over what's happened since Thanksgiving. I'm not even clear on before that, but I do remember meeting Ruth Ann when she came to Stockholm to rescue me and my necklace."

"That's the last thing you recall?" I asked, surprised. That was way back when Axel kidnapped me and brought me to his estate in Stockholm.

Axel intervened and told me not to push it just yet. He pulled me aside and whispered, "We really don't want her remembering everything yet."

"Good point," I said.

"What are you two talking about?" Viktor yelled. "Get back here and take care of Prunella or I will stick that needle in her and put her back to sleep."

Prunella handled him beautifully. "Please, Viktor, that is your name, right?" she asked sweetly, changing her tactic. He nodded, apparently mesmerized by her beauty. "I won't be a problem. I can't even walk yet, so I won't try any funny stuff."

He was convinced and put the syringe in his pocket. "If any of you try anything before we land," he pulled out the syringe and said, "this is what you'll get."

"Got it," I said, sitting at the end of the couch near Prunella's covered feet. I was tempted to ask him to give me the shot so I could sleep and forget this was happening to us, again.

Viktor left us alone and went back inside the cockpit. He reminded us he could see every move we made. Obviously, he had missed Nigel waving his cell phone in the air. It made me think this guy wasn't the smartest because he should've taken them away from us in the beginning. At least, that's what I would've done.

Chapter 17

I was hoping Prunella would let it go for a little while, but that wasn't going to happen. "Now," she said with conviction. "Spill it!"

"Prunella," Axel said. "We really don't know anything. You actually got more out of the guy than we have. He refused to tell us where we're heading and who's his boss."

"Really?" she asked, watching us closely to see if we were showing signs of lying.

"Really," I said.

Axel asked if he could go back and sit down so he could think of a plan to get us out of this alive. Prunella agreed, if I would stay with her. "Of course," I said. "I'm tired."

"Maybe you should close your eyes for a little while, Ruth Ann," Prunella said. "You haven't slept like I have."

I decided it might be best to take a short nap. I leaned back so my head rested on the back of the couch and my legs stretched out in front of me on the floor. Prunella told me she was getting groggy again, and would close her eyes, too.

I dozed off immediately. My mind took me on a journey to a tropical oasis where I was confronted with none other than

Meme, Isabella's dead grandmother. I stood on a remote sand-bar in the middle of the ocean with a few palm trees, and a perfectly formed wooden shack. I don't know how I got here, but I walked to the shack where Meme was waiting for me. She was standing in front of the doorway filled with long strands of beads. Her hand rustled the beads and called for me to hurry.

"Meme!" I blurted out, loudly. "You're alive!"

"No, Ruth Ann, I'm not."

"But, I'm standing right in front of you outside your shack!"

"It's kind of like a dream, Ruth Ann," she said, smiling.

I looked up at her and I realized Meme had all her teeth, and her skin was smooth and not aged like I remembered. Her hands were lacking the dry, harsh wrinkles that I so remember when she held our precious necklace trying to break the curse.

"The curse was broken, Ruth Ann," she said, watching me intently.

"So, you can read my mind even in a dream!" I exclaimed.

"I know all when it comes to you, Ruth Ann. We are forever entwined. You, Isabella, Prunella, and me."

"Nobody else?" I asked.

"Nobody you know, Ruth Ann."

"Why am I dreaming this?" I couldn't help but ask.

"Because, once again, you've gotten yourself in trouble. Last time, Isabella tried to help you, but, she got caught up with her feelings for the twin who was murdered in Axel's office."

"You know about that?" I asked, perplexed.

"Of course, I just told you I know all."

"Why are you doing this to me?"

"You need my help. You need to listen to me before my time is up. Do not hand over your gem, Ruth Ann."

"Blue Ice?" I asked, making sure she was talking about our necklace.

"Yes!" she bellowed. *"What other gem have I known other than your Blue Ice?"*

"Sorry, I'm not used to these kinds of dreams, Meme."

"It's okay. Now, listen, in a short time you'll be able to contact your family in Deer Creek."

"I'm not involving my daughters!" I snapped.

"No, no, not Lynne and Nancy. I'm talking about Isabella, Inga, Carlos, Cassandra, and even John and Judy if you must."

"Not John and definitely not Judy!"

"Fine. Call them and tell them exactly where you are so they can rush to save you, Axel, and Prunella."

"What about Nigel?"

"Him, too. I will get to get to him in a second. Now, listen carefully. Have Isabella bring the necklace. Tell her to put a safety hex on it so only she can wear it without anyone taking it off her."

"A safety hex?" I questioned her. *"Why should they bring it anyway?"*

"It's going to save Prunella, and you."

"How, why, and from what?" I asked, confused and frustrated.

"I don't have all the answers. I just know that Prunella needs the gem to protect her, and it'll protect you, too."

"Should Isabella transfer this safety hex to Prunella?" I inquired.

"Yes, tell Isabella even though she'll know."

"Then what? How do we get out of this?" I asked, hoping

she'd give me something concrete.

"I can't tell you the future in detail, Ruth Ann. I'm not allowed. Just follow what I've said so far. Then when Isabella gets to you, get that necklace around Prunella's neck and protect her. If you do not do this, she will die!"

"What?" I cried, loudly. "You're telling me if Isabella doesn't place the safety hex on the necklace and get it to Prunella she's going to die?" Meme nodded.

"Someone close to her will kill her."

"Who?" I asked, wondering what she meant by someone close to her. "Are you saying one of us could kill her?"

"I didn't say that, Ruth Ann. I said someone close to her."

"You're being too vague! Please tell me who and how we can save her."

"Get the necklace and put it on her immediately!"

"Then what? How do we get away from this drug lord and his guards?" I asked, nervously.

"You will find a way," she answered, ambiguously.

"No, Meme, this is unacceptable. I need answers, and you're the only one who can give them to me."

"I'm only allowed a short time to speak with you, Ruth Ann, and my time is almost up."

"But, you haven't told me hardly anything!" I cried.

"Yes, I've told you about saving Prunella, and I can tell you this man, Manual Marquez is a very dangerous man. Pretend to go along with him until Isabella and the others get there. He'll take an unusual fascination with your cousin, so that'll buy her some time."

"Wait, what? You're saying Marquez is going to fall in love with Prunella?"

"More like he will become obsessed with her. I don't

126

think a man like Manual Marquez could love anyone besides himself."

"You know him?" I couldn't help but ask.

"Oh, yes, I know of him, and I encountered him a few times years ago. This is why I was brought to speak to you."

"By whom?" I inquired.

She ignored my question and continued. "I have to hurry, Ruth Ann. There's more."

"More?"

"It's about Nigel."

"You know him, too?" I asked, feeling a headache beginning to throb in my temples even though I was supposedly in a dream.

"You know him, Ruth Ann," she said, elusively. "Or, I should say, you know a close relative of his."

"Who?"

"Sherman. Nigel is Sherman's long-lost brother," Meme disclosed. "Nigel and Sherman were separated when they were young."

"No way!" I shouted. "That's too much of a coincidence."

"Is it?" Meme questioned me. "Think about it, Ruth Ann. Do you think Nigel just showed up out of thin air at the hospital where Prunella was a coma patient? He is from England, not Sweden. He tracked you down, and once he heard you needed a caretaker for Prunella, he jumped on it."

"This is too much to believe, Meme. How do I know what you're telling me is the truth?"

"Ask him when you wake, Ruth Ann. He thinks he won't ever get caught."

"What does he want with us?" I asked, worried we had another dangerous situation brewing.

"He thinks he's being sneaky. He needs money and knows that Sherman was pretty well off. Watch him closely. He's a sneak and will sell you out to the highest bidder, including Manual Marquez."

"That's horrible!" I said, worried about him now. "I can't take much more of this, Meme. How am I supposed to fix all of this?"

"You are a strong woman, Ruth Ann. You have more fight and stubbornness than a woman in her twenties." She smiled, and I reached out to take her hand, but she pulled away and shook her head. "What? I can't touch you, can I?"

"No," she answered. "Nigel found you to stake his claim on Sherman's money. He found out somehow, and there's one major problem with this."

"Now, what?"

"Prunella doesn't know that her great uncle has died, does she?" Meme asked me.

"No, she doesn't remember yet," I said, sadly.

"When she does, it'll kill her. She'll want to take full responsibility for his death," Meme told me.

"But, she wasn't in her right mind! Cassandra and Mattie placed a curse on her and it changed her personality" It suddenly dawned on me. "Cassandra. She's back in Deer Creek with the others awaiting trial for her crimes. What's going to happen to her?"

"She'll be fine, Ruth Ann. Isabella and she are getting closer each day, but unfortunately, she can't come with them to help you. Tell her to stay in Deer Creek and then everything will be alright. She won't go to jail or be shipped back to Jamaica. She'll be able to stay with Isabella and Carlos in Deer Creek."

"What happened to Mattie, your sister?" I asked, hoping

she had time to tell me that story.

"Mattie went back to Jamaica, Ruth Ann. She's not a nice woman. Don't try to reach her. She will only bring your family bad luck."

"But, I thought she was sorry for everything?" I asked.

"No, I'm afraid not. Let her go and live what's left of her life alone."

"That's sad," I said.

"I'm not sad for her. She wasn't a nice person, so let it be, please," Meme said with anger in her voice. That was rare, Meme never spoke badly of most people. She always tried to save them, but obviously, there was too much bad blood between the two of them.

"What else?" I asked, quickly.

"My time is up, Ruth Ann. Remember what I said, call Isabella immediately. Watch out for Nigel, but maybe he can be saved unlike my sister, Mattie. Also, one last thing ... when you wake and tell Prunella and Axel, they'll think you were just dreaming. Convince them to listen to my words. Once you've told Isabella, she'll believe you immediately. That's what matters, Ruth Ann (her voice started to fade and her body was disappearing before my very eyes), stay strong, and keep Prunella safe. Axel and she will have troubles, and I don't think they'll stay together, but you'll be in both of their lives, and Blue Ice will always protect you. Remember that ... Blue Ice will always be on your side, and protect you ..." She was gone. I stood alone on the sandbar now. There was no shack or palm trees or ...

"Ruth Ann," a faint, female voice was calling my name.

"Meme, is that you? Where are you?" I said, seeing the oasis disappear and blackness surround me. I realized my eyes were shut tightly. I opened them to see Prunella sitting up shaking my shoulders.

"Ruth Ann, are you okay?"

"Yes, sorry, Prunella. I was dreaming," I said, trying to get my bearings. "Wait a minute!" I exclaimed. "I just dreamt about Meme!"

"Meme, your assistant at the antique store?" Prunella asked, confused.

"No, no, Meme, Isabella's grandmother," I said, regretting the words immediately after leaving my lips.

"Who?" she asked, puzzled. "Who are Isabella and Meme, and why would you be dreaming about them?"

Axel must've overheard and rushed over. "Don't worry about it, Prunella. They are people you don't remember yet, but you will."

"I want to remember now!" she howled. "I hate not having my mind working!"

"It will, but don't force it, remember?" I was thinking about the doctor's words; do not force her memories or she could have a setback.

"Fine," she stammered. "Then why don't you tell me about this dream?"

"I don't think it really was a dream. Meme reached out to me to tell me what we need to do to get out of this mess."

"She did?" Axel asked, stunned. "Your dream felt real, right?"

"No, no, it wasn't a dream, it was her. She told me exactly what we need to do to get out of this," I said, discouraged they weren't believing me.

Axel suggested I sit down in my seat and he would listen to every word of my dream. He tried to explain to Prunella that she wouldn't understand it because she didn't know who the people were. She fought vehemently until Axel basically told her, "No, you're not ready. We'll be back in a few minutes to tell you what you need to do." That seemed to satisfy her. I was astonished that she was willing to let it go for the moment.

Chapter 18

"Ruth Ann," Axel said, kindly. "I know you believe that's what happened, but it was just a dream."

"No, Axel, Meme even told me you wouldn't believe me at first. I promised I would convince you."

"Okay, Ruth Ann. Let's say I believe you. She really didn't tell you how to fight off these criminals, did she?" he asked.

"She said we'd figure it out along the way. Her concern was keeping Prunella alive!"

"I know, I heard you," he said, rubbing his temples with his fingers. "It's just so far-fetched."

"Don't you think I know that?" I asked, irritated. "Oh," I blurted out. "I almost forgot."

"What?" he asked exasperated, wondering what I was going to say next.

"It's about," I stopped, put my finger to my mouth to make sure he understood we had to be really quiet. He nodded, and I continued. "Nigel. There's more to him than we knew."

"What?" he whispered, eagerly.

"He's Sherman's long-lost baby brother!"

"NO!" he bellowed loudly, covering his mouth with his

hand. Catching himself, he said in a much lower voice, "Sorry."

Fortunately, Nigel was in his seat, fidgeting with his cell phone and didn't appear to hear Axel. "It's true. He tracked us down to get a hold of poor Sherman's money," I said.

"His money?" Axel inquired, mystified. "He had that much money?"

"Think about it, Axel," I started to say. "He worked for you for a long time and had no expenses, and you paid him handsomely, I assume."

"I guess that could add up, and if he invested wisely, he would be worth quite a lot."

"Yes, and Nigel knew that. He found out about his death, and once he heard that we were in Stockholm, he pursued us."

"Why didn't he just ask? I'm sure he's due some of Sherman's money. But, going about it this way, makes me wonder if he really is on our side. Marquez could easily sway a man like that to be on his side, don't you think?" he asked me.

"That's what Meme said!" I blurted out. "You believe me now, don't you?" I asked, thrilled I was finally getting through to him.

"I guess I do, Ruth Ann," he replied, surprised at his own words. "Unless, he isn't any of those things and just an old guy who wants to make a living caring for my wife."

"We need to confront him," I said. "But, when? We're in a bit of a predicament at the moment."

"Bad timing," Axel said, thinking hard. "I'm not sure we bring it up just yet. Let's see where this goes and if he succumbs to Marquez."

"Sounds like a plan. Now we wait until I can make the call to Isabella," I said.

"Well, we do have to speak with Prunella a little. We

can't tell her very much because it would be devastating."

"I agree," I said. "But, what should we tell her?"

"I'm thinking, Ruth Ann, I'm thinking," he said, beating the palm of his hand on his forehead.

"Just tell me!" Prunella demanded, watching Axel and I try and worm our way out of telling her who exactly Isabella and Meme were.

"Look, Prunella," I said, frustrated. "It's too long of a story. You have to trust me on this one. Isabella and Carlos can be trusted completely. Meme was very old and she died a short time ago."

"Was she murdered?" Prunella asked, opening her eyes wide open.

"No, no," I quickly replied. "She was very old and she just passed away peacefully."

"Oh," Prunella mumbled, almost sounding disappointed that it wasn't a murder mystery.

"Look, we don't have time to fill you in and the doctor warned us not to tell you too much too quickly. You have to trust us and once we get out of this insane predicament, I promise I'll tell you more!" I couldn't help but laugh at my gross understatement.

"What are you guys talking about up there?" Nigel asked, walking toward the couch where we were gathered around Prunella.

Axel and I had just finished telling Prunella we weren't sure if Nigel was to be trusted. She fought, but we asked her to listen to us and go along with us.

"Nigel," I said, cheerily. "Have you taken a nap?"

"Me?" he asked, surprised and annoyed with my question. "I do not need a nap!"

"Ruth Ann didn't mean anything by it, Nigel," Axel told

him, vexed. "What do you want?"

"I, I came up here to see what our plan was," he said, baffled that Axel would question him.

"Oh, we were just figuring that out," Axel said. "I think our best, and only plan, is to call the authorities the minute one of us gets cell service. I was wondering if you would be willing to let me hold your cell phone so I could be the one to make the call?"

"No way!" he snapped. "I'm perfectly capable of making a call too."

"Axel is just saying he'll take all of our phones, Nigel," I quickly said. "I'm giving him my phone too, see," I said, pulling it out of my coat pocket and handing it to Axel.

He put my cell phone inside his sports coat and held his hand out for Nigel to give him his. "Well?" Axel asked. "Unless there's some reason you prefer not to let me have your phone?"

"No, I have nothing to hide," he said, shakily. I noticed his voice had a slight change of pitch when he said that. He started to pull his cell phone out of his pants pocket but changed his mind. "I think it would be a mistake to give all our phones to one person. I'm going to hold on to mine for now"

"Have it your way," Axel said, turning his attention to Prunella. "Are you feeling strong enough to let us get you out of this?"

"In my mind I am, but my legs aren't. I feel helpless not being able to walk or run if I need to. I'm going to weigh you all down." Prunella put her hands to her face and tried not to sob. Her shoulders shook, but no tears fell down her cheeks. I felt an odd sensation that I didn't like. Almost as if I wasn't trusting her again. I shoved it out of my head and told her she is too important to us and she should never feel like she was a burden.

"But, I am a burden to you," she said, frantically. "I can't possibly get away from Viktor."

"Ah, but you have another power," I said, smiling devilishly.

"What is that?" Axel said, raising an eyebrow.

"Prunella has the power of persuasion, female persuasion. Didn't you see the way Viktor looked at her and actually calmed down when she spoke?"

"You're right!" Axel blurted out. "I think we can use this to our advantage."

"How?" Prunella asked, innocently.

"He was irate with Ruth Ann and me, but with you, he was kind and gentle."

"Gentle as in drugging me during this flight?" she asked, skeptical.

"Well, besides that part," he said. "I think if you charm him, he'll do whatever you want."

"I'll try," she said doubtful, but willing. "What should I do?"

"Smile, talk to him and ask as many questions as we can come up with before he comes back out here," I said. "See if he has any reason to doubt his boss and cast doubt in the way his boss uses him to do his dirty work."

"That's good, Ruth Ann," Axel said. "Maybe ask him if he has a family or any kids back home."

"Okay, and then what?" she asked. "You don't really believe he would just let us go, do you?"

"Well, maybe not, but he might be distracted enough that he won't notice what I plan on doing," Axel said.

"Which is?" I inquired, wondering that myself.

"Calling as we start to descend or once we've hit the

ground. I need a really good distraction so he won't notice me."

"I can do that!" Prunella exclaimed, excited. "I can figure some way for him to be by my side while the plane is about to land. Then, you can call while you're in your seat, belted in, right?"

"Exactly!" Axel replied, happy Prunella was excited and participating. "We don't have the luxury of any weapons or even manpower."

"True," I said. "Viktor's a big guy, he would either shoot us or knock us out with one punch."

"I'm not fighting anyone," Nigel cried out from the back of the plane. "I'm too old for that."

"You and I are about the same age," Axel told him. "You're just out of shape."

"Hey," he stammered, offended. "I'm still strong enough. I just choose not to fight anymore."

"*Anymore?*" I questioned him.

"I did a little boxing back in the day. It kept me in shape, but, well, it's been a few years since I've been in the ring."

"Quite a few years, I would say," Axel muttered.

"This isn't getting us anywhere," I snapped. "We have a plan. Prunella will occupy Viktor while the plane is landing, and Axel will make the call home. He'll try to get Inga on the line, but wait," I stopped, and realized we were going about this all wrong. "No, why didn't we think of this in the first place?"

"What?" Axel asked, confused.

"We don't have to call," I said, realizing how dumb we've been. "We text!"

"I can't believe none of us thought of that," Axel said, feeling stupid. "I can type it out right now, and all I have to do is pull it up and hit send. This is great!" he said, rushing to his seat and pulling out his cell phone to write out his text. "I can text Inga, Isabella, and Carlos," he said.

"What are you going to tell them?" I said, wondering if he would tell Isabella about my conversation with Meme and the safety hex she had to put on Blue Ice.

"Let me type all three messages and then I'll read them to you," Axel said, lowering his head and focusing on his phone.

I decided not to push him, so I turned my attention back to Prunella and we talked about what she could tell Viktor to keep him by her side. "I know!" I bellowed. "You could say you're scared, and need his big, strong body by your side."

Prunella chortled, "And why would I be afraid and need his body near mine?"

"Well, I don't know, but, we can say you're feeling woozy from the drugs and aren't thinking clearly."

"That could work," she said, nodding her head.

I quickly asked her, "You're not feeling dizzy from the drugs still, are you?"

"Nope, not at all," she said, proudly. "I feel alert and ready to go. Unfortunately, my legs haven't walked in a while so I can't physically move very fast."

"All good," I told her. "I think we've got your end worked out. Now, I'll go and check on Axel." I walked to my seat across the small aisle from Axel.

Prunella closed her eyes, making me suspicious of just how awake she truly was. "Axel," I whispered. "How's it going?"

He looked up from his cell phone with his glasses barely hanging on his nose. "Almost done."

"Read it to me!" I said, anxiously.

"Okay, I'm done," he replied. "Here's what I wrote to Inga."

"Inga, need urgent help. Come to a village named Santa Marta near Bogota, Columbia, South America. We are in danger. Look for the house of Manual Marquez. He's a dangerous man, drug lord and gem thief. We're on a plane heading there as their prisoners. Hurry! Tell Isabella to read her text next."

"Isabella," he began reading her text disregarding my arms waving in the air to stop him. "Isabella," he repeated. *"Meme talked to Ruth Ann in a dream and told her to tell you to take Blue Ice and put a safety hex on it. Talk to Inga, she has the rest of the details. Please hurry, we are in a dangerous situation."*

"Axel," I cried out. "There's so much more you need to tell them!"

"No, Ruth Ann. I know you like to get wordy on your texts, but this isn't the time. They know where to go and what to bring. I emphasized we were being held prisoner and in a dangerous situation." He smacked his forehead and said, "I almost forgot to tell them not to warn anyone. We just want Isabella, Inga, and Carlos to come."

"Tell them to make sure Cassandra stays in Deer Creek," I reminded him.

He nodded and started typing on his cell phone. "There," he said. "I made it clear that just the three of them come, and not to bring Cassandra or tell John and Judy."

"Good," I said, wondering if John should be told. He was the chief of police and trained for situations like this.

"You're wondering if I should've told them to tell John, aren't you?" Axel asked, suspiciously. "I can, if you want."

"No." I don't know why I said that, but I felt it was the right answer. "They're going to wonder how Prunella's doing and if her health is okay," I said, frantic. "You should add that Prunella's awake and in pretty good shape, except that she can't walk."

"Too much information, Ruth Ann," Axel said. "They'll find out soon enough."

We sat in silence for a short time, when I noticed my ears beginning to pop. "Axel!" I exclaimed. "I think we're beginning our descent."

"I think you're right," he said, standing and leaning over the inner seat so he could peek out the window.

"What time is it?" I asked. "I'm so confused with time zones and how long we've been up in the air."

"I think, we'll land around four in the morning, but then we have a car ride to their village. I'm not sure how long that'll take," Axel answered, clearing it up a little for me. "We should be there early morning."

"Okay," I said, trying to figure out how exhausted I really should be. "I'm not tired at all right now."

"Adrenaline, Ruth Ann," he replied. "You'll collapse eventually."

"I know, but hopefully at the right time."

"I wonder why Viktor hasn't come back to check on us lately. I tried to hide my texting, but who knows what he saw," Axel said, worried.

"If he saw you texting, trust me, he would've stormed out of the cockpit and smashed all of our cell phones," I said.

"True."

"Axel, we're starting to descend quickly. Try to send those texts," I suggested.

"I will, right now," he said, pushing the send button on his phone. "Now, we wait and see if they go through."

I sat and folded my hands across my lap, saying a little

prayer to give us a break. I knew there were more important things God may be taking care of right now, but we sure could use a little divine intervention!

Chapter 19

"DING, DING," I heard those high-pitched noises loud and clear. I quickly told Axel to turn off the sound on his cell phone.

"I forgot," he said, correcting the potential problem. "But, you do understand the implication, right?" he asked me, smiling broadly.

"They went through?" I inquired, crossing every finger and toe I could manage.

"Yep."

"What was that noise?" Nigel demanded, storming from the back of the plane to our seats.

"It was Axel's cell phone," I said, causing a glare from Axel. I eyed him suspiciously and wondered what he was trying to tell me. I suddenly got the distinct impression Axel didn't want to include Nigel in everything we were doing. I quickly caught on and said, "It was just making noise, but we still don't have service. Maybe after we land," I said, noticing a slight nod from Axel. "Why don't you go and seatbelt yourself in. I think we're starting to descend."

"I noticed that, too," Nigel said, turning to go back to his seat. "What's the plan now?"

Axel turned his head around so he could see Nigel standing next to his seat about to sit down. "We're going to try and contact the authorities, Nigel. Are you going to help us?"

"Why wouldn't I?" he asked, surprised with Axel's question. "Are you doubting me for some reason?"

"Should I doubt you?" Axel asked, trying to catch him by confusing him.

"No!" he shouted, too loudly because the cockpit door flew open and Viktor stormed out.

"What's all the yelling about?" he asked, angrily. "Nigel, you need to sit down in your seat. We're about to land."

"We are?" he asked, rushing to fasten his seatbelt.

"I'm going to give you a few rules and then I'm going back into the cockpit for the landing. First, no funny stuff," he said, waving a gun in the air. "This is loaded, and don't test me."

"No need for a gun with us," Axel said. "You're younger and much stronger than any of us."

"Plus," Prunella added. "I can't do you any harm. I can't even walk."

I felt Prunella was beginning to act helpless to keep him occupied. Go, Prunella! "I'm a tiny bit scared," she said, whimpering a little.

Viktor put his gun in the back of his pants and walked to Prunella. "Why, you've been on private airplanes before, right?" He added, "This is your husband's plane, Prunella."

"Yes, but I just woke up from a coma, Viktor. I can't walk, and I'm weak," she said, forcing a tear to fall down her porcelain cheeks.

"Nothing to be scared of. I'll come right back here after we land and make sure you're alright. I won't let anything happen to you, I swear."

Wow, Axel and I eyed each other and smiled. It was working. She was wooing this big thug and I bet loving every minute of it. I watched as the two of them started a quiet conversation that Axel and I couldn't hear. What was she saying to him? Whatever it was, he was smiling and even laughing a bit. Suddenly, he was alerted by Axel's pilot, Stephen, that we were almost ready to land. Viktor hopped off the couch where he was sitting with Prunella and disappeared into the cockpit.

"How was I?" she asked, grinning from ear to ear. "I think he warmed up to me, nicely."

"He sure did," I said. "What's the plan, Axel?"

"When we touch down, we let Viktor give all his attention to Prunella. I'll check my cell phone to see if Inga or Isabella replied. Once I know they're aware of our situation, then we'll wait to be transferred to Manual Marquez' place."

"And we do what there?" I asked, not liking our plan very much. There will be a lot of time before Inga and the others get here to help us. "We need Prunella protected right away," I said. "Isabella needs to put that hex on Blue Ice."

"She will right away," Axel said. "But, until Isabella gets here and puts it around Prunella's neck, none of us are safe. Once that necklace is safely around her neck, I will breathe a little easier."

"So, you believe what Meme told us to do, right?" I asked, happy he was cooperating.

"Yes, but, we still don't have a way out of this. The necklace will protect Prunella, but what about the rest of us?"

"Meme told me that we would find a way out. Her main concern was Prunella's safety, and," I whispered the next word, "Nigel."

"We can only trust him so much," Axel said, quietly. "He's a money hungry old guy, and he'll sell all of us out for the right price."

"Meme said that, but she also said he might reform, unlike her sister, Mattie."

"That surprises me, Ruth Ann," Axel said. "I thought Mattie came around."

"She went back to her home in Jamaica awfully fast," I reminded him. "She may have had a moment of kindness, but according to Meme, she's not able to change so we need to leave her out of our lives."

"Very sad," he said.

"Check your cell phone, Axel," I said, excited. "Maybe Inga or Isabella texted you back."

He pulled out his cell and held it low behind the seat in front of him so Viktor wouldn't catch him. "Well?" I asked, impatiently. "Any replies?"

"Yes!" he cried. "Inga got the text and she only replied with 3 words."

"What?" I asked, anxiously.

"On our way!" he answered me.

"What about Isabella?"

"No, but I would assume Inga took care of it with the one text. She probably knew we were in danger and didn't want a lot of texts going back and forth."

"Tell Inga to hurry!" I exclaimed.

"I'll do that right now, Ruth Ann. I know you want to be sure they understand the urgency of our situation."

"What about them flying down here? Don't we need tell them what to do?"

"No," Axel said. "Inga knows everything she needs to make arrangements."

"How?" I asked, confused. "Did you text her more information and not tell me?"

"Yes, I did. But, it wasn't that I left it out. I just didn't want us talking about it too much. I only told her who to contact at the private airport in Colorado."

"Fine," was all I replied.

Axel sensed the strain in my reply and tried to explain he didn't mean anything by it. "Please, Ruth Ann, not now. We have too many urgent matters to handle, and I can't worry about you being upset with me."

I saw the agony in his eyes and caved. "I'm okay, Axel."

"Thanks, Ruth Ann," he said, checking his cell phone to see if the last text to Inga went through. "Understood," Axel said, reading his messages. "They're already on their way to the airport. The pilot is ready to go."

"Wow, that was fast," I said.

"That's why we pay big bucks, Ruth Ann. Money can really buy a lot."

"Not everything," I mumbled, thinking about what Viktor would do to us if he knew we had used Axel's cell phone to get help.

I wondered if it was a mistake not trying to contact the local authorities. I figured they were in Marquez' pocket anyway and could only cause us more harm. I decided to sit back and wait for the plane to land.

Prunella was sitting, waiting for Viktor to return to her. She was happy, helping us in any way she could. "We'll be on the ground in a minute or two," she called out. "I can see the ground, but there's no runway!"

I leaned over the seat next to me and peered out of the window. "Hey, she's right! There's nothing down there but a jungle." Discouraged, I added, "Not another jungle!"

"What do you mean, Ruth Ann," Prunella asked me. "What other jungle are you referring to?"

I forgot, again, that Prunella didn't remember what happened in Jamaica not long ago. "I just meant I don't know where he's going to land the plane because it's a jungle below us."

"Not anymore," Axel called out. "There's a clearing coming up. I can see a bright green patch of land and here we go ..." Axel sat back in his seat as the pilot hit the ground roughly. We bounced back and forth until finally the plane came to an abrupt stop.

"Wow, that wasn't pleasant," Prunella stated. "Axel, I thought you hired an experienced pilot."

"He is, Prunella," Axel said. "But, I bet he's never landed in a tiny clearing in a jungle."

"Good point," she said, sitting up ready to take on her new admirer, Viktor.

We waited until the cockpit door opened, and Viktor came out. "Nobody gets out of their seats yet," he ordered. "I need to make sure my guys are waiting for us, and ..." he turned around and eyed the exposed cockpit. "And, we have two large items to dispose of."

"What did that mean?" I wondered. "What large items?"

Axel must've caught on immediately. "You didn't have to kill them!"

"Kill who?" I bellowed. "You killed the pilot?"

"Yes, he did, Ruth Ann," Axel said, furious. "And the flight attendant. They did nothing to you, you bloody fool!"

"Shut up!" Viktor shouted, pulling out his gun. "This isn't the time to get tough. Would you like to be my next victim?"

Prunella decided it was time to interrupt. "Viktor, please leave him alone. I need you now so forget about what happened. I don't want you to leave me alone. Are you going to stay with us?"

He fell to her side, and quickly changed from killer to pushover. "I won't let anyone touch you, Prunella. I'll carry you off this plane myself and I promise I won't let anyone hurt you."

"Thank you, Viktor," she replied, smiling ever so sweetly, almost making me sick. "Who's here to help you?"

Axel and I let her talk and ask the questions. He divulged way more information to her than he would've to us. "My buddy's here to help me. We'll drive you, your cousin and husband, and Nigel to my boss's compound. There, we will wait for our next orders."

"What are they going to do with us?" she asked, acting terrified, even though she didn't have to act, it really was terrifying.

"I don't know, honestly," he said.

Axel yelled out, "Maybe because your boss doesn't trust you completely. Have you ever thought about that?"

"That's not true!" Viktor screamed. "I'm his number one man, and he just hasn't told me what's next because I've been all around the world chasing you!"

"Okay, Viktor," Axel said, jeeringly. "I think you better decide if doing your bosses dirty work is worth spending your life in prison ... or worse."

"What are you blabbing about?" he exclaimed. "I'm safer than any of his employees. He trusts me completely."

"Then, why don't you know what he wants from us?" Axel inquired.

"I do know you fool," he hollered. "He wants that priceless necklace of yours."

"And why would anyone think we had that on us?" Axel asked, opening a huge can of worms. "If it's priceless, why would we carry it with us?"

Viktor appeared confused. I wasn't sure what Axel was trying to accomplish. I really didn't want Manual's men to seek out my family in Deer Creek.

"Shut up," he stammered. "You're just trying to goad me. I'm not falling for your rich man stunts. Just because you're not strong enough to overthrow me, you think you'll use your intelligence to do it. Don't bother."

"Alright, Viktor," Axel said. "But, if you ever feel your boss is using you to do his dirty work, and you want people who could really help you, we're here for you," Axel said, trying to manipulate him.

"Viktor," Prunella called to him. "Can you sit with me while we wait?"

"I have to open the door and let the other guy on board. He'll take care of the others, and I'll personally take care of you."

"Great," she said, cheerily. "I trust you, Viktor. You wouldn't let anyone or anything hurt me, would you?"

"No, way," he said, confidently.

"You know, the others are my family, too. I wouldn't be happy if they were hurt, either."

He eyed her suspiciously for a second, and they replied, "I'll do my best to see that they aren't treated too badly, okay?"

"Try really, really hard," she pleaded.

"Yes, yes, I will."

Amazing, she transformed a cruel killer into a teddy bear right before our very eyes. If only he stayed true to his word.

Chapter 20

"It's time to get off the plane," Viktor ordered, motioning to another man who just boarded. "You take Mr. Eklund but be careful with him. He thinks he's so smart, but remember, he has no power over us. The other two will follow you. I don't think they pose a physical threat."

Insulted, I wanted to lash out, but thought it unwise. I came to a quick decision that could prove beneficial for us. I would play a weak, dumb middle-aged woman, even though I clearly wasn't!

I stood and waited for a very petrified Nigel to meet up with me. "It'll be alright, Nigel," I whispered to him. "Just do what they want, and we'll be safe."

"How can you say that?" he snapped, causing Viktor's attention to fall upon us.

"Would you shut up," I muttered to him. "Can't you think before you speak?"

"What are you two whispering about?" Viktor demanded. "Do I need Sal to put a gag in your mouths?"

"No, of course not," I swiftly responded. "Nigel needs to keep quiet, that's all I was telling him."

"Very good, Ruth Ann," Viktor said, mocking me like I was a child. "Now you're getting it."

I wanted to smack him but didn't think he'd take kindly

to my action. I chose to smile and walk down the narrow stairs to the grassy runway. Even though we were far away from home, I felt better now that we were off the plane. I waited with Nigel and then Sal led Axel down the stairs. He had a firm grip on Axel's arm, but Axel wasn't restrained by any ropes or handcuffs. That was a positive sign.

Sal shoved Axel toward us, and the three of us stood waiting for Viktor to come down the stairs with Prunella in his arms. It took longer than we expected when finally, they appeared at the plane's doorway. Prunella was clinging to him with her arms tightly wound around his neck. He had a firm, but not aggressive hold of her around her body as he carefully came down the stairs. I spotted her head resting on his shoulder as he walked past us heading for a large, black sedan with blackened windows.

"Open the door, you fool!" Viktor snapped at Sal. "The others wouldn't dare take off without her," he said, referring to Axel, Nigel, and me.

"Yes, sir," Sal replied, bitterly. He rushed around the other side of the car and waited for Viktor to put Prunella inside.

Once Prunella was safely inside the car, Viktor ordered Sal to bring us over. "Move it!" the young, large, muscular man spat out. "C'mon, hurry up."

Axel grabbed my arm and led me to the car before Sal had a chance to hurt me. Nigel trudged behind slowly, but he did manage to keep up. "Get in," Viktor snapped at me. The back-door opposite the one Prunella used was wide open and Viktor was waiting for me to crawl in. I bent over and slid inside a surprisingly spacious area where Prunella was sprawled across the entire length of the side seat. The back part of the sedan reminded me of limousine with a long sitting area in the back and a lengthy couch along the side. The opposite side housed a bar with crystal glasses, water bottles, and quite an assortment of liquors. Axel was next; he slid in and sat next to me on the back seat. I waited for Nigel to be next, but he never came into the back area of the car. Unfortunately, Viktor entered and crawled past Axel and me to get near Prunella. He sat at the end of the couch near her feet. I noticed he actually lifted her legs and placed them on his thighs. I saw Axel's face redden, and I had to gently and inconspicuously touch his hand to calm him down.

"Are you jealous?" Viktor prodded Axel. He was caressing her calves with his large, rough, and un-manicured hands ever so tenderly. I watched Prunella tense as he ran his hand a little higher on her thigh. She swiftly took a hold of his hand and gave it a squeeze, stopping his hand from going any further.

"You're being so sweet to me, Viktor," Prunella said, nauseatingly nice. "Where are we going and when will we get there?" she inquired, hoping to get information from him so Axel could relay it to Inga and the others.

"Don't worry your pretty little head about it," he answered, releasing her hand and continuing his revolting, caressing up and down her leg.

"Please?" she begged. "I'm so tired of being cooped up. First, in the hospital, and then the plane. I'm ready to try and walk again."

"I'll help you regain your strength. I bet those two wanted you incapacitated," Viktor said, accusing Axel and me of trying to keep Prunella a cripple.

"I would never do that!" I snapped, unexpectedly. I didn't want to react, but he really ticked me off and it just spewed out of my mouth before my brain could stop it.

"Shut up!" he snarled at me. "You're just jealous of her because she's young and beautiful."

I was about to react, when Axel stopped me. Prunella directed his attention back to her. "Viktor, I really would love it if you helped me. You're so strong and I know I'd feel safe with you."

"You're right! You would be safe with me. Maybe I can convince the boss to let you stay in my suite of rooms."

Axel's patience went out the window. He lunged at Viktor, causing Prunella to raise her legs out of the way. We all froze, watching Prunella manipulate her legs. "Hey," Viktor cried, shoving Axel back into his seat. "You moved your legs!"

"I did!" she bellowed, thrilled. "Maybe I can walk now."

"Don't push it, Prunella," I said. "Take it slowly."

"I don't want to! I want to walk and go wherever I want to."

"With me, right?" Viktor asked, surprising us that he actually believed Prunella was going to have a relationship with him.

"You know, Viktor," she began. "I'm still married to Axel."

"We can fix that," he said, glaring at Axel. "One way or another."

"You promised Axel or Ruth Ann wouldn't get hurt, remember?" she asked, kindly.

"I did, didn't I?" he replied, questioning himself about his own motives. "Well, we'll see what I can do."

"Yes, you did," Prunella answered. "Let's get back to where we're going and, hey, what happened to Nigel?"

"I'm up here," a voice called out through an intercom.

"He's sitting next to Sal in the front," Viktor answered. I

looked toward the front and we couldn't see anyone through the dark tinted shield. "He's not a threat like you two."

"You said I was a weak, middle-aged woman, remember?" I asked, sarcastically.

"But, you're sneaky. I don't like sneaky."

Axel shook his head trying to signal me to shut my mouth. I wasn't helping our cause so I let Prunella do all the work. She seemed to be the only one who was getting through to Viktor, and I wanted her to get as much information out of him as possible before we were confronted by Manual Marquez. Everything could change once we were in his hands.

I closed my eyes, feeling the impending exhaustion creeping through my aching bones. I tried to listen to Prunella but found myself dozing in and out of sleep.

"Ruth Ann, can you hear me?" a strong, female voice called. "Come on, Ruth Ann, open your eyes!"

I didn't want to open them, I was so tired, and needed my sleep. It's been a long few weeks, but some unknown force made me do it. I opened my eyes, one at a time, and I was once again in an unknown location, but different than the last time. "Meme?" I asked, seeing her familiar face come into focus. "Am I dreaming, again?"

"Not exactly a dream, but you can call it what you want," she replied, smiling and displaying her perfect set of teeth.

"You have more to tell me?" I asked.

"Yes, Ruth Ann, but first I need to tell you that you did well. You made Axel believe you and Isabella, Inga, and Carlos are on their way with Blue Ice."

"It took some convincing, but he came around," I said, looking around at my new surroundings. "Where are we?"

Meme laughed strongly, "Ah, you noticed we're not in the same place as before. We are ..." I cut her off abruptly.

"We're in Felix's house in the basement, aren't we?"
Meme nodded. "We're in the room where you," I stopped,
gulped, and tried to say the words, but Meme did it for me.

"Where I died, Ruth Ann," she said slowly, looking
around the tiny bedroom furnished with a single, twin bed that
was so small I didn't think I would fit on it and I'm only
around five feet three. "A lot of good happened in here, too."

"You broke the long-time curse on our necklace," I said.

"Yes, I did. However, others tried to place another eviler
one on it, didn't they?"

"Yes, but they failed. Except for what Mattie did to the
necklace and Prunella. She doesn't remember any of it
though."

"That's a good thing, right now, Ruth Ann," Meme said,
sitting on the edge of the bed.

"Are you tired?" I asked her, surprised she would feel
tiredness or anything else.

"No, but you are, and I feel it through you. Soon, you'll
be able to rest, but not now."

"What's going to happen next?" I asked, hoping she
would be specific with me about how we were going to get out
of this mess.

"I can only tell you bits and pieces, Ruth Ann."

"Please, tell me as much as you can."

"You need to restrain your mouth, Ruth Ann. Viktor and
the others won't think you're funny. They will stop you, and it
could hurt you. Do you understand me?"

"I know. I tend to stick my foot in my mouth. I'll try,
Meme."

"Try hard. Now, I have spoken to Isabella and she has
already put the safety hex on Blue Ice. She will get here soon
with Inga and Carlos, and the three of them will sneak onto

Manual Marquez' property. But, you have to help them. There are many of his men guarding his property and you need to remain free to roam so you can let them in."

"I'm going to be able to roam around freely?" I asked, surprised. "Won't I be thrown into a cell or tied to a bed?"

"Don't be so dramatic, Ruth Ann," Meme said, seriously. "Axel won't be able to help you. They'll restrain him because they fear him more than you. Manual Marquez won't be happy that you don't have Blue Ice with you, and he will need a little time to come up with a plan to get it. So, that buys you a little time to strategize. Use your time well."

"Strategize what?" I asked, frustrated.

"How to get out of this mess!" Meme said, exasperated for the first time. "You need to think and use your resources wisely."

"What resources? I don't know anything about where we're going."

"Things will transpire that will be obvious in the near future. You and Axel will come up with a plan, and it should work. I can't tell you the plan, Ruth Ann, so don't ask me. I just know you'll have an obvious opportunity, and when you're faced with it, use it!"

"You're confusing me, Meme. I'm more anxious now than I was. You're telling me I'll know when we have an opportunity to escape, right?" Meme nodded slowly and smiled. "But, you won't tell me what that will be?" Meme nodded, again. "You didn't mention, Isabella, Inga and Carlos though."

"They'll be with you. I can't say much more. Just know that YOU will be the one who sees your chance for escape. Remember that! And, don't forget to stop talking so much. Manual's a very dangerous, powerful man down here. Don't

upset him or your opportunity will vanish."

"Fine, I'll do my best, Meme," I said, yawning.

"I'm going to leave you now. You're tired, rest for a few more minutes, and when you wake, you will be at the home of Manual Marquez. Be aware of your surroundings and stay free so you can sneak in Isabella, Carlos and Inga. Don't anger your captors!"

"I got it!" I snapped.

"One last thing. Isabella must put the necklace on Prunella's neck the minute she sees her. Do not wait! It's a matter of life and death. If she has it on her neck, she'll be safe. If not, she will die ..." Meme faded out and I felt totally relaxed until I felt my body being shaken.

"Stop it!" I cried, not yet able to open my eyes.

"Ruth Ann, it's me, Axel. Wake up, we're here."

I forced my eyes open. Meme told me to study my surroundings, so I wanted to memorize as much as possible about the place. I looked out the window and I didn't see a house yet, but we were on a gravel road surrounded by jungle. The rocks from the gravel were pounding the sides and bottom of the car replicating the sounds of a small gun. Axel was looking out the window just like me. I wanted to tell him to pay attention to every detail, but Viktor was too close. Prunella's eyes were closed, and her head was leaning against the side of the car. Viktor had both hands on her calves, watching her intently.

"She sleeps a lot," he said, out of the blue. "Why does she sleep so much?"

He looked at Axel and me for an answer, but I kept hearing Meme's words in my head. "Don't say too much." I hoped Axel would respond, but he was too full of rage to answer him, so I had to.

"She's been sick for a while, Viktor. She was in a coma. I think she's still weak and needs to get her strength back. She sleeps because she's weak."

"I'll make sure she eats as soon as we settle in," he said, turning his attention back to Prunella. I was beginning to think he was delusional, expecting that she would return his affection. He really cared for her, and I was wondering if this was my 'opportunity'?

"She has to be careful what she eats, Viktor," I said. "Nothing heavy or too hard to chew. Keep it soft, and bland."

"Yes, I will do that, thank you."

Whoa, he was kind to me, and even Axel gave me a slight grin. I decided to leave it at that. I wasn't going to continue the conversation even though I was dying to ask about where we were headed. It was a long, bumpy road until we finally came to a large clearing. The jungle gave way to a perfectly lined row of tall palm trees on both sides of the road. Ahead I could see a massive U-shaped estate. As we drove toward the circular drive with a large grassy area in the middle full of vibrant flowers, I noticed a white, stucco house that had three stories. It looked sturdily built, almost like a fortress, I thought to myself.

The large sedan came to a halt in front of the grand entrance. As I looked out the window, I tried to envision different ways in and out for our escape. I could only see one set of doors, apparently the main entrance. To my right and left were several sets of windows, but the first-floor ones had bars. Kind of like a prison cell. That wasn't a good sign. I looked up and noticed above the main entrance was a large semi-circular balcony supported by sturdy, ornate columns. The roof was flat, and I suddenly spotted movement up there; a guard holding a long rifle was walking back and forth. That wasn't a good sign for Inga, Isabella and Carlos. They would be spotted getting near the house no matter how cautiously they approached.

I felt deflated, but only momentarily. Axel was quiet and surveilling the area just like me. We always seemed to have this connection, as if we could read each other's minds. I took a deep breath in and sighed. "What was that for?" Viktor asked, just as he let go of Prunella's leg.

"I'm just really tired, that's all," I said, although I really felt dispirited.

"I'm sure after you talk with my boss, he'll let you rest. You and him, he nodded his head to Axel, have a lot to discuss with my boss."

"What about my wife?" Axel said, finally speaking.

"I will take her to her room immediately."

"Her *own* room?" Axel inquired. "Or *your* room?"

"None of your business!" he bellowed.

Axel didn't say anything more. He shook his head and waited for instructions. It didn't take long when the door near me opened and a large, heavy set man came into my sight. "Out," he said, nastily.

I slid my legs out of the car, and he took hold of my arm. I wanted to shove him away but decided against it. He was huge, smelled of tobacco and maybe even a little alcohol. "I'm coming," I said, trying not to sound angry.

Impatiently, he forced me out of the car and I stumbled and fell forward on the newly tarred part of the driveway. "Hey!" I hollered, thankful I was wearing pants because it saved my knees from getting scraped. "That wasn't necessary. I wasn't fighting you."

He didn't respond, and I wondered if he understood me. He obviously didn't speak much English, because I heard Sal get out of the car and shout at him in Spanish. I knew a few words, but not enough to hold a conversation. I didn't have to speak Spanish to figure out that Sal wasn't happy with this guy. He stormed over to him and was shouting and shoving him out of the way. Sal reached down and held out his hand to help me stand. I gladly took it, hoping I could get on his good side. I needed all the help I could get!

Chapter 21

"Welcome!" a man called out boisterously as he stood in front of the tall, double doored entrance. "Come in, come in to my beautiful home!"

By now, Axel was out of the car standing next to me. We were dumbfounded after hearing what had to be Manual Marquez invite us into his home. I glanced around to see if Axel and I were going to be escorted by one of his guards or walk up the stairs alone.

"Come, come," the man said anxiously, motioning his arms in the air to hurry us. "You don't need my men to drag you, do you?"

"No," I replied immediately, taking hold of Axel's arm and walking up the wide stairs to where this strange man waited.

Once we were within a couple feet of him, he turned and walked inside without introducing himself. "Follow me, please," he said, waving his arm in the air. His back was to us as he walked down a hall to the right, and I didn't notice any guards in sight. Axel and I walked through the oversized wide, foyer. The floors were tiled in red brick and there was a huge cement fountain in the middle. The water flowed out of a large fish's mouth into a basin and splashed against the curved sides. The colors on the fish were beautiful; bright yellows, blues, and greens were dominant with purple and reds appearing sparingly.

Axel didn't glance at the fountain, but only at the back of the man we assumed was Manual Marquez. With nobody watching us, we could've jumped the man, but that would've been reckless since I'm pretty sure there were plenty of guards floating around. We walked down a large hallway, passing several rooms with closed doors. He suddenly took a turn to the left and disappeared. Once we caught up, we thought we were entering an office, but it was another hall that led toward the back of the estate. That was the U-shape I saw. The front was the bottom of the 'U' and there were two wings off each side. He kept walking, whistling to himself, expecting Axel and me to be right behind him. I tried to pay attention to every detail as we walked, but every door we passed was closed. All I could memorize was beautiful artwork on the walls, and the niches filled with colorful pottery.

"In here," the man called back to us as he reached and opened a door on the right side of the hall.

Axel and I hurried inside and we were amazed to find Prunella already in there, lying on a turquoise colored leather couch. She had a blanket covering her bottom half, and Viktor standing over her. "What took you so long?" she asked, surprised to see us.

"We came right here," Axel said, about to rush to her, but Sal appeared out of nowhere stopping him.

"Do not move," he ordered Axel.

"Thank you, Sal," the man said, patting him on his shoulder. "Bring them to those chairs by the window."

I realized we were in a large, sun-filled room with floor to ceiling windows on the back side. There was a large, ornate wooden desk in the very middle of the room with chairs in front of it, but that wasn't where he told Sal to take us. He took us around the desk to a nice sitting area near the windows. The sun's early morning glare blocked me from seeing outside too well. There were no window coverings on them, making me wonder how hot it must get in the middle of the day around here. Or, perhaps it this man was so wealthy, it didn't matter what it cost to cool this massive place.

"Sit," Sal told us, pointing to several brightly colored upholstered chairs. We nodded and sat down next to each other. Sal stood behind us and waited for his boss to come over.

"What about Prunella?" I asked. "Can't we sit by her so we can all talk together?"

"No," Sal answered, just as Manual Marquez walked up to a chair directly across from Axel and me. Only a round glass table was between us now. I watched as the man waited for Sal to come around and make sure he was comfortable.

"Sal, get us a cold drink, please," he commanded. "Would you care for iced tea or lemonade? I'd offer you something stronger, but it is early in the morning. Oh, what about coffee or tea? I hear Ruth Ann likes to drink tea."

How would he know that? I didn't inquire, reminding myself to limit what came out of my mouth. I just replied, "I would like a cup of tea, thank you."

"Very well," the man said, and responded to Sal in Spanish for what I assumed was tea. Axel asked for nothing. I could see his temper rising and realized that he was used to being in control, not the other way around.

"So, Ruth Ann, I hope we made your trip down here comfortable?" he asked, resting his elbows on the arms of the chair and bringing his two hands together in front of his chest.

"Considering we were forced down here, yes, it was comfortable. Can I ask your name, sir?" I asked, trying not to sound condescending.

"Forgive me for my ignorance. My name is Manual Marquez. I am the owner of this estate and requested your visit."

"For what reason?" Axel barked.

Manual turned from me to Axel and obviously didn't like his tone. "You should be respectful in another man's home, Mr. Eklund. Especially when we could make your stay, well, rather uncomfortable, right?"

I whispered to Axel to please keep his cool when he straightened himself in his chair and responded, "I am sorry, Mr. Marquez. You're completely correct. I should show my respect for you while in your home. But, may I ask why this was necessary? I mean, if you wanted something from us, all you had to do was ask."

Before Manual could reply, another one of his guards walked past the windows and French doors near us. He was holding a large rifle as he strolled past us without looking in-side. Manual smiled after he watched him go by and said, "May I call you Axel?"

"Yes," Axel answered. "May I call you Manual?"

"Of course!" he responded, exuberantly. "Now, we're getting somewhere. We're on first name basis, that's moving forward."

"Manual, if I may," I said, hoping to get past their awk-ward conversation. "What are you going to do with us?" I also remembered Nigel. "Where is Nigel? Did you take him some-where else?"

"Ruth Ann, it really is very simple. I brought you three down here to inquire about a special, rare piece I'd like to ob-tain. I'm sure you're aware of what I'm referring to?" He brushed his hand in the air nonchalantly and added, "Don't concern yourself with Nigel. He's been taken back to the airport and sent home to England. He is of no more use to me or you. He's a greedy coward, and you're better forgetting about him."

"Of course. I'm not concerned about Nigel right now. We barely know him." I answered.

"Then, if you will tell me what I can pay you to get it, then we could possibly make this a short visit."

"*Pay us*?" I asked, baffled. "You aren't going to just take it?"

He laughed so loud I thought he'd burst his gut wide open. "I'm not stealing it from you. I will pay an enormous, ridiculous amount of money for it. Just let me see it, and then have my appraiser evaluate it, and then we'll come to mutual terms. How does that sound?"

"Why aren't you asking me?" Axel inquired. "Ruth Ann isn't a negotiator."

"I am too!" I snapped. "I own ..." Manual cut me off instantly.

"You own Ruth Ann's Antiques! Yes, you do know how to negotiate. You buy products and sell them all the time, correct?"

"Yes!" I said, glaring back at Axel. "Thank you."

Axel shook his head in disgust and told me through gritted teeth. "I'm not saying you can't do it, Ruth Ann. I don't think this is as simple as he's making it sound."

"What did you say, Axel?" Manual demanded, not hearing his last comment.

"I only told Ruth Ann that she is perfectly capable of handling normal, legal business transactions." I could tell Axel thought about his next comment before he said it. He took his time and finally said, "But, Manual, this isn't an ordinary, standard business deal, is it?"

"I guess it isn't."

"You had to hijack my plane and kidnap us. And, you murdered my pilot and attendant for no reason!" Axel's face reddened and I feared he was going to have a stroke. I swiftly grabbed his forearm to keep him in his chair. If Manual had Axel's pilot and attendant murdered, I'm pretty sure he wouldn't blink an eye having us taken care of, too.

"I didn't murder your pilot and attendant," he replied, carefully. "The pilot tried to take out Viktor, so Viktor defended himself."

"That's nonsense and you know it!" Axel bellowed. "This is preposterous. Let us leave immediately and maybe we won't come after you with the local and American authorities."

Manual laughed again, but this time he wasn't laughing happily. He was angry and he snapped his fingers. Sal rushed over from where he was standing with Viktor. He leaned over and Manual whispered something into his ear. Sal straightened, walked over to Axel and roughly grabbed hold of him. He dragged him toward the door with Axel hollering and frantically trying to escape. Unfortunately, Sal was much younger, bigger, and stronger.

Prunella didn't flinch as she watched her husband being dragged out of the room. I truly wanted to rush after him, and do whatever I could, but that would only cause the two of us to be restrained. I promised Meme I'd stay free to roam the estate until Inga, Isabella and Carlos arrived. It took every ounce of patience to turn back to Manual and not say a word.

"So, I'm sorry about that, Ruth Ann. Maybe Axel's overtired and chose to make an unwise decision. He shouldn't have had a temper tantrum. That was his mistake, and he will be paying for that shortly."

"Please don't hurt him," I begged. "We'll cooperate with you, but don't harm him. He's not used to being controlled. He's a prominent businessman, and not used to being treated this way." I really hoped I didn't insult Manual with my last comment, but it would look stranger if I didn't put up some sort of fight.

"Don't worry about it, Ruth Ann. Let's get back to our discussion."

"First, can I ask why Prunella's over there? It's her necklace too."

"Well, there you go, Ruth Ann. You admitted you know what I want. Good for you! Now, I will tell you something since you were forthcoming." For a moment, I had no idea what I spilled, but then I realized we never brought up the necklace. He just stated he wanted a rare piece from us, but never said it was a necklace.

"Go on," I said.

"Prunella is being treated with care because she just had a traumatic injury and we don't want her to relapse. I understand she still can't walk, and Viktor has taken a liking to her. I have to admit, he has good taste. She's a beauty. I wouldn't mind a chance with her myself." He held his hand to stop me from protesting. Thankfully, he did, because I might've said something I shouldn't have. "I know you think I'm too old for her, but Axel's just a little older than me, and she married him."

"Good point," I said for no reason. Shut your mouth, Ruth Ann!

"See, you agree. I'm allowing Viktor to keep watch over her until she and I get some time to get to know each other."

"But, I thought you said we could leave immediately!"

"Well, not too soon," he said, eyeing the couch where Prunella and Viktor were sitting. They were far enough away that they couldn't hear our conversation. "And, Axel made a fool of himself. He's to blame for detaining you even further."

"If you just let us go, I will let you buy the necklace!" I blurted out, stupidly.

"Ah, good choice, Ruth Ann," he said, thrilled. "Let me see it so I can get my appraiser in here."

"Do you think I have it with me?" I asked, amazed with his ignorance. "It's safely locked up far from here."

"Back in your hometown, Deer Creek?" he inquired.

I didn't want him snooping around town when my daughters were there. "No, no, we don't keep it there. That's a small town, and too risky. Axel keeps it at his place of business."

"You're telling me it's back in Stockholm?"

"Yes."

He watched me long and hard for several seconds, when I couldn't help but start to fidget. I knew it was a clear sign I was lying, but I was so uncomfortable I couldn't help myself. "Are you telling me the truth, Ruth Ann?"

"Why would I lie? You'd kill us, wouldn't you?" I asked, playing his game.

"Probably."

"So, we need to go back to Stockholm, get the necklace, come back and present it to you. Does that sound like a good plan?"

He stood up, walked toward me and leaned over my chair. "Do I look like a fool?"

I leaned back as far as I could in my chair and tried to get the stench of his breath away from my face. "No, Manual. I don't take you for a fool."

"Then, why are you lying to me?"

Before I could worm my way out of this, Prunella starting screaming she was in pain. Manual ran to her side as quickly as his short, stout body could carry him. I was surprised by how lithe he was. "What's wrong with her?" he yelled at Viktor, who was fervently trying to calm Prunella down. She was playing her part beautifully. She begged them to help her.

Manual yelled for me to come and help. I hopped out of my chair, grateful to leave our conversation behind. I wasn't sure what my plan was, but Meme did tell me I'd come up with one. Somehow, I didn't think suggesting to go back to Stockholm was what she had in mind, though.

Chapter 22

"Help me, Ruth Ann! I'm in pain. My legs are hurting so bad I think I'm going to faint." I held Prunella's hand as I told her she would be alright. She had real tears streaming down her face, confusing me. Was she really in pain or was she protecting me from Manual? I caught a quick glimmer in her eyes that assured me she was fine. Viktor and Manual panicked, exactly the reaction we wanted.

"You need to get her help!" I shrieked. "She needs medical help, now!"

Viktor started begging his boss to listen to me. Manual ran to his desk, picked up his cell phone and started shouting instructions into it. He slammed his phone down on his spotless desk and told us the doctor's in surgery. "We have to wait until he's available."

"How long will that be?" I asked, pretending to be hysterical. "She needs help!"

Manual ignored me and ordered Sal and Viktor to take her to a room upstairs. Viktor requested he take her to his own room, when Manual shook his head. "No, no, take her to ... take her to, Isabella's old room!"

Viktor turned pale, Sal backed away shaking his head.

"No, sir, no, please not that room, it's ..." Viktor stopped talking abruptly because he couldn't finish his sentence.

"It's not cursed!" Manual hollered. "It's a room already filled with woman's stuff, she can rest in there until the doctor comes."

Viktor didn't move, Sal remained frozen. "NOW!" Manual screamed, walking to Sal and slapping his face to rouse him from the trance he was in. "Move her, now!"

Viktor and Sal walked over to Prunella, who was a little calmer, and lifted her in their arms and gently walked out of the room. I should've insisted on following, but I was in such shock, I couldn't move myself. It couldn't be the same Isabella I knew, and who was on her way this very moment. Isabella had to be a common name. I was being ridiculous, but, after hearing Viktor say Isabella's room was cursed, well ...

"Ruth Ann," I heard a voice calling my name. "Are you alright?"

I shook my head to come back to reality. "What, what?" I asked Manual.

"You're awfully pale, do you need to sit down?" he took my arm and led me to the couch where Prunella was just lying. I didn't argue, I did feel a little dizzy. "I'll get you some water."

"Thank you," I said, taking a big gulp of cool water. "I'm alright now. I just had a dizzy spell. It's been long couple days."

"I think we should stop for today. You need rest, and Prunella needs to rest until the doctor comes. I'll take you to your room myself." He held out his hand and I took it. Why not? He wasn't being rude to me, even though I found myself kidnapped, again, in a man's home being treated quite nicely.

As we walked through the halls to the main foyer, I kept

a keen eye on everything we passed, just in case I spotted a possible escape route. He took me up a flight of stairs, not as impressive as Axel's, but still a fairly grand staircase made out of cement not wood. He hesitated on the second floor and glanced down the hall. I took a look to see what he was staring at, and that's when I saw a man standing outside a room about halfway down the hall to the right. That had to be the room with the large semi-circular balcony I spotted when we arrived earlier.

Instead of walking me down this hall, he went up another set of stairs to the third floor. "You'll be comfortable up here," he said. "I'll have food and drink brought to your room."

Before he stopped half-way down the hall, I asked, "Can't I sit with Prunella?"

"Not now. I want you to rest, Ruth Ann."

"What about Axel?" I asked, hoping he'd answer me.

"He's not upstairs at the moment. Don't worry about him right now. All I want you to do is rest. Soon, you'll hear a knock on your door and a tray will be delivered. You can have anything you like. Tell me, and I will request it for you."

"I'd love some orange juice and a bowl of cereal. Any kind will do right now."

He nodded, and then said, "Please feel free to wash and change clothes."

"But, I don't have any clothes to change into," I said, wondering what happened to my bag from the airport.

"Your bag is here, and there's other stuff in there, too."

He opened the door with a key and shoved the key back into his pants pocket. "That's it?" I asked, confused. "When will I know what's going on?"

"I'll send for you a little later. Just stay in here and you'll be safe."

He nudged me inside and shut the door behind me. I could swear I heard a click. He had to have locked me in. How was I to roam free if I'm locked in my room? I didn't want to check the door too quickly in case he was outside waiting for me to see if I would try to escape. So, I turned around and stepped into a luxurious, master suite. It was the size of a one-bedroom apartment. There was a large sitting room in front of me with beautiful, brightly colored couches and matching chairs. The back wall had floor to ceiling windows with a set of doors that opened onto a small balcony. I rushed over to the door, pulled it open and stepped onto the hot, sunny balcony. I leaned over the edge and there it was. Prunella's massive balcony was directly below mine, I just knew it. I wondered if I could get down there somehow, but that would be risky. Not only could I break something, I assumed the guards would see me.

I walked back inside and toured the rest of my room. The bedroom was to the right and it was a nice size. There was a king bed on one wall and a large bathroom with a jetted tub and a steam shower. I looked inside the cabinets, and they were all empty except for two drawers in the bedroom. All my clothes from my bag were neatly folded and stored inside. I rushed back into the bathroom to find my toiletry bag waiting for me. "Who did this?"

I also found a closet in the living area and opened it up. It was a long, narrow walk-in with not much there except a small supply of women's clothing, and a nice terry cloth robe. I pulled the robe off the hanger and walked into the bathroom. I decided I had some time to clean up, so I took a long, warm shower. It felt fantastic and I felt like a fresh, energized person. I put on the robe and went back into the closet. All my clothes were for a cold climate; however, it was blazingly hot down here, and I needed lighter clothes.

I went back to the walk-in and to my surprise, the clothes in there were my size! I hung up the robe and put on a bright pink tank dress. It was a beautiful piece and fit me perfectly. I looked down on the floor and noticed an assortment of flip flops and sandals. I bent down and picked up a pair of tan flip flops and slipped my right foot in. "Perfect!" Somebody definitely planned for me to be staying here, but who?

I went back into the sitting room and took a closer look around. On the round table my tray was sitting there with a bowl of bran and large glass of orange juice with ice cubes. Just the way I like it! Again, very odd, but how would anyone know that's how I drink my juice? I brushed it off thinking it might be common to put ice in juice in a hot climate. I sat down and gobbled the cereal down, and suddenly wondered if that was a wise idea. Could the juice or cereal be laced with a drug? It wouldn't be the first time I was naïve and found myself waking in a strange place because I ate something I shouldn't have.

I was pleasantly surprised when I didn't pass out. I started pacing around the room, finding nothing of importance. I decided I should see if I could get out of the room so I walked to the door and tried the handle. It opened! I carefully opened the door about a foot and stuck my head into the hall. Nobody was guarding my door, thankfully. I thought if Prunella's room had a guard mine would, too. Hey, I wondered why I wasn't good enough for a guard? I walked into the tiled hall, noticing the echo from my flip flops. Obviously, they would hear me coming a mile away.

It was a long, wide hallway with several doors. There wasn't any light coming from windows because all the doors were closed. I went the opposite direction from the stairs and checked a few doors. Every one of them was locked. I turned around and checked all the doors going toward the staircase and they, too, were locked. Why would it be necessary to lock all these doors? Were they all bedrooms, and if so, was anyone staying in there? Or, maybe there were prisoners inside them!

I walked down a couple stairs, wondering if I could check on Prunella. I didn't see anyone in sight, so I went down to the second floor and headed toward the room with the guard standing in front. He didn't notice me until I was about two rooms away. He jolted and aimed a small handgun at me.

"Whoa!" I cried, holding my hands in the air. "I only want to check on my cousin."

"No, you can't," the young man said. "You must go back to your room."

"Why? I'm not a prisoner here. Manual told me to rest, but I'm not tired. I just want to see how Prunella's doing."

"I need to get permission, Ruth Ann," he said, using my name. It took me by surprise at first, and then I decided to ask him.

"How do you know who I am?"

He eyed me oddly and shrugged his shoulders. "I just do."

"Oh, well, maybe I'll just go and find your boss and tell him to let me see my cousin."

"He turned his attention back to the door and ignored me. I walked to the stairs, carefully sneaking to see if the doors on this floor were locked, too. The guard didn't notice me as I wiggled a few door knobs. They were locked. I figured Manual's room was somewhere on this floor. I would've expected his to be the room with the massive balcony, but that's where Prunella was staying. Suddenly, I had a horrific thought pop in my head. Don't tell me Prunella is staying in Manual's bedroom, and if so, is he also staying there?

I marched down the stairs and headed to the left. I remembered exactly how to get to Manual's office. I wasn't confronted with any guards or staff along my way. I made another left and went down almost the entire length of this hall when I realized I didn't know which door led to his office. There were too many doors in this place! I grabbed one or two handles and they were unlocked. The first room I peeked in was a large gym. There wasn't anybody in there, but I noticed it was a shiny, spotless room with mirrored walls and treadmills, bikes, and lots of free weights. Manual's physique suggested that he didn't spend a lot of time in here. I shut the door and tried the next one realizing I opened a door on the other side of the hall. This room was completely empty, but sunlight streamed in from the exposed windows. I closed the door and went to the next door ... jackpot! This had to be Manual's office because I remembered it was double-doored. I was right.

I reached my hand to knock when I heard voices from within. My rational side warned me to not eavesdrop, but really, was I in a place to be rational? I leaned a little closer and realized Axel was in there. I wanted to rush in, but something held me back. I couldn't exactly make out their conversation, but it was clearly Manual and Axel.

"I'm not telling you!" Axel hollered, angrily.

"You don't have a choice. If you don't cooperate, you'll be eliminated."

"Go ahead, kill me. I will not let you take Ruth Ann back to my office in Sweden. She has no idea how to retrieve it."

"I will not let you go, Axel. You'll try and pull a fast one over my men. I don't trust you. Ruth Ann's easier to control."

Axel laughed heartily. "Really? You think Ruth Ann is a

pushover?"

"She's a woman! And, she's not young anymore."

"You're a fool if you think she can't take care of herself because she's a middle-aged woman."

"I'm not negotiating with you. I'm telling you that your life will be miserable until I get that bloody necklace!"

"I don't care what you do with me!" he snapped. "Your men already tried to break my face with their fists. I'm not letting you take Ruth Ann and that's final!"

I couldn't take it any longer. I didn't knock but grabbed the handle and threw the double doors open. I was furious, and not about to let Manual manhandle Axel any longer. To think he thought I was a feeble woman who couldn't defend myself. That was pure nonsense, and I was about to tell him that to his face.

"Ruth Ann!" Axel exclaimed, stunned by my sudden appearance. "Go back to your room, now! I don't want anything to happen to you. Manual and I were just having a calm, mutually agreeable talk."

"That's a load of bull and you know it!" I snapped. "I heard you two." I turned to Manual with steam pouring out of my ears. "How dare you demean me because I'm a woman. In my country, women are strong, resilient, and intelligent. I'll be happy to go to Sweden to get that necklace for you."

"Ruth Ann!" Axel screamed. "NO!"

"You will?" Manual asked, shocked at the turn of events.

"Under certain conditions," I said, trying to think as fast as I could about what I could use to delay this unexpected turn. I wanted to keep us here as long as I could until Isabella, Carlos and Inga arrived.

"What conditions?" Manual asked, interestedly.

Axel glared at me intently, knowing I had no idea what

conditions I was going to demand. I needed a distraction ... think, fast!

I had an idea. If it works, it would buy me a little time. "Before I tell you my conditions, I want to see my cousin. I was just upstairs and the guard outside her door wouldn't let me in. I demand to see her!"

"You demand?" Manual inquired, surprised at my boldness.

Axel interrupted, furious, "You have my wife's door guarded? Why? If she can't walk why is she be such a threat?"

"It's not your wife who's a threat, Axel. It's the people trying to get *in* her room that could be a threat."

"Like me or Ruth Ann?" Axel probed.

"Not exactly."

"Who then?" I demanded, confused. He couldn't have any idea that Inga and the others were almost here.

Manual was clearly uncomfortable with this conversation. He had little beads of sweat forming on his brow, and I noticed his hands trembling when he raised them to yell at us. "This little charade isn't going to work! I'm the one giving the orders, do you both understand me?"

Within seconds, two guards flew in his office with guns drawn. "Put those down!" Manual ordered. "Go away. There's no need for the two of you to come barging in here."

"But, sir, we heard yelling and thought you might need our assistance," the one guard said.

"Go, I don't need your assistance right now."

The two guards retreated and closed the door behind them. "Now," Manual began, much more calmly, "Let's try this again. I'm the one in charge, get it?" Axel and I nodded. "Good. Now that we've established that, I need to speak with

Ruth Ann about going to Stockholm to retrieve this very important piece for me. I'll send you in my private plane with all the luxuries you would ever want. Tell me what I can have ready for you? Chocolates? Champagne?"

"I want to see Prunella before I agree to another trip to Stockholm," I said, deliberately and very seriously. Manual studied my expression without speaking for a moment. Maybe I should try this approach more often because I believed it was about to work.

Chapter 23

"Why did you have to force him to let you see Prunella?" Axel argued with me. "All you had to do was pretend you were going to go to Sweden, and it would've bought us some time. Now look at the mess we're in!"

"You were the one who hollered 'NO' when I suggested going in the first place!" I snapped back at him. "Now, you're telling me I shouldn't have agreed to go?"

Axel pulled his arm as forcefully as he could, trying to unhinge the chain from the wall. "It's no use. I'm handcuffed to these chains, Ruth Ann. I thought when he brought me to his office I was through with this room."

"I'm sorry, Axel," I said, sitting in a hard chair with ropes wrapped around my body too. "He flipped out on both of us!"

"He sure did. All you asked was to see Prunella. Why on earth would that cause such a harsh reaction?"

"There is something weird regarding Prunella. First, Viktor was possessive of her, but now it seems that Manual is too. Why?"

"I don't know, but we'd better figure it out and quick. I'm surprised they brought you here, too. Where were you before?"

"In a bedroom suite on the third floor. I was right above Prunella's room."

"He could've just brought you back to your room instead of here with me," Axel said, looking around the small, windowless room.

"Are we in the basement?" I asked, confused with our location.

"Not exactly. There really aren't basements in these climates. It's a special room dug below ground to hold prisoners."

"How do you know that?" I inquired, curiously.

"He bragged about it when I was thrown down here the first time. It's just a single, cement room with no windows and ..." he paused for dramatic effect and said, "no way out."

"There has to be!" I cried. "I have to be free to wait for Isabella, Carlos and Inga."

"I guess you shouldn't have irritated him, Ruth Ann."

"I didn't think asking to see my cousin would irritate anyone!"

"Well, we're not dealing with a stable man. This guy's a dangerous narcissist."

"Interesting," I said, methodically. "I may have an idea."

"You do?" he asked, skeptically.

"Thanks, Axel. Give me a little more credit than that! I have a brain and can come up with ideas, too."

"Sorry, just tell me your idea," he said, genuinely apologetic.

"When dealing with a narcissist, you can't lay blame or be accusatory. You have to treat them with empathy."

"Empathy!" Axel barked, angrily. "I'm not going to apologize to the jerk!"

"No, no, that's not what I mean. Empathy is being able to put yourself in their shoes and understand their motivation.

It's not condoning or approving of their methods and behavior, it's letting them know you understand their feelings, as if you've been through it before. It's a way of calling them out for bad behavior without blaming them for their bad behavior."

"Okay," Axel said, trying to let the information sink in. "So, what on earth are you going to say?"

"I'm thinking, I'm thinking," I said exasperated, because I didn't have an answer for that yet. "I'll think of something, and then I'll call for the guard to take me to Manual. If it works, I hope he'll at least let me go back to my room. Then, I'll be free to keep a look out for Inga, Isabella and Carlos."

"Sounds like a great idea if you can think of something empathetic. He's a bully!"

"Bullying is part of a narcissist's behavior, but only one part. Manual snaps when he feels threatened. But, what made him feel so threatened?"

"Prunella," Axel mumbled.

"YES!" I exclaimed, energized. "He felt threatened when I mentioned I wanted to see her. Why? Something must be going on with her to cause Manual to have that reaction."

"But, what?" Axel asked, baffled.

"I don't think we'll know until we see her," I replied. "I'm going to call the guard and have him take me to Manual."

"But, you don't have a plan yet, Ruth Ann!"

"I can handle it. If they actually do take me to him, you'll be left alone down here." I looked at him seriously and asked, "Will you be alright?"

"I was in here alone before, remember?"

"I promise you I will come back and get you out of here."

"I know you will, Ruth Ann. I don't think you're weak. I hope you know that?"

I smiled and said, "I do, Axel. In fact, I know I drive you absolutely nuts most of the time."

He laughed and clapped his hands. The echo reverberated throughout the tiny room causing the guard to unlock the door and fly down the wooden stairs.

"What was that noise?" he demanded.

"What noise?" Axel asked sarcastically, knowing full well that his clapping caused the noise. "We didn't hear any noise."

"Stop lying," the guard snapped. I didn't recognize this one. I wondered how many men Manual had working for him at his estate. "What did you do?"

"I didn't do anything," I answered, truthfully. "But, I have a request." I figured I should sound authoritative, not wishy-washy.

"What?"

"I need to see Manual. I'm ready to talk."

He looked at me peculiarly, waiting for me to say more, but I remained silent. He started to walk up the stairs, turned, came back to me, and then shook his head and disappeared up the stairs.

"What was that about?" Axel asked. "I think he wanted to ask you more questions but changed his mind."

"I know," I said, smiling slightly. "I think it worked, unless he ignored my request and went upstairs to keep guarding us."

"We'll find out soon enough," Axel said, leaning against the wall and trying to lower his arms so they could rest. "These chains are causing my shoulders and arms to stiffen. I don't want to be worthless if we can get out of here."

"You'll be fine, Axel. Just keep moving them around every now and again. Keep the blood flowing to your arms and legs. Hopefully, you won't be shackled for long."

That brought up a horrific memory. Poor Helena, Axel's housekeeper back in Deer Creek, was murdered while being shackled to a wall in the basement. A vision passed through my brain, and I shuddered. I remember being shielded from the worst of it, but it was a nightmare that was still vivid.

"Ruth Ann," Axel called out to me. "Are you alright?"

"Yes, well no, but I will be."

"You just thought about what happened to Helena, didn't you? It won't happen again, Ruth Ann. Both of us will be fine."

"Yes, we will," I said, starting to feeling stronger. "We need that guard to take me seriously, and hope that he went to Manual with my request."

"All you really told the guard was that you were ready to talk. I didn't think Manual dumped us down here waiting for you to talk, but, if it works, it works!"

"I didn't have time to formulate a plan. You clapped your hands and the guard appeared."

I sat in my lonely chair observing our surroundings. It was a plain, empty room with Axel chained to one of the walls. The chair I was sitting on was the only piece of furniture in here. The floor was loose, and dirty. There were seven stairs that led to the door where we entered. The guard must be just on the other side of the door that opened into the gym near Manual's office.

"Ruth Ann," Axel whispered. "I hear something."

I listened carefully until I heard voices at the top of the stairs. "I think there's more than one guard up there," I said.

"I can't make out what they're saying, but I'm hoping they open that door!"

Our wish came true! The door swung open, but the arguing on the other side didn't stop. "What are they yelling about?" I asked Axel.

"I don't speak Spanish, so I have no idea."

We listened, even though we didn't understand what they were saying. I was hoping I could figure out a word or two, when I heard a man yell, "Get her!"

"That was clearly in English," I said.

"They're coming to get you, Ruth Ann," Axel whispered.

I had to admit, I was a little frightened. I told myself to remain calm and stay strong. I wasn't going to let them think I was scared. I'm pretty sure my eyes were bulging out of their sockets when a very large, nasty looking man hobbled down the stairs sporting a very long, knife. Axel watched intently but didn't move. I had a horrifying thought pop in my head wondering if he was coming to finish us off.

"Don't argue with him, Ruth Ann," Axel murmured to me. As if I would! The shiny, long, steel blade shimmered in the dim light.

I took the initiative and asked, "Are you taking me to see Manual?"

Axel's glared daggers at me after he just finished telling me to keep quiet. I thought it best to ask outright if he was taking me to see Manual.

He didn't respond but stomped through the loose dirt to me. He raised the knife in the air about to strike me when Axel hollered, "NO!"

The guard ignored him and the knife came swinging down with amazing accuracy cutting the ropes between my hands and leaving the rest of me intact.

"Did you have to do that?" I screamed, shaking so hard I nearly fell out of the chair. My free hands were trembling as I raised them in the air. I'm a very melodramatic person when I'm furious, and I was more ticked off than ever!

Axel shook his head and said loudly, without concern for the guard, "Ruth Ann, keep your cool. You're fine, right?"

I turned my gaze toward him and nodded, irritated, but unhurt. Before I had time to catch my breath, the guard grabbed my arm and forced me out of the chair. He whisked me away before I had a chance to say another word to Axel. It took all my strength to keep up with him as he dragged me up the stairs. He had such a tight grasp on my arm if I lagged a step or two behind, I'd be on the ground bouncing up the stairs.

At the top of the stairs, he took his free hand and banged on the door. The door opened it and I was suddenly blinded by bright light. I shut my eyes to adjust and when I opened them I found myself standing in the sun-filled gym with Viktor standing before me.

"Viktor!" I bellowed, trying to sound happy to see him. "I'm glad it's you."

He looked oddly at the other man and said, "Why is that? I'm not your friend."

Quickly, I recovered and replied, "I'm only happy because you speak English, Viktor."

"Oh," Viktor responded, eyeing the other man carefully, hoping he didn't think he was working with us. "I'll take her from here," he told the man. "You go back to your station."

The other man disappeared, and I was left alone with Viktor. I wasn't going to waste this moment so I inquired about Prunella. "Is she okay? Nobody will let me see her, and I'm so worried about her!" I laid it on a little thick, but I hit jackpot.

Viktor acquiesced, and said, "They won't let you see

her?"

"No, Viktor, and I'm really worried about her."

"She's good, she's resting in bed."

"Can you tell me why she is so heavily guarded and restricted from seeing us?"

He was about to speak but clammed up. I couldn't let this opportunity slip out of my hands so I added, "Please, Viktor. Prunella means the world to me, just like I see she does to you, too."

"What are you talking about?" he inquired, suddenly looking embarrassed.

"I've seen how much you care for her. I do, too. Can you bring me to her before I go talk to your boss?" I fluttered my eyelashes and pressed my hands together in prayer so he knew how desperately I needed his assistance.

"Well," he said, looking around the gym to see if anyone was listening or watching. "I don't know if I should."

"Why? Did your boss specifically tell you nobody was to see her?"

"No, but obviously, he didn't want *you or Axel* to see her."

"We're no threat, Viktor," I begged. "Please, I just want to see her for a second and make sure she's alright."

"I guess it wouldn't hurt to take a quick, and I mean fast, visit to the second floor."

I smiled and thanked him profusely. I let him lead me out of the gym, and instead of going to Manual's office, which was right down the hall from the gym, he went the other direction. Phew, I was wondering if he would change his mind once we were in the hall.

"Hurry," he snapped at me. "I don't want to get in trouble."

"Why would you get in trouble?" I asked. "From what I've observed, you're the lead guy here."

That made him smirk. "I am second in charge."

"See, you can make decisions like this then," I said, trying to keep rewarding him with compliments. "What about the guard outside her door?"

"I'll tell him to move aside and keep his mouth shut!"

"Good."

We went up the stairs and down the hall to the room where Prunella was being held. He told the guard, in Spanish, to give me a moment inside the room. He nodded, stepped aside, and Viktor opened the door. It wasn't locked I detected. That's a plus.

"I'll wait by the door," Viktor said. "You go check on her for only a minute, and then come back to me. No funny stuff!"

I turned around and gave him a thumbs up. I disappeared into the bedroom and found Prunella lying like a queen on her throne! A four-poster bed was smack dab in the middle of the room with white sheers draped over the posts. The bedding was pure white, fluffy, and airy. Prunella was propped up with several pillows behind her. She had a tray over her lap, and when she spotted me, she cried, "Ruth Ann! Finally, you've come to see me!"

I marched up to her, a little perturbed she was living like a queen while I was rotting in a cement prison, and said, "They wouldn't let me see you."

"Why not?" she asked, innocently. "I've been stuck in this bed since Viktor brought me here."

I lost a little control and blurted sarcastically, "Well, I'm glad someone's been treated well. Axel and I have been locked in a cement room below ground! And, Axel is still there, shackled to the wall!"

She looked down at her tray loaded with colorful fruits, and different breads and cheeses, and said, "But, why? No one told me you were being treated like prisoners!"

Exasperated, I said, "Prunella, do you remember that our plane was hijacked and we were kidnapped?"

"No," she answered, truthfully, as far as I could tell. "I'm a little foggy on why we're here. I know Viktor has been very kind to me, so I thought you and Axel were being treated well. I was about to inquire why I was here, but then I remembered I just got out of the hospital and still can't walk." She started to cry and added, "I just thought this is where we went for me to recover until I could get strong and walk again."

I didn't have the heart to say otherwise when Viktor called me to come to him. I grabbed her gentle hand and said, "Just rest, Prunella. Axel and I will be fine. You're recovering, so do whatever Viktor or Manual want you to do. I'll be back to visit you real soon."

"But, you just got here!" she cried. "I don't want you to leave!"

I didn't get a chance to respond because Viktor popped in the room and answered for me. "Ruth Ann will be back soon, Prunella. She has to meet with Mr. Marquez in his office. Right, Ruth Ann?"

"Ah, yes, I do have to go, Prunella. I promise I'll be back soon."

"You promised, don't forget," she said, and then lay her head back against the pillows. Viktor rushed to her side, grabbed the tray and put it on a table next to her bed. "If you need anything, just push that button, remember?"

I looked to see what button he was referring to. There it was! A button on the wall right to the side of her bed. She nodded, and Viktor led me out.

I didn't want to break his trust, so I didn't tell him I was disappointed with the amount of time he allowed. Instead, I said, "Thank you, Viktor. I really appreciate you helping me see Prunella."

"That's okay," he said, obviously not used to getting a compliment by the way his face blushed.

He led me out of her room and nodded for the guard to take over watching the door. We walked at a quick pace to Manual's office. Viktor tapped on the door, and we both heard, "Come in."

Viktor opened the door and gave me a slight push to enter. He shut the door behind me, leaving me standing alone waiting for Manual to tell me where to sit.

"Let's sit on the couch, Ruth Ann," he said in a loud, cheery voice. I was taken aback because my last encounter with him put me in a cement room! I walked to where Prunella lay not too long ago and waited for Manual to come over. He motioned for me to sit, and I plopped my tired body on the cool leather couch. He sat rather close to me, and I was tempted to move slightly over, but I felt my legs sticking to the couch.

"Would you care for a glass of lemonade, Ruth Ann? Or something a little stronger?"

"Such as?" I asked, wondering what he meant.

"I can have a couple margaritas whipped up for us, if you'd like?"

I do love a margarita, but I didn't think this was the right time. I opted for the lemonade and waited for him to pour us a couple glasses from the pitcher on the coffee table in front of us. I took a sip, and it was very refreshing. "Thank you," I said. "It's been a long day."

"Yes, it has for you and Axel."

"And Prunella," I added. "However, she appears to be quite comfortable." Why did I say that?

He eyed me strangely, and after a moment, he said, "How do you know that?"

Quickly, I replied, "I know she's in the room below mine, and if it's as nice as my room, then I know she's quite comfortable."

"Oh, I guess that makes sense. I thought for a moment you ..." he hesitated and decided to move on to another topic. "So, you wanted to talk to me?"

I knew I had to answer, "yes", but I wasn't sure what I needed to tell him! I figured I'd tell the truth, well partially. "I need to know why you put me with Axel in that hole in the ground? I told you I was willing to go to Stockholm. I didn't think it was very hospitable of you."

He laughed raucously at my bluntness, and then said, "You really don't know how to be an obedient guest, do you, Ruth Ann?"

"I didn't know I had to be obedient, Manual," I said, agitated. "Right now, I should be back home, not in South America. If you wanted my necklace, all you had to do was ask."

"And you would've given it to me?"

"Well, no, Manual. That piece is a part of us, and even though it's been a load of trouble lately, I don't know how to part with it."

"But, you just told me you were willing to retrieve it and bring it back here for me?" he asked, baffled and clearly irritated with me. "Were you going to try and trick me?"

"Of course not!" I bellowed. "I just want to go home," I said, honestly. "I'm not thinking clearly, Manual. Can you do me a favor and explain to me why you want the necklace so badly?"

"Ah, I was wondering when you were going to ask me that particular question," he said smiling, displaying immaculately white large teeth. Obviously, he calmed down with my candidness. "What made you think to ask me that now?"

"To be honest, we were both too scared to ask." I was trying to keep my cool, but rage crept up inside me and I snapped. "You kidnapped us, Manual!" I hollered. "You killed the pilot, and the poor attendant, and hijacked Axel's plane! How dare you ask us to be level headed after you did that to us?" I added before he could, "You might as well tell Viktor or one of your other guards to take me back to the cement hole."

I was so stupid to lose my temper like that. Meme had warned me to behave so I could be the one to let Inga, Isabella, and Carlos on to the property. I realized that I completely blew it.

Chapter 24

Manual's stare scared me to death. He didn't say a word for a long time, then he stood and slowly walked to the back of the couch. I was quivering in fear wondering if he was going to take his short, stubby fingers and wrap them around my neck. I could hear it in the papers now, "Ruth Ann Conroy, violently murdered because she was reckless with her big mouth, *again*!" I sat frozen, waiting for Manual to take some kind of action, when he told me to get up.

I didn't stand right away, but turned my head, and saw him walking toward an empty wall. Finally, I stood, walked to where he was standing and waited for my next order. He put his hand on the wall and forcefully pushed it. A section opened into a concealed room. It was so well hidden that I never would have spotted any cracks on the wall until Manual opened it. I figured it was just an empty wall waiting for artwork.

"Follow me," he said, walking into the darkness. I stood a few feet away, peering into the secret room. It was pitch black, but suddenly light flooded the room, and Manual stuck his head out and waved me in.

"Coming," I said, hesitantly. "Where are you taking

me?" I asked nervously, one step away from entering.

"It's okay, Ruth Ann. I'm not punishing you for your outburst. I want to show you something."

Trusting I wasn't walking into a trap, I entered the room. My eyes had to be playing tricks on me. It was the most FABULOUS room I'd ever seen in my life! "You like what you see, don't you, Ruth Ann?" Manual asked, smiling from a large glass display case in the middle of the surprisingly spacious room. In fact, I spotted glass cases covering every inch of wall space in the windowless room.

"What is this place?" I asked, stunned at the sight.

"My private showroom."

"Is everything in here real?" I asked him, still shocked at the beauty that surrounded me.

"Of course!" he bellowed, amused at my naiveté.

"But, how, why?" I inquired, wondering why he brought me inside this room.

"It's my passion, Ruth Ann. This is something I've been doing for many, many years."

"I think I'm starting to understand your motives now," I said, walking to the display case in the middle of the room where he was standing. "Where did you get all these?"

"All over the world, Ruth Ann. It's my obsession, my reason for living ever since I lost my ..." he clammed up and turned away from me.

"Your what, Manual? Your wife or girlfriend?" I asked, suddenly seeing a different side of this stranger, a more emotional side.

He ignored my question and reached inside his pants pocket and pulled out a set of keys. I watched him take a specific key, open the top of the case and pull a rod to prop it up. I almost forgot my question after seeing the spectacular gems inside the case. "Wow," I murmured. "Those are amazing."

"Yes, they are, Ruth Ann." He reached inside and picked up a necklace lying on a velvet holder. He walked behind me and placed the shimmering, ruby around my neck. "It fits you, Ruth Ann," he said, coming around to my front and admiring the necklace. "It's like it was made for you. Would you like it?"

"You want to *give* it to me?" I asked, baffled. I walked to a mirror near one of the wall cases. It was a full length oval mirror and as I approached it, I could see the magnificent sparkle bouncing off the mirror.

Manual watched me carefully, and said, "You would like to have it, no?"

"Of course, I would!" I declared. "What woman wouldn't want this?"

"I went to a heap of trouble to obtain it, Ruth Ann," he said. "It's worth hundreds of thousands of dollars."

"I'm sure it is, Manual. Why would you ask me if I wanted it, then?" I asked, touching the smooth surface of the center stone.

"Do you understand me now?" he asked, surprising me suddenly.

"You mean your desire to obtain beautiful gems and ..." I cut myself off because the word 'drugs' almost slipped out.

He quickly caught on. "And what, Ruth Ann?" he teased.

"I didn't mean anything, Manual. I was just caught off guard seeing all the unbelievable jewels you've collected." I thought to myself that many of these pieces weren't peacefully handed over to him.

"You think I stole most of these, don't you?" he asked, as if he could read my mind.

"I really don't know the answer to your question. Why

don't you fill me in," I said, hoping he wouldn't get offended with my effrontery.

"I'm not evil, Ruth Ann. I see something I want for my collection, and I stop at nothing to get it."

"So, you're talking about our Blue Ice now, aren't you?"

"I do appreciate your naming the piece, Ruth Ann."

"You didn't answer my question."

"Yes. I want that necklace, and I want it badly," he answered, truthfully.

"You're willing to kidnap, kill, and keep us prisoner until you get it, right?" I asked, not sure if I wanted to know his response.

"Yes."

"I'll give it to you for being honest, Manual. However, you have to know it terrifies me."

"I'm sure it does, Ruth Ann. In the last few months, you've had quite a few of adventures because of this gem."

"You did your research," I said.

"I always do."

"What if I tell you I can't give Blue Ice to you?"

"That's unacceptable."

"But, you didn't hear me correctly, Manual. I said I *can't* give it to you."

"Why not?" he asked, curiously.

"If you did your research, you'd know the piece has been cursed. The woman who broke the curse told me that I would always have it with me for protection. It could never be out of our family. Trust me, Manual, it has given me much grief lately, and I've thought many times about getting rid of it. But, I can't."

He stood watching me fixedly. I felt uncomfortable the way he watched me and the ruby necklace that still lay around my neck. I reached to take it off when he pulled my hand down. "No, keep it on, Ruth Ann. It really is meant for you."

"Are you bribing me with this?" I asked, wondering why he would give me a ruby necklace worth so much or ... was he letting me wear it until he kills me?

"It's not a bribe. I have many beautiful pieces, and this one was my first acquisition for my late ..." he stopped speaking, but this time he finished his sentence. "My late wife."

I felt a rush of dread run through my body. I was having many thoughts like was she wearing this when she died or did she betray him and he killed her while she was wearing it?

"Ruth Ann," he began. "I see those wheels in your head spinning to wild conclusions. Let me tell you that I loved my wife dearly and would never hurt a hair on her head. She saw this necklace right before we were married, and I purchased it for her as a wedding gift."

"I shouldn't have it on," I said, feeling awkward.

"Yes, please keep it on. I haven't seen it on a woman since she died."

I was about to ask how she died, when I decided against it. I decided to change the topic. "Where did you get all these other pieces and were they for your wife, too?"

"No, she was killed on our wedding night, Ruth Ann," he admitted, turning angry. "I found her wearing this necklace around her neck after someone stabbed her in the heart."

"That's horrible, Manual," I exclaimed. "I, I really don't want to wear this anymore."

"Please, it was years ago, and I've dealt with it for the most part. The people responsible for her death are long gone."

"Did you kill them?" I asked, not sure if I wanted the answer to that question.

"Oh, yes," he said, proudly. "We searched long and hard until we found who was responsible and I killed him myself."

"I'm sorry, Manual," I said sadly, strangely not afraid that he admitted to killing someone with his own hands. "How did you find who killed your wife, if I might ask?"

"I had help," he said, suddenly looking at me oddly. "In fact, I had someone you know help me."

"Excuse me?" I asked, confused. "You and I have never met before."

"But, we have a mutual acquaintance."

"Who?" I asked, but before he answered, I knew. "Meme," I said, quietly.

"Yes, Ruth Ann. You do catch on, don't you?"

"Let's just say Meme was very important to me, and I was there when she died."

"I heard."

"How?"

"I have contacts around the world, Ruth Ann. Meme and I worked hand in hand on a few of my acquisitions. She knew I wasn't a bad man or she wouldn't have helped me, right?" He watched me carefully, wondering if I believed him or not. "You do know Meme would never help me if she thought I was evil. You must know that! Answer me, Ruth Ann!"

"Of course, I know that!" I snapped. "I'm just so surprised about this connection." I thought for a quick second and added, "Then, you must know about her other family members." My mind was reeling. Here, this man we've never met, kidnaps us and hijacks our plane to this country that isn't anywhere near where Meme lived in her small village in Jamaica. Meme would never help anyone she didn't believe in, or would she? I was too confused to think straight, so I took a deep breath and let him talk some more.

"I've been to her village, Ruth Ann. I even knew her daughter, and her granddaughter, Isabella."

"You knew Isabella?"

"Not knew, but know her, Ruth Ann. I think there's more to Isabella than you're aware. She's been ..." he stopped, thought twice about his next words and said, "Forget about it. Let's just say, I know all of them, and several of these pieces were obtained because of Meme and her granddaughter."

"So, that's how you know about Blue Ice," I bellowed. "You knew Isabella and Meme and how they broke the long-time curse."

"Yep."

"But, that means you've talked to Isabella recently," I said, perplexed. "You wouldn't know who had the necklace unless ..." it suddenly dawned on me. "You've been working with Isabella, haven't you?" Please tell me this isn't so, please tell me I'm imagining this whole thing!

He watched me figure out the pattern, and finally, he said, "Isabella and I have been in contact since Meme passed away. I know all about you being in the room when she passed, too."

"I, I can't believe what I'm hearing," I said, so shocked I felt nauseous.

He grabbed my arm and led me to a chair in the corner of the room. I plopped down and tried to take in the cool air of the room. I wasn't going to get sick in here or in front of this man. It took me a moment, but then my nausea subsided. "So, you and Isabella planned to kidnap us?"

"No, no, Isabella had no idea about that," he quickly answered. "She was taking too long getting me the necklace, so I had to take matters into my own hands."

"Wait!" I hollered. "Isabella was going to steal our necklace and bring it to you?"

"No, not exactly, Ruth Ann. She was going to try and convince you to part with the piece because it's been so much trouble. She's not an aggressive person, but ... she can be kind of scary."

"Isabella?" I questioned him.

"Yes, my men fear her, Ruth Ann."

"What are you talking about?" I asked, getting very irritated.

"She's been here before," he said carefully, worried I'd get sick or faint.

"Here, as in South America?"

"Yes, Ruth Ann. She's traveled here on behalf of her grandmother who wouldn't travel."

"When?" I asked, turning my anger toward Isabella at the moment.

"She was here around six months ago. She stayed in the very room Prunella's in right this very moment."

"You've got to be kidding!"

"No, I never joke, Ruth Ann. If you want to learn anything about me, it's I don't mess around when it comes to my gems."

"I believe you," I replied, honestly.

"My men think she has great powers and they fear her. If she came back here, they would try and get rid of her."

My mind went into overdrive. She's on her way here at this very moment. If one of Manual's men caught sight of her, it could be her end. I had to figure out how to keep her away from here, but I needed the necklace to keep Prunella alive. What was I going to do?

"Are you alright, Ruth Ann?" he asked, watching me

closely. "You look like you're thinking about many things"

"I'm just stunned by all of this, Manual. I don't get why they would be so afraid of Isabella. She's so tiny, young, and definitely doesn't come across as a threat."

"She is if she has magical powers," he replied. "My men fear that most of all."

"That's nonsense."

"Not to us," he said.

"Please, tell me more about your involvement with Isabella. Did you and she have a good relationship or was it all business?" I had to stall. I needed to get this information back to Axel, but I really didn't want to go back to the hole in the ground where he was being kept.

He didn't want to answer me, but I kept on him. Finally, after the third time I asked, he stomped his feet on the ground and walked to the chair opposite where I was sitting. He sat down and put his hands on his head. "Why do you keep asking me that question, Ruth Ann?"

"Because I need to know."

"Isabella's a beautiful woman."

"So, you did have a personal relationship with her," I said, feeling nauseous again. How could Isabella have any kind of intimate relationship with this man? He was much older than her, and I couldn't fathom her being touched by him!

"No, not like that, Ruth Ann," he said, reading my mind. "I do like to admire beautiful women, but she was too young even for me. It took me a while to realize that, I'm afraid."

"What do you mean?" I asked, curiously.

"At first, when Meme introduced her granddaughter, I was mesmerized by her beauty and innocence. However, I found out she wasn't as innocent as I first thought."

"What do you mean by that?" I snapped, angry at his insinuation that Isabella was loose with men.

"No, innocent as in naïve, not that she wasn't a virgin or anything like that."

"Oh, sorry."

"Isabella wasn't like that. She was mysterious and it caught my attention. She has beautiful dark, velvety skin, and her eyes gazed into my soul when she looked and talked to me. I was attracted to her I admit, but after she came here and we spent time together, I realized it could never work between us."

Curiously, I asked, "Did Isabella want a relationship with you?"

"No, I don't think so. She was just being kind to me or trying to pull one over me." He rubbed his forehead and added, "I think she was trying to tease me in a way, perhaps for financial gain."

"So, you think Isabella flirted to get more money out of you because she found precious gems for you?"

"Yes, I do."

"Maybe Isabella was doing it because they needed the money. Isabella and her mother and grandmother lived quite poorly. I was there, I saw where they lived and what they had to do to make a living."

"Yes, they did live like they didn't have much money, but that's not exactly the truth, Ruth Ann," Manual said, surprising me with this new bit of information.

"I don't know what you're trying to tell me. Just say it, please," I said, irritated.

"I gave Meme lots of money, Ruth Ann. They actually were very wealthy."

"NO WAY!" I hollered. "I would've known that."

"You've barely spent time with them. Meme and you only spent a few days together, and Isabella just a few weeks."

"I don't believe you, Manual."

"I'll prove it to you," he said, standing and walking to the center display case. He reached into his pants pocket and pulled out the set of keys. He grabbed a tiny key and stuck it into a lock built into the cabinet below the glassed area that displayed the jewelry. "Give me a second, and I'll show you."

I watched as he bent down and pulled out a metal box and carried it over to where we were sitting. He placed it down upon the table in between the two chairs. He sat down opposite me and leaned over to open the box. He pulled out a large folder filled with papers. "I keep meticulous records, Ruth Ann. I have them by name and location so it's easy to find." He held up the folder and showed me the label.

"It has Meme's name and a bunch of dates," I said, wishing I had my glasses so I could see the dates clearly.

"Yes," he replied. "I had several deals with her, and they're all inside of this folder."

"Can I see it?" I asked, wondering if he would hand it to me to peruse.

"No, no, but I will show you myself. Nobody touches these but me."

He pulled out an invoice and read it out loud. "This one dates back to 1992."

"Wow, that's 25 years ago," I muttered.

"Yes, I've known Meme for a long time, and her mother, too."

"What did you purchase from them?" I asked.

"It was a rare emerald that Meme obtained after a local man died. She was in the poor guys will and his kids were left with nothing but a large debt. Meme wasn't going to accept it, until I got wind of it and offered her an enormous amount of money." He quickly added, "Well, an enormous amount of money to them."

"What's that supposed to mean?" I asked, thinking he screwed Meme out of what the emerald was truly worth.

"Meme's idea of a lot of money and mine are two totally different figures. I gave her enough money to live on for the rest of her life, but, Ruth Ann, I had several other deals with her for a lot more money."

"Why don't you just tell me the number, Manual? I know you're dying to tell me how much you've given them over the years."

"Millions."

I was flabbergasted. Did he just say millions? That's impossible!

"No response?" he inquired, watching me think.

"Did you say millions?"

"Yes, I said millions. I know it's hard to believe, but I have all the paperwork right here," he said, waving the folder in the air. "I'll read you each individual transaction if you'd like to hear them?"

"No, I don't need to hear anymore," I said, completely discouraged and disappointed in Isabella and Meme.

"Why are you looking so sad?" he asked, seeing the dejection spread across my face.

"I, I don't quite know. I would think that would be something Isabella might've mentioned to me, that's all."

"She's a very wealthy young woman, Ruth Ann. I told you, my men fear her."

"But, not because she's rich," I argued. "It's because she has those powers you mentioned."

"Don't act like you don't know what I'm talking about.

You've seen her work, and her grandmother's."

"Yes, I have. I saw the curse on Blue Ice broken," I admitted, willingly.

"That had to be quite the experience. Maybe some time you can tell me all about it. Right now, I need to get back to obtaining that precious Blue Ice of yours. What can we do to make this work?"

I sat staring at this stranger, wondering whom I should trust. Poor Axel was stuck in a hole under the gym while Prunella was living like a queen upstairs. Her memory was still spotty, but it could return at any moment. I was upset with Isabella and felt betrayed, but did I really have a right to? I was so confused I asked Manual if I could sit here and think for a little while. He obliged, telling me he would be right outside at his desk waiting for me. He stood, leaving me alone in a room filled with priceless gems and still wearing the ruby necklace.

Chapter 25

I sat wondering what time it was. It had to be late afternoon, and I was hoping to eat something soon. I had eaten a small breakfast, but totally forgot about lunch. My stomach was rumbling, and I thought of Axel. He had to be miserable, worried, and starving!

It was time to stop feeling sorry for myself because of what Isabella may, or may not, have disclosed to me. Their financial situation was none of my business, but it did hurt. I thought she was an orphan and I took her in hoping to help her. Obviously, that wasn't necessary. I knew I would confront her after Axel, Prunella, and I get out of here!

I was about to exit the room when I caught sight of the folder laying on the center display case. I casually walked to it, fighting with myself if I should or should not have a peek. Why not? He probably left it there on purpose to see if my curiosity would win out. I turned to see if he was watching me, picked up the folder and reached inside to pull out a few papers. Here is what I found under Meme's name:

DATE	ITEM	PAID	ITEM	PAID
1992	Emerald	250,000		
1993	Emerald	125,000		
1993	Diamond	400,000	Diamond	55,000
			(small but beautiful)	
1996	Sapphire	100,000		
1997	Fire Agate	20,000	Lapis Lazuli	10,000
	Larimar	5,000		
1999	Jade	25,000	Turquoise	5,000
	Spinel	20,000	Opal	10,000
2004	Quartz	3,000	Ruby	150,000
	Amber	15,000		
2008	Diamond	275,000	Ruby	125,000
2010	Sapphire	300,000	Topaz	50,000
2013	Aquamarine	*pending*	Malachite	10,000
	Larimar	15,000		
2015	Diamond	475,000	Aquamarine	*pending*
	Ruby	100,000		

"Wow," I whispered. "That's what he paid Meme for those stones!"

"Yes, Ruth Ann," a male voice called out from a distance. "If you think I didn't leave that there on purpose, you must be more tired than I thought!" He laughed as he stood in the doorway catching me holding the folder.

"I didn't want to look, but I couldn't help myself," I answered, agitated. "How did Meme get her hands on all those gems?" I asked, wondering if we were talking about the same person I thought I knew.

"Don't really know or care, Ruth Ann," he said, bluntly.

"As long as she knew I would pay good money, she kept coming up with them."

"Did Isabella know about all of them?" I added, "I mean, when she was old enough to be aware of it."

"She knew."

"But, why didn't she mention it to me?" Then it dawned on me. I had to ask, even though I was pretty sure I knew the answer. "Those two pending transactions ... were they ..." I stopped, swallowed, and spat out, "for Blue Ice?"

"Yep," he said honestly. "I wondered if you saw that."

"Are you saying Meme told you about my gem and told you she could obtain it for you?"

"That's exactly what was supposed to happen, however," he stopped for a moment, debating whether or not to finish his sentence. "She wasn't able to get it for me."

"But, I didn't even know about the piece until late summer! How would she know about it back in 2013?" My mind was reeling. Had Meme and Isabella played me and only pretended to get rid of some supposed curse? But, how could they have pulled off those amazing theatrics in Felix's basement where Meme passed away? They didn't have the technology to pull it off, or did they?

"Look, Ruth Ann," he said, walking toward me and taking the folder from my hand. "Meme wasn't a saint, and neither is Isabella. They wanted money, and I gave it to them. Obviously, Isabella lied to you about how wealthy she is. I don't really care about any of that. All I want to know is how to get my hands on Blue Ice!"

He saw the horror on my face, knowing I realized Isabella and Meme had used me. "Ruth Ann," he said, changing to a kinder tone. "I'm sorry if you were duped, but Meme knew about the gem, and you were aware of that. What you didn't know was she was using you to get the gem for me, not to break some ridiculous curse. That had to be a hoax to get you to hand it over so she could sell it to me."

"No, no," I exclaimed. "Meme didn't want the necklace! She told me it would always be with our family. So, you have to be mistaken."

"I don't think so, but whatever you want to believe." He grabbed my arm gently and led me into his office. "Look, I'm hungry. Why don't I give you a little time to think about it? We'll have dinner, and then we can discuss the topic again. Agreed?"

I was so confused I didn't know what to think or say. I nodded and we headed into the hallway. He led me back to the entrance and into a large, elegant dining room. There was a long, mahogany table that sat at least thirty in the middle of the room. There were only plate settings for three. The question was, who was the third person? Axel, Viktor, or Sal?

Manual walked to the far end of the table and pulled out a high-backed chair for me. I sat down, and he helped push the chair in so I was quite close to the table. He sat down at the head of the table and grabbed the linen napkin and placed it in his lap. I followed suit, looking directly across from me at the empty seat waiting to be filled.

"Who will be joining us?" I couldn't help but ask.

He didn't answer right away because the person who was going to join us for dinner just entered the dining room from the doorway that led to the kitchen.

"Axel!" I hollered, relieved to see him.

"Sit, Axel," Manual ordered, pointing to the seat to his left.

Axel walked slowly to the chair, watching me every second. "So," Axel started to say. "I guess a thank you is in order."

"Yes, it is," Manual replied.

"I wish I could've cleaned up first, but I'll take this as a positive step?"

I noticed Axel was in the same pants and shirt he traveled in. I was fortunate to have been able to shower and change, but he wasn't as lucky. "Maybe Axel can reside in a bedroom now, Manual," I suggested as nicely as I could muster. "I think he should be able to shower and change his clothes, right?"

Please answer, please answer, I thought to myself. Thankfully, I was rewarded. "Yes, I think that can be arranged. However, you'll have a man standing guard outside your bedroom so you can't try any funny stuff."

"We're out in the middle of nowhere, Manual," Axel said, causing me to fear he would lose the bedroom privilege.

"Axel," I quickly chimed in. "Manual is willing to compromise. I think you could cooperate with him, alright?"

"Yes, Ruth Ann, I can," he said, conceding. "Thank you, Manual. I would really appreciate a room where I can clean up."

"Then, it'll be done! Let's eat."

We waited silently until a host of women came in carrying large trays of food. "Wow," I muttered. "That's a lot of food for three people!"

"Yes, they outdo themselves," Manual said, accepting the large piece of beef being served to him.

There was steak, chicken, and some kind of fish. I chose the steak thinking I could use the red meat for strength. I scooped a pile of mashed potatoes on my plate, and a large serving of green beans. It looked so good I couldn't wait to dig in. A very large woman reached over me with a large basket of bread. I reached in and grabbed a large roll, almost drooling from the wonderful aroma of the freshly baked breads. I slathered some butter on the warm roll and took a large bite. The roll was soft, buttery, and fabulous! I devoured my meal in no time, not paying any attention to the two men sitting with me at the table. When I was finished, I sat upright and patted my stomach because the fullness was starting to set in.

"That was so good," I turned and said to the woman standing behind me. She stared blankly at me without any reaction. "Manual, do they speak English?"

"No, they don't, Ruth Ann," he answered, flatly. He looked at my clean plate and said, "You sure look like you enjoyed your meal."

"I was very hungry," I replied. "I haven't eaten anything since morning.

I looked across at Axel. He still had quite a bit of food on his plate. "Axel, aren't you hungry?" I asked.

He stared across the table at me without speaking. "Axel, are you alright?"

"Ruth Ann," he said, raising his arm and pointing to my neck. "What are you wearing?"

I had forgotten that the ruby necklace was still around my neck. "Oh, I, I forgot I had it on."

"But, what is it?" he demanded, looking irritated with me. "Is that yours?"

"Yes," Manual blurted and responded for me. "I gave it to her."

Axel slowly turned his attention to Manual. "You did what?" he snapped.

"I gave it to Ruth Ann as a gift. Do you have a problem

with that?"

"Yes!" he bellowed, starting to rise. I had to stop him before he made a serious mistake.

"Axel!" I said, sternly. "Sit down. A lot happened in the last few hours that you don't know about. I promise to tell you if you calm down. I never said I was accepting the necklace."

"Of course, you will!" Manual exclaimed. "It would be rude not to."

"Yes, Ruth Ann," Axel said, mockingly. "That would be rude of you not to accept a necklace that is already around your neck."

"Knock it off the both of you!" I snapped. "We're not getting anywhere with this conversation. I'll handle whether I accept the ruby necklace or not. Now, the two of you need to come to an understanding about why we're here and when we can leave. Does that sound reasonable?" I looked from one to the other finally feeling a confidence that I hadn't felt in a long while.

"You may leave when you've given me your necklace," Manual said matter of factly.

"That will never happen," Axel said, holding himself very rigidly.

"Now, neither of you are being very reasonable, are you?" I asked them, agitated.

"Ruth Ann!" Axel hollered. "What are you trying to accomplish?"

I turned to face him and said, "Do you want to go back to that hole in the ground or to a nice comfortable bedroom where you can freshen up and start thinking clearly?" I gave him a funny look, hoping he would catch my drift. We would do much better near each other instead of me upstairs in a bedroom on the third floor and him in a cement room four flours down.

He nodded slightly. Finally, Axel put his pride aside and pretended to go along with Manual. "Okay, I'll cooperate and help you get your hands on the gem you so desperately want." He stopped, and just as if a lightbulb went off in his head he added, "Why don't you tell me, not Ruth Ann, why you so desperately want the necklace? I'd love to understand better."

Good boy, Axel! I hoped Axel would be given the same tour of Manual's gem room as I was. "I won't only tell you, I will show you." He stood up, pushed his chair in and waited for us to do the same. He walked into the hallway, and we were joined by Sal, obviously, an extra hand since Axel was roaming free.

Chapter 26

"It's an amazing room, isn't it, Axel?" I asked, as we entered Manual's gem room.

"Amazing is a proper word for it," he said, skeptically. "Why on earth would you leave millions of dollars' worth of gems in this room?"

"Nobody knows about this room except for a few people I trust completely," he replied.

"And you add *us* to your list of people you trust?" Axel asked, baffled.

"I wondered about that, too," I mumbled, quietly.

"Or," Axel began. "Are you not concerned because you don't plan on keeping us alive?"

"That's nonsense!" I hollered. "Manual wouldn't kill us!" I said it so fast because it seemed so outrageous, until I thought about it for a moment. I turned to Manual, who was closing the wall to the gem room. "Right?"

"He's not going to answer you, Ruth Ann," Axel said, smirking. "And if he did, would you believe him?" He added, "Think about it. Does it make sense that he gave you that ruby necklace? No, he'll let you wear it until you're dead, and then he'll put it back into his precious collection!"

"No," I muttered, again quietly. "Manual?" I tried getting him to respond, again. "You don't plan on killing us. Please answer me!"

He walked to his desk and sat down. "Join me," he said, motioning his hands to the chairs in front of his desk. "Sit, we'll talk."

"That's not answering me," I said, nervously.

"Ruth Ann, let's sit and see what he has to say," Axel said, grabbing my hand and leading me to the chair. I plopped down heavily, feeling the weight of my life dropping onto that upholstered chair.

"Now, let me say that I do not plan on killing you, Ruth Ann. I'm not that evil," he said, looking only at me and not Axel.

"What about Axel?" I asked, noticing he purposely left him out.

"Him," Manual said, moving his head in the direction of Axel's chair. "He isn't cooperating. I don't want to kill him, either, but if he continues to be difficult, my mind may change."

"He's not doing anything but fighting for our lives and our possessions, Manual. Wouldn't you do the same thing?" I asked him.

"Yes, I would, Ruth Ann. However, I would expect my captor to threaten my life, too."

"You live a very different life than we do, Manual," I said. "We aren't used to people talking about ending other lives so casually."

"Casually?" he questioned me. "I take nothing casually. I'm a serious business man. I've tried the life of a loving, loyal husband, and look where it got me! My wife was murdered! I'll never let myself be vulnerable like that again."

"What about Prunella?" I couldn't help but ask. "Or Isa-bella?"

Axel looked at me oddly. "What are you talking about?"
"She's speaking nonsense, Axel. Ignore her!" Manual snapped. "Ruth Ann, I will not be able to speak openly with you if I feel you've betrayed me. Do you understand me?"

"Are you threatening her?" Axel said, looking even more furious than he was.

"I don't threaten, I act."

"So, did you just add Ruth Ann to your *kill list*?" Axel asked, sarcastically.

"Axel, shut up!" I bellowed. "Are you trying to get your-self thrown in that hole or worse?"

Manual looked at Axel and said, "You should listen to her. She's speaking wisely now."

Axel crossed his arms and made a, "Hmph" noise. I could tell it was taking every bit of his patience to not lunge forward and strangle the man sitting behind the desk. I thought it was time to get us back on track.

"So, can we knock off the schoolyard threats and get back to why we're here in the first place?"

"Yes," Manual replied.

"Fine," Axel said through gritted teeth.

"Good." I said. "Now, I'm going to suggest we sleep on things and do some serious thinking about how this benefits each one of us before we meet again."

"Are you calling the shots, now?" Manual asked, mock-ingly.

"No, but it's late, I'm tired, and I would really like to see Prunella."

"I will take you to see her. I'm sure she's anxious to see if you're alright," Manual said. He had no idea Viktor let me see her earlier, and I needed to make sure Prunella did not tip him off.

"Thank you. I would love it if you would escort me," I said. "What about Axel?"

"No," Manual declared. "He'll go directly to his room."

"His room *upstairs*, right?" I asked, hoping he hadn't blown it with his antics.

"Yes, I agreed to it, and I stick to my word."

I reached and squeezed Axel's forearm before he could make a snide reply. "Yes," Axel said instead. "Thank you."

"Phew," I mumbled under my breath. We waited for Manual to rise, and then Axel and I stood to follow him upstairs. Sal was waiting for us on in the hallway, and Manual instructed him to take Axel to the third floor. That's all I could make out. I was crossing my fingers and toes that he would be in a room near mine.

Sal nudged Axel to move. He didn't have a choice but to follow Sal down the hall away from Manual and me. I wanted us to go up together, but that wasn't going to happen. "Let's go, Ruth Ann. It's time you get to see your cousin."

We headed up to the second floor and walked toward the guard outside her door. The guard gave me a strange look after Manual told him I was finally going to see Prunella. I shook my head, hoping the guard wouldn't tattle on Viktor or me. He caught my eye, and I felt he understood my action because he pulled out a set of keys and opened the door without saying a word. I wanted to make sure I remembered the guard's good deed because he could be beneficial to me in the near future.

"The light's still on in her bedroom; she must be awake," Manual stated, as we walked in.

I needed to be the first to speak so I could make it clear to Prunella that we hadn't seen each other yet. When Manual and I reached the double doors to the bedroom, I spotted her sitting upright in her bed, holding a book.

"Prunella!" I exclaimed, cheerily. "I'm so glad I finally got to see you! I was worried about your health, how are you feeling?"

It took her all of two seconds to catch on, thankfully. She's been up and down lately, I didn't know what to expect. "Ruth Ann! You're finally here!"

"I wouldn't keep her from you, Prunella," Manual said, hurrying to her side and sitting on the edge of the bed. "She's your cousin. We've been very busy, though."

"With what?" Prunella asked, harmlessly.

"Making sure your recovery goes as planned, of course," I said, lying for her own good. She was still very confused, and hardly remembered her past.

"Oh," she replied, disappointed. "I thought maybe something else was going on."

"Like what?" I asked, wondering what she could be thinking.

Manual decided it was time to control the conversation. "Prunella, my dear, we're working very hard to make sure you get stronger and start walking again. That's why I've sent for a physical therapist to come here and begin working with you tomorrow."

"You have?" I asked, dumbfounded.

Prunella looked from me to Manual. "If you two have been working together, why didn't Ruth Ann know about the therapist?"

"I did, Prunella," I quickly stated. "You know me, I get dippy when I'm tired. I was about to go to my room to catch up on some sleep."

Prunella eyed me suspiciously. "You never get dippy,

Ruth Ann. What's up with you two?"

"Absolutely nothing," Manual swiftly replied. "It's late, why don't we get some sleep and we'll be back to see you in the morning before your first physical therapy session."

"Okay," she agreed, conceding. But she noticed my neck and cried, "Ruth Ann! What are you wearing around your neck? It's stunning! Is it yours?"

"Oh, no, Prunella," I quickly replied, reaching up to feel the large ruby necklace. "Manual just let me wear it for fun. It's going back in his safe tonight."

"Oh, that's too bad. It looks like it was made for you."

Before it got even more awkward, Manual hopped off the bed and grabbed my hand to lead me out of her bedroom. I barely had time to say good night when I was whooshed into the hallway. Manual closed the door behind him and displayed an angry scowl at me.

"Are you purposely trying to blow it?" he snapped.

"What?" I asked.

"You were supposed to go along with my physical therapy speech, Ruth Ann."

"I'm sorry, I really am exhausted and not in my right mind. Excuse me for being scared for my life!" "Don't be so dramatic, Ruth Ann," he said, laughing. "Since you didn't do anything on purpose, I'll let it slide ... this one time."

He waved the guard away, and personally escorted me to my room on the third floor. When we reached my door, he stopped me. "Hold on, Ruth Ann."

He walked to the room right next to mine. There was a guard standing outside in the hall. He whispered a few words, and then marched back to me. "What was that about?" I asked him, even though it was obvious Axel was inside the other room and the guard was being warned.

"Nothing that concerns you." He waited for me to argue, but I stayed quiet. "So, I'm going to let you in your room, and I'm not going to lock you in or tell my guard to not let you roam freely. Can I trust you to behave?"

I smiled, happy that just as Meme predicted, I was free to walk the premises to look for Isabella, Inga and Carlos. "Of course, you can, Manual. I pose no threat to anyone."

"We'll see about that. From what I've heard, you can be quite a spitfire."

"Me?" I questioned, innocently, even though I liked his analogy and planned to live up to it wholeheartedly.

He laughed, let me inside my room and closed the door behind me. I waited a few minutes and tried the door knob. It turned without resistance. I opened the door and stuck my head out. I looked toward the right and spotted the guard sitting in a chair outside Axel's room. I wondered if he would fall asleep, allowing me to sneak into Axel's room? I decided it might be too risky, so I walked inside my room and went into the bedroom. I reached up and unclasped the ruby necklace and placed it in the nightstand drawer. I didn't plan on wearing or looking at that necklace again. I hurried onto my balcony and looked to see if Axel was allowed on his.

Axel and I shared a nice balcony, divided into two sections by a high cement railing. I leaned over the railing edge and wondered if it was possible to jump onto Axel's side. I grabbed one of the chairs, stepped on the seat and looked down onto Prunella's massive balcony directly below me. "It's pretty high up," I muttered, nervously. I shook it off and told myself it was necessary to make it over to Axel's balcony. We had to conspire together, and he wasn't anywhere in sight!

Chapter 27

I was staring three floors down at the cement walk below, encouraging myself to make the leap, when I heard, "RUTH ANN!" "What on earth are you trying to do?"

"Axel," I called, secretly relieved that he stopped me, "Look, it's only a large step to your balcony."

He rushed to the edge of his balcony and ordered me to step off the chair. "Are you crazy? Don't you dare climb over that edge."

"Look, it's not that bad, Axel," I said, trying to sound courageous.

He looked around to make sure the coast was clear, and then swung his legs over and kneeled on the thick cement railing. Within a second or two, he was standing on my balcony and grabbed me into a strong embrace.

"Thank God I felt drawn to the balcony!" he exclaimed, holding me tightly. "I looked out here when the guard, Sal, brought me in here, but had no idea you would be right next door."

"I told you I was right above Prunella," I reminded him.

"Oh, I guess I forgot." He rubbed his head and added, "Maybe from the blows to my head."

"Are you alright?" He nodded, and I asked, "Why do you think they would put us next to each other? I mean, they must know we'd try and get to each other and the balcony is the obvious way."

"I don't think it matters to them," he replied. "It's not like we can jump down three floors and escape. Plus, they know we'd never leave without Prunella."

"True, just seems odd, that's all," I said. "Manual also told me I could come and go from my room at my leisure. I have no restrictions."

"I do," he stated. "My door is locked, and I can't get out. However," he stopped, raised his hand to his face and rubbed the stubs on his unshaven face. "However, I could leave from your room."

"There's a guard outside in the hall, Axel. That's impossible."

"At some point in time they must change guards or maybe he'll use the bathroom or eat. We might have a moment when my door is unguarded."

"Actually, there's a chair for the guard to sit on. Maybe he'll fall asleep?"

"Bingo!" Axel exclaimed, thrilled. "It's late, and I bet he'll doze off. We need to keep an eye on him without him noticing. You can open the door and check, but not too often or he'll get suspicious."

"I guess I have to be the one to do that, don't I?"

"Yep, but I'll make sure you're discreet."

"Gee, thanks."

We decided to go inside my bedroom just in case an outside guard spotted us. "Wow, we have totally different rooms," Axel said, looking around. "My room is barren except for a twin bed and a bathroom."

"Really?" I asked, surprised. "This is such a luxurious room, why wouldn't the one next door be the same?"

"Mine must be saved for prisoners or unwelcome guests."

"At least you're not stuck in that hole anymore," I said, trying to make his situation sound positive.

"True. We need to come up with a plan, Ruth Ann. Who knows if they'll keep us here, and we need to take advantage of the time we have. What are we going to do?"

"I plan on roaming around looking for Isabella, Inga and Carlos."

"That's right!" he bellowed. "They should be here by now. I wonder if they've made it to Manual's compound?"

"I think they're around, but he has so many guards outside. I think walking outside at night could be fatal for me."

"They might mistake you for an intruder, and shoot first, ask later," he agreed. "Maybe you could walk around this mansion and look for secret entrances. Those three could be hiding inside, too."

"How?" I asked, doubtful. "With all those, guards, they would never miss someone getting in."

"I'm sure there's a way. There's always a way."

We sat down on the sofa and didn't speak for several minutes. Finally, Axel came up with a plan. "Ruth Ann, peek outside your door a few times until you notice the guard getting sleepy, then pretend you're hungry and tell the guard you're going to grab a snack from the kitchen. He'll shrug it off without a thought, and hopefully lean his head back and fall asleep. Once you leave, I'll watch and wait for him to doze off. Then, I'll sneak out of here and meet up with you."

"If, and that's a big if it works, how will you know where to meet me?" I asked. So many things could go wrong with his plan, it terrified me.

"I'm thinking. We don't know our way around, but what we do know is where his office, the gym, that underground room and the dining room are."

"Those are too public of places for me to wait for you," I answered.

"Not necessarily," he mumbled, thinking more than speaking. A lightbulb went off in his head and he proudly said, "When I was being taken out of the gym I noticed a sauna room. We could meet in there."

"I guess it could work. Who would take a sauna this time of night?"

"Exactly," he replied, pleased with himself for thinking of it.

"But, what if the guard doesn't fall asleep?" I asked him.

"Stop thinking so negatively. I'm sure it'll happen, it's getting late."

"But," I stopped when Axel told me not to be a downer. "Fine, but how long should I wait for you? I'm not going to stay in there all night!"

"Give it an hour. If I don't get to the sauna room by then just go to the kitchen and really grab something to bring up-stairs. Then, if the guard sees you, he'll think that you took your time, but did get food."

"Okay," I said, unsure about the plan. "I'm going to take a look now and see what he's doing." I started toward my bed-room door when Axel reminded me to stay unseen. "I know, Axel!" I barked, quietly.

I slowly turned the door knob and opened it a couple of inches. I was thankful it didn't squeak. I couldn't see anything so I opened it a little more. "Careful," Axel whispered from behind the door. After the door was opened about six inches,

I was able to stick my head out enough to get a glimpse of the guard. He was leaning back in his chair with earphones on and his eyes were ... . yes! They were closed.

I shut the door gently and whispered, "He's not only asleep, he's got earphones on. He must be listening to music because I could hear what sounded like Latin music."

"Great!" Axel blurted out. "You should go, but let the guard see you're leaving."

"Wake him up?" I asked, confused. "Why don't I just leave, and when I come back with something to eat, I'll tell him then that I was hungry and went to the kitchen."

"I guess it would work that way, too," he admitted. "Go but be careful not to run into anyone else, especially when you veer off toward the gym and not the kitchen!"

"You're right. It might look awfully suspicious of me walking around hallways where I didn't belong."

"It'll be fine, Ruth Ann. I trust you. You can feel it out when you're downstairs. Listen, and keep your eyes wide open."

I nodded, opened the door and stepped into the hall. I glanced at the guard, and he was out cold. I wasn't about to wake him, so I headed the opposite direction toward the staircase. The third-floor hall was fairly dark, lit only by a few dim sconces. When I got to the second-floor landing, I desperately wanted to check on Prunella, but I realized that could be reckless so I went to the main level and stood in the large foyer. I knew I had to go left to get to the gym, and right to the dining room. I figured the kitchen was near there, but I didn't know for sure. So, if I was caught wandering the halls, I could honestly say I was looking for the kitchen.

I quickly found the long hallway that led to Manual's s office and I knew the gym was nearby. I had noticed several doors earlier and decided to take a peek in a few again.

The first door on the right side was locked, just as I thought it might be this time of night. The next door on the right was also locked. I looked to the left and spotted the door to the gym. I panicked wondering if they locked the gym, but before I checked, my curiosity led me to the next door. The gym filled the left side of the hall, but on the right, there was one more door until I reached Manual's office. I figured it was locked, but was stunned to find the door knob loose, almost waiting for me to turn it. I stepped back, terrified that I had just gotten myself caught, when I decided to be brave and stick my head against the door to listen for any sounds or voices.

"Nothing," I muttered quietly to myself. I decided it was safe and opened the door. What I found when I entered dropped me to my knees. I couldn't believe my eyes!

Chapter 28

"RUTH ANN!" a female cried, lowering a large glass vase from her raised arms. "How did you know where to find us?"

I was so flabbergasted I couldn't speak. Inga set down the vase and helped me to my feet. "Are you alright? We didn't give you a heart attack, did we?"

"No, no," I was able to say. "I'm so shocked to see you three standing before me, that's all."

Carlos put a small gun he was aiming my way back into his waistband. "How did you know to look here?"

"I didn't," I said, truthfully. "I was snooping around. I'm supposed to meet Axel in the sauna soon. Axel" I exclaimed. "He'll be so happy to see you three!"

Isabella looked at me with her usual sweet, innocent smile. I suddenly didn't feel so happy to see her. She had betrayed me if what Manual told me was true. She must've noticed my expression change, and asked, "What's wrong? You look almost mad to see me!"

Was I going to tell her the truth right now or wait until we were safely far away from here? I chose the latter, and quickly changed my tone. "I'm fine, Isabella," was all I could muster. I've always been bad at hiding my emotions. If I am mad or hurt it is written all over my face.

"Oh, okay, Ruth Ann," Isabella replied. "I brought what you asked me to. I have ..."

"Don't say it out loud!" Inga snapped at her. "You put another curse on it, and I don't want to be near that thing again."

"It's not a curse," Isabella fired back. "It's a safety hex. That's the opposite of a curse, Inga."

"I don't care. All this funny stuff scares me," Inga admitted, surprising me. She was such a tough, strong woman, and admitting she was afraid of anything wasn't something I ever thought she would publicly announce.

"If you didn't want to come and help save Prunella, Ruth Ann, and Axel, then you should've stayed in Deer Creek!" Isabella bellowed.

"Would you two knock it off!" Carlos snapped, obviously irritated. "I'm so sick of you two fighting. We're here, deal with it!"

"Wow, what's been happening with all of you?" I asked.

"Nothing, Ruth Ann," Carlos declared, glaring at the other two to stop their nonsense. "It's been a trying experience getting inside here. We had no idea where to go and how to find you, but here you are!"

"Dumb luck," I said, smiling. "I'm just thankful none of you were shot by Manual's guards."

"He does have quite a few," Carlos mentioned.

"We had to wait until it was late and really dark outside," Inga said. "There was no way we could've made it in here during the day. We'd have been an instant target."

I spent the next several minutes filling them in on what happened from the moment we took off from the airport in Sweden. Their mouths were gaped open in disbelief, but none of them spoke until I was finished. Even as I heard myself describe what happened, I could barely believe it. "That's it," I ended. "Now we're trying to figure out a way to get out of here. I'm not sure what Meme meant in the dream about Prunella being in danger, though. She's living like a queen up on the second floor."

"But, why?" Inga asked, observantly.

"Why is she living like a queen?" I asked, making sure that's what she meant.

"Yes."

"I think she's made some admirers around here."

"What are you implying, Ruth Ann?" Carlos asked. "Are you saying someone has romantic feelings for her?"

"Not *someone*, but more than one!"

"You've got to be kidding!" Inga gasped, irate. "Who are you talking about? I'll strangle them with my very own hands!"

"The first man was our captor, Viktor. I told you about him, and I don't want to make him mad because we might be able to use him to our advantage. The other man is ... well, this may sound crazy, but Manual Marquez." I waited for a gasp or argument, but they didn't say a word. "No comments?" I asked curiously, watching Isabella closely to see if she had an odd reaction. "You have to be surprised about Manual, right?"

Carlos replied first. "Well, she's very pretty and has a kind, sweet personality. I'm not surprised a man would fall for her."

"How's Mr. Eklund taking it?" Inga asked, inquiringly. "He has to be furious."

I pondered Inga's question, and realized Axel really hadn't seemed too upset.

"Ruth Ann?" Inga asked, waiting for my answer. "Are you going to tell us how he's handling this?"

"Sorry, Inga. I was just thinking about that. I don't know how Axel is. We don't talk about it, and maybe he brushes it off thinking once they get home, they'll go back to being a normal married couple."

"Normal?" Inga inquired. "When have they ever been normal?"

"Good point, Inga," I said. "Axel probably assumes Prunella's being extra sweet so they'll stay on her good side. Then, hopefully, we can use that to help us get out of here, alive."

"Alive?" Carlos asked, worried. "I'm not ready to put my life on the line again."

Inga swirled her head around and faced him straight on. "Then leave!"

"I was kidding," Carlos said, rolling his eyes. "Just trying to lighten the mood. Give me a break."

I wasn't so sure Carlos was joking, but I knew him well enough to know he definitely would risk his life to help us. That's just the kind of man he is. "I guess I keep going over Meme's words in my head. Get the necklace on Prunella's neck so she'll be safe. Meme said that without Blue Ice she could die."

Isabella nodded. "That's exactly right, Ruth Ann. My grandmother is right."

"But, how do you know?" Inga asked, confused. "The woman is dead."

"We just do," I told Inga. "Don't bother trying to understand. I know Meme came to me in my dream or whatever it was. I'm not willing to risk doubting her."

"I'm confused," Carlos chimed in. "If this Manual wants

Blue Ice, and you're about to put it around Prunella's neck, won't he just take it from her and get what he wants anyway?"

"I've thought about that, Carlos," I said. "We need to hide it somehow."

"But, how?" Inga cried. "It's a huge blue gem!"

"I know, but if she wears something high on her neck, we can keep him from seeing it."

"In this climate?" Inga questioned, again. "It's so hot I feel like we're on the surface of the sun!"

"We don't have a choice. We have to get that necklace to Prunella for her safety, and then get out of here right away," I said, not sure how we would go about any of it.

"Didn't you say you were to meet up with Axel?" Carlos inquired.

"Oh, I almost forgot! I have to get to the gym right now," I said, turning for the door.

"We'll come with you," Inga said.

"I want us to stick together, but we can't risk you three being seen. Let me look in the hall and if the coast is clear, and we'll head to the sauna in the gym."

I opened the door and took a peek down the dark hall. There was no one in sight. I waved my hand directing them to follow. They quickly came to my side and we headed to the gym. I opened the door and let the three of them enter before me. Once safely inside, I pointed toward the door where Axel was supposed to be meeting me.

"Let's get in there," I said, anxiously. "I don't want to risk anyone coming in here besides Axel."

"It's the middle of the night," Carlos commented. "Who would be in the gym now?"

"I don't know, and don't care. I just don't want you three to get caught. That would ruin everything!" I said, hurrying to the sauna. "But first, I'm going to show you where Axel and I were held earlier today."

"They put you in the gym?" Inga questioned, baffled.

"Not exactly," I said, hastily deciding to make the quick detour to show them the door that led down to the cement hole in the ground. They walked behind me until I reached a dead end. I held out my hand and said, "This door takes you down a flight of stairs into a home-made prison."

"What?" Inga cried.

"Axel was chained to a wall and I was tied to a chair. He was down there for hours and hours, but I wasn't. Manual only put me down there to teach me a lesson because I was being difficult."

"Surprise, surprise," Inga murmured. I ignored her remark, but Isabella came to my defense.

"He's a monster!" Isabella cried, upset. "How could a man do that to a woman?" I wondered myself, and I also wondered how Isabella and her grandmother could ever do business with this man!

"Don't ask," I said, thinking of all the times I've been uncomfortably detained this year. "We don't need to go down there because no one is being held there anymore."

"How do you know?" Carlos asked, curiously.

"First, there's no guard, and second, I was the one who helped get Axel moved to a room on the third floor."

"Good for you, Ruth Ann!" Isabella cried. "Now what?"

"We wait for Axel," I said, turning around and walking to the sauna. "In here." I opened the door and we filed in.

Carlos stopped just before entering. "I'll wait for him here."

"Why?" Inga demanded. "We need to hide."

Carlos glared at her and snapped, "Because I feel like it!

If I hear anyone coming I'll get inside. But, until then ..." he stopped, peaked inside the tiny sauna and shook his head. "Nope, I'm not going in there."

"Are you claustrophobic?" Isabella asked, surprised. "I never knew that."

"I'm not claustrophobic, I just don't want to go in there."

"Leave him alone," I ordered, just as Inga was about to go on the attack. "He'll alert us when Axel is coming."

"As long as it's Axel and not one of his guards," Inga said, irritated. "Or Marquez himself."

I looked a little closer at Carlos standing right outside the door of the sauna. Little beads of sweat were forming on his brow, and it wasn't from the heat. The room was quite cool, therefore there had to be another reason why Carlos was sweating.

I stepped out of the sauna, leaving Inga and Isabella alone. "Carlos," I said, startling him and causing him to jump back.

"What? Why did you do that?" he asked, quickly wiping his damp forehead.

"I'm sorry," I said, reaching to touch his arm. He pulled away, allowing my hand to hang in the air. "What's going on with you?" I asked, trying not to sound irritated, even though my patience was running thin.

He glared at me and shook his head. "Nothing, Ruth Ann. Just leave me alone." He added, "Go back in and I'll let you know when I hear someone coming, hopefully it'll be Axel."

I turned around and walked into the sauna. He obviously wasn't willing to confide in me, so I chose to drop it. The heavy, wooden door closed behind me, and I peeked out the sliver of a window to see if Carlos was doing any better.

"What's going on?" Inga asked, always the curious one.

"Why wouldn't he come in here?"

Isabella answered, "He must have had a bad experience in a small enclosed area."

"You don't know about it?" I asked.

"No, I had no idea, actually," Isabella replied, sitting on a long bench against the back wall.

"Maybe he just doesn't feel well," Inga said, bringing up a different angle.

"True, but I don't think that's it," I said, feeling there was more to it. "It's up to him to tell us, if he ever does."

I went and sat on the bench next to Isabella. Inga started pacing, making me anxious and dizzy. "Please stop, Inga," I barked. "Sit down and rest a moment. You've had a long day."

"I'm completely fine, Ruth Ann. I slept on the plane down here, and now, my adrenaline is keeping me fired up."

Instead of arguing, I closed my eyes to calm myself down. I wasn't sure if I fell asleep or if my mind was taken over by Meme again.

"Ruth Ann, open your eyes. I need to speak with you." I recognized her voice, but I felt so sleepy I didn't want to awaken. "Come on Ruth Ann," she said, exasperated. "I don't have much time!"

I opened one eye, and there she stood, right in front of my face. "Not again," I said, frustrated. "I see you more often now than when you were alive!"

"You need to listen to me!" she snapped, showing those perfectly white teeth. "Look at me!"

"Fine, what do you want now," I answered. "Isabella and the others are here. We're just waiting for Axel and then we'll come up with a plan to rescue Prunella. We'll be out of here by morning."

"No, you won't."

I was definitely awake after she said that. "What do you mean by that?"

"I need to warn you about Manual," she said.

"Oh, you mean the man you've done business with and made a lot of money from," I said, angrily. "You left that part out when you visited me before, didn't you?"

"Yes, Ruth Ann, I did. There's a lot more to the story than what he told you. But, I didn't use any of that money for myself, except for bare necessities."

"Then what happened to the millions of dollars?" I asked, skeptically. I started to doubt this woman. She wasn't the same woman I remember from Jamaica. This woman looked similar, just younger and cleaned up.

"I'll tell you another time, I promise. Right now, I only have a short time. Just trust that I did good with the money."

"Does Isabella have the money now?" I asked, curiously.

"Some of it," she replied. "Don't be mad at her, Ruth Ann. She's young, and alone now without her mother or me."

"She's become close to her half-sister, Cassandra," I reminded her.

"Yes, but that's a new relationship. She needs time to fully trust her."

"When this is over, and we're safely back in Deer Creek, I will ask Isabella to explain it all to me. I feel ..." she stopped me by holding her hand in the air.

"She didn't betray you, Ruth Ann. She's embarrassed and worried that you would treat her differently if you knew about the money."

"I wouldn't do that! Look at how close I am with Prunella, and she's very wealthy."

"First, she's part of your family, and second, she's rich because of Axel, to whom you're also very close."

I watched her facial expression change when she mentioned how close she thought Axel and I were. "What are you implying?"

"You and Axel have grown close and have a tight bond, do you not?"

"Yes, but there's nothing improper going on."

"You both have stronger feelings than you're willing to admit. In time, you will come to see this and your lives will change forever!"

"You're scaring me," I said, not wanting to hear any more. "Just tell me why you're here and warning me about Manual."

"Yes, you're right, Ruth Ann. I was momentarily distracted." She sat on a rickety wood chair in her hut on the beach in Jamaica. I didn't notice we were there until just now. "My time grows short, I'm getting tired." I noticed her slump in her chair, and her eyes sunk in their sockets a bit deeper. "Manual's nice to you, right?" I nodded. "Keep it that way. Don't argue with him!"

"I'm trying, but it's hard, Meme. He kidnapped us!"

"Just listen to my words! Do not argue with him. If you follow my words, all of you should get out of here alive."

"Should?" I questioned her. "What does that mean, exactly?"

"I, I only know so much. Just trust me, and don't upset Manual."

"What else?" I asked her. "What are his plans for us?"

"You and Axel? He doesn't know about the others showing up."

"And Prunella," I mentioned. "Don't forget about her."

"She's safe, Ruth Ann. Manual's falling in love with her, but he's terrified."

"Why?" I asked, curiously, even though I shouldn't care.

"He's afraid because of how he felt after his wife was murdered, and then with Isabella."

"He was in love with her, wasn't he?"

"Oh, yes, definitely. But, all his men warned him about her. They called her a witch and brainwashed him against her."

"But, you wouldn't want her to be with him anyway, right?" I asked, wondering if Meme actually wished Isabella married this criminal.

"Well, it would've gotten her out of her miserable life back in our village. She would've lived like a queen."

"Kind of like how he's treating Prunella right now," I said, observantly.

"Yes, Ruth Ann, exactly like that."

"So, Manual's falling for Prunella, and he's afraid she could be a witch too?"

"No, but he's aware of the connection with Isabella and Prunella. He knows about your trip to Jamaica, and that Isabella was involved."

"So?"

"He doesn't want his men to figure it out. He's the boss, the man that's in charge. He doesn't want to appear weak."

"Once again, so? How does this affect me?" I asked, confused.

"Ruth Ann!" She barked. "Listen. Manual plans on keeping Prunella and not letting her go home. Don't you see that? He will allow you to have limited contact with her, and Axel will never get to see her. He plans on murdering him!"

"Because they're still married, right?" I asked, horrified

with this news.

"Yes, finally you're seeing the bigger picture. Manual wants her, and Axel's in his way because they're still married. I think Prunella and Axel aren't meant to be together, but that doesn't mean he should die."

"You don't think they should be together?" I asked, surprised.

"No."

"But, I have John in my life."

"Where is he now?" she asked me.

"He has no idea what's happened to us."

"When's the last time he tried contacting you?"

She had a point. I hadn't given John too much thought lately and I barely talked with him while I was spending my days at the hospital. He had been distant and non-communicative, but he might just be busy with work.

"Well?" Meme asked me, again. "I see you're deep in thought."

"Who's kidding who, Meme?" I asked smiling, even if it wasn't funny. "You probably know what I was thinking about!"

"That doesn't matter, Ruth Ann. You answered my question, though. You haven't heard from him lately."

"No, I guess I haven't," I admitted. "Can we get back to why you're here warning me about Manual. All I know so far is he's falling in love with her and wants to keep her here. And, he wants Axel dead so their marriage would be dissolved."

"Here's the worst part," Meme started to say, rising from her chair. "He isn't planning on letting you ever return to Deer Creek!"

Chapter 29

Suddenly my eyes flew open, and my heart was racing so fast I felt I had just finished running a marathon. "Ruth Ann," Isabella shrieked, worried. "What's wrong?"

I looked around and saw Isabella sitting next to me, holding my hand, and Inga hovering over me. "I'm fine. I guess I was sleeping, and I ..." I stopped, realized what had happened, and decided to share with them. "It was Meme, she came to me in a vision again."

"It's okay, Ruth Ann," Isabella said smiling, and patting my hand gently. "She does it quite often with me."

"That's ridiculous!" Inga snapped.

"No, it isn't, Inga," I responded. "Let me tell you what she told me." I relayed everything I could remember, except for the part about the money and the betrayal. I figured that subject would be best broached when Isabella and I were alone.

"So, she told you that Manual was a threat to only *you*?" Inga questioned.

"No, to Axel too. He wants to kill him so he can keep Prunella for himself." I watched for any strange reactions from Isabella, but I got nothing.

"But, why can't *you* leave?" Inga asked, confused.

"I don't know. That's exactly when I woke up," I said, truthfully. "I didn't get Meme's reason why Manual won't let me go home."

"Not that any of us would allow him to kill Mr. Eklund or leave you and Prunella here," Inga stated, with the resounding strength I needed to hear.

"What's going on in here?" Carlos asked, sticking his head barely inside the sauna.

"Nothing, Ruth Ann had another conversation with Isabella's dead grandmother," Inga replied, sarcastically. I heard a tinge of skepticism in her voice, making me question my conversation with Meme.

"Oh," Carlos replied, and shrugged his shoulders. "Doesn't surprise me."

"Really?" Inga asked, surprised. "You think those encounters are real?"

"Of course, I do," Carlos answered, shutting the door and going back to his post.

I stood and pushed Inga out of my way. "Let me take this. I'll go and talk to Carlos. Maybe he'll be more willing to talk now." I left a dazed Inga and Isabella alone, and found Carlos pacing around the door toward the hall. "Carlos," I whispered. "Any sign of Axel? Or anyone?"

"Nope," he replied disappointed. "I'm getting worried about Axel. He should've been here by now."

"Me, too. I wonder if the guard woke up and caught him sneaking out of my bedroom."

"If he hasn't been caught, it sure is rude of him to make us wait this long!" Carlos snapped.

"Carlos, he doesn't even know you three are here," I reminded him. "Maybe I should go and have a look?"

"No, it's not safe walking around in the middle of the night."

"Why?" I asked. "Outside of a guard or two, everyone inside the place is sleeping."

"But, if Axel was caught, then they'll have figured out you aren't in your room, either."

"Good point," I said. "But, we can't sit here and speculate. I need to find Axel."

"I'll go with you then."

"No!" I replied, a little too loudly. "You might be spotted. They know I'm here already, so I'll look."

"I'm not letting you go alone. You either let me go with you willingly or I'll follow you."

"Fine, but we need to tell Inga and Isabella," I said, turning to go back inside the sauna. "Inga isn't going to take it well."

"No way, Ruth Ann!" Inga shouted before I could get the words out of my mouth. "You're not going without me."

"Hey," Isabella cried. "I'm sure not going to stay here by myself."

Carlos pulled me aside and whispered, "Maybe we should all go. We're safer together."

"It's too risky," I told him.

"There's risk in whatever we do, Ruth Ann," he said, making sense. "I think we stay together and sneak upstairs."

"That won't be necessary," a strange voice called out from the sauna door.

"Viktor!" I exclaimed. Inga and Carlos looked terrified, wondering who this tall stranger was. Isabella, on the other hand smiled at the young man, convincing me that my encounter with Meme was real.

For a moment, Viktor didn't realize the young, beautiful woman was Isabella. But, when his eyes met hers, he took a step back, his eyes full of fear. "Isabella, is that really you?"

Inga's and Carlos' heads turned from Isabella to Viktor in total confusion. Carlos was the first to speak as he aimed his gun at Viktor. "Wait, how do you know this man, Isabella?" Before Carlos finished his question, Viktor ripped the gun from Carlos' hand and shoved it in his pocket.

Viktor remained speechless so I answered his question. "Yes, Viktor, this is Isabella. I heard you knew her."

Viktor's eyes remained fixed on Isabella, but he couldn't or wouldn't speak. Inga was shaking her head trying to figure out what on earth was happening. I said, "It's a long story, isn't it Isabella?" I watched her eyes leave Viktor's gaze and look at me, anxiously.

"I'm sorry, Ruth Ann," she said. "I'm a terrible person. I should've told you everything."

"Yes, Isabella, you should have trusted me enough to tell me what your grandmother did."

"Then, you know about ... the money, too?" she asked guiltily, just like a young child who had been caught behaving badly.

"Yes, I do," I said sternly. I was angry with her, but it wasn't the right time to get into it. Instead, I walked to Viktor and snapped my fingers at him, waking him out of his trance. "Viktor, get over it!"

"What?" he snapped at me angrily. "I was just surprised at seeing her again."

"That's not it, and we know it," I said, making sure it was obvious I knew what had happened when Isabella was last here.

"You know?" he questioned me. "How? Did she tell you?" he pointed at Isabella and I shook my head.

"It doesn't matter," I replied. "Just tell me you're not going to turn them in."

"Why wouldn't I?" he asked, confused. "They broke in!"

"No, no," I said. "They came because I asked them to."

"But, you didn't have access to a phone."

"I did on the plane," I said. "Manual took our phones away after we arrived here."

"Smart of you," he said. "But, they shouldn't be here. My boss will be furious when he finds out she's back in his home again."

"Again?" Inga and Carlos said in unison. "Somebody better tell us what's going on around here!" Carlos bellowed.

"Shhh," Viktor said, raising his finger to his mouth. "If they see me with you and find out I didn't immediately turn you in, I'll be killed!"

"By Manual?" I asked him.

"Of course," Viktor replied, stunned I would even ask him that question. "Even I can't figure out why I've waited this long."

"Because you want to help us, and Prunella, don't you?" I asked. "I noticed how much you cared for her while we were on the plane."

"She is special," he answered with a hint of a smile. "But, you and that man you flew with are a real pain!"

"Axel," I said. "You said when you found us that it wouldn't be necessary to go look for him. Why?"

"He was caught leaving *your* room," he said, pointing at me.

Inga, Isabella and Carlos eyed me suspiciously. "What

was he doing in your bedroom?" Inga asked slyly.

"Not what you think!" I exclaimed. "He was in the room next to mine so he hopped onto my balcony and we figured out how to get out and look for you three. I was free to roam, so I walked out of my bedroom and noticed the guard outside of Axel's room was falling asleep." Viktor grumbled some incoherent words, probably admonishing his friend for sleeping while on duty. "Axel was going to sneak out and meet me here after making sure the guard was sound asleep."

"That's when I came into the picture," Viktor chimed in. "I practically walked right into Eklund in the hall. He was so preoccupied watching the guard, he didn't see me coming down the hall." He shook his head and added, "Not very smart of him."

"Who, the guard or Axel?" Carlos asked sarcastically.

Viktor glared at him, and I thought it wise to intervene. "Carlos, do you really think this is the time to be funny?"

"You better listen to her," Viktor suggested, scowling. "All I have to do is drag your skinny butt across the hall and you'll be dead."

"Wait!" I cried. "Are you telling me Manual is in his office right now?"

"And," Viktor added, "he's not alone."

"Axel's in there, isn't he?" I asked.

"Yep. He's in big trouble right about now."

"Take me to him!" I demanded, terrified for Axel's life.

Inga stopped Viktor by pulling on his arm. "Hey, get away from me!"

"I need you, Isabella and Ruth Ann to come clean to us first. Nobody leaves here until I understand what's going on!"

Viktor laughed and swiped her arm away. "I'm the one giving the orders around here, don't forget that."

"If you're the one in charge, why did you look like you saw a ghost when you saw Isabella?" Inga asked, rightfully so.

"I'll take that one, Viktor," Isabella said. "My grandmother and I did business with Manual Marquez before."

"Business?" Carlos and Inga questioned together. "What kind of business would you have with this man? Isn't he a drug lord?"

Viktor snapped, "He's a legitimate business man."

"Who happens to sell drugs, and illegal gems," I added.

Viktor was about to protest but changed his mind. "None of this matter right now. I have to decide what I'm going to do with all of you."

"You'll leave Inga, Isabella and Carlos here while you take me to Axel and Manual," I suggested. "Please."

He appeared to be weighing the odds in his head when he finally spoke. "I could do that, but if it gets out that I harbored those three, I'm a dead man."

"Who's going to tell?" Inga asked him. "We won't say a word."

"Well ... I'll agree for now, but that means you three stay here. No following us into the hall, got it?" he asked us.

The three of them nodded and Inga crossed herself, swearing to keep quiet, even though I knew her well enough to know she'd lie to him in a heartbeat.

Viktor walked to the door that led into the hall. "You'll tell my boss you ran into me in the hall. You tell him you were wandering around because you couldn't sleep and got lost looking for the kitchen."

"Sounds perfectly reasonable," I said. "But, why are you helping *me*?" I asked, curiously.

"Because you were right. I do care for your cousin, and I

can tell she cares a great deal for you. If I hurt you, in turn I hurt Prunella."

"You're way too good to work for Manual," I said, hoping he didn't take it the wrong way.

"He's been very good to me. I came from a poor household, and now I have more money than my parents made in their lifetime," he added, "several lifetimes, and I'm only in my early thirties."

"If you have a lot of money, why don't you leave this job?" I asked just as we walked up to Manual's office.

"I can't," he said, disappointed. "Once you get to my level, you're in for life."

"That's ridiculous!" I exclaimed, softly. "You can do whatever you'd like."

"No, it doesn't work that way, Ruth Ann." He held up his finger to his mouth to silence me. "I'm going to knock. Remember what I told you to say. I may act like I forced you in here, so go along with me, okay?"

"I guess that would keep up the charade that we're enemies."

"I never actually said I wasn't," he stated. "I said I cared for your cousin, and she wouldn't want anything bad to happen to you."

"Or Axel, right?" I asked, wondering if he had the same attitude for him.

"Yeah, right," he said, sarcastically, knocking on the door.

I heard a muffled voice telling us to come in. Viktor grabbed the handle and took hold of my arm. He definitely was doing a good job of pretending to force me inside. The way he held onto my arm, I felt pretty sure there would be a bruise forming soon.

We walked inside the dimly lit office and I immediately spotted Axel sitting in one of the chairs in front of Manual's desk. His back was to me, but I was grateful he appeared unharmed.

"Axel," I exclaimed, trying to break free of Viktor's grip. "Let me go, Viktor!" I demanded, but he wouldn't release me.

He led me toward the desk where Manual was seated, elbows leaning on the desk with his hands folded together. He looked tired. When I reached Axel, I noticed he was tied to the chair with a gag in his mouth. "Why is he restrained?" I demanded.

Manual sat straight in his chair and smiled at me. "Well, I knew you wouldn't be far behind." He looked at Viktor and asked, "Where'd you find her?"

"In the hall by the kitchen. She said she couldn't sleep and was lost searching for the kitchen for something to eat.

"Viktor's right. You told me I was free to roam around so why was I dragged in here like a criminal?"

Manual laughed boisterously. "Good one, Ruth Ann. I know you and Axel had some kind of plan to try and escape."

"No, we didn't," I answered, truthfully.

"Then why did Axel get caught coming out of your bedroom a little while ago?" he asked me.

"I have no idea!" I retorted. "I wasn't in there, remember?"

"You're lying to me, Ruth Ann," he said, his smile replaced with a nasty scowl. "I've been very accommodating with you, but you're trying my patience."

"I can't force you to believe me, but I won't admit to something I didn't do."

Manual took some time to think about what I said. "Well," he began. "Maybe you were innocent in this situation, but I refuse to be taken for a fool. I'll let you off the hook this time, but if you do anything against me, you'll be sorry."

Axel shook violently in his chair. "Ease up Eklund," Manual said, standing and walking to him. He reached and took the gag out of his mouth.

"Don't you threaten her!" he screeched with a hoarse voice.

"Shut up, Eklund! What are you going to do about it? You're tied to this chair and my guard is right here ready to kill you if I give the order."

Axel eyed me desperately but didn't say a word. "Manual," I said, "Why is he tied to the chair?"

"He wasn't cooperating, Ruth Ann." Manual looked back at Axel and asked, "So, are you ready to tell me what you were doing coming out of Ruth Ann's bedroom?"

"I already told you everything!" he barked. "I jumped over the railing and walked out Ruth Ann's door. She wasn't in there, and her door was unlocked."

"It sounds too simple," Manual replied, rubbing his chin with his stubby fingers. "But, I guess it could've happened that way." He looked at Viktor and asked his opinion.

"Sounds logical. He probably went in search of her," he answered, pointing to me and surprising Axel. Axel eyed me suspiciously, and I ever so carefully nodded my head hoping he would understand that Viktor was an ally.

Manual waved his arm in the air. "Enough. It's almost morning, and we have to prepare to fly to Sweden to retrieve your necklace." He looked only at me and asked, well, more likely ordered, "You are coming, Ruth Ann. I need you to lead the way."

If he only knew the necklace was only a few feet away with Isabella. "Ruth Ann can't go," Axel bellowed. "Only I can get the necklace out of my safe."

"I don't trust you," Manual said. "I think you can tell Ruth Ann how to get into your precious safe."

"My safe can only be opened with my fingerprint. Ruth Ann can't do it."

I was stunned at how fast he came up with that lie. I knew for a fact the safe had a simple digital combination, and I even knew what it was. Axel, however, didn't take his eyes off Manual. "Can you untie my hands, please? I'm not so young anymore, and my arms are killing me." I laughed inside at how nonchalant he was.

"Oh, uh, fine, Viktor, cut the ropes."

Viktor walked to Axel, pulled a large knife out of the back of his pants, and cut the thick ropes from behind the chair. "Done, boss," Viktor said, placing the knife back in his pants.

"There, Eklund," Manual said, watching Axel rub his hands together. "Now, how are we going to solve our little dilemma?"

"Easy, you take me."

"I think you're trying to trick me," Manual said, irritated. "You wouldn't try to pull a fast one, would you?"

"Why would I? If you don't get what you want, you'll kill me, and come back here and kill Ruth Ann," Axel said, casually.

"You have a point," Manual replied. "I'm tired, and not thinking clearly. Your stupid stunt woke me out of a peaceful night's sleep. I think I'm going back to bed, and in a few hours, I'll let you know my answer." Manual stood and started to walk toward the door.

"Hey," I hollered. "What are we supposed to do?"

"Go back to bed," he stated.

Axel said, "I'd rather wait in here. My room is not exactly comfortable."

"Ah, yes, I accidentally put you in a spare room, not a bedroom," Manual said, laughing. "I guess you can wait in here." He turned to Viktor and told him to keep watch at the door and check on Axel every now and again. "Ruth Ann, don't you want to head up to your bedroom? I believe it's quite comfortable in there."

"Yes, but I'm not tired," I said, truthfully. I wanted to remain down here so I could get to Isabella, Inga and Carlos.

"Suit yourself," he said, shrugging. "However, if you remain in here, the door will be locked."

"I never said I wanted to stay in here with Axel. I'd like to pop into the kitchen and get some hot tea. It'll help me fall asleep."

"I'll take you," Manual said, holding his hand out for me.

"You go, I'm fine by myself," I answered fearing if he joined me, I'd never figure out a way to get back to Carlos, Inga and Isabella. "You said you were really tired, so I'll walk with you to the stairs, and then I'll be fine."

"Fine, let's go," Manual said, lowering his hand. "I'd join you for a bite, but I need to get some sleep. I think better when I'm well rested."

I hoped he'd never rest! Then we might have a chance of distracting him until we could devise an escape plan.

Chapter 30

"Here we are," Manual said, pushing the door to the kitchen. He reached around and hit the light switch. "Just turn it off when you're through."

"I sure will," I said, chipper. "I hope having some tea will make me sleepy. I also need sleep to think clearly."

He nodded, said good-night to me and disappeared into the dark hall.

"Finally," I whispered. I figured I had to make this look good, so I walked to the stove and grabbed the stainless-steel teapot. I filled it with some water, turned on the heat, and gave it a few minutes. While I was waiting, I grabbed a mug, put a tea bag in it, and even grabbed a biscotti from a glass jar on the counter. I took a bite and left the crumbs clearly visible on the white marble counter. Once the water was hot, I poured it, dunked the tea bag, threw it out and took several sips, which did taste excellent! I felt my ruse was good enough, so I turned and headed back to Manual's office and the gym.

"What took you so long?" Viktor barked.

"I had to get rid of your boss, and make it look like I spent time in the kitchen. Why, did anything happen?"

"No, I'm just a little jumpy, that's all."

"I'm going to get the others from the sauna. You unlock the door so Axel can come out." I was shocked at how fast he obeyed my orders.

"Finally!" Inga exclaimed, looking pale and a little sweaty.

"Are you alright?" I asked her, worried.

"Carlos turned on the damn sauna, and we couldn't get it to turn off," she turned and glared fiercely at poor, wet, Carlos.

"Sorry, I set the timer."

"For forty-five minutes!" Inga snapped. "I'm soaking wet!"

"Forget about it," I said, anxiously. "Let's go."

They followed me into the hall where Viktor and Axel were waiting. "Mr. Eklund," Inga bellowed. "You don't look too bad."

"No, I'm fine, Inga. But, we don't have a lot of time."

"Yeah," Viktor chimed in. "What's the plan? I cannot get caught helping you!"

"We need to get up to the second floor and put this necklace on Prunella first!" Isabella said anxiously, opening her blouse to reveal Blue Ice.

Viktor looked like he saw a ghost. "Are you alright?" I asked, reaching out to catch him as he wavered.

"I'm fine," he said, regaining his balance. "I just didn't expect to see that!" He quickly added, "Hey! What's that thing doing here? I thought we had to fly to Sweden to get it."

Axel answered swiftly, "We had to buy time with your boss. We were waiting for Isabella to get here with the necklace so she could save Prunella."

He eyed Axel oddly, "What do you mean *save* Prunella?"

"She's in danger, Viktor," I answered. "Blue Ice could

252

protect her from Manual."

"Mr. Marquez wants to kill her? I don't believe that for a second. He's obsessed with her and wants her for himself."

"It's a long of a story, and quite unbelievable," I said, starting to doubt my visions with Meme.

"Fine, but I don't see why we have to put that thing on her neck," he said, pointing with a shaky hand. "Plus, she's a witch!"

"I am not a witch!" Isabella barked. "I've told you that before, and you need to believe me."

"Well, if you're not one, that grandmother of yours is," he said.

"She's dead," Isabella stated, upset. "You don't have to fear her, or me, again."

"Well," he said, thinking about it. "We do have to go to Prunella anyway. I guess it wouldn't hurt to put that thing on her."

"Finally, can we go now?" Inga asked impatiently. "I don't want that Manual or any of his guards catching us."

"I can get us there without being seen," Viktor retorted. "Follow me."

We agreed and followed behind Viktor closely as he led us down the hall, stopping near the foyer. "Shhh," he whispered. "Let me make sure the coast is clear." We huddled against the wall and waited for Viktor to wave us forward. "Don't make a sound, understand?" We nodded and moved toward the wall near the stairs.

Instead of walking up the stairs, he put his hand against the wall at the bottom of the staircase. The lighting was minimal, but I managed to see him push a hidden button and suddenly a secret door slid open. "No questions," he quickly said, looking directly at me.

He disappeared inside the wall, and we all hurried in. We followed Viktor through a narrow, stifling tunnel. "Whoa, it's so hot I can't breathe," I said, feeling it was safe to speak.

"There's no air circulating in here," Axel said, wiping his brow with his sleeve.

"He's right," Viktor said. "Only a few trustworthy people know about this tunnel."

"And you're one of them, I assume," Inga said, sarcastically.

He gave a little growl her way, and I stepped in because Viktor was our only chance of getting to Prunella. "Back off, Inga," I said, calmly. "Viktor is kind enough to help us, so please give him a break."

"Fine," she stammered. Inga wasn't easy to win over. She was so used to protecting Prunella that trusting a stranger was rare.

We trudged on in spite of the lack of air and daunting heat. I usually didn't handle these conditions well, but I took a few deep breaths and told myself it was just temporary. "Don't we have to get to the second floor?" Axel inquired, wiping the sweat that continued to drip down his cheeks.

Axel's question was soon answered. We hit a dead end and I didn't notice Viktor take a slight turn to the left. "We go up here," he said, taking hold of the metal handrail and stepping onto the narrowest set of stairs I'd ever seen. "Be careful, the stairs are small, and very steep."

I went after Viktor, and Axel was right on my heels. I had to turn and ask him to give me some space so I didn't trip on his feet as he took each step. "I don't want to be too far behind in case you miss the step." he said.

"I won't miss a step, but I'll trip if my foot gets caught on yours," I snapped, knowing I shouldn't have. He was only trying to protect me, but in these conditions, I wasn't thinking clearly. "Sorry, Axel," I said.

We trudged on, Isabella and Carlos behind Axel, and Inga in the rear. "How far up are we going? I thought Prunella was on the *second* floor?" Inga called out from several feet below me.

"She is," I called back just as Viktor reached the top and disappeared left down another tunnel.

"Shhh," Viktor whispered from several feet ahead of me. "We need to be more careful up here."

"These walls are thick cement," Axel said, touching the rough walls on both sides of him. "Nobody could hear us inside here!"

"I don't trust anyone or anything right now," Viktor said, waiting for us to catch up with him. "I need to think of a plan just in case we're spotted going into Prunella's bedroom."

"So, this tunnel leads right into her room?" I said, happy we didn't have to go into the hall first.

"Yes," he said. "I just can't remember which opening it is."

"Are the rooms on either side of hers occupied?" Inga asked.

"Yes!" he exclaimed. "My boss is sleeping in the room next to her."

"Great," Axel muttered, angrily. "And he knows how to maneuver these tunnels, so he probably goes in there and watches her."

"He wouldn't do that!" I snapped at Axel. "That's an invasion of privacy."

"And you think he cares about that?" Axel spat back, aggravated.

"Can we just get to Prunella?" Isabella begged. "I feel a

strong sensation that she needs to put on this necklace right away!"

"Is she in danger?" Viktor asked, terrified. "I just can't risk going in my boss's bedroom."

"I'll look first," I offered.

"NO!" Viktor barked. "If you walked into his room instead of Prunella's, he'll figure out that I told you about the tunnels."

"Look, Viktor," Axel said, interrupting. "If Ruth Ann is caught, it's all of us against him. We could restrain him in his room until we get to Prunella and escape."

"You'll never get out of here unseen," Viktor bellowed.

I carefully took hold of his arm and said, "With your help we can."

"Me?" he questioned, perplexed. "I can't leave here. They'll kill me."

"Not if you come with us," Axel said. "I'll get you protection."

The whites of Viktor's eyes were so huge I could see the horror in them even in the tunnel's dim lighting. "No way! I'll never agreed to this. It doesn't matter where I go or who you have protecting me, he'll find me and kill me!"

Carlos, who had been extremely quiet so far laughed. "Don't be so dramatic. I find it hard to believe Manual Marquez would care if you left the country."

I knew that wasn't going to go over well. If Carlos was in punching distance of Viktor, I'm pretty sure he would be on the ground unconscious. I noticed the regret in Carlos' expression once the words left his mouth. If Carlos had learned anything since meeting us, it's that anything is possible. "I'm sorry, Viktor," Carlos said, humbly. "I'm overheated, tired, and ready to get out of these tunnels. I'm sure you're worried your boss will seek revenge against you, but we don't even know if we'll get caught or not."

"He's got a good point," Axel said. "I think we count the openings in this tunnel and then think about how many rooms are on this side of the floor. What do you say?"

"I'll go back and count door openings," Inga said, noticing the slight cracks in the walls shaped like doors. "I see them now that my eyes have adjusted." She took off without waiting for an answer. I soon lost sight of her in the darkened tunnel.

"How many rooms are on this floor, Viktor?" I asked, curiously.

"How do I know?" he snapped.

"You live here, don't you?" Axel inquired. "Think, man, it's not that hard."

Viktor rubbed his temples with his hands and shut his eyes. "There have to be about seven or eight doors on each side of the hall."

"About or exactly?" I asked, telling him to imagine each room. "Where's your room?"

"Mine?" he asked, confused. "My room and the other employees who live here stay in another building out back."

"You don't even get to live in this massive mansion?" Carlos asked, baffled.

"No, I don't," he replied, looking like a deflated toddler. "I guess I never thought about it before, but I should be living in here! There's a million bedrooms in this place!"

"You're right, you should," I said.

Inga reappeared and said, "Up to here there are three doors on this side of the hall. If Prunella's smack dab in the middle, there should be three rooms on the other side of this door." She waited for us to compliment her deductive reasoning and shot us a nasty glare when I suggested she count the doors on the other side before coming to conclusions.

"She'll be back to prove her point. I did tell her that Prunella's room was in the middle and has a huge balcony."

"And that balcony's right in the middle of this estate," Viktor said, proudly. "It's got to be hers!"

"It is," Inga said, huffing and puffing a little. "There are three doors and then another door that's open right next to the main staircase."

"Nobody saw you, did they?" Viktor asked, anxiously.

"No, it's still pretty early, and I don't think anyone is up yet," she answered, grateful she wasn't the one who blew our cover.

"We feel fairly confident this door leads to Prunella's bedroom," I said. "Let's go in."

Viktor nodded reluctantly. His large hand shook as he pushed the tiny button. "It opens into a closet right off the door from the hall."

Axel shook his head as the door slowly released and slid open. "If it opens into a closet we shouldn't have been so worried about being seen by Manual."

"I guess not," Viktor said, calming down since he realized what Axel said made sense.

"Let's go in," Axel said, stepping around Viktor and disappearing inside the closet. I went next, and then Isabella, Carlos, Inga and lastly, Viktor. He showed us the button to close the tunnel door and turned to face us.

"We're safe in here, but we still don't know who's on the other side of those doors," he whispered, pointing to the double doors to his right. "They lead to the living room, and my boss could be sleeping on the couch in there."

"No, he's not," I said confidently. "When he left Axel and me in his office, he said he desperately needed sleep."

"You're right!" Viktor blurted out loudly, immediately covering his mouth.

"He wanted to go to his bedroom and sleep. So, he's not in here," I said, feeling pretty smart that I figured that one out. "I think we have plenty of time to go inside and find Prunella. We might have some convincing to do to get her to understand what's really happening here."

"What on earth are you talking about, Ruth Ann?" Inga inquired. "Why wouldn't she want to leave here?"

"Her memory isn't back," I said, regretting I hadn't entirely fill her in on Prunella's condition. "She actually cares for Manual at the moment, and he promised her therapy that would help her get stronger."

"Tell her he's lying!" Inga barked, angrily. "I thought she could walk again, and she remembered everything?"

"Well," I began, but stopped.

"It'll be fine," Isabella said, displaying the necklace around her neck. "Once I get this on her, she'll be protected and willing to listen to us."

"Why?" Viktor asked, curiously. "Is that some magical stone or something?"

"Something like that," I answered for Isabella. "However, it sure seems like it's been more bad luck than good luck to me."

"And to everyone who has touched it for most of its past," Axel mumbled under his breath, but loud enough for me to hear.

"Who's going in first?" I quickly asked, before anyone could ask further questions.

"I'll go," Axel stated, walking toward the doors.

"We should go together," Inga commented.

"But, if there's even the slightest chance Manual's around, he doesn't know you guys are here. If Axel, Viktor, and I go in and get caught, you three will still be able to rescue us."

"That's a brilliant observation, Ruth Ann," Axel said. "Even though you're exhausted, you're really on the ball."

"I'll collapse after this is over," I admitted, truthfully.

"We'll make sure you don't," Axel said, kindly. "I agree that Inga, Carlos and Isabella stay in the closet until we make sure it's safe, and we talk to Prunella. If we all go marching in her bedroom, we might scare her. She could scream, unintentionally and alert the guard to come in and check on her."

"I doubt we'd *scare* her," Inga said, irritated. "But, she might scream out of *happiness*."

Viktor, watched our banter and decided it was time to go inside her room. He stepped into the darkened living area. I quickly followed his steps with Axel in the rear. He shut the door behind him, leaving only about an inch opened. I turned and heard rumbling noises from the closet, and three sets of eyes peering through the opening in the door. I giggled to myself wondering who was stuck kneeling, who was on top and who was in the middle. Isabella was the tiniest, so she was probably on her knees, Inga was the tallest, so she must be the set of eyes on the top, leaving poor Carlos in the middle.

Viktor walked toward the bedroom doors where Prunella was more than likely sleeping. As I walked closer, I noticed a digital clock's red light shining brightly. It was morning, five in the morning. We didn't have much time before Manual and his guards would be rouse and begin looking for us.

"Shhh," Viktor whispered as he gently pushed the half-opened bedroom doors. Axel was standing next to him, and I was behind the two of them. Axel looked inside her bedroom, and quickly turned to tell me she was in her bed asleep.

I nodded, and watched as Viktor let Axel in first, and motioned for me to follow him. Viktor respectfully stayed back, giving me confidence that he truly was on our side. Axel grabbed my hand and we quietly tiptoed to Prunella's bed. She was on her side with her hands cradled under her cheek. She looked so young and innocent lying there that I hated to wake her, but we didn't have the time to let her wake up on her own. Axel nudged me closer to her. I took the hint and laid my hand gently on her shoulder, but she didn't move. I gave her a soft shake, and still, she didn't flinch. I turned and looked at Axel, confused. I whispered, "She's not waking up!"

"Give her a more forceful shake, Ruth Ann," Axel said. "She's a heavy sleeper."

"Oh," I reached and took hold of her arm, picking it up and wobbling it around. She did not rouse and there was no reaction.

"What's going on?" Viktor complained from across the room. "I don't hear Prunella's voice."

"That's because she's not waking up!" I snapped loudly, irritated.

Axel and I quickly turned to see if my voice woke her up, but again, nothing. She didn't move an inch. A sudden rush of dread flowed through my body as I reached and took hold of Prunella's limp wrist. "Oh, my God!" a female voice cried from the doorway. "Is she dead?" I didn't need to turn to see who said those words because I knew Inga's voice well enough. I was only focused on finding a pulse in Prunella's wrist.

Thankfully, I felt a slow and faint pulse. "Phew," Inga said, now by my side. I backed off a little and realized I had been holding my own breath. I took a deep breath and looked at Axel. He was pale as a ghost. "It's okay, Axel. She's alive," I said. "Someone's drugged her." I said, secretly fearing that she had slipped back into her coma.

Carlos intervened, holding an empty syringe and a tiny glass bottle. "Where did you get that?" Viktor snapped.

"Your boss must've drugged her," Carlos answered. "It was on her nightstand," he said, pointing to a few empty glass vials and used syringes lying on her nightstand.

"He wouldn't drug her!" Viktor spewed. "Somebody else must've done it."

"Who?" Axel asked, angrily.

Viktor didn't respond but walked to the nightstand and picked up one of the bottles. Suddenly, without warning, the glass shattered in his hand. "Viktor," Isabella bellowed. "You're bleeding!"

He looked down at his hands and realized that he had crushed the bottle. He grabbed a tissue and held it in his hands. "This stops now!" he declared, furious. "I won't let anyone inject Prunella again. We will get her, and all of you, out of here today!"

Finally, I thought to myself. Even though we had a long way to go to get out of here, I felt quite sure we would be leaving and never coming back.

Chapter 31

I was surprised at Viktor's immediate denial that Manual would drug Prunella since he had drugged her himself on the plane ride here. When I mentioned that, he emphatically stated that she was sedated on the plane to keep her calm. He was angry, but it looked to me that she was being sedated here, too. Thankfully, he came around after examining a bottle on the nightstand and realizing it wasn't the same drug he gave Prunella on the airplane. I noticed his hand was bleeding through the tissue so I quickly ran into her bathroom and grabbed a hand towel. Before leaving, I spotted a pile of makeup on the bathroom sink counter. I recognized that makeup! It was Prunella's, but why would it be spread all over the counter? There were remnants of blush sprinkled in the sink, but how could Prunella stand at the sink putting on makeup if she wasn't able to walk yet? I had a sick, funny feeling in the pit of my stomach and knew something was terribly wrong. "She can't be," I said to myself. "She isn't faking her condition, is she?"

"Who's faking what?" a male voice called out from the door.

"Oh, it's just you, Carlos. I was talking to myself. Nothing to worry about."

"Don't even try to brush me off, Ruth Ann," he said, walking toward the sink. "What's taking you so long in here?"

"It's nothing, Carlos," I tried to say, but he wasn't taking it. "Fine. What do you see at the sink?"

"A mess."

"Besides that, Carlos. Think about it. *Who made the mess*?"

"Ah, I see where you're going with this. But, what's the big deal? You told us that Prunella was getting stronger and standing at a sink to put on her makeup isn't too taxing."

"Axel and I haven't exactly told you, Isabella and Inga the entire truth."

"What do you mean, Ruth Ann?" Carlos asked, becoming impatient with me.

"When we left the hospital, I told you three that Prunella needed a lot of therapy, but what I haven't told you is that she's still unable to walk or even stand. And ..."

"There's more?" Carlos asked, stunned.

"Yes. She has no recollection of anything that happened since around Thanksgiving. She doesn't remember what happened in Sweden at all. She thinks we were there for business and that she had an accident. Remember, she was in a coma! I'm sorry, Carlos. I didn't do this to deceive you. I knew once we got back to Deer Creek, you would find out anyway. And, once she woke up, all I wanted to do was get her home. Until this happened, and we were kidnapped!"

I could see Carlos' brain spinning. Finally, his tightened, angry expression relaxed when he realized Axel and I only did what we thought best. "It's okay, Ruth Ann," he said. "You didn't intend to deceive us. I probably would've done the same thing."

"Thanks for understanding, Carlos. I'm pretty sure Isabella has already figured it out, but when Inga does ... watch out. She may not understand our reasoning so easily. She's going to be furious with me for not letting her stay in Sweden to take care of Prunella."

"She'll get over it," he declared, and suggested we get the towel back to Viktor.

"What took you two so long?" Inga bellowed. "Was it that difficult to find a towel?"

"Let it go, Inga," Carlos said, taking the towel from me and handing it to Viktor, who was sitting on the edge of the large bed.

"How's your hand?" I asked him. "You shouldn't have done that."

"I was so mad I didn't think clearly," he said, wrapping the small towel around his hand. He looked at Prunella and shook his head. "What are we going to do now? My boss or Sal could come in here at any moment."

"It's still early, Viktor," I said, looking at the clock in the living area. "It's not even six yet. Do they wake up this early around here?"

"Not usually," Viktor answered. "I'm just getting nervous, really nervous that I'll get caught helping you."

An idea popped in my head. "Hey, why don't we take turns keeping watch at the main door? If anyone hears someone coming toward her room, we'll hide."

"Hide where?" Inga asked, looking around the big bedroom. "Outside of that closet and the bathroom, there's nowhere to hide. And, I doubt we'd make it all the way back to the closet if someone was coming. It's right next to the door!"

"I get it, Inga," I snapped. "Anyone else have a suggestion?"

"Yeah, I do," Axel said. "Let's put the necklace on Prunella and carry her into the tunnels. We can figure out where to go once we're safe in the tunnels."

"Great plan!" I agreed. "Viktor?"

"Um, well, I guess we could do that. But, if they come in here and find Prunella missing, the first thing my boss will do is check the tunnels."

"Maybe he'll think the guard outside her door fell asleep and someone took her out that way," Isabella said. "It would buy us more time anyway."

"I guess," Viktor said, giving in, skeptically.

Axel asked if Carlos and Inga would help carry Prunella. Viktor put up a valiant fight, but because his hand still bleeding, he backed off. I volunteered to be the lookout at the door while Isabella grabbed Prunella's possessions. As I waited by the door, I realized the necklace was still around Isabella's neck! I was about to hurry back to the bedroom when I heard voices coming from the hall. I looked for the others hoping they were on their way to meet me in the closet, but they were still in the bedroom. What was taking them so long?

I was torn deciding whether I should tell them to hurry up or keep listening at the door. I figured by the time I went back to the bedroom, they'd be coming anyway, so I chose to lean the side of my head against the door and eavesdrop. "You idiot!" Manual hollered very loudly, obviously very close by. "How dare you fall asleep guarding her! How do you know if anyone got inside?"

"Boss, nobody got by me. I only just dozed off. It was a long night, and nobody tried to get by me, I swear."

"Sal, do you understand how valuable that woman is to

me? She's my everything, and if anyone got in there and touched a hair on her head ... I will ... murder them with my own bloody hands, and then come back and do the same to you! DO YOU HEAR ME, FOOL?" he hollered, furious.

"Yes, sir, I do. I promise nobody came through this door. The keys are attached to my body," he said, lifting his shirt and showing Manual the rope tied around his waist with the key to Prunella's room shining at the end. "See? The rope hasn't moved, and the key's still here."

"Well, you better hope nothing has happened inside there. Now, open the door!"

"Uh-oh," I whispered, frantic. "We gotta get out of here, now!" I whipped my head around and saw all of them, except Prunella standing behind me. I was about to react when Inga placed her hand, rather forcefully, over my mouth and pulled me inside the closet.

"Hey," I complained. "I wasn't going to yell. You didn't have to do that!"

"I thought we surprised you. You were so focused on listening at the door you didn't notice us until you turned around," Inga explained. "I thought you were going to ask why Prunella isn't with us."

"Actually ..."

"We didn't have enough time to get her out of the bed and over here," Carlos said. "She's dead weight right now."

"We can't leave without her," I exclaimed, when we heard the keys in the door. "They're coming in."

"Shhh," Viktor said. "Let's listen and make sure they don't realize anyone was in there."

"What about the stuff on the nightstand?" Isabella asked. "You smashed a glass bottle of whatever drug they were injecting her with."

"Hopefully, Manual won't notice," Axel said. "Before we rushed out of the bedroom, I took a quick look. It looks the same as it did when we went in here."

"What if he opens this closet?" Inga asked, worried. "We're sitting ducks in here."

"He has no reason to come in here," Viktor said. "He only cares about checking on Prunella. Let's listen."

Viktor and Axel leaned against the door with the rest of us standing back. "Hey," I said, thinking of an important point. "How did you know to get out of the bedroom so fast?"

"We heard Manual screaming at the guard," Axel said, turning and answering me.

"Oh, he was pretty loud," I said. "Can you hear anything yet? Is Sal with him or did Manual come in alone?"

"Stop asking so many questions, Ruth Ann!" Inga barked, quietly. "Nobody can hear anything if you keep yacking."

I scowled at her, but she was right. I guess I was just nervous, and when I'm nervous, I babble.

Axel turned around and said, "Sal was in there."

"Was?" Carlos inquired.

"I heard Manual order him to wait in the hall," Axel responded.

"So, Sal's relieved that Prunella is still safe in her bed," Inga said. "Anything else?"

"Manual's talking to Prunella," Viktor said, his ear against the door.

Viktor cracked the door an inch. "If you see him or hear him coming out of her bedroom, slowly shut the door."

I waited while Viktor peeked out through the door. "He's with her. I can hear and see him right now. He's next to her bed and just sat on the edge. He's talking to her, which is strange since she's drugged."

"Can you hear what he's saying to her?" Isabella asked, suddenly realizing she forgot to take Blue Ice off her neck and put it on Prunella's. "Oh, my God!" she cried. "I can't believe I forgot!"

"It's probably best," Axel said. "If Manual spotted it on her, we would be big trouble."

"But, that's what he wants in the first place!" Inga cried. "Maybe if he got it, he would let us go."

"He doesn't even know you're here, Inga," I reminded her.

"He will if that necklace suddenly appears!" Inga said, making a good point.

"Yeah, I think we played it safe for the moment," Axel agreed. "Manual would've blown a gasket if he found the necklace around her neck. Unless," he stopped and looked at Isabella. "Hey, this isn't like last time when ..."

"No," Isabella stopped him before he finished his question. "It can be removed this time. I just put a safety hex on it as my grandmother requested."

Viktor turned slowly toward Isabella with a terrified look in his eyes. "What do you mean, your grandmother requested? Isn't she dead?"

"Yes," I chimed in instantly. "But, Isabella has these dreams, and Meme's in them. I have them too, but it's just our subconscious telling us what we need to do. Don't worry, Viktor. Just keep listening at the door and see what he's doing now." I hoped that settled his nerves.

Isabella gave me an odd look. I shook my head, hoping she understood that Viktor and Manual didn't understand visions and were very frightened of Meme.

Chapter 32

"That's crazy, Ruth Ann!" Carlos bellowed. "If we try and trick Marquez and he finds out, we're goners."

"But, it might work," I said, hoping the others would be open-minded.

Axel had a tiny, evil smirk on his face giving me the impression he might be on board. Viktor wasn't listening because I had pulled the others to the back of the closet out of earshot. "No way, Ruth Ann!" Inga said, adamantly.

"Think about it, if we can pull this off, we'll be home free. We could be home by the end of the day!" I said.

"Let me try and understand this," Carlos began. "You want us to turn out the lights and have Isabella march out of the closet exposing her chest with that, that," he refrained, pointed to Blue Ice, and continued. "That pain in the ass necklace!" He added, "And then, you want Isabella to float across the room and chant a few words that convince Manual he'll be cursed if he keeps Prunella or the necklace. Did I get that right? Sounds pretty far-fetched to me."

"Well, sort of," I replied, realizing how unbelievable it sounded after Carlos replayed it. "The curtains are still drawn, so if one of us can sneak out and turn off the lights, there'll be a nice dim glow in the room. Then Isabella can quietly sneak out of the closet and suddenly appear in the doorway to the bedroom. Manual will be so startled, he won't know how she appeared. Remember, Sal is still guarding the door and nobody will be able to get in here. It's perfect, and I might add, the only option I've heard that could work," I said, feeling confident. "If Isabella can convince him she's cursing him, it may work. He told me she and Meme really frightened him." I turned to Isabella and asked, "You can chant words that sounds like you're cursing him, can't you?"

"Of course, I can, in fact," Isabella smiled devilishly and added, "I could put an actual curse on him!"

"No!" I insisted.

"Why not, Ruth Ann?" Axel asked. "Let him rot."

"I'm not looking to curse the man, just get him out of our way so we can rescue Prunella and go back to Deer Creek. We can contact the police after we're safe," I said, frustrated. "However, if everyone else wants the man cursed, then I'm outnumbered."

"Curse the fool!" Viktor called out from the door. He must've heard our conversation despite our attempt to be discreet. "He should be drugged, kidnapped, and tortured for what he's done to all of you."

"Thanks, Viktor," I said.

We went and huddled near the door where Viktor was keeping watch. Axel asked if he could look, and Viktor willingly obliged. "He's talking to her," Axel said. "Why would he be talking to Prunella if she's unconscious." He looked at Viktor and asked, "Are you sure Sal didn't sneak back in?"

"No."

"But, either he's crazy or ..."

"Prunella's awake," I finished for Axel.

"Is that possible?" Inga questioned. "I mean, just a few minutes ago she was out cold."

It was the right time to mention what I found in the bathroom. "That doesn't mean Prunella was able to stand and put on her own makeup," Isabella said. "Maybe she had help from a maid."

"I haven't seen a maid," I said, confused.

Inga looked confused, and I knew why. It was time to tell her, the last person on earth that I wanted to tell, the truth. "I'm sorry, Inga. I knew if you were aware of Prunella's true condition, you would never have left Sweden. And, we needed you to go home with Cassandra, Carlos and Isabella. "Please understand, you knew almost everything."

"I knew she was awake and in physical therapy to regain her strength," Inga spat, angrily. "I *didn't* know she couldn't walk or had no memory of what happened in Stockholm, and in Axel's office when she collapsed. So, she has no idea she was cursed in Jamaica and wanted us dead?"

"No, Inga," Axel answered her. "The doctor told us not to force any information on her. She needs to remember on her own."

I wanted to make Inga feel better and said, "Inga, I know how close and protective you are of Prunella. I didn't want you worried she'd never recover. I did it to protect you, all of you actually."

"It's okay, Ruth Ann," Inga said, calming down. "I don't like it, and please don't ever do that to me again, but I kind of understand your motives."

"Thanks," I replied, grateful for her compassion. Inga exudes toughness, but inside, she's a soft, caring person. Well, when she wants to be!

"I think someone's inside the bedroom with Manual and

Prunella," Axel quickly said. "He's asking questions, and I swear I hear another voice."

"What questions? What voice?" I asked, worried. "Is it a male or female voice answering?"

"Do you think it's Prunella? Maybe she's been fooling us again!" Carlos said. "Remember, she was against us and tried everything to get rid of us."

"That's because she was wearing the cursed necklace," Isabella reminded him, frustrated. "We fixed that, remember?" She added, "That's when she collapsed in Axel's office."

"I know, Isabella. I was there, too! But, something very odd is happening in that bedroom. First, we find her unconscious with empty syringes on the nightstand. Then, Ruth Ann finds her makeup all over the bathroom sink implying she was *standing* at the sink. Now, Manual's in there talking away and you're hearing a response. It leads to only one conclusion, doesn't it?" Carlos waited for our response. "Come on people! Prunella isn't unconscious or a cripple, she's playing us and working with Manual Marquez."

Nobody could speak at first after hearing Carlos lay it out for us. It sounded outrageous, but what else could it be? Viktor ended up being the first to speak. "Nonsense!" he barked. "She's too kind of a person to be so deceitful. I don't believe it, and I hardly know the woman."

"Viktor's right," I said. "It can't be Prunella. I think Manual's gone a bit crazy. What's he asking her anyway? Can you make out any of the words from inside here?"

"No," Axel and Viktor answered.

"But," Viktor started to say, "we've heard another voice. Whose voice is that?"

"We need to find that out right now," Axel said, grabbing

the door and opening it another inch.

"Be careful, Axel," I said. "We can't risk getting caught."

"I thought we were going to turn off the lights and let Isabella out," Inga said.

"Only if Manual is alone," I said. "If there's someone besides Prunella in the room, it won't work. We only know that Manual is superstitious when it comes to Isabella and her grandmother."

"What are we going to do now?" Inga cried, anxiously. "I need to find out if Ms. Prunella's alright."

"I've got a funny feeling she is," I mumbled. "Maybe putting on the necklace would've avoided this."

"I'm sorry, Ruth Ann," Isabella said, feeling horrible. "I totally forgot about it. It was my main duty, and I let you down. I'll never forgive myself if anything happens to her or us."

"We don't have time for pity right now," Axel snapped. "We need to see who else is in there. I'm going to try and sneak around the room and get near that bedroom opening."

"No!" I cried. "Too dangerous. He'll see you for sure."

"We don't have a choice, Ruth Ann," Carlos said. "Go ahead, Axel, do it."

Everyone else agreed so I conceded.

We struggled to get into position so we could all watch Axel tiptoe his way toward the double doors to the bedroom.

"He made it!" Isabella said, relieved. "Look, he's trying to peek around the door so he can see better."

We watched carefully as Axel got on his knees and looked inside the bedroom. I crossed every finger hoping Prunella wasn't the one talking back to Manual.

Axel only took a moment, and then stood and made his way back to us. "She's awake!" he said, out of breath as he shut the door almost all the way before delivering this distressing news.

"Awake?" I questioned him. "Are you sure? Maybe you heard another woman's voice, like a maid."

He vehemently shook his head. "No, it was Prunella."

"Tell us what you heard and saw, Axel," Viktor said, ignoring my comments.

"When I got to the bedroom door, I leaned over and looked inside. It took me only one second to see to see that Prunella was sitting up, smiling and conversing with him."

"I don't believe it!" I exclaimed, horrified at his news.

"I'm not lying," Axel adamantly responded. "She was smiling and being very sweet to him."

"Ruth Ann," Isabella said. "Just let Axel finish. I know you're really upset right now, but we don't know the reason what Prunella is doing. It could be an act."

"She tried to hurt us before!" Inga spewed.

"I've explained that hundreds of times to you, Inga," Isabella said exasperated. "It wasn't her, she was under a curse. Let it go!"

"Can I go on?" Axel inquired, anxiously. "We don't have a lot of time."

He waited for me to argue, but I chose to keep my comments to myself until he was finished. "Good. Manual was bragging about some physical therapist that was coming today. He said she would be running up and down the stairs in no time.

"And," he said, elongating the word. "Prunella told him she was pretty strong already and didn't understand why he was having someone come to help her. Then he tried to convince her to let the therapist work with her. He said he would do anything for her, and he wanted her at her best for the up-coming event."

"What event?" Inga asked, confused. She looked at me as if I knew what Manual was referring to.

"I don't know, Inga. Why you looking at me?" I asked.

"Because you seem to omit pertinent information." She swiftly added, "For our own protection, of course."

Axel was growing impatient. He started to rub his head in frustration. "We don't know what he's planning, but it's something that includes my wife!"

"You don't think he needs Blue Ice for this event, do you?" I asked.

"But, he thinks the necklace is in Sweden," Inga stated, getting more and more muddled.

"We only did that to buy time, Inga," Axel answered. "What are we going to do now? My wife's looking forward to some unknown event. Maybe Manual wants Blue Ice so he can present it to her? What else could it be?"

"That does sound possible," Carlos said. "You know, he's about to leave Prunella in her bedroom and fly you two to Sweden to get the necklace."

"Our plan to have me appear out of thin air wearing Blue Ice could still work," Isabella said.

"Not here," Axel said. "The curtains have just been opened and the sun is flooding the room."

"I have an idea!" I said, hopefully. "I'm sure Manual will be calling us into his office, right?" Axel and Viktor nodded. "We can have Isabella, Inga and Carlos hide in the tunnels and wait for us to be called in to see him. I think it would be totally hilarious if Isabella came floating in his office and Axel and I pretend not to see her. Manual would think he was seeing things and freak out. I'm sure Viktor can get Isabella to his office without anyone catching them."

"I could do that," Viktor replied.

"That would be great!" I said, excited.

"This could work," Axel mumbled, obviously imagining all the scenarios that could pop up.

"What if he doesn't take you to his office?" Inga inquired, pessimistically. "He could order you to the dining room or the kitchen."

"Thanks for ruining the plan, Inga," Carlos retorted.

"No, Carlos," Axel jumped in to save Inga. "She's got a point. If he takes us somewhere else, this won't work."

"So, what are we going to do now?" Viktor asked, frustrated.

We stood in silence as Viktor went back to check on what was happening in Prunella's bedroom. He told us they were still talking, and his boss was smiling away. He couldn't see what Prunella was doing from his vantage point, but figured they were having a pleasant conversation.

"Okay," Axel began. "I think it's up to you, Viktor, to lead your boss into his office."

"What am I supposed to do?" Viktor responded, exasperated. "I have no say with him."

"I think if Manual starts talking about Blue Ice, you could whisper something like he might be overheard by a staff member, and it could be risky. You could suggest having the conversation in the privacy of his office with you guarding the door."

"That's brilliant!" I bellowed. "We've covered most angles. I think we wait until he leaves. Then Axel and I can change clothes and get into the foyer. We'll wait for him there and see where he wants to meet with us. I am hungry, so eating isn't such a bad idea."

"Hey!" Inga chimed in. "We're starving, too."

"We'll get you food," Axel said. "I'll find a way."

"I'll figure out a way to get some food to you wherever you three are hiding," Viktor said.

"Let's see what's going on in there," I suggested. "He can't stay here for too much longer. Obviously, he's planning something. I wonder if I could ask him. Maybe he'd confess and tell us what he's planning to do."

"You think he's going to tell us?" Axel asked, cynically.

"Who knows," I said. "He's slipped and said too much to me a few times since we've been here."

We took turns watching Manual talk and talk *and* talk to her. I was confused, scared, and suspicious about Prunella's behavior.

Chapter 33

When I took my turn listening, Manual raised his voice to an alarmingly loud level. At first, I jumped, but then regained my composure and listened intently. None of the others seemed to hear Manual's voice, probably because they were chatting amongst themselves further from the closet door.

"Prunella," Manual called loudly. "I know we just met, but the minute our eyes met, I knew you were the one for me. The only one!"

I listened for Prunella's response, but I couldn't hear anything but a mumbled female's voice.

"Don't worry, my dear, I know you are, but I can fix that immediately."

Oh, no, he had to be referring to that fact that Axel and Prunella were still married. What did he mean he could fix that immediately?

"Prunella, please, *I promise I won't touch a hair on his head*," Manual said, emphasizing the last part. That's a load of bull! He would just have one of his men *handle* Axel. Is she buying this?

"My turn," Inga said, trying to shove me aside.

"No! Wait, Inga," I said, standing my ground. "Give me

a minute longer. Manual's spilling good information."

"I can listen too, Ruth Ann," she insisted. I wasn't about to move an inch. I held my arm up to tell her I meant business, and that she needed to step aside for a little longer.

"Prunella," Manual continued. "You'll be the most beautiful woman in the room, and everyone will be jealous of you ... and me."

He paused, waiting for Prunella's response. Inga's head was now close enough to hear their conversation. She didn't know what was going on, but stayed quiet, waiting.

"I won't hurt anyone, Prunella, dear," he pleaded. "What can I do to convince you? I'll place the piece around your neck, and you'll be my queen. You'll never want for anything ever again."

"What on earth is he saying, Ruth Ann?" Inga asked, anxiously.

I quickly filled her in on what I'd heard. She was horrified and questioned every word. "She won't betray us, Ruth Ann. Ms. Prunella has to be going along with him for some reason. Maybe she's afraid for her life, or worse, your life."

"I didn't think of that," I admitted, hoping Inga was correct. I couldn't imagine her being so cruel, again. And this time, I couldn't blame it on a curse!

"What's going on over there?" Axel Inquired, curiously. "You two are pressed against that door so tightly something must be going on."

I didn't want to miss another word from Manual but I had to tell the others what I overheard, and they were stunned.

"Prunella's turned on us again!" Carlos cried, nervously. "Can she be under another curse? I find that hard to believe."

Isabella answered for me because to tell you the truth, I had no idea. "No, Carlos, she isn't. She's got to be pretending.

Why else would she agree to betray us and wear the necklace to some event he's planning?"

"If she's faking, then why didn't she wake up when it was just us in the bedroom with her?" Carlos asked, picking up on the same thought Inga and I had.

"I, I don't know, Carlos," she admitted, choking on her words. "Something has to be going on we're not aware of," she said. "There has to be."

"Ruth Ann," Inga called out, quietly, but urgently. "Hurry, I think he's about to leave her bedroom!"

Axel beat me to the door, and so did Carlos. Isabella and I were last to hear Manual's voice getting louder as he got closer to the door. I could hear his footsteps get close to us, and I held my breath, hoping he would walk past the closet door, and go into the hallway.

Inga looked terrified as she watched through the tiny opening. Axel was looking over her head, and Viktor over Axel's. The three of them were huddled so close, I didn't have a chance to look. I was so nervous I started pacing around the large, narrow closet. There wasn't anything really in here except for some clothes and a small electric broom. I wondered if Manuel had purchased these clothes for Prunella. I grabbed one of the sundresses and looked at the label. Yes, it was her size! I immediately felt a surge of anxiety run through my body. At any moment, someone could come in here to grab clothes for Prunella. I was just praying it wasn't Manual!

Thankfully, he left her room. I took a long, deep breath, and said, "He left, right?"

"Yes, I think we're safe, for now," Viktor replied, calming down himself. "We should head back into the tunnel and begin our plan."

"I agree," Axel said. "Ruth Ann and I need to get back to

the third floor for a quick change of clothes. It'll make it look like we were in our rooms all night. Then, we can head down and see if we can get Manual into his office so Isabella can do her magic!"

We let Viktor lead us back inside the dark tunnel. Now that we were familiar with the layout, it didn't take long for us to reach the narrow, cement stairs to the third floor. Viktor went first, making sure the coast was clear. "Nobody's around," he said, waving us into the hall. "Hurry up and get to your rooms."

Inga and Isabella followed me into my room to make sure I'd be quick. Axel disappeared into his room with Carlos. Viktor kept watch in the hall and told us if he spotted anyone to have Inga, Isabella and Carlos hide. We didn't want to take any chances, so Inga and Isabella waited in my bathroom as I changed, quickly washed and refreshed.

"I wish I could change clothes," Isabella stated. "I look horrendous!"

"You look beautiful as always," I said, truthfully. She was dressed in a sleeveless sundress and cute sandals. I wondered if she should change before her performance but figured it wouldn't matter.

Both of them threw some water on their faces. "I'm ready," I said. "Let's go and see if they're in the hall."

We hurried out of the room and found the others inside Axel's doorway. "We'll go back inside the tunnels and head down as close to my boss's office as we can get. Axel and Ruth Ann don't have to hide, but I think they should exit in the foyer and wait for my boss there. That way, you three can know if they're headed to the office or to the dining room. If they go anywhere else, I'll find you and let you know right away. But," he said seriously. "Where I leave you, you stay put and don't go anywhere else, got it?"

Inga, Carlos and Isabella nodded. "What time is it?" Isabella inquired.

"It's seven-thirty," Axel replied. "Manual must be ready to eat breakfast now. Does he usually eat at this time, Viktor?"

"He always eats at eight in the morning, so we have plenty of time."

"But, that means there's not enough time to talk to us before breakfast," I mentioned. "We'll have to eat and then hope he wants to discuss his plans for us in his office."

"If he doesn't, remember I'll suggest it's better to discuss the necklace in private. That way, he'll take you to his office," Viktor said, beautifully recalling the plan.

"I sure hope so," Axel said with a hint of skepticism in his voice.

Viktor led the way through the tunnel down two flights of stairs until he stopped dead in his tracks. "Okay, we're just outside the foyer. I'll check to see if anyone's hanging around and if not, I'll let Ruth Ann and Axel out to wait for my boss. I'll take you three around to the hall where his office is."

"Where will we end up?" Carlos asked curiously.

"Right inside the gym," Viktor answered.

"Hey, that's great!" I exclaimed. "You'll be able to go in the hall and listen outside Manual's office door."

"That would be our ideal situation," Axel said. "Let's hope Manual follows our plan."

Viktor pushed a section of the wall and a narrow door popped open. "Shhh," he said. "Give me a second." He disappeared into the foyer. It didn't take long when he waved his hand, signaling for Axel and me to follow. "Okay, I'm leaving you both here, and taking the others to the gym. They'll have to be careful not to roam around the gym because this time of day some of the guards typically go and use the equipment."

"But, how will they be able to get outside Manual's door when we're in there?" I asked, worried. "They can't be seen by anyone or our plan won't work."

"I'll be there and it'll be fine. If anyone's in the gym or hanging around that hallway, I'll give them a job that takes them away from there."

"You're second in command, aren't you, Viktor?" Axel inquired.

"I believe so, but I kind of feel like I've been betrayed by my boss, too."

"Not anymore," I quickly said.

"We'll see," he said, cautiously.

Once Axel and I were in the foyer, we decided to wait for a while before looking for Manual. It was now seven forty-five.

"This place is massive," I mentioned, looking around the expansive foyer filled with artwork.

"I think Manual likes expensive things." remarked Axel. "These paintings look like originals by some Mexican artist. They are very colorful with abstract shapes and objects. I can't figure most of them out!"

"Me either, but I think this one," I went and stood under a large, ornate gold framed picture near the front door. "I think these shapes suggest a palm tree." I twisted my head to the right and said, "See, those are the palm fronds, and the brown swirly strokes appear to be the trunk. It's hard to tell, and I'm no art connoisseur," I was suddenly cut off by a strong male voice.

"Why Ruth Ann, you've got quite the eye," Manual said, walking to my side. "That's exactly what it is, but most people who see it don't have a clue. Would you have, Axel?"

"Nope."

"See, Ruth Ann, you've got an eye for art." he blurted out loudly, "Aha, that must be because you own an antique store."

"What else do you know about my personal life, Manual? "I asked, still aggravated, but curious.

"Let's see ... I know you lost your husband many years ago in a plane crash and he left you to raise twin daughters, Lynne and Nancy." At this point, I felt the heat building inside me. Axel was now at my side, touching my elbow to keep me calm. "Oh, and your store, Ruth Ann's, is run also by a young woman named Meme. Your daughter Lynne, is a baker and owns Sinful Sweets, and she recently opened a little store in your town's resort. Nancy's a high school history teacher, and both of them are unmarried." He looked at me as if he was concerned. "How does that make you feel your thirty-some-thing daughters haven't got married yet? That's getting a little old, at least in my country."

I was close in screaming, but Axel stepped in and saved me. "Manual, before you insult Ruth Ann any further, can we get on with your plans for us today?"

"Oh, yes, I guess that's a good idea." He looked at me amused that I was red-faced and angry. "I need to eat first. Let's go get some breakfast, and then we'll discuss what I've decided."

Decided? I asked myself. It sounded like he had already made up his mind about he wanted to do with us. I sure hoped his 'vision' of Isabella fluttering around his office would change his mind!

Axel grabbed my hand and led me behind Manual into the dining room. There was a large table elegantly set with fine china and three perfectly spaced crystal candelabras on top of a white linen tablecloth. The china and even the silver-ware was gold. Manual went to the head of the table and mo-tioned for me to sit on one side of him and Axel on the other. "Please, sit," he said, plopping his stout body into one of the large end chairs.

Axel and I sat down and waited for what was to come. It didn't take long for several men and women to come in carry-ing silver trays full of food. "How many of us are eating?" I asked, surprised at the amount of food.

"Just the three of us," he replied, placing a white napkin in his lap. "Wait, four or five actually. Viktor and Sal will be joining us, too."

I was happy Viktor was coming, but a little worried about Sal. He seemed very loyal to Manual and didn't show the same affection toward Prunella that Viktor did.

As the silver trays were passed around the table, Sal and Viktor waltzed in and sat next to Axel and me. "I'm starving," Sal announced, eyeing the tray filled with salmon. The smell nearly made me lose what little I had in my stomach when the woman offered it to me. I shook my head, and she moved to her employer. He took a large serving, along with everything else they brought to him. I thought I took a lot, but nothing compared to Manual.

Axel and I both ate heartily, not knowing when our next meal would take place. I surveyed my plate filled with a stack of waffles, rye toast and butter, and even a small pile of scram-bled eggs. But, what looked best was my large bowl filled with cantaloupe, pineapple, apples, bananas, and a handful of red grapes.

"You like your carbs, Ruth Ann," Manual said, stuffing an entire piece of thick bacon in his mouth. The man had no manners. He had egg stuck in his day-old stubble and a drop of maple syrup clung to his thin mustache. He didn't even seem to notice. Then, the most ridiculous thing happened, one of his maids rushed to his side and actually wiped his mouth clean! "Enough!" he snapped at the poor woman. She bent over and scurried back to the kitchen.

"So, we need to have a serious discussion," he said, after finishing a large bite of sausage. "Sal, Viktor, you need to hear this too."

I was worried Sal would blow our plans. Hopefully, Viktor would be able to keep Sal away from us when, and if, we went to Manual's office.

"Sir," Viktor quickly interrupted before his boss divulged his plans. "I think it would be best if we take this discussion to your private office."

"Why?" Manual asked, brushing Viktor's comment aside. "We're alone in here."

Viktor stood and hurried to his boss's side. He whispered some words in his ear while Manual nodded and muttered, "Ahem, yes, you're right." He waited for Viktor to sit down, when he said, "I think it would be best if we talk in my office when you're through eating."

Viktor threw a slight grin my way, and then continued eating. "Sounds good to me," I said, finishing my waffles. "Thank you for breakfast. It was delicious."

"You have a healthy appetite, Ruth Ann," he said, smiling. "I like a woman who's not afraid to eat."

"Uh, thank you," I said, not sure if that was a compliment or insult. I really didn't care either way right now. All I wanted to do was get inside his office and wait for Isabella to do her act. Break a leg, Isabella!

Chapter 34

Manual devoured a couple hearty platefuls and rubbed his expanding belly. "That was delicious! When you're ready we'll head into my office."

Axel wiped his mouth delicately with his napkin and placed it on his empty plate. "I think we're ready now. Right, Ruth Ann?"

"Yep," I replied cheerfully, ready to get this over with. I stood, and the two other men joined me. Viktor and Sal shoveled in as much food as they could before following us into the foyer.

"Viktor, I want you to come with us," Manual said. "Sal, you go back and take over for Lennie. Tell him to grab some breakfast in the kitchen. There's lots of leftover food in there."

Phew, Sal wasn't going to be a problem. Axel winked at me, and I returned a quick grin. Our plan was going to work, I just knew it!

"Here," Manual said, opening his office door. "I have much to discuss with you two."

"Boss," Viktor called out, surprising Manual. "Would you excuse me for one minute? I need to take care of another matter of great urgency."

"Oh, um, that's fine, Viktor. But, don't be long. I may need you."

Viktor pretended to take off down the hall. Manual stepped inside and Axel and I followed. "It's really bright in here, Manual," Axel stated, covering his eyes with his hand. "Would you mind if I close the curtains a little? I have a nasty headache."

At first, I was worried about Axel, but then realized he was faking to make sure the ambience was just right for Isabella's performance. I went into actress mode and told Axel to sit down and I would close the curtains.

When Manual noticed me marching for the long wall of windows, he said, "That's fine. Go ahead and shut them. It's too bad though, it's a beautiful morning filled with bright sunshine and warm air. Not what you would have this time of year in Deer Creek!"

"No, it's much colder and darker there," I said, keeping him in a light mood as I shut the last of the curtains. The sun was still peeking through, but the room had a glow perfect for Isabella's entrance.

Manual directed us to his desk and the two chairs in front of it. Axel was already sitting holding his head as I sat down. If I didn't know any better, I would think Axel was in a lot of pain. Manual looked a little concerned. "Do you get these headaches regularly?" he asked Axel.

"Sometimes. When they come on, they're ferocious and the bright light makes it worse."

"I can call one of my staff in here with some medicine if you'd like?" Manual asked, making me feel a little guilty for fooling him.

"No, thank you, Manual. I think the darker room will do just the trick," Axel replied. I wanted to giggle because it sure would do the trick!

Once we were settled in our chairs, Manual laid his hands on his desk and said, "Now, let's get down to business. We might have a problem if you're sick, Axel."

"I'll be fine, just give me a little while."

"This is where I see it. I'm waiting to get my hands on your precious Blue Ice, but it's in your office safe up in Stockholm, correct?"

"Yes," Axel answered.

"And, *you're* the only one who can get inside that safe of yours, correct?"

"Yes," Axel repeated.

"This is where we have a problem. I don't trust you."

"What have I done to earn your distrust?" Axel inquired.

"You're slick," Manual said, eyeing him intently. "You're a successful businessman, and you've proven that you can get yourself out of prison even when there's a stack of evidence against you."

"I was legally pardoned, Manual."

"And that proves you are very shrewd."

"Can we get down to business, please?" I asked, irritated. This cat and mouse game wasn't getting us anywhere. "Yes, Axel's a smart businessman. He's paid his dues for any alleged crimes he supposedly committed."

"Such careful words, Ruth Ann," Manual said, smiling.

"Well, just say it, Manual. You want me to go to Sweden to get Blue Ice for you, but you don't want to waste valuable time if Axel is telling the truth and he's really the only one who can get it. Am I right?"

"Well, yes," he responded. "I don't trust him, but if I'm wrong, and he's actually telling me the truth, I wasted a lot of time and money."

"Then just take me!" Axel snapped. "This is getting ridiculous."

Manual was about to argue with Axel when suddenly, a shadowy figure appeared at the door. I didn't hear the door open, and I knew the tunnel didn't come directly into his office. At least I didn't think so.

"Who's there?" Manual barked, noticing someone on the far side of the room. "Answer me!"

Axel and I turned and watched as Isabella's body came into focus. She was wearing a flowing white dress and had white flowers in her smooth, long, dark hair. Where did she get those? I didn't know whether to watch Manual or Isabella. She was mesmerizing as she flowed to the middle of the office.

"What's happening?" Manual bellowed, trying to stand from his chair behind the desk. If I didn't know better, I would say he was glued to his chair. "It can't be!" he mumbled, terrified at the vision standing not too far from him. "Ruth Ann, Axel, do you see her?"

"See who?" Axel asked, perfectly on cue.

"Are you alright?" I asked Manual, playing it up. "You look as white as a ghost."

He got his legs working, and stood, holding on to his desk with his hands. "It's you!" he said, shakily. "What are you doing here? Why are you here?"

It was Isabella's turn. Her voice was magical as she said, *"Ah, my dear Manual. It is I, Isabella. Do you not remember me?"* Manual nodded, his eyes fully opened in horror. *"Are you happy to see me again? It's been a while, and you've been a bad man."*

"Bad?" he muttered, confused. He looked at me again, "Ruth Ann, tell me you see and hear Isabella? You know her."

"Manual, are you okay? You're asking strange questions. Maybe you should sit down and take a drink of water," I said, thrilled our plan was working.

"I need to speak to you, Manual. Ruth Ann and Axel can't see or hear me. You'll look crazier than ever if you keep asking them if they see me. They can't."

"What do you want with me?" he asked angrily, ignoring Axel and me completely now.

Isabella pulled a section of her new white dress away so her neck was in full view. *"This is why I'm here,"* she stated, shocking him back into his seat. *"Ah, you see it! The famous Blue Ice that you so desperately desire. You even stooped low enough to kidnap poor Prunella, Axel and kind-hearted Ruth Ann."* She watched a speechless Manual for a quick second before continuing. *"You remember I left you because you were ruthless and would go to any lengths to get what you wanted. I can't live that way. And I also recall you professing your love to me just like you're doing with Prunella. You do realize how wrong you are, right?"*

Manual's mouth opened, but no words came out. Either he was about to have a stroke or he was scared to death. Axel and I remained calm and cool without any reaction.

"Manual, you kidnapped a woman who is frail, can't walk, and has no recollection of events that have occurred in her life. She was ripe for your picking, wasn't she?" Isabella paused again, but still no response from Manual. *"She's married, Manual! You can't possibly believe this will work for the two of you! Once she gets her memory back, she will despise you for what you've done to her, and to Axel and Ruth Ann. She'll never agree to be your true love! Just like me, I hated you once I found out how evil you were!"* Isabella's expression went from ghost-like to bitter and angry. Unfortunately,

that snapped Manual out of his stupor.

"This is not real!" he bellowed. "What are you doing here?" he looked over at Axel and I sitting in our chairs, still looking at him without any reaction "Ruth Ann! Axel!" he hollered. "Stop it! I know you see her too."

"What are you talking about?" I asked, trying to get him back on track. "I think I should get you something stronger than water. What would you like?"

"Shut up, Ruth Ann!" he screamed, furious. "You three had me going, but not anymore." He stood up, walked toward the curtains that were shut and pulled them wide-open. "There, the sun will put an end to this."

Before he turned around, Isabella rushed out of the room. Viktor must've heard the conversation and knew things had taken a dangerous turn. He got her out of the room so quickly, I almost missed it. "Hey," Manual cried out. "Where'd she go?"

"Who?" Axel asked, hoping he would fall prey to our scheme again.

"Isabella," he said, his face turning white. "You know she was just standing here in the middle of the room."

"Boss," Viktor called out from the doorway. "I heard a lot of yelling in here. Everything okay?"

"Viktor!" he yelled, relieved. "You were guarding the door the entire time, right?" Viktor nodded. "So, you must've seen Isabella leave my office a second ago."

"No," he replied, a worried look upon his face. "Nobody went through this door since the three of you came in here." He played his part even further. "Wait, did you say Isabella? As in Isabella who used to come here with that, that grandmother of hers?"

"Yes, that's the one and you know it. She left here in disgrace, remember?"

"Yes," he replied, even though he knew Isabella didn't leave out of shame. She left because Manual's a criminal.

"She was in this room! I swear, but where'd she go to?" he asked, looking frantically around the room. "Look over every inch in here, Viktor. She must be hiding here somewhere."

Viktor walked around the couch and chairs, behind the curtains, and even around Manual's own desk and chair. "There's nobody in here."

Manual rubbed his head messing up his graying locks. "This can't be happening. I knew her grandmother was a witch, but I thought she was just a sweet, young girl. She's just like her grandmother, a witch. A horrible, mean witch!"

"Isabella's not a witch or horrible!" I quickly recovered and said, "She's back home in Deer Creek. Why do you keep saying she was in this room?"

"Because she was," he muttered quietly. "She was here, wearing your necklace. That's impossible, right? It's in Sweden, not right in front of my face!"

"Of course, it's not here, Manual," Axel said. "You're imagining things. Maybe you ate something that made you sick. You did have a huge breakfast."

"That's ridiculous!" he exclaimed. "That wouldn't cause me to see her!"

"Boss, why don't I take you to your room so you can lie down? Maybe you'll feel better if you rest for a little while."

Manual became fuming mad at Viktor. "Don't tell me to lie down! I feel terrific, and now I think you're turning on me too!"

"Never, boss," Viktor quickly answered.

Manual didn't know what to do. Axel and I stayed quiet, waiting for his next move. Viktor had risked his life for us in here, and I wanted to make sure we did everything we could to protect him once we get out of here.

Chapter 35

"Search the entire estate!" Manual ordered, regaining his composure. "I want every available man to help you, Viktor. Where's Sal?" he snapped. "He should've been here, too."

"I'll find him," Viktor said, turning to leave. "I'll personally make sure the entire house gets searched.

"Now, let's get back to why we came here in the first place," he said, stunning Axel and me. "I want that necklace more than ever now." Great, I thought to myself. We just made it worse, but how did that happen?

"Why is this necklace so important to you?" I asked, trying to figure out what was causing such panic. "I'm sure there are other pieces just as beautiful and rare as ours."

Axel gave me a little glare. "I mean, you have so many pieces, why add this one? It seems to me it's been nothing but a pain for you."

"It has, but I need it. I just have to have it, and now, with her," he stopped, realizing he had said too much.

"Her?" Axel asked, irritated. We all know he was referring to Prunella. "Are you referring to my wife?"

"Um, well, yes," he answered. "I might as well confess."

"Confess what?" Axel demanded. "She's my wife, you know."

"She isn't happy."

"How on earth would you know that?" Axel hollered. "You've only known her for two days!"

"But, we've bonded, and she admitted that when she woke from her coma that she had no feelings for you anymore. She told me you and she have grown apart."

I was stunned by his announcement. Did Prunella really tell Manual this or was Manual lying? I felt conflicted and terrified. How Axel was going to take it?

"You're a fool if you believe her," Axel said. "She's lying to you so you'll let her go, and you know it."

"Never!" Manual loudly replied. "She doesn't want to go back to your boring little town in Colorado. She told me she's done with the cold weather there and in Sweden. She told me the bright, warm sunshine has filled her with new hope and she wants to start a new life down here, with me."

"I don't believe you," I interrupted. "Prunella would never do or say those things. She loves her family and her friends. She wouldn't tell you before telling us."

"Well, she did," he said. "I'm planning a huge party that will introduce Prunella to my people, and she'll be wearing," he smacked his lips shut, even though Axel and I knew what exactly what he wanted her to be wearing. For a moment, I wanted to give it to him and be done with it. But, a familiar voice in my head told me, *"You will always be a part of the necklace, stop fighting it. It's never leaving your family."*

"That can't happen. Meme told me that the necklace would never leave our family, and I believe that."

"It won't actually be leaving your family, Ruth Ann," Manual plainly stated.

"How can you say that?" I asked, questioning his remark.

"If it stays with Prunella, then it doesn't actually leave your family. Prunella's still your cousin even if she's not living near you. Unless," Manual paused for just a moment and added, "Unless you stay here with her, too."

"WHAT!" Axel shrieked. "That will NEVER happen!"

"Whoa, Eklund," Manual replied, stunned by Axel's sudden outburst. "What was that about? Are you upset that Prunella won't be coming home or that Ruth Ann might be staying here, too?"

Before Axel unleashed anymore wrath, I interrupted and asked Manual "What's this huge party you're throwing? Did you say it's to introduce Prunella to your family and friends? It seems a bit premature, doesn't it? Even if what you told us is true, she's still married."

"Of course, it's true! Prunella likes the idea of a party," he said. "She was very excited about it."

"You're lying," Axel stated, irritated. "Prunella hates attention. She would never agree to a party in her honor."

"Well, you must not know her very well," Manual replied, smugly. "She told me she couldn't wait to find a dress that will highlight her necklace."

"*Our* necklace, Manual," I quickly corrected. "It's shared between her, Axel and me. Don't forget that!"

He shrugged his shoulders and sat down at his desk. "You both might as well get comfortable. We're not going anywhere until Viktor comes back with Isabella. I know she was here, and you two must've been involved with her little performance." He waved his hand in the air displaying a thick gold band ring with the biggest diamond I've ever seen. "Don't try and tell me I was imagining things. I'm not crazy."

I wanted to say something in our defense, but Axel gave

me a quick look that clearly told me that I needed to stay quiet. "So," Manual continued. "You know what that means then, right?" He waited for us to respond, but I didn't dare. I knew exactly what he was implying. That if Isabella was really here, she also has Blue Ice and that Axel and I made a monstrous mistake lying to him.

"I see you, Ruth Ann. I can tell you're thinking hard about what will happen to the two of you if I find out you lied to me. That was a cruel joke, and I am not happy."

"I would never joke about my safety," I snapped. "I had nothing to do with some far-fetched plan to scare you, Manual."

"We'll see," he responded to me. "You'd better hope you weren't. I won't be as accommodating with you as I've been."

"You bloody idiot!" Axel stood, screaming loudly. "You have the nerve to admonish us for supposedly lying to you? You and your men kidnapped us and flew us halfway around the world to rob us! Are you mad or just totally delusional?"

I watched in horror as Axel yelled at Manual. This wasn't going to help our case no matter how right Axel was. I looked at Manual and saw his smug expression turn to fury. He waited until Axel was done then stood, leaned over his desk and slowly and carefully said, "Did you just call me mad or delusional?"

Axel leaned in, uncomfortably too close for me, and said, "You have to be, Manual. You've committed a huge crime taking us by force. How could you think you'll actually get away with it?"

"When I'm finished with you, nobody will ask me any more questions. Trust me, you won't be capable of speaking to any police."

"What's that supposed to mean?" I exclaimed, interrupting their stand-off.

Manual turned his attention to me, unfortunately, and swiftly said, "Stay out of this Ruth Ann. I believe you had nothing to do with this rebellion, but if I find out I'm wrong, you won't be excused. I know I just offered you the chance to stay here with your cousin, but that's not set in stone."

"I have no intention of staying here," I announced. "I'm going back home, immediately. This has gone on long enough. I want to leave, NOW!"

Manual straightened up, grabbed his round belly and started to laugh, loudly and heartily. "You're cracking me up, Ruth Ann! Do you really think you can just march out of here on your own?"

"Yes, I do."

He looked at me with amazement and instead of replying, he shook his head and stomped to the door. Suddenly, Axel and I heard him holler, "VIKTOR! Where are you?" Axel smiled at me as we watched an infuriated Manual yell Viktor's name several times.

It didn't take long before Viktor met Manual near the office doors. Viktor was clearly out of breath as he leaned over and whispered some words into Manual's ear. "UNACCEPTABLE!" Manual replied, furious. "She's hear, I know, I feel it!"

"I'm sorry, boss, she is nowhere to be found."

Manual came back inside his office and made his way back to his desk. He plopped down, shaking his head in disbelief. "I know she was here," he mumbled. "You are playing me, aren't you?" he asked, Axel, Viktor, and me.

"No boss," Viktor replied, trying to show a little empathy. "I'm just saying we couldn't find any sign of her. But," before Viktor veered down a dangerous path, Axel chimed in.

"She's not here, Manual. Just accept it."

"Shut up, Eklund," he said, agitated. "I need time to think. Viktor," Manual waved him closer to his side. "Take them away for now. I can't think clearly with them jumping down my throat."

Inside, I was thrilled. Manual was caving, and if we could keep Isabella out of sight, I thought our plan was going to work. I wasn't sure what we were going to do next, but once we found Inga, Carlos and Isabella, we would discuss our next move.

"Take them to their rooms, but don't leave their doors. I want you to watch them closely." Thankfully, he said our rooms and not that hole in the ground we stayed in before. "Better yet, put them in the same room and don't allow either of them to speak. I don't want any conspiring behind my back, and I don't trust Eklund not to jump his balcony to get inside Ruth Ann's room. If you're in the room with them, they'll behave."

"Yes, boss," Viktor responded, dutifully.

Viktor led us out of the office after asking his boss how long he was to keep us confined. Manual told him to bring us back to him in an hour. Axel threw me a tiny grin as Viktor grabbed his arm and lead him toward the door. Once the door was closed, Viktor released Axel's arm and gave him a nasty glare. "Did you have to get him riled up like that?"

"I didn't, Viktor," Axel answered. "He's nuts!"

"I don't like this," Viktor murmured, shaking his head. "But, I'm in so deep, I might as well keep going." He walked a few feet, and instead of heading straight down the hall and into the foyer, he stopped in front of the gym. He turned nervously making sure nobody was around, and then hurried us into the gym. "Shhh," he said to Axel and me. "Nobody's in here now, but that could change. I'm taking you back into the tunnel where I brought Isabella after that fiasco of a performance."

"It worked, Viktor," I cried. "We said we couldn't see her, and when you told him nobody found her, he had to think he was seeing visions!"

"Maybe, but he's pretty stubborn. He still thinks Isabella is physically here, and he'll knock down every wall searching for her."

"But, he forced us out of his office so he could calm down and think," I said, walking toward the opening of the tunnel with Viktor and Axel. "He's petrified that he saw a ghost!"

"I sure hope so," Viktor replied, as he pushed the hidden door and it opened. He motioned us to hurry inside, and then shoved the door closed. "They're right around the corner," he said, pointing to a sharp turn ahead.

"Ruth Ann!" Isabella cried, grabbing me and hugging me tightly. "That was really scary."

"You were perfect!" I said. "Until Viktor had to drag you out of there. I'm just glad you didn't get caught. That would've been horrible."

"Well, it didn't happen," Viktor barked. He told them what his boss made him do, and Isabella looked pale and scared. Calmly, he said to Isabella, "It's alright, he doesn't suspect my disloyalty, for the time being."

She smiled innocently and thanked him. I asked Viktor where we were going and he told me back to my bedroom on the third floor. However, it wasn't just Axel and me; all of us were going up there. We had a lot to figure out, and only an hour to do it.

Captive Ice

Chapter 36

"Why didn't you take Ruth Ann and me up the stairs?" Axel asked.

"Because I needed to get the others up to her room, too," Viktor replied, crabbily. "They would never find their way without being seen. The entire staff is on the lookout for Isabella."

"Good point," Axel said, following him down the dark tunnel. Inga was at the back of the group, awfully quiet. I let the others go ahead so I could walk with her.

"What are you thinking, Inga?" I asked her. "You don't think we're handling this correctly, do you?"

"No, I don't," she snapped, through gritted teeth.

"Why don't you tell me what you would've done?" I asked, feeling annoyed.

"First, I would've never put Isabella in such a dangerous position. That man could've pulled a gun out and shot her."

"I didn't think of that," I admitted, truthfully.

"Second and third, I would've never brought that necklace down here, and I would've either brought the cops with us or dragged that boyfriend of yours down here to save you, again."

"John?" I questioned her. "He has no authority down here. And, well, I didn't want him involved. And, you heard Isabella, she had to bring the necklace for Prunella's safety. She put a hex on it to protect Prunella."

"That's ridiculous!" Inga snapped.

"You know that this is real, Inga. Blue Ice has been cursed, and re-cursed. You've seen it with your own eyes."

"I really don't know what I believe anymore. I would've left the necklace safely back in Deer Creek and forced them to come to us. We'd be on home turf."

"I wish we could've done that, Inga," I said. "But, Prunella may have been killed before we made it home. Meme told me so."

"Isabella told me the same thing. I'm just having a difficult time believing this is happening over and over."

"Me, too," I agreed. "But, what I really like is that my stout, stalwart and crusty, old friend has returned. You're one tough woman!"

"I guess I'll take being called tough a compliment."

"And you're my friend!"

"Yes, Ruth Ann, thank you for that. You're my friend too."

The rest of the way we remained silent. It didn't take long until Viktor told us we were on the third floor. "I'll go first and check out the hall and your room. Once I know it's clear, I'll come back for you. But, when I do, you have to move fast down the hall. We can't risk getting caught after everything we've accomplished."

Viktor disappeared leaving the rest of us in almost complete darkness. I stayed near Inga a few feet back from the others. Inga took hold of my arm and whispered, "Do you have a plan? I can't figure out how we're going to get out of here. Prunella will never be able to escape as fast as we can."

Inga still placed Prunella high on a pedestal. She was so loyal to her that it made her unable to think rationally. Inga would never believe that Prunella wanted to stay here with Manual. I wish I had the same loyalty. I was beginning to believe that Prunella really did want us to go away and leave her alone.

"Let's go," Viktor whispered into the tunnel. "Nobody's up here right now. My boss must still trust me or he would've sent Sal up here too."

We rushed down the hall and into my bedroom. "Wow, this is nice," Carlos remarked. "You not slumming it too much in here."

"I was only here one night, Carlos," I said, irritated. "I also spent time in a hole in the ground, too."

We walked to the couches near the balcony. Axel sat next to me on the couch and Isabella sat on my other side. Inga and Carlos sat in a couple chairs while Viktor paced around the room. "You're making me nervous, Viktor," Isabella said. "Please stop pacing!"

"Sorry, I do my best thinking while I'm moving."

"What are we going to do next?" Carlos inquired. "I think the best thing we can do is have Viktor go down to the second floor and grab Prunella. We plan a meeting place and then we get out of here. If we do it when it's dark, we might get out of here without being caught."

"Too many men patrolling the house," Viktor said, shaking his head. "We need a distraction."

"Ah, and then the men will leave their posts and we can escape," Axel said, smiling. "What kind of distraction do you have in mind?"

"I don't know, yet. I'm trying to think of one," he said,

starting to pace again. He looked at Isabella for her approval. She nodded sweetly, and he slowly walked around the room.

"What about an explosion of some sort?" Inga asked. "Like in the back of the house."

"We can set a small fire in the kitchen or something," Carlos suggested. "Or, set off an alarm inside and sneak out somewhere and run."

"All good suggestions," Axel said. "I like the idea of a small explosion. I'm sure Viktor can get his hands on an explosive."

"I can," he answered, devoid of any details.

"How?" I asked, confused. "You have dynamite just lying around?"

"Don't worry about how, Ruth Ann," Axel said to me. "In the line of business Manual's in, I'm sure it can be handled."

"I don't want anyone hurt or killed," Isabella said. "No more bloodshed."

Inga wasn't as kind. "I could care less who gets killed down here. Let Manual get blown to smithereens!"

"But, one of us could get caught in the cross-fire," Isabella said, worried. "I'm getting a bad feeling inside."

"You're just scared," I said, trying to reassure her even though I knew Isabella's *feelings* could be very real.

"When are we doing this?" Inga asked, excited. "I say tonight."

"How am I supposed to rig an explosion in just a few hours?" Viktor asked. "I need more time."

"We don't have time," Axel said. "We need to get out of here before one of them," Axel pointed to Inga, Carlos and Isabella, "get caught."

Viktor shook his head. "It's not possible. I need help."

"Can you trust anyone else here?" I asked him. "What about Sal?"

"No way, he's totally devoted to my boss. And, the other guys are weak-minded fools. They answer to me, but if I order them to go against my boss, they will probably turn me in for a reward! They all want my position. I don't trust any of them."

"Better to get out of here," I said. "You have no life here."

"I thought I did, but I guess I'm wrong."

"Viktor," Carlos interjected. "Can you get this done to-night?"

"I don't know. Let me think for a moment. I can't go anywhere now because I'm supposed to be watching Axel and Ruth Ann for an hour."

"Okay," Axel said thinking out loud. "It's almost noon and from the size of him, I have a feeling Manual keeps a tight eating schedule." Viktor held back a laugh with a muffled cough. Axel continued, "He'll probably tell us to meet him in the dining room to eat first, and then force us back into his office. I just hope he comes to the conclusion that his vision of Isabella was real and drops the whole ridiculous plan of getting his hands on Blue Ice. Maybe he'll think Prunella's too much work for him and let her go home with Ruth Ann and me. He has no idea the rest of you are here. So," he took a breath after that mouthful and finished saying, "So, I think it's best if Inga, Carlos and Isabella remain in the tunnels or in Ruth Ann's bedroom."

"I agree," I said. "When I'm in my room, you three can be with me, but when we're down in the dining room or his office, the best place to hide is in the tunnels. I turned to Viktor and asked, "Nobody uses those tunnels, right?"

"Well, my boss has used them, but if he's with you or Axel, then we're safe."

"That makes me a little nervous, but what else can we do until Viktor figures out how to come up with a big enough distraction to send his men away from the exits so we can escape."

"Just give me the afternoon," Viktor asked. "I'll do a little reconnaissance and see what I can get my hands on. I know he has some explosives in a locked-up building not far from here. He's used them to blast through rocks to get inside caves where he was told there were diamonds."

"Here?" Axel asked, doubting there were diamond mines near here.

Viktor rolled his eyes and replied, "My boss goes all over the world to get what he wants. That's why he's willing to fly you to your office in Sweden to supposedly retrieve the necklace from your safe," Viktor said to Axel.

"Well, we all know it's not there!" Isabella said, opening her blouse to display the dazzling blue aquamarine. "I still think I should get to Prunella and put it around her neck."

"NO!" Axel and Viktor bellowed together. Axel added, "If Manual notices the necklace around Prunella's neck, we're done for. He'll probably kill Ruth Ann and me and search every inch of this place until he finds Isabella. It's too risky. Prunella will have to wait to put it on until we've decided if we're taking her with us or not."

"*Or not?*" Inga questioned, infuriated by the slightest doubt we had in Prunella's allegiance. "She's faking, and we have to believe that!"

"Inga," Axel said in a gentle, soft tone. "We might have to accept the fact that Prunella has changed and doesn't want to come home with us. She may really want to stay here and live with that disgusting man. I don't know why or remotely understand her thinking, but we may have to face it."

"I'll never accept that," Inga stated, and then walked to the balcony. She slid the drapes open a little bit, and the sun came blaring in. "It's a beautiful day outside," Inga said, closing the curtains. "I spotted a couple men with rifles walking outside. They're probably guarding your room so neither one of you climb down and escape."

"We're on the third floor!" I cried. "That would be impossible. Axel or I aren't exactly stunt people."

"My boss probably told his men to keep a close eye on the front. Maybe he's starting to doubt my loyalty," Viktor said, worried.

"You'll have to make sure he doesn't," Axel said. "When you take us to him in about thirty minutes, shove me a little or do something to show him you're irritated with me."

"That won't be hard to do," Viktor mumbled, clearly starting to regret ever getting involved with us. Axel heard him but ignored his comment. I have to agree with poor Viktor, we were making his life difficult, and possibly fatal!

"I'm starving," Carlos blurted out of nowhere. "Is there anything to eat in here?" he asked, looking around the living room.

"I have a whole bowl of fruit and nuts next to my bed. It was delivered this morning by one of the maids. Go and eat, Carlos." Carlos rushed and grabbed a large basket filled with ripe fruits and nuts. Inga and Isabella dug in, too. I was fairly confident I'd to be eating again soon, so I didn't touch any of it.

"I feel much better," Carlos announced. "How much time do we have left in here?"

"It's time," Viktor stated, walking toward the door and

opening it. He looked both ways down the hall and told us to follow him. "I'll take us to the foyer, and that's where Inga, Carlos and Isabella must wait. Ruth Ann, Axel, and I will exit into the foyer and if we don't run into my boss, I'll take them to his office."

"Hopefully, he'll be in the dining room. Maybe we can check there first," Axel suggested.

"We can do that," Viktor answered, rushing us into the tunnel. "Hurry up, we're running a little late."

Within a couple minutes we were just outside of the foyer in the tunnel. Even though we've gone through these tunnels a number of times, I was still getting twisted and turned around. Thankfully, Viktor was leading the way.

Viktor leaned his ear against the wall, listening for any sounds from Manual or his men. "I think we're safe," he whispered. "I'm going to push the door and step out. Ruth Ann and Axel follow right behind me."

"See you soon," I said, stepping through the door. I felt bad leaving the others inside the dark, claustrophobic tunnel, but we didn't have other options at the moment.

Viktor headed toward the dining room and kitchen, holding Axel's arm rather forcefully. "Hey," I said. "Ease up until you have to be rough with him."

"Oh, sorry," Viktor said, loosening his grip a little. He didn't lay a hand on me as I walked behind the two of them. Just as I was about to follow them into the dining room, they stopped abruptly. "Hey," I said, nearly crashing into Viktor's backside.

It took me about a half a second to see why they stopped, and what I saw horrified me beyond my wildest dreams.

Chapter 37

"Prunella!" Axel cried, astonished. "You're here."

There was my cousin, sitting to the right of Manual, smiling and giggling at whatever he was whispering in her dainty little ear. Axel was about to punch Manual in the face when Viktor grabbed his arm more tightly and pulled him back. I knew that Axel wasn't acting, he was fuming and wanted to kill Manual with his own bare hands.

"Aha!" Manual exclaimed, happily. "You found me. I was a bad host and told you to come to my office. But, alas, it is lunchtime, and I thought it would be nice for you to eat with my dear Prunella. Please, come and sit down." Manual took his hand off Prunella's shoulder and waved us in. He was at the end of the long table with Prunella to his right, and he invited me to sit to his left. I obliged, of course. Viktor dumped Axel into a chair roughly, causing his boss to hide a nasty smile. Viktor still seemed to be in Manual's good graces. Manual even asked Viktor to sit on the other side of Prunella and he happily agreed.

"So, how was your time together?" Manual inquired. "I assume they behaved, Viktor?"

"Yes, I had them separated the entire time. Ruth Ann was

sitting on her bed and Eklund was on the couch with me hovering over him. I don't think he likes me, boss."

Good touch, Viktor!

Axel couldn't help himself. "Why would I like you? You're a bloody criminal like your boss."

"Whoa," Manual said, his smile fading. "We're in the presence of ladies, Eklund. Mind your manners." Obviously, he was trying to look good in front of Prunella. It was rather sickening, to be honest.

"Prunella, dear, why don't you tell Ruth Ann and Axel our plans?" Manual urged, gloating.

She leaned over and whispered to him, "I don't want to, Manual. It's going to be very hard to tell them what I want to do. Can't you tell them?"

He replied in a softly, "You have to, dear, they won't believe me. They have to hear it from you."

She nodded and lowered her head, nervous and scared. I was sitting on pins and needles waiting to hear what she was about to tell us. I noticed Axel stiffen in his chair. I felt horrible that he was about to hear his wife tell him she wanted to leave him for this short, stocky, disgusting criminal!

"Go on, Prunella," Axel said surprising me. "I want to hear it from your own lips."

"Axel," she cried, a tear falling down her pale cheeks. "I, I don't want to hurt you." She turned to Manual and said, "Tell them, Manual. Tell them I told you not to hurt them."

"I don't care what *he* does to me, Prunella," Axel said, angrily. "I only care what *you* do to hurt me, and Ruth Ann."

"I, I don't know what to say," she replied, tears now streaming down her cheeks. "I haven't been the same in a long time. I don't fit in with you and everyone else in Deer Creek. You must've sensed that for a while."

"You've been through a lot, Prunella," I interrupted and said. "Maybe you need to go home and see a doctor that we trust. You remember Doc Albert at our hospital, right?"

"NO," she snapped, turning her attention solely to Axel. "That's not what I meant. Sure, maybe the coma did change me, but you and I have been growing apart for some time now. You and Ruth Ann are a better fit than we are. We have such an age difference, and you and Ruth Ann are closer in age."

Wow, I thought quietly to myself. Perhaps she's picked up on Axel's feelings toward me. Even so, I'd done nothing to betray her. "Nonsense," I couldn't help blurt. "You're not thinking clearly. You've had too many upsetting things happen lately, like losing Sherman." Oh, no, I wasn't supposed to bring him up.

She looked at me intently, but not surprised. "Wait," I said, noticing her oddly calm reaction. "You remember, don't you?"

Axel watched nervously as his wife recalled what happened not too long ago. "Yes, I remember. I killed him. I killed my great uncle, and I have to live with that for the rest of my life. Don't you understand that I can never go back to my old life? I need, actually, I *want* to start over, and that means cutting ties with everyone."

"That makes no sense," I exclaimed, stunned. "This is exactly the time you need your family. We can help you recover and heal."

"No," she said, with a finality in her voice that brought chills up my spine. "You should be with Axel, I'm too young and tarnished for him."

"Hold on, Prunella," I began. "There's nothing going on between Axel and me. Plus," I hesitated and peered over at Manual who was sitting watching closely. "Plus, he's almost as old as Axel!"

"I am not!" Manual bellowed. "He's like seventy, and I'm only sixty."

"Seriously?" Axel asked mockingly, entering the conversation again. "Sixty isn't exactly young, is it? Prunella's in her mid-thirties. And," he said, turning to Prunella, "if you think I believe our age difference is the reason you want to leave me, try again!"

"And, Prunella," I said loudly, pointing at Manual. "He's a criminal!"

Prunella glared at me and before Manual could protest, she spat, "And my husband isn't?"

"That's not fair," I replied. "Axel's been cleared, and he's proven his loyalty and willingness to lead an honorable life. Why are you being so cruel, Prunella? I don't understand what's gotten into you!"

Prunella popped out of her chair, leaned over the table and shouted, "THAT'S WHAT I'M TRYING TO TELL YOU!" She sat back in her chair, and we watched her in shock.

I decided to take another approach. I slowly and calmly responded, "So, can you tell me when you were able to stand and walk? You've been lying to Axel and me for a while, haven't you?"

"No," she answered, flatly.

"When?" Axel inquired, bitterly.

"In the hospital I knew I had feeling back in my legs, and I was getting stronger. I didn't say anything to anyone because I was confused about my life and what I wanted to do. And then," she stopped, turned to Manual and grabbed his hand with a smile. "He miraculously came into my life. I knew after talking with him that he was going to give me my new start in life. I'm not saying this to hurt either of you, but it's time for me to be honest with you, and myself. Can't you try and believe me?"

Axel and I sat in disbelief watching Prunella's stare at us intensely. She was waiting for us to say something, but I couldn't. I felt angry, betrayed, and miserably depressed. I couldn't imagine how Axel was feeling at this moment. I wanted to get up and walk out of this house and never look back. For one fleeting moment, I wanted to find Isabella and take the necklace from her neck and throw it at Manual and Prunella. I'd had it!

"Enough," Manual stated, standing. "Prunella's explained how she feels, and the two of you need to accept it."

"She's still married to me," Axel said, very quietly.

"We can take care of that," Manual answered.

"How? Kill me?"

"No," Prunella responded. "Manual promised he wouldn't do that. I think once we dissolve our marriage you and Ruth Ann should go back to Deer Creek."

"That could take months!" I proclaimed. "I'm not staying here that long."

Manual barked, "You'll stay here until I tell you to leave."

Just then Sal entered the dining room, but he wasn't alone.

Chapter 38

"I KNEW IT!" Manual hollered, hoisting his round body out of the chair. I couldn't imagine how Prunella could be attracted to this disgusting man. He was nothing next to the distinguished, handsome man she married.

"I'm so sorry," Isabella cried, looking at me and Axel. "Sal caught me peeking out of the tunnel just as he was coming down the stairs. He grabbed my arm so fast, I didn't have a chance of getting away from him."

"Sal, great job!" Manual bellowed, thrilled. "You'll be highly rewarded for this." He walked close to Isabella and parted her loose, white blouse so he could see her neck. "Magnificent," he muttered, amazed at the sight of our doomed Blue Ice.

"Release her!" I demanded, hoping to draw him out of his trance. "Prunella, tell him to let her go."

"Ruth Ann," she said sweetly, but condescendingly. "Isabella has the only thing I want from my old life. Can't you forget you ever saw that necklace? It's brought you nothing but trouble and sadness since you laid eyes on it, right? And, you've only known of it for a few months. You can't be too attached to it. Axel and I have been around the necklace for most of our lives, and I doubt Axel would care if he never saw it again, right Axel?"

"You're wrong, Prunella," Axel answered her. "That necklace belongs to Ruth Ann, too, and you can't just think we'll walk away from it, do you?"

"Yes, I do." She continued, "I don't want anything else from you, so why can't you just agree? I'm sorry that I've hurt all of you, but this is what I want."

"Do you remember Isabella?" I asked, curiously, testing her memory.

"Yes. She's Meme's granddaughter," she replied. "I know where you're going with this, Ruth Ann, but it won't work."

Manual looked confused. "What are you talking about, Prunella? What is Ruth Ann doing?"

"She wants to remind me that Meme died breaking the curse on Blue Ice and told us that it had to remain in our family forever. She said it was destined to be with us, and nothing we do can change that. Correct, Ruth Ann?"

"Yes," I said. "So, you can't be the only one to possess it."

Prunella didn't respond, but Manual turned back to Isabella. "Take it off!"

"No," she said, confidently.

"Don't make me force you," Manual stated. "You don't understand that you, Axel and Ruth Ann have lost. If you cooperate, maybe the three of you can leave here, alive and unhurt."

The first thing that went through my head was Inga and Carlos were still undiscovered. They and Viktor were only hope now, unless Manual found out that Viktor helped us.

"I will not cooperate," Isabella stated, boldly. "You'll

have to rip it from my neck."

"Don't tempt me," Manual said, reaching his shaking hand to touch the perfect, clear, blue gem. "Ouch!" he hollered, pulling his hand away. "I just got a shock."

Isabella smiled, "That's what you get!"

"Shut up!" he screamed. "What's wrong with that thing? Did you hex it or something?"

She answered, "Just something."

"Witch!" he shouted, and waved Sal over. "Take her to Prunella's room and don't leave her side."

Manual whispered into Prunella's ear and she nodded several times. What happened next still haunts me. Prunella stood, backed away from her chair and walked with ease out of the dining room. Axel and I glanced at each other in shock and disappointment. Prunella was more deceptive than we thought. She was in perfect health.

"Now, Viktor," Manual said, walking behind my chair. "What to do with the two of you. I think you two will be my personal guests at the party! Yes, that's a fantastic idea."

"What?" I asked, not turning to see Manual's snide look. "Party?"

"I'm throwing a huge party, tomorrow night!"

"Tomorrow night?" Viktor asked, confused. "I wasn't informed of that, sir."

"That's because I decided just now. It'll be perfect. Prunella will wear a magnificent dress to accentuate the blue of her necklace."

Axel grabbed my arm just as I was going to respond. He shook his head slightly, and whispered, "Don't say a word. He's playing us."

I unenthusiastically cooperated. I wanted to turn and slug him in his fat, ugly, stomach, but I resisted. Axel was right.

He was goading us and wanted me to fight back. I wasn't going to give him the satisfaction.

Viktor didn't dare look at Axel and me as he asked his boss what he wanted him to do with us. "They can wait in Ruth Ann's bedroom until I send someone up to fit them for their party clothes. First, Prunella will choose a dress for herself and then she'll select party clothes for both of them."

"Okay, boss," Viktor said, walking toward me. Axel and I stood, but just as we were about to exit the dining room Manual stopped us.

"Viktor," Manual called out. "You don't have any idea how Isabella got inside the tunnels, do you?"

Bless this new friend of ours. He swiftly replied, "No, Sir, but I will get to the bottom of it. I'll find out who helped her."

Manual clapped his hands loudly, and said, "Wonderful! I knew I could count on you, Viktor!"

Phew, that was close. Viktor thought quickly on his feet and didn't turn on us. "That was too close," Axel said as we headed up the first flight of stairs.

"I thought I was a dead man," Viktor said, reaching the landing on the second floor. He looked down the hall and spotted Sal outside Prunella's room. "I want to go and help Isabella. She's in there with Prunella."

"I think Manual wants my wife to talk her into releasing the necklace," said Axel.

"Do you think it'll work?" I asked, worried.

"Isabella might still think that if she puts the necklace on Prunella that it will protect her," Axel said, softly. "Remember, Meme told her to place a safety hex on the necklace and then get it around Prunella's neck."

Viktor said he'd figure it out and walked with us to the

third floor. "We have one problem," he started to say as we headed down the hall. "We still have Inga and Carlos in the tunnels."

"I forgot about them!" Axel exclaimed.

"I wouldn't be surprised if my boss wants those tunnels checked now. He might not think Isabella was in there alone."

"Oh, no," I cried, stepping into my bedroom suite. "We need to find them!"

"No, you don't," a voice called out from inside the bedroom.

"Inga!" I howled, thrilled to see her. She and Carlos were sitting on my couch lounging as if they hadn't a care in the world.

"How did you get in here?" Viktor asked, confused.

"We remembered the way," Carlos replied, proudly. "Once Isabella was grabbed out of the tunnel, we knew we had to get out of sight. This was the only logical place."

"Smart thinking," I said, walking over to the couch and sitting between them. "This has been an exhausting day, and there's so much we need to discuss."

"Tell us, what happened once Isabella was captured?" Carlos asked. "Hey, where is she? They didn't harm her, did they?"

"No, she's with Prunella," I responded.

"Oh, that's good," Inga said. "But, why aren't they treating her like a prisoner?"

"They are," Axel answered. "Isabella's in grave danger."

Carlos flew off the couch and ran toward Viktor and Axel near the door. "Why? What happened?"

"She was dragged into the dining room by Sal," Viktor explained.

"Let me tell you everything that happened," I said, beginning with the fact that Prunella has her memory, and her ability to walk.

"No, she wouldn't do that," Inga muttered, upset. "Ms. Prunella wouldn't betray us like this."

"Well, get used to it because she did," Axel said, bluntly. "I don't even recognize her anymore."

"We'll get her away from here and then we'll make sure she gets professional help," Inga said, frantic. "That'll do it! We'll be the ones to make her better."

"No, Inga," Axel said, depressed. "She wants to remain here with that vile man. There's nothing we can do about it."

"No, I won't accept that," Inga said, desperately. "I've known her too long to just give up on her." She looked wildly at the rest of us. "Why aren't you with me on this?"

"Because you weren't there when she talked to us, Inga," I said, sadly. "She was totally lucid and wants to start her life over, with that man. We can't force her."

"Yes, we can," Inga demanded. "I'm not leaving without her. I can't believe you all are so willing to leave her!"

"We aren't giving up, Inga," I said. "We need her to come to her own conclusion. If she wants to stay here, then we have to let her." I added, "I hope someday soon, she'll change her mind and we'll be home waiting for her."

Inga's mouth opened to speak, but she closed it and wound her arms around her body. I never thought I'd see the day when Inga looked defeated. I felt horrible, but I had to stay strong. I told myself it would all work out, somehow.

"We don't have much time before my boss sends in party clothes for Ruth Ann and Axel. We need to get Inga and Carlos out of sight. I'll stand by the door and wait for someone coming."

Carlos and Inga refused to wait in the closet but agreed to stay off to the side just in case the door opened suddenly. We tried to explain Manual's party to them, but the words sounded so absurd, I had a difficult time believing it.

"But, why would he want you and Mr. Eklund at the party?" Inga asked, baffled. "You could get lost in the crowd and escape."

"I'm pretty sure we'll be heavily guarded," I said.

"He wants us to watch first-hand how Prunella's introduced to his peers as she wears Blue Ice," Axel said, making it more plausible. "He's disturbed, and dangerous."

"We don't have any choice, do we?" I asked Axel.

"No," Viktor called out from the door answering for Axel. "You have to go, but maybe we can figure a way out or a distraction at the party."

"With everything that's happened, I think our explosion idea is out of the picture," I said, confused. "How can we pull something off with a room full of people?"

"That's a brilliant idea!" Axel exclaimed, excited. "We can figure some huge distraction, maybe not an explosion, but something. We have to think fast!"

"Why not an explosion?" Viktor asked.

"We don't want anyone hurt, Viktor," Axel said. "It's too dangerous to play with explosives at a party."

"You're right," he acknowledged. "What can we do now?"

"Any ideas?" Axel asked Inga, Carlos, and me.

None of us spoke up. "Think hard," Axel insisted, when suddenly Viktor turned and called out in a quiet voice, "Someone's coming. Get Inga and Carlos out of here!"

Inga and Carlos ran into the bedroom and hid behind a tall, painted panel. The bright colors of the flowers and palm trees were something I enjoyed looking at while I lied in bed. The scene was serene and calming, however, at the moment I didn't feel very tranquil. My heart was racing so fast, I could feel it pounding.

"In here," Viktor said to the older woman who was holding a few items of clothing. "Place them on the couch, and I'll call you back inside when they're ready."

The old, hunched woman nodded, but didn't speak. She rushed in tiny, muffled steps to the couch and dropped the dresses and suits on the couch. She backed away, bowing as she exited the room to wait in the hall for Axel and me to try on the clothes.

"That was weird," Inga said, peeking around the corner of the bedroom. "Does she not speak English?"

"Yes, she understood," Viktor replied. "She's old and knows to do as she's told."

"I thought that kind of treatment was long gone," Inga said, insulted. Thankfully, she was never treated like a servant in Axel's employment.

I walked to the couch and separated the dresses from the suits. "Why so many?" I asked, counting four dresses for me and two suits for Axel.

Inga answered as she came out into the open near me. "They gotta fit, don't they?"

I held up the first long dress. It was a beautiful teal colored gown filled with sequins and beading. "This is so fancy!" I said, wondering how I would look in it. I felt a rush of excitement inside of me, but then I shoved it back down. This wasn't for fun, I reminded myself.

"Make sure you pick a dress you can run in, Ruth Ann," Inga said. "We might have to get out of here in a rush, and you may not have time to change."

"Good point," I agreed, setting the tight-fitting gown down. I picked another one up, and it looked just as beautiful, but in a totally different way.

"This one should work," I said, holding the flowing, sheer dress high. The colors were gorgeous! "I love this pattern, too. The large flowers remind me of the culture here, and it's so airy and light. I think this could work." I went into my bathroom, took off my casual sundress and slipped the long dress over my head. The neckline was a tad low, but it fit me perfectly. I loved the draping in front and back. The length was perfect for our escape, too.

I called Inga into the bathroom. "What do you think?" I asked her, turning around and admiring the way the dress twirled.

"It's not a bloody fashion show, Ruth Ann!" Inga snapped. "However, it'll do. I'm happy you picked something that you won't keep tripping on."

"Gee, thanks, Inga," I said, a little disappointed she didn't tell me I looked good. I knew it wasn't the right time, but it wouldn't have hurt to give me a tiny compliment.

"Take it off and meet back in the living room," she said, stomping out of the bathroom.

I pulled it off and hung it neatly on the hanger. Axel had tried on a cream blazer, and a pair of black dress pants. He looked fantastic! His tall, slim frame pulled the ensemble off so elegantly. He looked very dapper. I felt a twinge of attraction toward him, but I had to shake it off. If we were in a different time, and a different situation, I would've been interested in Axel. It can never happen, though. Prunella is my cousin, no matter how she's behaving right now. I could never cheat with Axel, it would be so very wrong!

"Perfect," Carlos said, fidgeting with Axel's handkerchief in his front jacket pocket. "You look very distinguished, Axel."

"Thanks," he answered, slipping the jacket off and hanging it up on the hanger.

"Not bad for someone your age," Viktor blurted out near the front door.

"Hey, he's not that old!" I blurted out.

"That's okay, Ruth Ann," Axel said. "He's just being sarcastic. However, compared to him, I am old."

"I'm not far behind, Axel," I said, feeling depressed. I felt great for my age, but just saying, 'for my age', meant I'm not young anymore.

The old maid was called in and Viktor handed her the pile of clothes we didn't need. She mumbled something to Viktor, and he said, "No, no, they're fine."

She became agitated and babbled more to Viktor. He turned to me, frustrated, and said, "She wants you to put it on so she can see if it needs any alterations."

"It fits me perfectly," I interjected. "No alterations needed."

"Just pacify her, please," Viktor begged.

"Fine," I said and marched into the bathroom and took off my clothes again so I could slip the dress on. The old lady appeared out of nowhere and walked very close to me. She grabbed my waist and roughly turned me around so she could eye the dress and how it fit. She pulled some fabric here and there and pulled out a little plastic container full of pins. "No, no, it fits me perfectly," I said, pulling away.

She pointed to a couple areas and nodded repeatedly. "No, I like it looser," I said, taking the container off the sink and placing it back in her hand. "I'm fine with it like this."

She nodded and smiled with a mouth missing several teeth. She took off and disappeared out of the room. "There, that wasn't too bad," Viktor said.

"I wonder what she brought to Prunella?" I couldn't help but ask. "I'm sure she'll look beautiful."

"Who cares!" Inga barked. "This isn't a beauty contest. We're here to figure out a distraction for the party. We don't have time to play dress up!"

"Calm down, Inga," I said. "We have time now. Maybe you need something more to eat."

"We both do," Carlos chimed in. "I'm starving."

Viktor said he would go down to the kitchen and get some food.

"But, we just ate, they might get suspicious!" I reminded him.

"So?" he asked. "You've got an appetite, what's the big deal?"

"Plus, I'm sure Viktor won't run into Manual. He's busy making arrangements for the party tomorrow," Inga said. "I vote for letting him go and get food."

"I'm going," Viktor said, opening the door and heading out. Before he was all the way out the door, he stuck his head in to make sure we'd post someone at the door.

Once he was gone, Carlos asked, "Are we sure we can trust him?"

"I think so," Axel said. "He's risked a lot helping us so far."

"I wonder what's happening with Isabella and Prunella?" I asked, wondering if Prunella was able to get Blue Ice off Isabella's neck.

"Isabella really wanted to get that necklace on Ms. Prunella's neck," Inga said. "I bet she caved, and it's on Ms. Prunella's neck right now."

"I hope not," I said. "What are they going to do with Isabella then?" I was worried for Isabella. If she didn't have the necklace around her neck, then what use would she be for them? I was terrified for the young girl's life, and what they would do to dispose of her.

Chapter 39

We spent the next couple hours in my bedroom thinking of a way to escape during the party. None of us had any success, but at least Viktor was able to scrounge food for Inga and Carlos. He only encountered an angry cook in the kitchen who was working on the evening meal, and the huge event that was sprung on her earlier that day.

"I don't care how mad she was," Carlos declared. "She's a fantastic cook!"

Inga glared at him, probably because he's never told her that. "She's okay," Inga replied, stuffing a mouthful of rice in her mouth.

"No disrespect, Inga," Carlos quickly amended. "I'm just so hungry, anything would taste good right now." He finished shoving a large bite of steak in his mouth. "This meat is so juicy and tender, I can't get enough."

Viktor had been standing at the door starting to get anxious. "I can't believe my boss would want me to stay locked in here with you two. Maybe he really doesn't trust me."

"Viktor," Axel said. "I'm sure that's not the case, and he wouldn't leave you with us if he didn't trust you. You'd let us escape."

"True," he replied. "I think I'm going to check around. I'll be back," he said, exiting into the hall.

After he was gone, Axel turned and asked, "So, nobody really has any ideas for tomorrow night?"

Carlos quickly answered. "I do. I didn't want to say anything just in case Viktor would reject my idea."

"What is it?" I asked, anxiously. "I've drawn a blank."

"You two have to participate at this party in some way or Manual wouldn't make you attend," Carlos started. "I think he only wants you there to brag about how happy he and Prunella are."

"So?" I asked. "We already knew that much."

He threw me a nasty glare and continued. "Yes, but what about the other guests? Do we know who's coming to this party? Is it a bunch of other criminals or just locals he wants to make jealous of his new-found riches?"

"Prunella and Blue Ice, right?" I asked.

"Yep," Carlos answered. "If it's criminals, we're in trouble. There'll be guards everywhere. But, if it's just locals who don't know any better, we can have Viktor slip you two past them and out the door. There won't be so many guards roaming around, and then Inga, Isabella and I can meet you at a specific location."

"Sounds too easy," Axel replied. "I wonder if Viktor can get his hands on a drug that will make everyone at the party immediately sick after eating it?"

"That's horrible!" I exclaimed.

"Not kill people, Ruth Ann. Just give them something that'll make them throw up. There's a pill that makes one violently ill right after a sip of alcohol."

"Not a bad plan," Carlos remarked. "But, can Viktor get his hands on that pill?"

"The man's a drug lord!" Inga spewed. "If Viktor is as high-up in the chain of command as he's told us, I'm sure he knows how to get something like that."

"I think that's our best plan so far," I said. "But, we have to make sure we don't eat or drink that drug."

"What about Ms. Prunella?" Inga asked, nervously. "We can't let her ingest it either."

"We might not have control over that, Inga," Axel said, sadly. "If we let her know, we might get caught. She could tell Manual what we did, and then we're all dead."

We felt it was the most promising plan. Now, we had to convince Viktor to get his hands on the drug. He was only gone a short time when the door flew open, scaring Inga and Carlos. They threw their bodies behind the couch so fast that I heard Inga let out a groan. "She landed on my belt buckle, which is on me!", said Carlos.

"Sorry, Carlos," Inga said, recovering. "I didn't mean to squish you."

"Shhh," Axel swiftly said. "Someone's coming in."

The old lady entered. She was carrying a duffel bag. She placed it on the coffee table, unzipped it and pulled out an assortment of sandals for me, and a few pairs of black shiny shoes for Axel. "On," she said with a thick accent.

I nodded and grabbed the pair of sandals with the lowest heel. They were a shimmery gold color, with barely an inch heel. I slipped them on, and they were a perfect fit. I smiled and nodded at the old lady. I then had an idea. I was going to try and communicate with her. "Thank you," I said, kindly. "What is your name?" I asked, accentuating each word hoping she would understand me.

"I speak English," she replied, displaying her decaying teeth, "My name is Ramona."

"That's a pretty name, Ramona," I said, noticing the others eye me strangely. "My name is Ruth Ann."

"Yes, yes, I know that," she replied, getting a little nervous.

"What do you do here?" I inquired, curiously.

"I take care of many things for," she hesitated, looked around and realized nobody but strangers were here. "Manual. He's my sister's son."

Well, that wasn't what I wanted to hear. I was hoping I could persuade another one of Manual's employees to help us, but discovering she was his aunt wasn't a good thing. However, what she said next took us by surprise!

"He's a bad man," she said, standing very close to me so I was the only one who could hear her.

I bent over and asked, "Did you just tell me your nephew's a bad man?"

She nodded fervently. "Yes, yes, he's very bad. He breaks laws, and hurts people, and steals things from innocent people like you."

"Yes, he does," I said, standing straight again. The poor woman was under five feet, making me look gigantic. "How do you know we're innocent?" I couldn't help but ask.

"I listen and hear things my nephew thinks I don't. He thinks I'm a stupid old lady and only keeps me around because he promised my sister, his mother, on her deathbed to keep me close to him." She added, "He's not my family anymore. I can't watch him hurt you and that pretty lady in his new mistress's bedroom."

"Wait!" I bellowed. "Have you seen Isabella in Prunella's bedroom?"

"Yes, yes, I have," she replied, proudly. "Shall I tell you what I heard?"

"Please," Axel interjected. "I'm Prunella's husband, for now, that is."

"I know. My horrible nephew thinks he can just wave his hand and get rid of you," she was talking to Axel now. "But, I want to help you."

"How?" Axel asked. "Do you know a way out of this place?"

"Of course, I do!" she proclaimed. "I've lived here since it was built twenty years ago. I know every tunnel and escape route. He thinks I'm useless, but I bide my time until I can turn the tables on him. This is the time!"

Wow, she almost looked younger and stronger as she spoke. I wanted to let her in on our plan to drug the guests at the party, but we needed help creating a diversion. I pulled Axel aside for a second and he agreed to tell her. "It's a chance, but what else do we have?"

I asked her to sit down, and I explained how we wanted to find a way to get our hands on a drug that would make people violently ill within minutes of swallowing it. "Yes, I know of that drug. It's called Antabuse."

"What?" Inga asked, stunned the woman answered so quickly.

"Antabuse. It makes you very sick if you drink alcohol after you take it."

"What happens?" Axel asked, a little worried about believing her ability to know any of this.

"After swallowing the pill, the person's face becomes flush, and then a terrible headache hits them. After that, their blood pressure drops and their heart races causing them to get dizzy and finally become so nauseas they vomit."

"Whoa, that sounds terribly dangerous," I said.

"It can be, but if it's controlled it's okay," Carlos said out of the blue.

"How on earth do you know about Antabuse?" Axel asked, confused.

"My father took it. He was an alcoholic for many years. Remember, my parents are very wealthy. They can get treatment for many things most people in my village can't afford."

"Did he use it?" I couldn't help to ask.

"Yes, but only once."

"Why only once?" Inga inquired.

"Once you take that drug and then take a drink, you never want to take it again."

"What happened to your father?" I asked.

"He went through all the stages like Ramona told us, and then he swore off alcohol forever."

"Has he drunk since then?" Inga asked.

"No."

"That's a blessing then," I said, trying to make it a positive comment.

"Yes, I guess," he said, quietly.

"So," Axel said loudly, causing us to jump a little. "I think it's a perfect plan. Ramona, do you know how we can get this drug?"

"Yes, I can get it for you." Manual does many things for the local pharmacies, so they will do anything for him.

"Really?" I asked, surprised, but not too surprised.

"You haven't told us what you saw in Prunella's bedroom?" Inga reminded Ramona. "We got sidetracked with the drug, but I want to hear how Isabella's doing."

"I have to hurry if you want me to get the pills. I will bring them to you with the excuse I have to fix your dress. You need to tell Viktor everything when he comes back and he will figure out how to make sure everyone, but you two, ingest those pills."

"Wait, you know Viktor's helping us?" Axel asked, stunned.

"Yes, he's a good man. He only worked for Manual to make money. My nephew pays well for loyal service."

"I bet," I mumbled. "Can you tell us about Prunella and Isabella before you have to leave?"

"Isabella gave the other lady the pretty blue necklace everyone is talking about."

"NO!" I screamed, falling on to the couch in disbelief. "Why would she give it up so easily?"

"She might not have had a choice, Ruth Ann," Axel said, standing over me. "Are you alright?"

"Yes, I'm just tired, and so disappointed Prunella has our necklace. I'll never get to hold it again, will I?" I felt a heavy pressure and sense of loss fall upon me.

"I have to go now," Ramona blabbed, nervously. "Isabella was taken out of her room by Manual and Sal. I don't know where they took her yet, but I will investigate. I promise I'll let you or Viktor know as soon as I find out. I'm sorry I don't have better news," and with that she turned and hurried out of the room.

"This is terrible!" Inga blurted out. "We're done for now."

"No, this can't be it for us. We can get the necklace back before leaving here," Carlos said. "Maybe when everyone's sick, we can get it off Prunella's neck without anyone seeing us."

"Us?" Axel asked Carlos. "You're not going to the party."

"Well, we won't be out in the open, but we'll be close by. And when mayhem breaks out, we'll come out and help," he said.

Axel let that remark go for now. We had another, huge problem. Well, two huge problems. "So," I began, feeling less hopeless. "We need to find out where Manual and Sal brought poor Isabella. I'm worried they threw her into that hole in the ground. And," I said, barely taking a breath in case someone interrupted my thought. "And, there's something none of us have thought about." I said as I raised my hand. "If we give this drug to a large number of people, there'll be, excuse the disgusting use of the word, but, there'll be vomit everywhere!"

"Gross, Ruth Ann," Inga cried.

"She's got a valid point," Axel replied. "Do we even know how many people are coming to this party?"

"Thirty," a male voice answered from the door.

"Viktor!" I bellowed. "We didn't hear you come in."

"I told you to watch and listen for anyone coming. You failed miserably!"

"Sorry, we were so busy talking about what Ramona told us," I said, wondering if he knew we had spoken to her.

"Don't worry, Ruth Ann. I ran into her a minute ago. She told me she talked with all of you. It's not good about Isabella. I haven't located her yet, but Ramona said she has a few ideas and she'd get back here right away."

"So, we have to just sit here and wait?" Inga asked, worried.

"I can't be too obvious," Viktor mentioned. "I have to stay on my boss's good side."

"Leave him alone," Axel said, disappointed. "We don't have a choice but to wait for Ramona. Now, you mentioned thirty guests? Any other details about the party?"

"Yes. I'm afraid it's not good," he said, staying close to

the door and opening it every minute or so to make sure we were still alone. "He invited some high-powered business acquaintances of his, and let's just say, they aren't the most upstanding individuals."

"They're criminals, aren't they?" Carlos inquired.

"Most of them, I believe, have dabbled in acquiring rare gems and other illegal activities. I wouldn't mess with any of them."

"That's great, just great!" Inga howled. "What are we going to do now?"

"We stick with our plan," Axel replied. He walked closer to Viktor and told him, "We came up with another idea instead of an explosion. We asked Ramona if she could can get her hands on a drug called Antabuse."

Viktor's eyes popped wide-open. "What? That's a crazy idea."

"Think about it," Axel said. "It lessens the risk of killing anyone. Do you know what Antabuse is and does to a person who takes the pill?"

"Yes, I do. I've seen it," he hesitated, and shook his head. "No, it's impossible."

"Why?" I asked, concerned. "You started to say that you've seen it ... what? You know of someone who's taken the drug?"

"Well, no, and yes. I know what happens when a person ingests that drug. It's pretty severe, don't you think?"

"Yes, but isn't that what we need?" Axel asked him.

"So, you want to slip this pill into all thirty guest's drinks?" Viktor asked.

"And into Manual's and Prunella's," I added, waiting for him to explode.

"NO WAY!" he hollered, utterly opposed to drugging

Prunella. I didn't think Viktor cared what happened to Manual anymore.

"We have to give it to everyone," Axel said. "And that includes Prunella."

"That's hard to believe you want to cause such harm on Prunella," he said, shaking his head in disbelief. "She'll be so sick, and she's just recovered from her coma."

"We know, but she appears quite strong now, Viktor," Axel said. "I think it's the lesser of two evils. Our choices are creating an explosion that could kill innocent, well maybe not so innocent, people, or slip a pill and make people throw up."

"Throw up violently, after they thought they were having a heart attack!" Viktor said.

"You would rather cause an explosion?" I asked, wondering if he was right. It was awfully mean to inflict this kind of sickness.

"I don't know," he answered, rubbing his shaven head. "Let's wait for Ramona. She's always helped me when I've been conflicted."

"She has?" I asked, surprised. "You two are close?"

"Oh, yes," he replied. "She knows I've had a lot of trouble staying here and witnessing the things I have. She told me when I was younger that once I make some more money I could disappear and live a better life."

"You still can," I said, smiling. "We promised to help you."

"I know. I'm nervous this won't work like we're planning. I'm not sure what to do."

We left Viktor to keep watch at the door and the rest of us clustered near the balcony. It was getting close to dinnertime, and I wondered what Manual was going to do with Axel and me. Not long after, Viktor motioned for Inga and Carlos to hide. He opened the door to Ramona, and unfortunately, Manual.

"Viktor," his boss said, loudly. "Are they behaving in here?"

"Yes, Sir," he replied, standing tall and rigid.

"Ramona tells me they picked out clothes, but she wants to alter Ruth Ann's dress a little. That's why she's back with me."

"Thanks," I called out from the couch where I was trying to sit casually.

Manual gave his aunt a little shove and she rushed to me and we disappeared into my bedroom. Luckily, I could still over hear them talking.

"So, Axel, I have some news for you," Manual said with an odd smile on his face.

"Go ahead," Axel said, unenthusiastically.

"Isabella gave the necklace back to your wife!" he blurted it out hoping for an angry reaction from Axel, but Axel sat calmly and didn't say a word. "Did you hear me, Eklund?" he asked, irritated.

"Yes, I did," he answered. "What am I supposed to do about it? We knew it was going to happen."

"You did?" he asked, baffled. "You and Ruth Ann told me that the necklace can't leave your possession!"

"Well, we were wrong," he said, matter of factly. Manual's temper flared and he stormed out of my room and slammed the door.

"Whoa," I said, sticking my head into the living room from the bedroom. "He's ticked off."

"It was quite amusing," Axel said, grinning. "You know that I'm seething inside about losing the necklace, but I won't let him know that."

"I wish I could be like that," I said. "I'm such an open book. I would be hysterical, crying on the couch if he said that to me."

"You're stronger than you give yourself credit for, Ruth Ann," Axel said. "Now, get Ramona in here and let's hear what she has to say."

Ramona, Carlos and Inga hurried into the living room. Viktor rushed into the hall after his boss to find what he was going to do.

"He's a fool," Ramona said in English. "He wanted you to storm after him so Viktor would have to hit you. You played my nephew perfectly, Mr. Eklund."

"Axel, please call me Axel."

She ignored his request and continued. "I know where the pretty young girl is."

"Isabella?" Inga asked, making sure she wasn't referring to Prunella.

"Yes, yes," she said, agitated. "She's not hurt. She's been sequestered in Manual's bedroom."

"What?" I exclaimed. "Why?"

"My vile nephew thinks he can have *both* women."

"That's horrible," I said. "What does he want with Isabella?"

"He wanted her before, but she disappeared," Ramona said. "Everyone here thought she and her grandmother were witches. I never did," she said, proudly. "I knew they had some strange powers, but they weren't evil."

"No, they aren't," I replied. "Or weren't. Meme is dead."

"I heard," Ramona answered. "Isabella told me."

"Have you spoken with her?" Axel asked, curiously.

"Yes, I was just with her."

"Why?" I inquired.

"I had to bring her dresses to try on for the party."

"She's going to the party?" Carlos jumped in and asked. "But, why?"

"Manual wants her there," Ramona answered. "He's disturbed, and I don't know why."

"Greed," Axel suggested. "He's greedy with his money, his gems, and his women."

Inga retorted, "Well, he's not taking Ms. Prunella or Isabella for his own!"

"We can agree on Isabella, but Prunella wants to be with him," Axel said, bitterly. "If I could only understand why she wants him it would be easier to handle."

"Money, power, and her need to run away from us," I said, feeling the latter was the most compelling reason. "She's confused, and I believe the curse that put her into a coma messed up her thinking."

"Finally," Inga mumbled. "You understand how I feel."

"Of course, I do," I said, empathetically. "But, we can't force Prunella to live somewhere she doesn't want to. Maybe someday she'll return to us."

Inga huffed, but didn't argue. I think she was starting to get what we were saying. I knew she was a tough woman, but even she couldn't force her beloved Prunella to come home with us.

Chapter 40

Ramona told us Isabella was staying strong knowing we would rescue her soon. "She feels horrible guilt over the necklace," Ramona said. "She doesn't want you to be mad at her, and she sobbed when she told me so."

"We're not mad!" I bellowed. "You must tell her that. Our only concern is to get her away from that man and get us out of here." I asked Ramona if she could get the drug. "Oh, yes, but I need a little time to fetch it. One of our pharmacies is getting it for us and delivering it to one of our outbuildings"

"How are you going to be able to get it?" Axel asked. "Isn't this building heavily guarded?"

"Yes, of course it is," she barked. "But, I've had to retrieve many items stored there, so they won't give me a second look. Don't worry, it'll be fine. Did you ask Viktor if he thinks this could work?"

"He's not happy about it," Axel said.

"What other choice do you have?" she inquired, sitting in a chair next to the couch. It was hard to believe this woman was so old, my guess in her mid-eighties, because her mind was so active.

"How soon can you get back here with the drug?" Axel

asked, getting back to business. "We need to figure how to get people to take it."

The old woman smiled and answered Axel's question. "I have a plan. My nephew is planning a grand dinner. He wants everyone to be sitting in his dining room when he introduces Prunella and the necklace. He plans on making a grand toast and bragging about his latest acquisition. Everyone will be sipping champagne. That's where the pills need to be placed. I will make sure all the glasses are filled in the kitchen, and the waiters will carry them out on silver trays. No one would dare not drink to a toast made by our host. It'll work beautifully."

"Wow," Inga said, impressed. "You've really thought this out."

"Yes. I've been waiting for an opportunity like this for years." She smiled broadly, displaying her horribly repulsive mouth. "I despise him."

"You have a lot of hatred aimed at him. Can I ask why?" I hoped I wasn't being intrusive, but she wanted such vengeance against him.

She looked me straight in the face and said, bitterly, "He murdered my husband."

"I'm so sorry," I said, not knowing if I wanted to know why.

"He did it for no reason. He never trusted my beloved husband, and when he felt he had reason, he executed him."

"What did he think your husband did?" Inga asked.

"Stole from him, but he never did. It was just an excuse to get rid of him."

"Why did you stay here for so long after it happened?" I couldn't help asking.

"For this day."

"So, you're not doing this to help us, but to unhinge your revenge on him, right?" Carlos asked.

"Yes!" she spat. "But, I do want to help all of you, too."

"Thank you, and we're all so very sorry for what happened to you. Once this is over, can you leave here?" Axel asked.

"No. I'm stuck here, but he'll never suspect I had any part of this. But, I'll know, and it'll make the rest of my life here bearable."

I wanted to tell her she still had time to be happy, and leave this horrid place, but Axel placed a gentle hand on my forearm. He whispered, "Let her be." I nodded, agreeing it was best to leave it alone.

"Do you know more about this dinner party?" Inga asked, trying to get us back on track.

"There will be thirty people dining, and the staff is fervently cleaning the silver and setting the table with Manual's most expensive china. He's sparing no expense. There will be food catered since there's not enough time to cook that much food. I know the champagne and wine will be flowing, and there will be a lot of guards roaming the grounds. That's going to be a gigantic obstacle for your escape. I can help you with that, too."

"How?" Axel asked, feeling grateful we met this woman.

"In due time. Let me get my hands on the drug first, and then I'll discuss how you'll leave this place and never return."

She took off in a hurry, and Viktor closed the door. "She has taken control over the situation, hasn't she?"

"Not everything, Viktor," I said, realizing he wasn't feeling needed. "She's just getting the pills for us."

"And making sure the staff pours the champagne in the kitchen while she sneaks the pills in the glasses. And, she's going to come up with an escape route."

"You're going to have your hands full, Viktor," I said, hoping to persuade him that he was invaluable to our plan. "You can't let Manual see you helping us escape!"

"But, I thought I was coming with you?" he asked, anxiously. "You promised."

"Of course, you are," Axel quickly interjected. "We'll have a place to meet after all hell breaks loose. Ramona will tell us where to go, and you'll be there, too."

"Oh, I guess that'll work," he said, looking slightly convinced. "I have to bring you and Ruth Ann down to the kitchen soon. My boss wants you there to eat."

"In the kitchen because everyone's working in the dining room, right?" I asked.

"Yes. He wants me by your side at all times. I don't think he trusts you two."

Axel laughed. "He shouldn't! But, what he isn't counting on is you. He shouldn't be trusting you anymore!"

"Good point," Viktor replied, sufficiently convinced and amused. "I'll make sure to bring dinner up here for you both," he added, referring to Inga and Carlos.

"I hope Manual brings Isabella to eat with him," I said, nervously. "He wouldn't keep her hostage in his room, would he?" I asked, Viktor.

"I wouldn't doubt it. He's furious with you and Axel for betraying him with her. He just can't figure out how Isabella got here. He confiscated your cell phones and there's no house phones for you to use. What's worrying me is that he believes there's an insider helping you both and is suspicious of everyone in his staff."

"Really?" I asked, surprised. "Would he suspect his Aunt Ramona?"

"I doubt it," he replied. "She's family, and I can't imagine him thinking she would do anything to betray him. He thinks she's kind of worthless and old. Boy, does he have that one wrong! She hates her nephew!" Viktor added, emphasizing the last comment.

"She told us that, too," I said. "As long as he doesn't suspect her and lock her up. We need her to get her hands on those pills."

"I could get them," Viktor exclaimed.

"We don't want any suspicion to fall on you," Axel said right away. "You're are only way out of this hell-hole."

Viktor smiled, apparently satisfied with Axel's comment, and said, "I'll get you out of here. I don't know about Prunella though."

"She's not coming," Axel snapped. "I won't force her to come with us." He looked at Inga, Carlos and even me and added, "Nobody argues with me again about my decision. If I had even the slightest sense that she's pretending to have feelings for Manual, then I would get her out of here, but I don't believe that's the case. If she wants to come home, we'll be there."

"But," Inga started to say, but clamped her mouth shut. She looked exhausted. It had been a grueling couple of days and I felt it too.

"So," Viktor said, walking back toward the door. "Let's go you two. It's dinnertime. Try and behave down there, would you? It'll make my life a little easier if I don't have to react when Axel pushes him too far."

"You mean hit me?" Axel asked. "If you have to, you have to."

"No, Axel," I bellowed. "Don't do or say anything to get Manual that angry, please!"

"I promise I'll try, but that man has a way of pulling the worst out of me."

We left Inga and Carlos and headed down into the kitchen. I promised to bring food back because it was going to be a long, but hopefully our last, night stuck together. Viktor worried Axel and I would be separated if Axel irritated Manual again, but Axel promised to behave.

"What time is it, anyway?" I asked, just as we stepped into the foyer.

"It's 6:30," Viktor asked, looking at his large, shiny gold watch. He noticed my look, and quickly added, "I bought it, Ruth Ann. It's not a stolen watch."

"I wasn't thinking that, Viktor. I was only admiring it, that's all. It's an expensive watch, isn't it?"

"Yes, and I earned every penny to purchase it."

"Yes, I'm sure you did," I said, smiling. "I really wasn't accusing you of anything. Axel and I trust you, Viktor."

"Thanks," he said, less defensively. "I've been on my own for so long, I'm not used to anyone believing me."

"That's changed now," I said quietly as we stepped inside the massive kitchen.

"Here they are, boss," Viktor said, giving Axel a little shove toward the long wooden table. "Sit," he ordered Axel. He turned to me, and I quickly took a seat next to Axel.

Manual was standing at the end of the large island, holding a water bottle. He walked toward us and sat across from me. "I hope your accommodations are comfortable still?"

"Yes," I answered before Axel could give a snide remark. "I thought I wasn't going to be locked in a room, Manual."

"That, Ruth Ann, was before you and Axel lied to me about Isabella. She's not a figment of my imagination like the two of you were trying to convince me. That was a cruel

347

trick!"

"You would've done the same thing," I snapped. "If you were kidnapped and being held prisoner, you would have tried anything to get out of here."

His face mellowed, slightly. He thought it over for a moment, and then actually smiled. "I guess you're right, Ruth Ann! I would lie and kill to keep myself free."

"Thank you," I said, looking at Axel to see if he was going to remark.

"Nothing from you, Eklund?" Manual asked sarcastically.

"Nope," Axel replied.

That seemed to anger Manual more than if Axel argued with him. "Eklund? You're trying my nerves! If you want to get out of here alive, try being respectful."

"Respectful?" Axel couldn't help but ask. "You just admitted you'd kill to get out of a situation like this. I'm being a perfect prisoner for you then, because I haven't laid a hand on you!"

Manual appeared confused. Thankfully, he let it go and waved for his cook to bring the food over. A large, rotund woman with a bright yellow apron rushed over holding a tray filled with an assortment of sandwiches. "Excuse the informal dinner. We're busy preparing for our dinner party tomorrow night." He grabbed a huge ham sandwich and took a bite. Before his mouth was empty, he asked, "I heard you picked out a lovely dress, Ruth Ann."

I looked at him in disgust as a glob of mayonnaise spilled down his chin. "Um, yes, I did." I got my focus back and asked, "May I ask why Axel and I are attending this dinner? I mean, we're your prisoners."

"It'll be the final blow for you to see how happy Prunella

is here. And why she's chosen to stay with me."

I laid a hand on Axel's thigh, and felt it tense. I knew he might not be able to ignore Manual's words. Instead of swatting my hand away, he grabbed it and gave it a tight squeeze. He didn't let go but hung on firmly. If it helped keep him calm, I happily obliged.

I used my other hand to take a turkey and swiss sandwich on soft, rye, marble bread. Thankfully, there wasn't any mayonnaise on it, but a generous spread of yellow mustard. I took a healthy bite and relished every chew. A minute later, Axel pulled his hand away and grabbed a tuna sandwich with lettuce and tomato. He ate slowly, trying to keep us in the kitchen until Manual left and Viktor could snatch a few extra sandwiches for Inga and Carlos.

I laid the other half of my sandwich down and asked Manual, "What's being served tomorrow at your party?"

"Much, much food!" he bellowed, proudly. "There will be an abundance of food and champagne served tomorrow night. You'll be very pleased at my abilities to throw a party at such short notice."

I glared at the man and said, "If you're looking for a compliment from me, you'll be waiting a very long time. This isn't an event I care to be a part of!"

"There's that sense of humor in you, Ruth Ann," he cackled, loudly. "You should be very happy to be at the dinner table instead of in my secret little room. Would you rather sit in a dirty hole or at an elegant table sipping champagne and consuming delicacies?"

"The table, Manual," I admitted, truthfully.

"So, you'll behave like a good girl?" he asked, sarcastically.

"Yes, Manual. I'll behave appropriately," I answered,

knowing that appropriate for me meant drugging the entire table and waiting for the symptoms to appear."

Chapter 41

The rest of the evening was uneventful. Manual didn't stay in the kitchen long. He had one of his staff fix a plate for Isabella and then disappeared out of the kitchen. I finished the rest of my food and waited for Viktor to come a little closer. "Can we sneak some of those sandwiches upstairs?"

"I'm already on it," Viktor said, reaching over my shoulder and taking two huge sandwiches with one of his bulky hands. He shoved them into a plastic bag that appeared out of nowhere. He grabbed a couple more, prompting the cook to yell at him. He whipped his head around and hollered words in Spanish that I couldn't understand. She growled and turned her attention back to the pile of potatoes she was peeling at the sink.

Once we arrived on the third floor, Viktor said he thought it went well in the kitchen. His boss didn't kill us or separate Axel and me for duping him with our part in Isabella's performance. Viktor opened my bedroom door and Axel was almost greeted with a nasty concussion. "Inga, it's me and Axel!"

"I thought it was that other man," she exclaimed, lowering a long piece of wood.

"What man?" Viktor immediately asked her.

"Sal," Carlos answered for Inga. "He came in here while you two were dining."

"What? Why?" Viktor hollered, worried.

"He didn't say," Carlos replied, sarcastically. "He came in and started searching the room. Inga and I were terrified and ran out to the balcony. I'm just thankful he didn't go out there!"

"What could he be looking for?" I asked, nervously. "They have the necklace. That's all they wanted, right?" I turned and asked a pale-faced Viktor. "I'll be right back," he said, and then disappeared down the hall.

"I'm just glad we didn't get spotted," Inga said, walking into the closet and getting rid of the wooden shelf she held.

"Me, too," Axel said.

"Viktor will find out and let us know," I said, exhaling loudly. "Oh, here's some food," I handed Inga a bag stuffed with deli sandwiches. She reached in, handed one to Carlos and took one for herself.

We waited for about a half an hour before Viktor returned, furious. "He's a moron!" he thundered. "He thought Ruth Ann might have some other priceless jewels hidden in here, and he took it upon himself to search her room. I chewed him out good and said if he ever pulled a stunt like that again, he'd be answering to our boss. The guy cowered and swore it would never happen again."

"Good," I said.

"That was too close," Axel mumbled. "I'm happy we're getting out of here tomorrow night."

"I sure hope so," Inga said. "Nothing ever goes as planned with us, does it?"

"It has to," I answered. "We don't have any other choice."

Viktor informed Axel and me that we were to bunker down in my room until breakfast. Manual clearly told Viktor that I wasn't to take one step out of this room or he wouldn't treat me so graciously anymore. "He's delusional!" I bellowed, angry that he actually believed he'd been kind and generous to me.

"Let it go for now," Axel said. "Soon, we'll never have to look at him again."

"Good!" I replied. I turned back to Viktor and asked, curiously, "Manual wants Axel and me to spend the night together? He's not only delusional, he's sick."

"Ruth Ann," Inga interrupted. "I highly doubt Mr. Marquez wants you and Mr. Eklund to have an *intimate evening* together, if you know what I mean."

"Yes, Inga, I get it," I said, rolling my eyes. "I just figured he put us together hoping we'd fall into each other's arms." The moment the words left my mouth I regretted them. Inga and Carlos stared oddly at me. I quickly corrected my comment. "You know what I meant! If Axel had another interest, then he'd give up his wife willingly so Manual could have her."

"Oh, yeah, that makes sense," Inga said, nodding her head. "But, that'll never happen."

Neither Axel nor I responded, but Carlos did. "Who cares?" he blurted. "We should get some rest so we're ready for tomorrow. We can discuss our plans in the morning."

"Wait!" I cried. "We haven't heard from Ramona."

"She's handling your request, Ruth Ann," Viktor said, pulling a couple chairs to the door and pushing them together. "She'll come in here as soon as she has her stash."

"First, it's not *my request*," I corrected him. "It's a group decision."

"Yes, that's what I meant," Viktor said, trying to fit his enormous body on the two chairs. He groaned and tried several positions before kicking one of the chairs to the ground in frustration.

"Why don't you take one of the cushioned chairs and use the harder chair for your feet?" I suggested. "I think you'll be more comfortable."

Viktor agreed, got himself settled and hunkered down for the night. "This isn't so bad," he said, leaning his head on the back of the chair and closing his eyes.

"I'm going to lie down on the bed," I said, walking into the bedroom area. "Inga, why don't you join me? Axel and Carlos can sleep on the couches."

"I wish we knew what was going on with Isabella," Carlos said, trying to get comfortable on the couch. "That man better not touch a hair on her head!"

"I think he's trying to scare us," Axel said. "He's too afraid of her to do anything else to her."

"That's true," I called out from my bed. "She's probably sleeping on his couch. He's not enough of a gentleman to let her have the bed!"

"Probably not," Inga said, yawning and closing her eyes. She laid flat on her back with her arms crossed, fully clothed including her shoes. She was ready to flee in an instant.

Surprisingly, I was able to relax and drift off to sleep. Unfortunately, I had a visitor interrupt my beautiful dream of lying on a sunny beach, the fluffy warm sand between my toes. I was sipping a tasty, cold Pina colada, looking out at the calm, blue-green Caribbean Sea when someone stood right in front of me.

"Meme!" I cried, not so happy to see here this time.

"I didn't have a choice, Ruth Ann," she said, not looking

pleased with me. *"You know I love seeing you, but can't it be under better circumstances? I'm trying to get out of this place, but it's been difficult figuring a viable plan."* I said.

"I told you what to do!" she snarled, displaying her new set of bright white teeth. *Wherever she was, she'd had a total transformation. She was still old, but her skin wasn't wrinkled, and her teeth were beautiful.*

"No, Meme, you didn't. You told us we'd figure it out once we were here! I'm trying the best I can!"

"I'm referring to Prunella. She's not safe. Isabella risked her life to dissuade Manual from taking the necklace instead of placing it on Prunella's neck. That was a foolish scheme, and now Isabella's in the clutches of that imbecile!"

"I'm sorry, we didn't plan on her getting caught. Hey," I hesitated, thinking of something very important to tell Meme. *"You were the one who told me that necklace would never leave me! That's why we planned to fool Manual and convince him he didn't want the necklace."*

"Yes, Ruth Ann, but you have it backwards. You cannot control the necklace; the necklace has control over you!"

"What!" I cried. *"That's impossible."*

"The necklace will always make its' way back to you. You don't have to play games."

"But, Prunella has the necklace around her neck now, and she doesn't want anything to do with us anymore."

"I realize that, Ruth Ann. I didn't plan on this misfortunate turn of events."

"What am I to do? We can't force her to come home with us. Manual brags and brags about how they want to be together, and Prunella doesn't deny it. She wants to start a new life, here, with that maniac."

"You're right about letting her go, for now. I don't have

a good feeling about this, Ruth Ann. Isabella is fine, right now, but that party tomorrow night is going to be very dangerous."

"We're going to drug everyone and grab my necklace and get the heck out of here."

"You think it'll happen just like that, do you?" she asked, grinning at my naiveté.

"I hope it will. We have to wait for Manual's aunt to get her hands on the drug."

"Ramona," Meme said. "She's due for some peace in her life. She's trustworthy, so let her help you."

"I'm glad you think so. Is there anything else I should be aware of?"

She shook her head and told me she couldn't see what was going to happen and didn't understand why. "I'm losing my abilities, Ruth Ann. My time is growing short. I need to alert you to a couple things, though."

"Please, hurry," I said, anxiously.

"First, Isabella needs to be filled in on your plans. She's stuck in that room with him right now, but you'll see her in the morning. For now, she's safe. You'll have to be careful Manual doesn't catch you two conspiring. Have Viktor or Axel cause a distraction. You'll have to be fast and give her all the details."

"Okay," I said, knowing I could handle that much so far. "What else?"

She grabbed her head with her hands. "My head hurts, and it shouldn't. Something very bad is going to happen, but I can't see it! I think," her voice became inaudible, but her mouth kept moving. Then I caught, "yes, they are in grave danger. Protect them, Ruth Ann." Then her body dissolved into thin air and I was back in my dream, holding my Pina Colada in my lounge chair.

"*Meme!*" *I hollered, looking everywhere for her. "I didn't catch who was in grave danger! Please, come back and tell me!" And then it was over.*

"Ruth Ann," Inga called my name. "Wake up! You're having a nightmare."

I opened my eyes and saw Inga's face about two inches from mine. "Inga, I'm fine, I think," I said, pushing her away and sitting up. "Did I talk in my sleep?"

"Yes, you were yelling for Meme to come back. Come back from where? She's dead, Ruth Ann," Inga said, confused.

"Carlos and I heard you hollering for Meme, too. You said something about someone being in grave danger. Who are you talking about?" Axel asked anxiously, sitting on the edge of the bed on my side. "Did you have another one of those encounters with Meme?"

"Yes, I did," I answered, still feeling hazy. "I was having a terrific dream, and she interrupted it. That's so weird how she does that. It has to be real if she interrupts a dream, right?" I asked, trying to figure out if Meme was in my dream or interrupted my dream.

"Tell us what happened," Axel pleaded. "You're making me nervous!"

I tried to recall everything she told me, and when I was done, the three of them were staring at me like I was crazy. "Really, that's what happened."

"So, Meme was losing her *powers*, and then she warned you someone was in danger, and poof, she disappeared!" Inga said, skeptically. I knew it was hard to believe, but her previous encounters with me were accurate.

"I believe you," Axel said. "Meme's worried our plan is

going to put one of us in serious danger."

"Who?" Carlos asked, worried. "As long as we don't drink the champagne, we'll be fine."

"Carlos," I began. "You won't be at the party to drink any of the champagne, remember?"

"Oh, yes, I just meant one of you two or Isabella."

"Isabella," I cried out, startling them. "I forgot to tell you about Isabella!"

"Tell us!" Carlos demanded.

"Meme said she has to be warned of our plans. It's very important we tell her what we're doing and when, so she can be ready to act with us."

"How are we going to see her?" Axel asked.

"At breakfast," I answered. "Meme told me to tell you or Viktor to cause a minor distraction so I can speak briefly to Isabella."

"I'm sure that can be arranged," Viktor said, walking into the bedroom. "What's going on in here?"

"You slept through Ruth Ann's dream!" Inga spat, angrily.

"I'll fill him in, quickly," I said, replaying everything that happened.

"This is insane!" Viktor said afterward. "How can a dead person just show up in your dream?"

"I don't know, Viktor," I admitted, truthfully. "But, it's happened, and she's been correct each time."

"I can get to Isabella, somehow," he said.

"No, Meme specifically told me to do it at breakfast. Plus, we don't have our final plans yet," I said.

"Let's get some more sleep, and to talk further in the morning," Axel said, yawning. "Hopefully, Ramona will be here before breakfast."

We agreed and went back to sleep. I had a difficult time drifting off, but when I did I had no more dreams. I woke alone in my bed with the sun filling the bedroom.

"What the ..." I said but stopped when I saw Manual hovering over me.

"Good morning, Ruth Ann," he said, smiling cheerily.

Fuming, I sat up and snapped, "What are you doing in here, and how dare you come into my bedroom!"

"*My bedroom*," he reminded me.

"It's rude and uncalled for. What do you want?"

"I'm here to wake you so we can have a nice breakfast. It's going to be a very busy day, and I need your cooperation."

"For what?"

"The party, of course!"

"Oh, yeah, that's right. I'll be counting the minutes," I replied sarcastically, wiping the smile off his face. I swiftly amended my remark. "Sorry, you woke me up, and I wasn't expecting you to be standing over me."

He calmed down, and said, "You're right. That was rude of me to hover. I'll be in the kitchen waiting for you and Eklund. I'll wake him now."

He turned to leave, and I called out, "I'll do it. I'd hate to see him react in a way you wouldn't appreciate, Manual."

He nodded and said, "Now you're getting it, Ruth Ann. Cooperation will take you a long way"

"Cooperate my ass," I mumbled quietly to myself. If he thinks I'm going to help him, he's more delusional than I thought.

I got out of bed, wondering where Inga fled and how she knew Manual was sneaking in. I found her out on the balcony waiting for him to leave.

"There you are!" I cried. "Quick thinking."

"I heard Viktor holler as Manual tried to open the door. His chair was leaning against the door and he went backwards. He was very loud, alerting Carlos and me, so we fled outside."

"Is Carlos still out there?" I inquired.

"No, he went inside the other room by Mr. Eklund."

"I didn't hear anything," I said, wondering how I missed all the commotion.

"You have a tendency of doing that," Inga said, shaking her head. "You must've really been in a deep sleep. Any more Meme visions?"

"Nope."

Inga and I walked into the living room and found Axel and Carlos sitting on the couch. "That was close," Carlos said. "Thanks, Viktor," he called to the grumpy young man by the door.

"He bashed my head when he opened the door, but at least it bought us enough time for you and Inga to hide."

Inga and Carlos agreed, and we began our day of intense planning.

Chapter 42

"Ah, there you three are," Manual said sitting at the kitchen table. "Please, join us."

I couldn't respond because I was thrown off guard when I saw Prunella on one side of Manual, and Isabella on the other. Prunella was smiling at him and sipping tea, while Isabella was scowling with her arms crossed across her chest. "Good morning," I said, trying not to let Manual or Prunella see how horrified I was at seeing the two of them happy. I didn't think Axel would say a word, and Viktor had already walked to the island and grabbed a cup of coffee. Axel and I sat directly across from them. There was an assortment of pastries and some cut fruit on a large platter.

"I told the cook to not worry about us for breakfast, Ruth Ann," Manual said, noticing my disapproval. "We didn't have time to make a full breakfast. I do hope you understand?"

I nodded, and grabbed a chocolate filled croissant, and filled a small bowl with fruit. It still was more than I usually ate, so I was fine, but, I didn't want him to know that.

Axel didn't take anything, and I gave him a slight nudge. "You need to eat something," I muttered, quietly. "It's going to be a *long* day."

He obliged, and grabbed a cinnamon roll, and some cranberry juice. "What are we supposed to do all day, Manual?" Axel inquired. "Are we to stay hidden in Ruth Ann's bedroom again?" He kept his gaze on Manual, ignoring Prunella's baby blue eyes staring at him.

"No, I think you can get a little exercise today," he said, rubbing his protruding belly. "I'll have Sal or one of the others take you for a walk around my property. It's quite large, and there are lots of beautiful flowers to see and smell."

"It's too hot to walk around outside," Axel stammered. "I'd rather stay inside."

"Have it your way," Manual replied, shrugging his shoulders. "Ruth Ann?" he turned his attention to me. "Would you like to take a walk outside?"

I actually did, but what would Axel think? I needed to have a clear head, and it was going to be a long day. Plus, wouldn't it be helpful to familiarize ourselves with the property? "I would like to, Manual," I said cheerily, prompting a confused look on Axel's face.

"I need fresh air," I said. "Plus, I'd love to see *all* of your property."

"Well, you can't see it all, but a nice portion of it. I'll have one of my men take you, and Viktor can take Axel to my office."

"Your office?" Axel asked, confused. "Won't you be in there working?"

"I don't need it today," he answered. "I want you close by, though."

"What for?" Axel asked.

Manual didn't answer him but turned to Isabella and told her to eat. She clearly stated she wasn't hungry. I tried to get her to eat, but she refused. It was at that moment I remembered we needed a distraction so I could get Isabella alone for a second. I thought fast, and out of nowhere Viktor hollered that there was a stranger looking in the kitchen window. The poor cook dropped a large pot filled with hot water and screamed. Manual, Prunella, and Axel rushed to her aid, as I grabbed Isabella's arm and whispered as fast as I could.

"Please don't be mad at us! We had no way of getting to you. Did he hurt you or ..." she cut me off and told me no, he did nothing to her but force her to sleep on the lumpy couch.

"I'm not mad, but what are we doing tonight? We have to get out of here!"

"We are. Manual's Aunt Ramona is going to help us."

"Yes, I know, I spoke with her briefly. She filled me in on the plan with the pills in the champagne."

"We haven't seen her in a long time. Do you know where she is?"

"She's right behind you, Ruth Ann," Isabella said, shutting me up quickly. I spun around and saw the short, old woman smiling. She gave me a tiny wink and went to help the others.

"There's nobody out there, sir," Sal said, entering through a back-kitchen door. "If someone was there, he's gone now."

"I want every guard on high alert. I want nothing to interfere with tonight's dinner party, got it?" Manual ordered.

"Yes, sir," Sal and Viktor responded. Sal left the kitchen and went back outside. Manual turned to me and Isabella standing near the table with an odd look on his face, and asked, "What were you two talking about?"

"Nothing," I quickly replied. "We wanted to come and help your poor maid, but there was no room over there. You were panicking about an intruder."

"Oh, don't worry about intruders," he said, waving his hand in the air brushing off what happened. "I have top notch guards, and they won't let anyone inside."

I wanted to blurt out that Inga, Carlos and Isabella snuck in, but obviously that would be unwise. Manual, probably realizing the same thing changed the subject. "I don't think you'll be able to take that walk, Ruth Ann. Not with a possible intruder out there. It could be dangerous."

"Nonsense!" I cried. "I need some air. I can go alone."

"Not a chance," he said, laughing.

Stunned, I said, "I wouldn't leave without Axel and the others."

"What others?" he retorted, causing me to panic.

"Isabella, and Prunella." Before Prunella, who was silent this entire time, could speak, I said, "I know, I know. You're staying here. It was a slip of the tongue."

Manual quickly became bored with our conversation. "Fine, I'll let Viktor take you, and Sal will guard Axel in my office. I need Viktor to speak with the guards outside anyway and they listen to him better than Sal. Got that Viktor? Don't let her out of your sight for one second."

"I won't, boss," he said. This put us in a great position. I could check out possible escape routes with Viktor's help.

Sal escorted Axel and Isabella to Manual's office. Unfortunately, they wouldn't be able to speak freely with Sal hanging around. Prunella remained in the kitchen with Manual, and I left with Viktor out the back door.

"That was close. Did you get to tell Isabella everything?" Viktor asked.

"I couldn't say much because we don't know what Ramona uncovered. Too bad she couldn't walk with us."

"There she is," Viktor said as we started down a stone

path toward a beautiful outdoor pool.

I turned and spotted Ramona coming out the back door. She wasn't fast, but she made it to us quickly. "Does my boss know you're out here?" Viktor asked, worried he'd get in trouble.

"No, he doesn't care what I do around here."

"I'm so happy to see you, Ramona," I said, gently putting my hand on her shoulder. "Any luck?"

"Oh, yes, it's all done."

"Tell us," I said, eagerly.

"I've got a bottle filled with 100 pills of the drug you asked for. I also know exactly how we're going to get you out of here."

"How?" I asked, thrilled with what I've heard so far.

"Guests will be running to the bathrooms and outside to get sick, and your group will meet up right where we're standing. None of the guards will think much of it because others will be out here vomiting! They'll think that's what you're doing too."

"But, Inga and Carlos will be out in the open, and the guards will spot them," I said, worried.

"No, they'll be too busy figuring out what's going on," she said, calmly. "This will work but let me continue before I'm spotted talking to you." Viktor and I nodded. She raised her arm and pointed to a destination past the pool. "There are three buildings back there. One's a garage filled with cars and trucks. I've arranged for someone to drive you out of here as soon as you show up."

"Who?" Viktor bellowed, terrified of what Ramona had arranged behind his back. "This person could be telling my boss right now what you've done!"

"No, don't worry, Viktor," she said, smiling. "This man

isn't in my nephew's pay. He hates him as much as I do."

"I want to ask why, but we don't have time," I said. "Then what?"

"This man will be sitting in a black SUV with the motor running. He knows how to get out of here the back way, and nobody will notice you leaving."

"What's his name?" I asked. "We need to make sure we get in the right truck."

"No name, Ruth Ann," she said, sternly. "We don't want him implicated once you leave. He has a family and lives nearby."

Viktor looked skeptical. "I don't know, this sounds too simple."

"It has to be or someone will mess up!" she spat. "We get the guests to the point where they're so sick they need to run outside. There are not enough bathrooms on the main level to handle them. Ruth Ann and Axel grab Isabella. Inga and Carlos will be waiting in the tunnel near the back of the house. It'll work perfectly!"

"And you'll never be discovered as the one who helped us, will you?" I asked, worried for the old woman.

"No, he'd never suspect me," she said. "He thinks I'm too old and weak, so it's the perfect plan."

"Sounds great!" I said, feeling that this plan had a good chance to work. Ramona left us and went back inside the kitchen. Viktor and I walked toward the pool. "Let's see this garage, can we?"

Poor Viktor looked dazed as he walked down the path past the large pool. A huge stone waterfall flowed into the beautiful, clear blue water. It looked so inviting that I wished we could hang out at the pool during the day but I wasn't going to push it.

"Here it is," Viktor said, pointing to the far building on the right. "My boss has around ten vehicles in here, and sometimes more. He likes cars."

"And jewels, and drugs," I mentioned, but he ignored my comment.

Viktor opened the garage door after making sure nobody was looking. "I see the SUV Ramona told us to find." It was a large, black SUV with blackened windows. I felt comfortable now that I'd seen it. "Can we walk around a little more?"

"Yes," he said, leading me past the other buildings. "Those two buildings hide many of my boss's illegal possessions. He has hidden rooms below ground underneath the tractors, pool and gardening items." He pointed to the last building and said, "That's where I sleep with the other guards. I realize now that it's degrading to be second in command and be sent to this building."

"I agree, Viktor, but it's over soon." I said.

"When we escape, will we go the police? I asked.

"Not a chance!" he bellowed. They would make a show of coming here, but he has them in his back pocket. We leave, and never look back!"

"You're still planning on coming with us, right?" I asked him.

"Yes. I have to, Ruth Ann. Are you sure Axel will be able to help me start a new life?"

"Yes, he promised, and he keeps his promises."

Viktor took a deep breath in. "I sure hope so."

We walked around a beautiful piece of land, filled with palm trees, exotic flowers, and lots and lots of sand. I was getting hot and thirsty. Viktor noticed my red face and said we should head back. We needed to share our plans with Inga, Carlos, Axel, and somehow Isabella. Viktor told me not to worry; he would make sure she knew exactly what to do.

"Wait, she's with Axel in Manual's office!" I remembered.

"Sal's with them. I can relieve Sal and then you three can talk. I'll pretend I'm guarding you in his office."

"Sounds perfect," I said, feeling like the end was near. It was time for action and ... leaving Prunella behind. I was sad but getting out of here was necessary.

Just as we started to walk up the steps to the kitchen door, Viktor stopped me and said, "It's time to take control! Let's do this!"

Chapter 43

"That's a great plan!" Isabella cried, tears rolling down her cheek.

"Why are you crying?" Viktor asked, concerned.

"I'm happy, Viktor. I want to get out of here!"

"Oh, I'm not used to seeing people cry from happiness," he said, perplexed.

There was a knock on the door and Viktor rushed to open it. It was a strange young man I'd never seen before. He whispered a few words to Viktor and disappeared. Viktor closed the door and said, "My boss wants you three to go to your rooms to rest, and then get ready. The guests will be here at five o'clock for cocktails."

"When is Ramona planning on putting the pills in the glasses?" Axel inquired.

"Before the toast right as they sit down for dinner. Then my boss will introduce Prunella and his newest possession. He wants everyone's attention and that won't happen during cocktail hour."

"Egomaniac," I blurted.

"Yes, that's exactly what he is," Viktor answered. "Oh, you'll have food brought to your rooms for lunch so nobody

will be coming back to the main floor until it's dinnertime."
Before I could ask he added, "No, none of you are invited to
the cocktail hour. He wants to see shock on his guests faces as
Axel, Isabella, Ruth Ann, and Prunella enter the dining room."

"Why us?" I asked, following Viktor out of the office and
up the stairs.

He stopped on the second-floor landing. Sal was waiting
for us. "I'll be taking Isabella to her room."

"I want to stay with them!" she cried.

"It's okay, Isabella," I said, trying to reassure her. "We'll
be together really soon. Go and make yourself beautiful." She
nodded and went willingly with Sal.

"There you are!" Inga said, angry and thrilled to see us.
"You've been gone so long we were scared something happened."

Axel, Viktor, and I filled them in on where we'd been
and the plans we made for the evening. "Sounds too simple,"
Inga said, causing Viktor to slap his hands.

"I said that, too!"

"It's perfect," Axel said. "Nobody will get confused if it
goes as planned."

"*If?*" I asked.

"Yes, there's always a chance something could change,
but don't worry, I think we'll be fine," Axel answered.

I lay down on my bed and tried to close my eyes, but I
was too nervous about what was going to happen. We heard a
knock on the door and Ramona came in with a young woman.
They carried a tray with sandwiches and chips. After setting
the trays down on the small table in the living room, Ramona
shooed the other woman away. She bowed and rushed out of
the room.

"Everyone needs to eat," Ramona stated just as Inga and

Carlos came out of the closet.

"Anything happening in the kitchen?" I asked, curiously.

"They're running around frantically getting everything prepared."

"How are you going to get the pills in the champagne glasses?" Inga asked, dying to know.

Ramona cackled, and replied, "My nephew is so gullible! I suggested I get the glasses out and clean them. I told him I'm too old to help prepare or serve the food, but I am capable of filling glasses with champagne for his toast."

"And he agreed?" Carlos asked, stunned at Manual's ignorance.

"Yes! He thinks I'm upset because I can't help more, and he gave in to my only request."

"Wow, things are going too smoothly," Axel said, looking worried.

"I agree," Viktor said, grabbing the first sandwich.

"Are we going to see you again, Ramona?" I asked, feeling sadness that I may never see this woman again.

"No. I can't come back here anymore. It'll look suspicious. You may see me in the kitchen as you head outside to escape.

"We can't change your mind in coming with us?" Axel asked. "We'll take care of you, I promise."

"No, no," she said, waving her arm to brush his comment aside. "My life is here. What's left of it."

I desperately wanted to convince her to come, but I knew she would continue to refuse. Her entire life was here, and I wasn't going to take her from the comfort of her homeland.

As she left, she grabbed an item out of her apron and shoved it toward Viktor. He accepted it and opened the door for Ramona. She took one last look at us and smiled. "Be careful and thank you!" Thank her? We're the ones that should be thanking her!

Surprisingly, time went fast. It was time for me to shower and get ready for the ball! It didn't take long to get cleaned up and dressed. I looked at my reflection in the bathroom mirror and thought I didn't look too bad. "You look beautiful!" Axel said as I walked into the living room.

"Thank you," I said, remarking how handsome he looked in his ivory suit coat and black pants.

"This isn't prom!" Inga snapped. "We've got business to take care of."

"We know that, Inga," I retorted. "How much time do we have left?"

Carlos was standing by the balcony doors and replied, "The guests are pulling up now. There are a lot of fancy cars lining up in front of the house."

"I'm sure there will be a lot of guards getting out of those cars, too," Axel said with a shaky voice.

"We'll be fine," I said, hoping to reassure everyone, and myself.

It was five o'clock on the dot. Viktor had switched guard duty with Sal for a short time so he could get dressed. Inga and Carlos hid in my bedroom watching the guests pile out of their limos and luxury cars. Sal left as soon as Viktor came back. "It's almost time," he said. "It looks like we're ready to do this."

"I can't wait!" I said, anxious to get this over with. "Just make sure to fake drinking the champagne," I said to Axel. "And we need to remind Isabella, too."

"She knows," Viktor stated.

"I'm a little nervous," I said. "When I'm nervous, I ramble."

"We know!" Inga, Carlos and Axel said in unison.

Carlos was still keeping watch at the balcony doors when he turned to us and said it looked like everyone was here. There were no more cars pulling into the front drive. "They're down there innocently sipping cocktails," he said. "I should feel a little bit guilty, but I don't because most of them are criminals anyway."

Viktor told us it was time to go. He took Inga and Carlos to an exit in the tunnel close to our meeting place. He was back in a flash and said, "It's show time!"

We checked the bedroom and made sure we had everything we needed. I glanced once more at the stunning ruby necklace glimmering up at me and for a second, I considered taking it. Inga and Carlos held my belongings. I carefully walked down the stairs, anticipating an unforgettable party!

We walked into the foyer and found Sal standing with both Isabella and Prunella. Prunella looked magnificent in her stunning light blue gown, and our spectacular aquamarine necklace shimmered in the low light. "Wow," Viktor said when he saw her and Isabella. Isabella looked very pretty too, but not nearly as glamorous as Prunella.

"The boss is going to come out in a moment to escort us to the dining room," Sal explained. "It should be any minute. The guests are taking their seats right now."

We could hear voices laughing and talking from the foyer, and I felt a little uncomfortable about what would soon happen. Then, out of nowhere, Manual appeared in a black tux with a white ruffled shirt. It was hideous! His stomach was so large the ruffles buckled at his midsection.

"Prunella, you're stunning!" he said, grabbing her arm

and beginning to walk toward the dining room. "The rest of you follow me."

We walked single file until reaching the doorway to the dining room. What happened next stunned Axel, Isabella and me. One of his staff actually used a microphone to announce Manual, Prunella, Axel, me and Isabella. How tacky was this man?

The guests stood and clapped as we marched in and took our places next to Manual and Prunella at the head of the table. Axel was across from me, and Isabella and I were seated next to each other. Manual pulled the chair out for Prunella and she delicately sat. Isabella and I pulled our own chairs out and sat. Axel sat down as the other guests took their seats again.

Manual stood and broadcast loudly, "I want you all to remember this evening. My precious new love and her family members are here to help celebrate my union with this lovely woman, Prunella." I could see the heat rising in Axel's face because it turned an ugly shade of red. Manual continued, "You're not here to only meet this beautiful woman, but to be the first to set your eyes on my newest acquisition." He took Prunella's arm and helped her to her feet. He placed his hand on her neck and rubbed the sparkling gem. "This is Blue Ice."

It was my turn to blow up. I was about to fly out of my chair when Isabella grabbed my arm to keep me sitting. Manual quickly glanced at me but didn't react. People oohed and aahed at his introduction of *my* necklace. As he soaked it in, I wanted to strangle the man for calling it by my name! Axel glanced sympathetically at me. He knew I wanted to kill that man and it was taking every ounce of strength not to react. Thankfully, the guests were so enamored with Blue Ice that they didn't notice me at all.

"Now, I want everyone to pick up their champagne

glasses and toast not only to the most amazing gem you've laid eyes on, but to the most beautiful woman any man could desire." He clapped his hands for the filled champagne glasses to be served.

"This is it!" I said anxiously to Isabella. "Remember to pretend to drink."

She nodded and watched as three waiters strolled in with ten glasses on each of the silver trays. They set the glasses near each one of us and stood back, waiting to be dismissed. Manual grabbed his glass and held it high.

"Everyone, please take a sip." He slowly brought the long-stemmed crystal glass to his lips and poured the liquid into his grossly large mouth. I could hear him swallow as he downed the entire glass of champagne in one long swig.

I held my own glass to my lips and pretended to take a sip. I watched carefully, and so did Axel and Isabella, as everyone drank heartily of their champagne. My gaze went to Prunella. She was standing next to Manual, but she didn't drink any champagne. Manual noticed and told her quietly to drink or his friends would be insulted. She nodded and took her dainty hand and raised it to her lips and took a tiny sip. Manual's stubby hand held went to her glass and forced her to drink more of the champagne. Poor Prunella choked a little but remained composed. This was the man she wanted to spend her life with! It was painfully difficult to believe.

It was over. Everyone drank, and now we waited. Plates of food were brought in and placed in front of the guests. The gold rim on the china was glistening as I saw the dinner put in front of me. It looked delicious! There was a large piece of filet mignon, a pile of asparagus with hollandaise sauce, and a twice baked potato. Outside of the asparagus, which I can't stand, it looked quite tasty. Isabella, Axel, and I waited for

Manual to take the first bite. The three of us dug into our food, waiting nervously for the first signs of distress from the guests. The beef was so buttery and tender that it melted in my mouth. I was half-way through my filet when Manual belched loudly, surprising himself. He apologized to those around him when I noticed little beads of sweat beginning to form on his brow. I nudged Isabella and she looked over at him just as Axel noticed too. Manual wiped his forehead with his white linen napkin and continued to eat, much to our amazement.

Chapter 44

It all happened so fast, I barely had time to remember our plan. It started with a large woman at the far end of the table. She stood up, screamed, and cried, "I'm having a heart attack! Please help me!" she slumped over her plate and grabbed her head in distress. "My head, my head!" she bawled. "It hurts so much!"

Then, one by one the guests started experiencing the same reaction. The men hollered at Manual, accusing him of poisoning them. "No, no," Manual replied, experiencing the same symptoms. "If I did, why am I feeling the same as everyone?" he tried to stand, but he became so dizzy he tumbled to the floor grasping his head and his heart. "I'm having a heart attack!"

Axel, Isabella and I waited patiently for the drug to hit everyone at the table. There were screams, moans, and threats flooding the room when finally, the first guest grabbed his mouth and rushed out of the dining room. I suddenly remembered Prunella; she drank the champagne too. I looked over at her and she was as calm as could be. It didn't appear she was having any symptoms at all, but how could that be?

Axel rushed around the table to Isabella and me and

grabbed our arms. "We gotta go!" he pushed passed the herd of people trying to get out of the dining room. Prunella watched us intently as we headed through the doors into the kitchen. Ramona was waiting for us in there. She was pleased when the three of us appeared.

"It's happening!" I bellowed.

"You need to run out the back door, NOW! Follow those guests," Ramona said, pushing me toward the group of people trying to get outside. "Go!"

I didn't have to be told more than once. Axel, Isabella and I looked around for Inga and Carlos. Ramona told us they had just made their way to the back and were waiting for us outside as planned. Thankfully, when I stepped outside, it was pretty dark. There were a few lights, and people were bent over throwing up everywhere. It was so disgusting, I had to cover my mouth to keep myself from losing it from the stench. It actually looked as if I was sick too as I ran past the people covering my mouth.

"There you are," I said, running into Inga as she popped out from behind a bush. Carlos was behind her, plugging his nose from the horrendous stench.

We were all together, finally, and about to head down the path to the garage when a loud, female voice halted us. Axel was the first to see who it was since he was at the back of the pack.

"Prunella!" he hollered. "Go back inside!"

"NO!" she screamed. "Where do you think you're going? Are you escaping?"

"Don't worry about us anymore," Axel snapped. "You gave up your family when you chose to stay here with that maniac."

She was quick to ask, "It was you! You made everyone

get sick, didn't you?"

"Yes, *we* did!" I fiercely hollered back.

"Ruth Ann?" Prunella asked shocked, turning to face me directly. "You wouldn't hurt a fly!"

"We didn't have a choice. You stole my necklace and you want to stay here."

Prunella reached to her neck and was shocked to find the necklace was missing. "Where is it?" she asked, horrified.

Ramona appeared out of thin air holding my precious Blue Ice in her shaky hand. "It's right here!" The woman looked so proud, I wondered how she pulled it off without Prunella noticing.

"You!" Prunella howled. "You're an evil old woman!"

"Prunella!" I bellowed. "You leave Ramona alone. She's been kind and helpful and she knows her nephew's a horrible human being. I will never believe you're attracted to him."

Prunella's glower was so menacing it terrified me. For a split second I thought she was going to lunge and wrestle me to the ground. Inga threw herself in front of me and held her arms out to protect me from Prunella's wrath.

"How dare you threaten Ruth Ann? She's done nothing but try to save you." The tears were streaming down her face, shocking the rest of us. Inga didn't cry, I didn't think she knew how! "I've been loyal to you for so long, and I've refused to leave here without you until this very moment. You're not the person I've known and cared for all these years. *You're the evil one!*"

Prunella turned away from us and marched into the darkness. Ramona rushed to me as fast as she could and put Blue Ice into my hands. "This is yours. You leave here with it, and never look back." I remembered Meme's words. Blue Ice is mine and would always be a part of me.

"Thank you, Ramona," I said, taking my lovely blue gem out of her hands. "I don't know how to thank you for saving my necklace, and our lives." Axel and the others nodded to agree. "I'm going to ask you one last time ..." she stopped and grabbed my hands and shook her head. "Okay," I said, understanding her completely.

We turned to leave when out of nowhere a gunshot went off very close to us. Axel threw himself in front of me and Inga protected Isabella. Carlos looked to see where the shot originated. As we stood on the stone path, so close to our destination we were met by none other than Manual, Viktor, Sal and Prunella. Prunella must've found Manual and told him everything that happened.

"I knew it!" Manual screamed. "You poisoned me!"

"And me, Manual," Prunella added, irritated that he left her out.

"Yes, we did!" Axel answered, taunting the nasty man.

"It isn't poison, you fool," Isabella shouted. "It's a curse, and you need to back off or it'll get worse."

Good one, Isabella!

Manual turned paler than he already was. "No, you didn't."

"Yes, I did." Isabella teased. "I can do more if you'd like."

"No, no, leave us alone!" he cried, falling to his knees. "Sal, Viktor, help me up!" The two men rushed to his side and each grabbed an arm. Once he stood, he raised the gun and aimed it at ME! I wouldn't let Axel stand in front of me this time. I wasn't afraid. For some reason I felt stronger than I had in a very long time.

"Go ahead, shoot me," I said, standing tall and proud. "I'm not afraid anymore."

Manual turned toward me. I really thought my time was up when Viktor grabbed his boss's arm and the gun went off, hitting Prunella in the leg. Viktor struggled to grab the gun from Manual, but Manual was stronger and ordered Sal to shoot. He turned and shot Viktor in the chest, the blow throwing both Viktor and Manual to the ground. Viktor was under Manual. Manuel reached up to check Viktor's pulse. "He's dead.", screamed Manual. "That's what he gets for helping you. He's a traitor and had to be killed!"

"He's a hero!" Isabella cried, trying to get to Viktor, but Carlos wouldn't let go of her. "He hated living here and doing your dirty work. You're nothing but a disgusting coward who robs and tortures people. You should be the one who's dead!"

Manual turned around on all fours and took hold of his gun before any of us could react. He shot Isabella right in the middle of her chest. She crumbled to the ground so gracefully I thought for a split second she was pretending, but she wasn't. I rushed to her and fell to her side. I screamed and screamed knowing there was nothing I could do to save her. Her beautiful blue eyes were open, staring into the clear night sky.

"Ruth Ann!" Carlos shrieked. "Move, let me try and revive her!"

"It's too late, Carlos," I said, trying to stand but my legs felt like rubber. I couldn't believe what was happening, and unfortunately it wasn't over yet.

Axel rushed toward Manual. Prunella was on the ground, holding her wounded thigh and writhing in pain. Sal was about to shoot Axel when Manual hollered, "NO, he's mine."

"Go ahead you lunatic, take your best shot," Axel answered, eerily calm.

Manual stood close to Axel, his gun aimed at his chest. Out of nowhere, Ramona showed up with a large knife and charged at her nephew. Sal jumped in to save his boss but took the blow from Ramona's knife right in the stomach. Sal fell to the ground, instantly dead.

So much happened so fast, I couldn't believe my eyes. Sal was dead. Viktor was dead. Poor, sweet, Isabella was dead. Prunella was shot, but alert and in pain on the ground. Manual and Axel stood face to face when the sound of sirens wailed in the distance. "I called the police," Ramona said. "I don't know if my nephew will ever be thrown in prison, but I had to call."

"You did the right thing," I said, pulling her away from Axel and Manual.

Carlos was on the ground putting pressure on Prunella's leg. She didn't appear grateful but scowled only at me. I felt chilled to the bone.

The last thing I remembered was Carlos screaming into Prunella's face as he held her bleeding leg. "This is all your fault! You caused *all* these deaths. How dare you kill Isabella?" Everything went black, until ...

Chapter 45

"Ruth Ann," I heard a voice in the distance calling my name over and over. I was so comfortable I chose to ignore it. The voice called my name several times until I couldn't take it any longer. I opened my eyes and looked around the familiar setting.

"Isabella, I thought you were dead! I'm so happy you're alive!" I looked saw Isabella in a beautiful flowing dress standing in the soft sand near the hut I remember so well.

Isabella didn't speak so I asked, "How did I get back to your village? This is the hut where I met you and your grandmother so many times. Is Meme here, too?"

"Yes, Ruth Ann," Meme answered from the doorway of the grass hut. "I'm here with my precious granddaughter." I turned and spotted Isabella walking closer to me. She looked so peaceful and relaxed. I was happy she was smiling. "It was too soon for her to be with me, but it was out of my hands. Fate intervened, and my sweet Isabella was a hero."

"Yes, she was," I said. "But, why can't she speak like you?"

"I can, Ruth Ann," Isabella's kind voice answered. "I'm okay, really. I am very happy, and I want you to know that.

You need to wake up soon and be with your family. They need you now more than ever."

Recent events flooded my brain. "Too many died this time because of my necklace," I said, reaching and feeling Blue Ice around my neck. "Why is there so much pain and suffering associated with this?" I asked, angrily. "It needs to stop!"

"Someday, Ruth Ann," Meme said. "You're safe, Axel, Carlos and Inga are safe and will be stronger when you get home and mourn those that you lost."

"You didn't mention Prunella's name, Meme," I said. "Where is she?"

"She's recovering from a bullet wound at Manual's estate."

"But, why? Didn't she see that he's a monster?" I asked, horrified with the news.

"Let her be, Ruth Ann," Isabella said, thoughtfully. "She's where she wants to be right now. Axel's willing to let her go, and you need to also. I know it's wrong, but it is what it is."

"Did the police arrest Manual? He's a killer and a criminal!"

"Unfortunately, that won't happen," Isabella replied. "Sometimes life isn't fair, and right now, it isn't for you. But, you're strong and have lots of support from those that love you. Go home! Go be with your friends and family."

Meme added, "Stay close to Axel, Inga, Carlos and Cassandra. They'll need you a lot right now, especially Cassandra. Her trial will begin soon, and she needs you to be strong and supportive." She added, "Everyone's been through so much and they'll move forward and recover just like you will."

"Yes, I will! Thanks," I said, and then they were gone. Everything went black, again.

"Ruth Ann!" a nagging voice repeated. "You need to wake up!"

I slowly opened my eyes. I was lying in a hospital bed with Axel hovering over me, and Doc Albert next to him. "Where am I?" I asked, trying to sit.

"Take it easy, Ruth Ann," Doc said, gently moving Axel to the other side of him. He asked if Axel could step out of the room for a moment while he examined me. Axel nodded and left the hospital room.

"Where am I?" I asked, confused.

"You're in the hospital in Deer Creek," Doc replied.

"How did I get here? Last I remember I was at Manual's estate."

"You were in shock and passed out. You've been out since you arrived two days ago."

"Two days!" I exclaimed. "Am I okay? Did I miss Christmas?"

"Yes, I believe you'll be fine," Doc answered, checking my vitals. "Christmas is tomorrow, Ruth Ann. You woke up just in time."

Suddenly, as memories of what happened at Manual's estate flooded my brain, I couldn't bear to think about Christmas. "Who's here besides me?"

"You're the only one admitted, but Axel, Inga, Carlos, Cassandra, Lynne and Nancy are in the waiting area. John's been here as much as he can."

"John," I said, forgetting all about him. I knew I had to have a serious talk with him very soon.

"You're doing pretty well," Doc said. "I'll let your

daughters in right now."

I waited for my girls to come in, knowing full well they were going to be furious with me, again, but once they saw me lying in bed they burst into tears and made me swear to never scare them like that again! I promised, well, tried to promise because with me, one never knew!

After Doc pricked and prodded me, he decided to release me later that evening. I was probably driving the staff nuts with my demands! Doc made me promise to rest at home but which home? My little ranch in town or Axel's massive estate up the mountain? My decision was made for me when the next person burst into the hospital room unannounced.

"Nigel!" I exclaimed, stunned. "What are you doing here?"

"Good afternoon, ma'am," he said, dressed in a black suit and tie. *Oh, no, don't say it ... don't say it!* But, he did. "I'm here to bring you home. I'm your new butler!"

END

About the Author

Karin Richardson graduated from The University of Iowa with a Communications Degree. She currently resides in a northwest suburb of Chicago with her husband, Kerry.

Richardson has always aspired to develop a series of books that can be enjoyed by readers of all ages, and the result is the Deer Creek Mystery Series.. She has currently published the fifth book -- CAPTIVE ICE -- in the series that began with BLUE ICE. Other books are ICE QUEST, CURSED ICE, and BLOOD ICE.!

Richardson loves to travel and is always thinking of new ways to incorporate her adventures into her next novel. As well as the continuing saga of Ruth Ann and her friends, Richardson is hard at work developing a new, exciting mystery series. "But," she says, "I will cherish and continue the never-ending series with my beloved Blue Ice."

About Blue Ice

The necklace in the book has an interesting story. Oh, yes, it's an actual necklace! Originally it was a ring and Richardson confessed that she used to play with it when she was a small child. "I thought it was just a pretty piece of costume jewelry!"

Richardson said that one of her relatives wore the ring when she came over from Sweden as a young bride. "Later my mother had it made into the necklace that was the inspiration for this series of stories."

If you enjoyed this book, you might enjoy the rest of Ruth Ann's exciting adventures with the fabulous aquamarine necklace. The Deer Creek Mystery series includes:

BLUE ICE

Ruth Ann's life was finally on track. Her children were grown and doing well, she had a great place to live, her business was taking off, and she was dating two of the town's most eligible bachelors. So, what could go wrong?

Apparently, everything!!! For starters, Ruth Ann inherits a rare aquamarine necklace, but before she can claim it, the bank is robbed and the necklace disappears. Now everyone is looking for the necklace, and some of them are not so polite about it!

With millions at stake, the under currents of the quiet little town of Deer Creek, Colorado are surging into a raging torrent bullets and fists are flying as old feuds erupt and people start taking sides.

ICE QUEST

They thought the mystery of the legendary necklace called Blue Ice had been solved and life in the sleepy little town of Deer Creek, Colorado could settle down again.

Well, of course they were wrong! Suddenly the fabulous aquamarine necklace disappeares AGAIN! And now Ruth Ann and her friends have a race to solve this new mystery and find the necklace before some else is killed!!

CURSED ICE

"Who are you?" the old woman asked me, her voice shaking with panic. "Why are you in here? You don't belong here! You must leave before it's too late!" But I was alone ... I was back on the beach in Jamaica, searching for John after the monster wave had knocked him down and dragged him under.

Book three of the Deer Creek Mysteries sees Ruth Ann and her friends return for yet another adventure starring the fabulous necklace known as Blue Ice. This time Ruth Ann travels to Jamaica on what was supposed to be a romantic get-away until where an ancient voodoo curse nearly costs John his life. Return to Deer Creek and find out what happens next!

BLOOD ICE

You hope you know who your friends are, but in a case like this one, it's hard to know who to trust! This is the fourth book by Karin Richardson about Ruth Ann and her friends in Deer Creek, Colorado. At first glance, it's a peaceful little town in the Rocky Mountains, but in reality, it's plagued by a series of mishaps centered around a mystical aquamarine necklace. This time Ruth Ann has to solve a mystery in a remote mansion, complete with hidden passages and inexplicable deaths. And the strangest thing of all is that the beautiful blue stone in the mythical necklace has turned bloody red! There's magic at work here, and it's not nice!!!